FINAL ORBIT

ALSO BY CHRIS HADFIELD

FICTION
The Apollo Murders
The Defector

NON FICTION
An Astronaut's Guide to Life on Earth
You Are Here: Around the World in 92 Minutes

FOR YOUNGER READERS
The Darkest Dark

FINAL ORBIT

CHRIS HADFIELD

QUERCUS

First published in Great Britain in 2025 by Quercus
Part of John Murray Group

1

Copyright © 2025 Chris Hadfield, Inc.

The moral right of Chris Hadfield to be
identified as the author of this work has been
asserted in accordance with the Copyright,
Designs and Patents Act, 1988.

All rights reserved. No part of this publication
may be reproduced or transmitted in any form
or by any means, electronic or mechanical,
including photocopy, recording, or any
information storage and retrieval system,
without permission in writing from the publisher.

This book is a work of fiction. Names, characters,
businesses, organizations, places and events are
either the product of the author's imagination
or used fictitiously. Any resemblance to
actual persons, living or dead, events or
locales is entirely coincidental.

A CIP catalogue record for this book is available
from the British Library

HB ISBN 978 1 52943 595 5
EXCLUSIVE HARDBACK ISBN 978 1 52944 815 3
TPB ISBN 978 1 52943 596 2
EBOOK ISBN 978 1 52943 597 9

Printed and bound in Great Britain by Clays Ltd, Elcograf S.p.A.

MIX
Paper | Supporting
responsible forestry
FSC
www.fsc.org   FSC® C104740

Papers used by Quercus are from well-managed forests and other responsible sources.

Quercus
Carmelite House
50 Victoria Embankment
London EC4Y 0DZ

John Murray Group
Part of Hodder & Stoughton Limited
An Hachette UK company

The authorised representative in the EEA is Hachette Ireland,
8 Castlecourt Centre, Dublin 15, D15 XTP3, Ireland (email: info@hbgi.ie)

To Cheryl-Ann, Murph, Madison and Abbas.
Without you, this book would never have found space to be written.

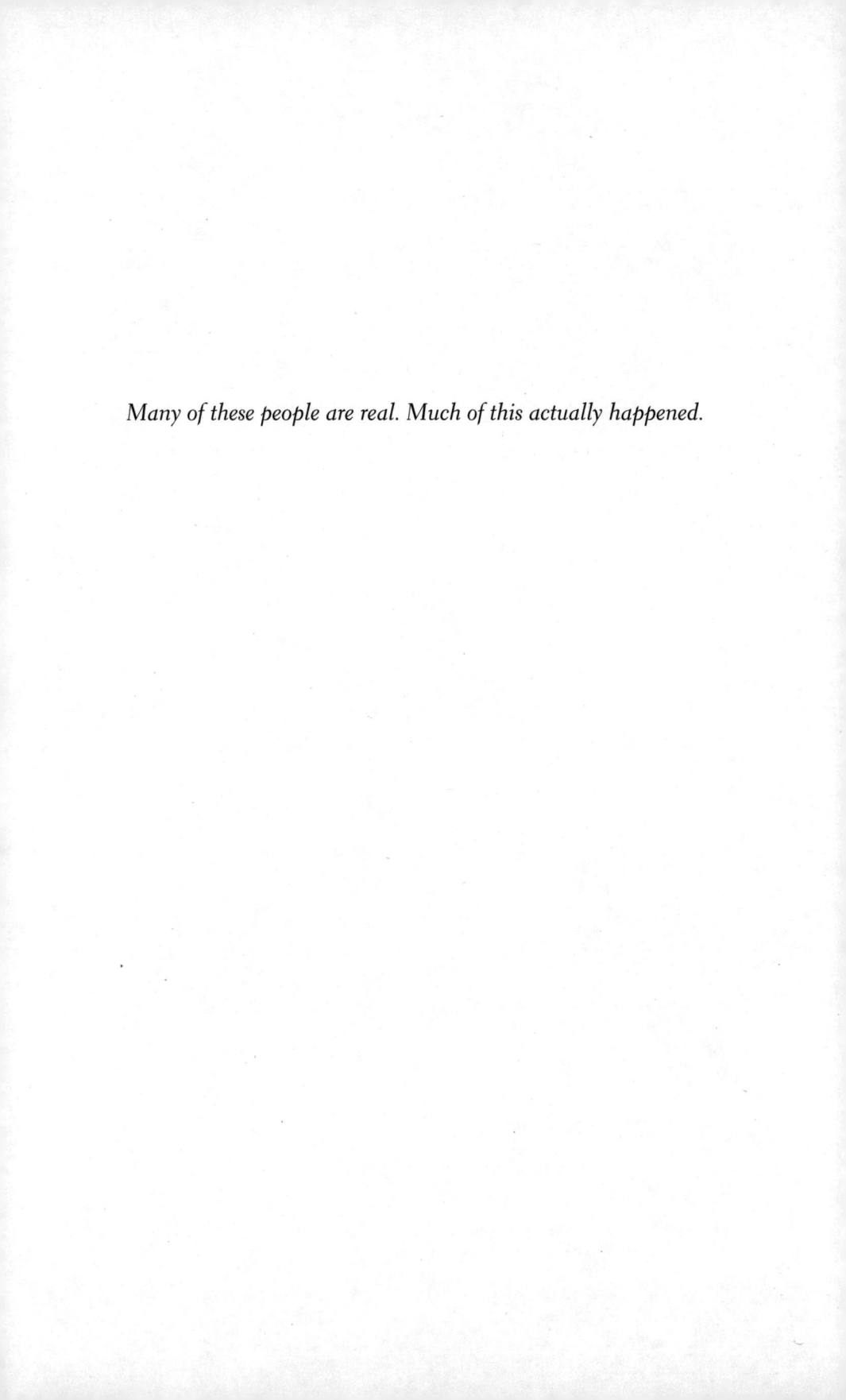

Many of these people are real. Much of this actually happened.

PROLOGUE

Great Wall of China, February 24, 1972

The late February weather was unusually warm and sunny. Up in the Badaling Mountains, an hour northwest of Peking, there was usually a frigid winter wind blowing down from the dry plateau of Inner Mongolia. But today it was just nice enough that President Nixon wasn't wearing a hat as he walked with his wife along the Great Wall.

Kaz Zemeckis surveyed the long stone wall, his good eye—the other lost to a flying accident years ago—tracing the worn walkway, crenellated battlements and regularly repeating watchtowers snaking along the ridgeline, the gray-brown structure hazily fading into the matching colors of the rocky hills. He tried to imagine what it had been like for the conscripted Ming Dynasty builders and soldiers 500 years earlier: clearing the jagged, rocky ground, cutting every stone and hauling each one into place by hand, living in makeshift tents on basic rations. An endless job of construction, maintenance and repair. Something for the soldiers to do as they patrolled the ramparts against an enemy that seldom came.

Military life.

Kaz nodded to the American standing next to him, his breath visible as he spoke. "You can bet there was a lot of blood mixed into the mortar between these stones, Jimmy."

"No doubt." Dr. Jimmy Doi was a US Air Force flight surgeon, son of a Japanese father and Chinese mother, immigrants to America who had taught their son both mother tongues. He was detailed as part of the president's medical team, chosen for his language skills.

Kaz was listed in the official roster as "aircrew," one of the military personnel cleared to accompany the president. He was careful to maintain that cover, but he'd actually been sent by General Sam Phillips, commander of the USAF's Space and Missile Systems division. The Chinese had been making rapid progress in rocket and satellite technology, and Nixon's visit had promised a rare opportunity for direct observation. State officials had pretended not to notice that Air Force One, the presidential Boeing VC-137C transport jet that had flown everyone to China, had carried a much larger crew than normal, approving all the names on the manifest. But they had taken care to assign escorts and translators to everyone. Kaz's escort was a military man about his age, lean, fit and tight-lipped. Apart from giving Kaz his name—Fang Kuo-chun—he had said nothing else, and today stood a short distance away, a compact figure, quietly observing.

Intelligence-gathering went both ways.

President Richard Nixon was irritated. He'd flown halfway around the world but had only been granted a short photo op with Chairman Mao Tse-tung, who was in far worse health than he'd been led to believe. Nixon had been pawned off ever since on underlings, and today's visit to the Great Wall was turning out to be all tourism, not statesmanship. Nixon worked hard to keep smiling, but his deep jowls kept settling into lines that made him look like he was waiting to spit out something distasteful. His eyes were fierce with impatience under heavy, frowning eyebrows, and his ski-jump nose dripped in the cool, dry air. When he bent over to shake hands with preselected photogenic children, he scared them.

It had snowed the night before, so to be sure President Nixon could make his planned visit to the Great Wall, hundreds of workers had been tasked with shoveling and sweeping the mountain road and the wall's steep walkway. Some had stayed after the work was done, joined by their children, all hoping to see the US president, even from a distance. It was a quiet crowd, uniformly dressed in plain blue Mao suits and soft, pleated, short-brimmed caps. Even so, security forces were keeping them well back from where Nixon and his wife, Pat, strolled on the wall. Many of the women workers' eyes were drawn to the extravagance of Pat Nixon's deliberate choice of a bright-red coat and brown fur hat.

It was Kaz who was the first to notice.

With everyone's attention on the Nixons as they stopped and waved, about to turn around and walk back down the Great Wall, a child of about five had wandered away from his mother and up the sloping walkway. The wide square cutouts built for Ming soldiers to fire arrows through were just the right height. The boy wanted to see, so he reached up with both hands, got a solid fingertip grip and scrabbled with his feet to pull himself up into the stone notch.

Kaz started running. He'd looked over the edge and knew it was a sheer drop of 20 or 30 feet to the bare rock below.

As he was closing in, the boy gave one last hard pull and, with a swinging kick of one dangling foot, he disappeared.

Running full tilt in his leather dress shoes, Kaz grabbed the edge of the adjoining cutout to slow himself, banging chest-first into the stone. Hearing a startled cry from the child, Kaz leaned hard to reach the next gap and saw the top of the boy's head disappearing over the edge, leaving him hanging from one arm, fingernails desperately scraping across the bare rock. Kaz slammed his hand over the boy's wrist and squeezed as hard as he could, tearing three of his own fingernails with the effort.

But he was way off balance and the surprising weight of the boy dragged him into the gap. He splayed his legs and slapped his right hand flat against the wall, trying to counter the inertia, but it wasn't enough to prevent the boy from pulling him through.

They were going to fall. Kaz strained hard, bending his left elbow to try to bring the boy closer into his chest—hoping to pivot them both in the air and take the brunt of the impact on his back and side, cushioning the child. Just as he was about to let go and wrap his right arm around the boy's head to protect his skull, he felt a sudden vicious yank on his right leg, stopping their fall.

Kaz's arm was pulled straight and the boy swung through the air, slamming into the wall's outer face. With his damaged fingers and thumb locked around the boy's wrist, the back of Kaz's hand smacked into the wall and went numb.

Kaz was upside down, dangling from the Great Wall of China, with a child's life depending on his grip. *I will not let go!*

He heard urgent voices speaking Chinese, and then Kaz and the boy were lifted back up, scraping against the cutout's sharp edge. Finally, enough of him was securely in the gap, and he was able to pull the boy to safety.

Sliding clumsily back through the hardness of the gap, still holding the boy, Kaz tumbled down onto the inner walkway. He quickly released the child into the outstretched arms of his mother, easy to identify by her wide, tear-filled eyes. Dr. Jimmy Doi bent to kneel next to her, talking quietly in Chinese as he gently probed the child for injury.

Kaz shook his head, trying to sort out what had just happened, as a small crowd of Chinese workers clustered around the child and his mother, stealing awed glances at him. Standing slightly apart, against the wall to Kaz's left, was his silent escort, Fang Kuo-chun, staring at Kaz, his face expressionless.

That's who grabbed my ankle, Kaz realized. *Who is he, really?*

Beyond him, down the steep walkway, Kaz saw the backs of the American delegation in the far distance. The president and first lady must have started back down before he had raced to save the boy, and they hadn't noticed what was going on. He played the sequence back in his head. There had been no shouting, apart from the child's one cry, so it was no wonder only the doctor and his minder had noticed.

Satisfied that the boy was unhurt, Doi came and knelt by Kaz. "Okay, hero, let's see if you're suffering from anything besides an adrenaline crash."

As the doc ran his hands over Kaz's legs and arms, feeling through the torn clothing for cuts or breaks, Kaz met Fang Kuo-chun's unwavering eyes. "Thank you for saving me," he said, in a sudden rush of emotion and post-action shakiness.

Jimmy translated.

Fang blinked, then nodded, holding Kaz's gaze for several seconds, each man clearly sizing the other up.

Way stronger than he looks, Kaz thought, impressed, remembering the vise-like grip on his ankle, and knowing the confidence and muscle it must have taken for Fang to haul him and the boy back up. Kaz had a sudden intuitive feeling that he was looking at a fellow fighter pilot.

Jimmy frowned as he inspected Kaz's torn fingernails and scraped, bleeding hands. "We need to get you to my first aid kit, back on the bus." He shook his head as he stood. "You're lucky that's all that was damaged. What you did was nuts."

Kaz closed his hands into fists to protect his injured fingers, then pushed himself to his feet. He felt a wave of dizziness, took a deep breath and steadied himself against the wall with one hand as he carefully started back down the steep slope.

The child's mother, clutching the boy in her arms, intercepted him. Looking up to meet his eyes, she thanked him, her voice full of emotion, with Jimmy translating.

"I'm glad I could be here to save your son," Kaz said, smiling as he reached out to touch the boy on one shoulder. Then he continued down the walkway, Jimmy beside him in case he needed help, Fang silently trailing.

By the time they reached the bottom, Nixon's limousine had departed and the rest of the entourage was already on the bus, save for a few members of the press corps who were loading their cameras in through the back door.

They climbed onto the bus and Jimmy retrieved his medical bag from the overhead rack and joined Kaz on a bench seat in the back. Fang took the seat opposite. Jimmy found some disinfectant and bandages and quietly cleaned the abraded skin and tightly bound the broken nails.

When he was nearly done, Kaz said, "Don't tell anyone what happened."

"Why not?" Jimmy Doi frowned. "I'd sure want people to know if I'd saved a kid's life."

"No need to distract from the president's visit," Kaz responded, and then leaned close, speaking just loud enough for only Jimmy to hear. "No need to highlight my being here."

He glanced across the aisle at Fang's impassive, watching face, and a thought flicked through his head: *What report will he be filing to his superiors?*

FIRST DAWN

FIRST BORN

1

Kennedy Space Center, July 3, 1975

General Tom Stafford was getting angry—it was almost launch date, and he needed the spaceship's primary systems to work.

They didn't.

Seated in Mission Control at the Johnson Space Center, near Houston, Kaz Zemeckis was equally frustrated. As military liaison CAPCOM for the first-ever American–Soviet spaceflight, he was supposed to be making everything smooth and efficient for the US crew, including General Stafford, the mission commander. This morning had been anything but.

Tom Stafford shifted in the reclined seat of the Apollo Command Module. His spacesuit was uncomfortable enough without the increasingly annoying lumpy pressure points pushing up into his back. Worse, they were way behind on the mission timeline.

He pressed the transmit button. "Houston, I say again, how do you read the Apollo crew?"

Kaz's reply in Tom's headset was still garbled and full of static. Unintelligible.

Tom swore to himself. *Dammit! We're inside two weeks from launch. And we still can't even talk to each other?*

He leaned forward in his seat and turned his helmet to make eye contact with the two astronauts lying on their backs beside him in the capsule, checking to see if they could hear Mission Control any better than he could. Both men frowned, shaking their heads.

A Russian spoke, very scratchy and distant-sounding, but understandable. "Tom, this is Alexei. We hear you good enough." Alexei Leonov, commander of the Soyuz.

Good enough? Tom was disgusted. *Is this what the nation's space program has sunk to?* He said, "Alexei, moy droog, great to hear your voice. I hear you good enough too. Just need to get our Mission Controls on the line with us."

The Apollo crew were in their spaceship, sitting on top of their Saturn 1B rocket, pointed at the sky on Launch Pad 39B at NASA's Kennedy Space Center in Florida. Alexei Leonov and his cosmonaut crew were on the other side of the world, lying in their Soyuz simulator in Star City, just outside of Moscow. Today was meant to be the Countdown Demonstration Test, one last chance to make sure everything was ready for launch.

But it wasn't.

The plan had been to follow the countdown procedures with the clock running, all the way until just before engine ignition. It would give every system a chance to misbehave now, with enough time left to get things fixed before they filled the rocket with fuel and launched for real. On Tom's previous spaceflights they'd checked communications with the launch team in Florida and also with Mission Control in Houston. But this time, since they were headed for a space rendezvous and docking with the Soyuz, NASA had included Russian Mission Control in Kaliningrad, near Moscow, and the Soviet crew in the communications check.

Tom looked up at the Apollo instrument panel in front of him. At least the vehicle was healthy. He tried another tack. "Launch Control, are you hearing Alexei and us okay?"

The launch director, three miles away, staring out at the rocket through the thick windows of the Launch Control bunker, answered immediately. "Roger, Tom, we hear you both loud and clear. Be advised we have Houston on the phone, and they're trying a different switch config to try to patch in Moscow as well." He'd heard the frustration in Tom's voice, and added, "Appreciate your patience."

A new voice broke in on the communication loops. "Apollo, Houston, how do you read us now?"

Everyone on the loop heard Tom's sigh of relief. He said, "Loud and clear as a bell now, Houston. How do you hear us, Kaz?"

Kaz stamped hard on the transmit button. "You're loud and clear too, Tom. Stand by for a voice check with Kaliningrad." He glanced at the Ground Control console, and the officer there gave him a thumbs-up. "Moscow, Houston, go ahead with your voice check with the Apollo crew."

Kaz held his breath. It had been a challenging morning, trying to get the whole complex communications system lashed together, but the backroom technicians were certain they had it right this time.

"Apollo, this is Moscow, how do you hear?" The Russian flight director was reading from a script, his English heavily accented.

In the Apollo capsule, Tom clenched a gloved fist where his crewmates could see it. He decided to use some of the Russian he'd learned, in return. "Slooshayoo horoshow, Moscow." *I hear you great.*

The Russian voice came back after a few seconds—the inherent time lag of the long vocal relay.

"Prinyata." *Copy.*

From Star City, Alexei's voice broke in again, clearer now. "Apollo, this is Soyuz. I hear everybody good too."

Tom replied, "Adleechna, moy droog. Spasiba!" *Excellent, my friend. Thanks!*

In Houston, Kaz looked at the countdown checklist. "Launch Control, this is Houston. We show our part of the comm checks as complete."

The launch director responded, "Copy, Houston, we concur. We'll discuss the snags at the debrief, but for now we're picking back up with the countdown timeline at L minus seventy minutes."

Kaz turned the pages in his checklist, verifying that all of today's actions for Houston were done. He pictured his counterpart in Moscow Mission Control, and the Soyuz crew still in their simulator in Star City, soon to fly to Baikonur and go through the final stages of their launch preparations.

Still lots of moving parts, but Houston and the Soviets were ready for Apollo to launch.

Despite today's aggravations, Kaz loved the psychotechnical intricacy of the work. Some of the most complex, capable machines and people in the world, docking spaceships together as a counterpoint to the menace of the Cold War—a job requiring all his skills and responsibilities.

He glanced back at Flight Surgeon JW McKinley at his console. His friend was peeling off his headset, smiling with relief.

Kaz realized he was smiling too. "What's up, Doc?" he called. "Wanna go grab a coffee?"

Kaz pivoted the small black toggle at the bottom of the large silver coffee urn towards himself and watched as the hot brown-black liquid splashed into his white ceramic mug, filling it. He released the handle, caught the last few drops and stepped back to make room for other flight controllers keen to get their needed shot of caffeine.

Coffee was the lifeblood of Mission Control.

He took a tentative sip, then asked his friend, "Were you watching their heartbeats during all that?"

"Sure was. What else do flight surgeons do?"

Dr. JW McKinley was a head shorter than Kaz, squarely built, with a high-and-tight dark crewcut and a naturally smiling face. His thick black glasses failed to hide the amusement in his eyes. He asked, "Whose do you think was beating fastest?"

Kaz considered. Vance Brand and Deke Slayton were rookie

spaceflyers, so they'd feel the most uncertainty, but veteran Tom Stafford was in command and had done the talking.

"I'm guessing Vance," he said.

JW's eyebrows lifted in surprise. "How'd you know?"

"Tom's done it all before, knows when to apply pressure, and Deke's been chief astronaut for years. Vance is the only true rookie."

JW shrugged. "You're right. Tom barely registered, Deke hit 110 beats per minute, and Vance peaked at 130." He blew on his coffee and took a tentative slurp, then a large swallow. "Though at the end there, when things were a little more heated, Tom was breaking 100."

"Even generals are human," Kaz said, smiling. Tom Stafford was a brigadier general in the US Air Force, the first general officer ever to fly in space. He'd been to the Moon on Apollo 10.

JW looked past Kaz and made a beckoning gesture. "Someone I'd like you to meet."

Kaz turned in time to see JW catch the eye of a tall Asian man. As he walked over, JW said, "He's a USAF flight surgeon, new to NASA, just getting up to speed to work console for mission support."

To JW's surprise, Kaz broke into a wide smile and reached to shake the man's hand. "Well, look who the cat dragged in! Jimmy, how are you?"

Dr. Jimmy Doi pumped Kaz's hand, his large, crooked teeth showing in a broad smile. "Kaz! I've been watching you on console all afternoon. It's been a while since China!"

JW looked between the two men, nonplussed. "China?" He shook his head, squinting at them. "How do you two know each other?"

Kaz held Jimmy's gaze while he explained. "We were both part of Nixon's boondoggle to China in seventy-two. Jimmy was medical staff, and I was officially aircrew." He winked at JW with his good eye. "Mostly we hung around and learned to drink baijiu together."

Kaz found himself smiling again at Jimmy. The slightly mismatched eyes he remembered, with the left one higher and rounder than the right. A long, straight nose and a grinning mouthful of teeth.

"How did you end up at NASA?"

Jimmy shrugged. "I could ask you the same question! Weren't you at the Pentagon?"

"Yeah, but the Navy had other plans. I've been working missions as military liaison and crew support." He raised an eyebrow. "NASA even sees fit to let me fly their T-38s. You back-seat-qualified yet?"

Jimmy squinted at him. "They let you fly front seat with just one working eyeball?"

Kaz nodded and pointed a thumb at JW. "Doc McKinley convinced them I was worth the risk. So long as I keep landing on the right part of the runway, everybody's happy." He tipped his head to one side. "Where have you been since the Great Wall?"

"Working on Vietnam vet rehab in Washington, keeping my hand in doing surgery at Walter Reed, and occasionally flying Thud two-seaters with the 113th Wing guys at Andrews." He smiled. "Occasional joyrides on Air Force One too."

Kaz snorted. "Cushy. Why would you leave all that for beautiful Houston-by-the-sea?"

"Tropical breezes and sandy beaches, like everybody who moves here." Both men knew it was sweltering outside and the nearest beach was in Galveston, 30 miles away. "And a chance to be part of this last Apollo mission, and, even better, to help with selection for the new Space Shuttle astronauts." President Nixon had approved the shuttle program in 1972, and the first flight was planned for 1978.

Jimmy glanced at JW. "Rumor has it we'll select women this time."

JW nodded. "The Soviets have been flying women since sixty-three—it's about time we caught up." He looked at his near-empty coffee cup. "Don't know about you two, but I need a refill." He headed for the coffee pot.

Kaz glanced at his wristwatch and then looked at Jimmy. "I'm gonna be mostly tied up on console until the Apollo-Soyuz mission is done, and I want to take my girlfriend out somewhere different tonight to make up for all the time I'll miss. You been here long enough to suss out any good Chinese restaurants?"

2

Chinatown, East Houston

The restaurant was busier than Kaz had expected for a Monday, and it took a couple of circuits of the nearby side streets until he found a good spot to park. He'd recently bought a 1955 Ford Thunderbird, a three-speed manual shift with electric overdrive, white with red interior. He'd always liked the look of the sporty little two-seater, especially the '55 model, the first year Ford had made it. He didn't want it to get dinged in a crowded, poorly lit restaurant parking lot.

It was a hot, humid July night, but no rain was forecast, so he left the T-Bird's top down. He pulled the parking brake, shut the motor off, pulled out the key and looked across at his passenger. It had been too noisy to talk driving up on I-45 from Clear Lake, and the quiet felt suddenly intimate.

Laura Woodsworth was smiling at him, taking off her NASA baseball cap and running her fingers through her long brown hair to detangle it. "So how'd you hear about this place? I've never been to this part of Houston."

"A new doc, Jimmy Doi, recommended it. Said the cooks and staff are all recent immigrants, so the food is the real deal. He said we should definitely try the shrimp dim sum." Kaz smiled. "I'm not really sure what dim sum is, but I got him to write out a few dishes to order."

He'd been admiring the view while he spoke. The sun was nearly setting, and its angled rays, filtering through the overhanging live oak trees, dappled Laura's face in light and shadow. They'd been dating on and off for a couple of years, and he'd been glad when she accepted the dinner invitation.

Laura swung her door open and climbed up and out of the low-slung T-Bird. She was wearing a T-shirt and cutoff jean shorts, the tawny brown of her long, tanned legs flashing as she closed the door.

She looked down the dark block at the bright lights in the distance.

"Let's go get us some dim sum."

The China Star restaurant was at the center of a row of one-story brick buildings linked by a long, covered high veranda, just north of the constant truck tire hum of I-10. *Converted store from an early strip mall*, Kaz thought, as they climbed the three cement steps up from the concrete parking lot. *Right height for unloading a delivery truck.* As he and Laura had walked up the side street where they'd parked, they'd seen an abandoned set of train tracks out back. He looked at the restaurant's covered outdoor seating, listened briefly to the traffic noise and asked Laura if she wanted to go inside. She nodded, and he opened the single door for her.

He'd expected the entrance to lead straight into the restaurant, but the owners had added a small reception area. An obese Asian man with black hair, wearing a bulging white suit and a black bow tie, sat impassively behind a built-in desk facing them. The wall behind him was papered with posters of the Chinese countryside and the Great Wall. A green paper dragon and two red paper lanterns hung from the ceiling, and there were potted plants at each end of the desk. The man surveyed Laura for several long seconds and then, without moving his head, he made and held eye contact with Kaz, then nodded. Kaz heard the click of the door to his left unlocking. He pulled it open and held it for Laura.

Rough neighborhood.

A waiter wearing a slender version of the same white suit and bow tie stood just inside the busy restaurant, menus in one hand, a water jug in the other. He bowed slightly and said to Kaz, "Welcome to the China Star. Indoor table for two?"

"Yes, please," Kaz said, and they followed him past a couple dozen tables filled mostly with Asian families to an empty one next to the far wall. The waiter set a menu at each place, poured water and retreated through a door in the back into the bright light of the kitchen. Kaz caught a glimpse of dark-haired men in frantic motion over hot burners.

Laura looked bemused. "What was up with the guy at the entrance?"

It had seemed odd to Kaz too, but they were on a date after a long day, so he opted to make light of it. "They have beauty standards, and you got us in."

She gave a lopsided smile at the compliment. "Thanks, handsome." She picked up her menu, written in a mix of English and Chinese. "I'm starving."

Kaz shifted in his seat to get at the front pocket of his jeans and pulled out the list Jimmy had written out for them. "Wanna just go with Jimmy's recommendations?" He squinted with his good eye at the bad handwriting. "Assuming I can read what the doctor wrote."

Laura shrugged. "Sure, so long as it's not too spicy." She dropped the menu and sat back. "I'm a midwestern girl, remember. We think paprika on deviled eggs is pretty crazy."

Kaz laughed and scanned the menu for drinks. "How about we try a beer called Tsingtao?"

"Why not? When in Peking, and all that."

Kaz waved at a tiny waitress in a red silk dress who was standing near the kitchen entrance. When she came over, he ordered two beers and consulted with her on Jimmy's list. The combination of bad handwriting, Kaz's poor pronunciation of unfamiliar words and the waitress's lack of English meant ordering took a while. By the end, Laura was openly laughing.

After the waitress left, she asked, "Any idea what we're going to be eating?"

Kaz chuckled ruefully. "I'm confident we're getting two beers. Everything after that is a crapshoot." He raised his glass of water. "Until then, here's to a good day in simulated spaceflight."

Laura clinked her glass against his. "Nice job keeping everybody calm today, Space Boy." She took a sip. "Sounded like there are still lots of problems."

"Yeah. Trying to connect all the different communications systems is a nightmare. But I'm glad we ran into it today and have a workable solution. Communications are bound to screw up in some form or other once we get launched."

He took a deep breath and exhaled slowly, deliberately shedding the events of his day. "How'd things go on your console?"

"Fine. Mostly prep work for the docked phase." Laura was a planetary geologist, but she worked all types of science support during missions. "We have a bunch of microgravity experiments inside the ship, as well as a solar observatory and my favorite, Earth observation." The Apollo crew were scheduled to have five days of free flight after undocking, and Laura was hoping they would come through with photos of many hard-to-access Earth geology locations. "I made them a long list," she said with a smile.

Kaz was nodding but realized he didn't want to talk about work. They were out on a date, after all. He looked around the restaurant. "Jimmy said this place hasn't been open for long. I wonder where they hire everybody."

Laura leaned forward, crossing her arms on the table. "I get my nails done at a place near the Johnson Space Center, and the manicurist there is Chinese. I bet her story is similar."

"What did she tell you?"

"Apparently, things really opened up ten years ago, when President Johnson changed the Asian immigration laws. Used to be we let in almost no one from China. But suddenly it was like twenty thousand a year, mostly from Hong Kong, plus lots from mainland China as well." She paused, recalling what the manicurist had told her. "There's also some loophole that once an immigrant gets naturalized, spouses and kids can get in too, beyond the quota."

The red-silk-clad waitress arrived with two bottles and two tall glasses on a tray. As she set the glasses down, she asked, "I pour?"

"Sure, please," Kaz answered, once he'd sifted her accent and understood what she meant.

As he watched her, he tried to guess her age. *Maybe twenty-three?* He also tried to picture her childhood and the uncertain path she'd followed to be here serving beer at the China Star on Jackson Street in Houston. The way she was concentrating on carefully tipping Laura's glass to get the right amount of frothy foam, Kaz guessed that pouring a beer was a recently learned skill.

"Are you from Hong Kong?" he asked.

The waitress gave a quick side glance at Kaz as she brought Laura's glass vertical to catch the last drops from the bottle. "Hong Kong, yes." She pronounced it "Heung Kong," and nervously nodded twice as she began on Kaz's beer, eyes down to concentrate. Conversation with patrons wasn't part of her job.

Kaz glanced towards the door to the kitchen, where the white-suited head waiter was standing watching them. Watching *her*, he realized.

He stayed silent until she'd finished, bowed and retreated through the swinging kitchen door, out of sight, the head waiter right behind her.

He picked up the brightly labeled green beer bottle and looked at Laura. "Does your manicurist seem that nervous?"

Laura pursed her lips, considering. "No, but it's an all-girl place and her English is better. No fat man guarding the door either."

Time to change the mood. Kaz smiled and raised his glass, holding it out for Laura to touch with hers. "Think this Chinese beer is gonna taste good?"

"It'll be the best one I've ever had," Laura answered, laughing.

The meal ended up being several small courses served haphazardly, apparently brought directly to the table as soon as they were ready. One dish came in a round wooden basket with an internally raised perforated platform, maybe to let the cooking liquid drain off the four glistening white and pink dumplings within.

"Dim sum," the waitress said as she set the basket amongst the many plates. "Shrimp," she added, rolling the "r."

Kaz and Laura had fumbled for a while with the chopsticks, laughing at each other's ineptness, but eventually settled on knives and forks. The dumplings were moderately spiced, and the mix of food textures went well with the Chinese lager, so Kaz ordered two more. By the time they arrived, he and Laura were mostly picking at the small amount of food that remained.

"So, what's the verdict?" he asked. "Jimmy's choices okay for an Indiana girl?"

Laura sipped her beer, had to cover a sudden burp, and laughed. "Sure were! Laura likes."

At the surrounding tables, many families had also finished their meals. Some were paying their bills as the kids restlessly waited to leave; at other tables, the men leaned back, smoking an after-dinner cigarette. The smoke smelled different to Kaz, more like herbs or plums than the Marlboros and Camels a lot of the NASA guys smoked. The head waiter was seating another wave of guests, and the kitchen door swung open repeatedly, the cooks even busier now.

Kaz realized that with the sun fully set, the restaurant looked more like a nightclub than an eatery; the head waiter had lowered the lighting and turned on some twinkling lights that were strung across the ceiling. *Makes sense*, he thought. *Serve two crowds, double the profit.* The volume was rising with the incoming, more adult crowd as well. *There'll be music soon*, he guessed.

The waitress in red silk approached their table with a tray carrying two small plates. On each was a small, yellow-orange curved pastry. She smiled as she set the plates in front of them and said, "Fortune cookie, made here." She nodded encouragingly and said, "Break open," and retreated to the kitchen.

Laura glanced at Kaz and smiled. She grabbed the two upper wings of the cookie and snapped it in half, revealing a small white slip of paper within. She slid it out and spoke the typed message aloud, her eyes sparkling as she read it to him: "You will be awakened in the morning with a kiss."

"I like the sound of that fortune!" In turn, Kaz carefully broke his cookie in half, pulled out the slip and read, "Good fortune takes preparation." He made a wry face. "The cookie knows I'm a CAPCOM." He looked at Laura. "I like yours better."

Laura took a tentative bite of her broken cookie and was surprised at the hardness of it between her teeth. "I'm not sure we're supposed to eat these."

The waitress had returned and was reaching past them to clear the plates and glasses.

"Maybe they glue them back together and reuse them," Kaz joked.

The waitress, with the beer bottles and glasses now balanced on her tray, turned too quickly. Kaz saw the tall bottles starting to topple and reached to catch them, but too late. One tumbled past his hands and clattered noisily onto the table, knocking over a water glass, which fell and shattered on the tile floor. The sudden crash momentarily stopped conversation in the restaurant, all eyes naturally turning their way. The waitress froze, seeming stricken. Looking enraged, the head waiter came bursting through the swinging door and strode purposefully to their table. As soon as he was close, he laced into the waitress in intense, blistering Chinese, making her cringe even smaller, then flee past him towards the kitchen, clutching her tray.

Kaz frowned at the white-suited man. "Hey, it was just an accident, man! No harm done."

The waiter's face was once again a mask of calm as he picked up the larger pieces of broken glass from the floor and cradled them in a napkin, avoiding Kaz's gaze. "We are very sorry, sir," he said, eyes on the floor. "It was a clumsy mistake. This will not happen again."

Kaz and Laura made eye contact, both uncomfortable. The head waiter stood, carefully folding the ends of the napkin over the broken pieces, then waved for a man to come with a dustpan and broom. He looked at Kaz. "Our apologies, sir, we'll get this cleaned up." He walked stiffly back to the kitchen, his raised voice immediately audible once he was through the swinging door.

Concerned, Kaz pushed himself to his feet and walked towards the kitchen, past the dishwasher approaching with the broom. Conversation in the restaurant had started to pick back up, but he was aware that a few of the patrons were watching him. He gave the door a hard rap. It opened a crack, and the white-clad waiter slid through to face Kaz.

"Yes, sir?" he said, looking blandly up at the taller man.

"I want to make sure you know we have no problem with what happened. It was just an accident—not her fault." He stressed, "I was reaching for the bottle and it fell."

The waiter held Kaz's gaze for several seconds. Then he said, "I understand, sir. Don't worry. We will take care of it."

The kitchen door swung wide as a waiter came through carrying a tray of food, and Kaz leaned to look past him. The girl in red silk was nowhere in sight.

The head waiter bowed to Kaz and disappeared again through the swinging door. Frowning, Kaz returned to his seat.

"It was good of you to try to check on her," Laura said.

Kaz shrugged. "Yeah, for all the help I was. Seems like she's on pretty thin ice here." He shook his head slowly. "Different cultures."

They sat together in silence for several moments, each of them wondering what was facing the waitress whose only sin was to break a glass.

Then Kaz took a deep breath and let it out slowly. "Enough," he said. "How about I pay the bill and we go compare our fortunes?"

3

Buffalo Bayou, Galveston Bay, Texas

She was a rust-stained hulking saltwater ship, her peeling blue paint and faded ivory lettering a testament to both her long years at sea and the indifference of her owners. The name on her bow and across her stern was *Pacific Triumph*, but any pride of victory was long since gone.

The flag hanging limply from her stern showed the faded red and blue squares with opposing stars that denoted registry in Panama. A salt-yellowed flag of convenience to avoid paying taxes. With 1,600 Panama-registered ships plying the world's oceans, the vessel was as anonymous as a 165,000-ton floating behemoth of welded steel could be. She could have come from anywhere. Just a working ship doing her job, hauling goods to market around the globe.

The *Triumph* was tied up at a Port of Houston unloading dock, deep in the brackish Buffalo Bayou, two hours of winding maneuvers inland from the Gulf of Mexico. Tall cranes were slowly swinging back and forth, lifting large packaged blocks out of the deep hold and placing them on pallets and trailers on the wide cement pier. Small teams of stevedores met each suspended load to guide it into place, unhook it, inspect it for damage, ensure customs compliance, then move it to temporary storage in the massive wharf warehouse or load it directly onto waiting transport if the cargo was perishable.

Most of what the men unloaded was exactly what was printed on the manifest. But like any large-scale operation, there were time-proven ways to slip certain items through, avoiding special notice.

Smuggling was as old as money.

The paperwork accompanying one large, square, cross-strapped cargo block showed that it was documented for direct delivery. It was said to contain several dozen bags of gypsum plaster for a Houston construction company and dozens more sacks of rice and beans, along with industrial-sized plastic jugs of soy sauce and peanut oil, meant for a distributor to the food markets and restaurants of Houston's growing Asian community. The crane set the heavy block gently beside a delivery van, its driver already waiting in an idling forklift to load it.

After the stevedores had released and cleared the lifting cable, the agent from the customs broker and freight-forwarding company pulled the paperwork out of the heavy reusable sleeve strapped to the pallet load and checked it. A quick count of visible plastic-wrapped bags and jugs matched the bill of lading, and there had been zero alerts and no history of smuggling from the *Pacific Triumph* or the receiving companies. A roving canine handler with a drug-sniffing German shepherd on a leash walked around the pallet, the dog showing no interest.

Satisfied, the agent compared his list to the driver's, signed and stamped the forms for the ship's loadmaster, slapped the side of the load for luck, like he usually did, and folded the page over on his clipboard, already walking and looking skyward, ready for the next crane load.

The driver revved up the forklift and maneuvered to expertly slide its long twin forks into the pallet slots. Barely pausing, he pivoted up the lever to lift the load off the ground and continued raising it as he drove forward towards the waiting open hold of his truck. He gently eased it squarely into place and lowered it down, the truck's heavy springs and shock absorbers compressing with the added weight.

After returning the forklift to its parking spot, the driver clambered into the back of the van to strap the load down. He jumped to the ground, leaving the rear door open for now, then climbed into the cab, started the engine and moved slowly to join the small, patient line of similar vehicles waiting to cross the exit weigh scales. When his turn came, he drove onto the familiar large metal plate, left the motor running, opened his door and walked around to clear his paperwork with the scale operator. He'd left the rear door open in case the operator wanted to have a look, but the new weight he'd picked up made sense compared to when he'd come in empty, and port policy was that random inspections saved time and manpower and were just as effective. The scale operator nodded as usual, signed and stamped the forms, took his copy and gave the driver a silent thumbs-up. Too many trucks for conversation. The driver pulled the heavy tailgate door down, latched it into place and drove off the scale and out through the gate.

Clear of all the formalities that protected the safety of the United States of America.

The truck handled with a familiar ponderousness as the driver turned right onto the winding service road that would connect him to the main highway to downtown Houston, the skyline visible in the distance. He rechecked his delivery clipboard, verified the two addresses, checked his watch and mentally pictured the best route into the city.

A dozen feet behind him, squarely held down by its own weight and the truck's cinched straps, hidden in the center of the surrounding gypsum, beans and oil, a special Chinese cargo awaited delivery.

4

Baikonur Cosmodrome, Launch Day, July 15

Lying on their backs, sealed inside custom-fitted rubberized pressure suits, the three cosmonauts' ears were filled with music.

It was Rachmaninoff's Prelude in G Minor: Major Svetlana Gromova's choice. The Star City psychologists had decided amongst themselves that music would calm the crew in the tense minutes leading up to engine ignition on Launch Platform 1. The Baikonur launch control team had limited each crew member to one selection with a maximum length of four minutes. This recording, played by Sergei Rachmaninoff himself, ran for 3:39.

Svetlana smiled behind her visor as the music rose and soared and fell. She thought a classical Russian composer who had moved to America was a fitting choice for their spaceflight. For the first time in history, a Soviet spaceship was going to dock in orbit with an American one.

The mission was called Soyuz-Apollo, and Svetlana was Flight Engineer #2.

She was strapped into the right seat of the compact Soyuz space capsule, her left shoulder and knee bumping against Colonel Alexei

Leonov, the mission commander. Similarly constrained on Alexei's left was Flight Engineer #1, Valery Kubasov. Their seats were reclined to ease the effects of acceleration during launch, their knees drawn up in front of them like they were reading in bed. The position gave them a natural place to rest their checklists, but more importantly, it decreased the overall room needed to accommodate them, so the Soyuz could be smaller and thus easier for the rocket to push up through the air.

Svetlana was a military test pilot and, as she always did, once all her checklist items were complete before takeoff, she assessed how she was feeling.

Calm, she decided. *I feel calm, and ready*.

This was her second spaceflight, planned to be a much simpler venture than her first: launch into Earth orbit, dock with the American Apollo ship, spend two days together demonstrating cooperation in a Cold War world, undock, re-enter the atmosphere and land the Soyuz on the Kazakh Steppe under parachute. A highly symbolic six-day flight, but not a challenging one.

On Svetlana's first space mission, things had gone terribly awry. She'd been part of a two-person Soviet crew on the USSR's secret spy space station Almaz, which had been clandestinely intercepted by an American Apollo spacecraft. There had been significant conflict—three crewmembers had died—and she'd ended up aboard the Apollo capsule. But she'd also walked on the Moon. Though most of the details had been kept classified on both sides of the Atlantic, Svetlana had been publicly hailed as the first Soviet and the only woman to have walked on the Moon.

In comparison, Soyuz-Apollo was going to be a piece of cake.

A calm, slightly self-conscious male voice from Baikonur Launch Control replaced the music, reading off his checklist: "Odna minuta do starta." *One minute before launch*.

Svetlana glanced at the clock above Alexei's left knee and nodded to herself: 15:19, Moscow time. Her eyes scanned the square central signal panel and the rectangular one above her right knee for yellow or red lights. None, as expected. The vehicle telling her it was ready too.

In the nearby Launch Control blockhouse, they had inserted and turned the thick metal key that permitted the automated launch process to proceed. It was the final safety check before sending the launch command and setting fire to the half-million pounds of refined kerosene and liquid oxygen in the Soyuz-U rocket's fuel tanks. Over 80,000 gallons of high explosive, about to erupt directly under the cosmonauts' backs in a focused blast of orange-white flame.

Just below Svetlana's right hip, on the outside of the rocketship, plumbing connections made a lip-smacking sound as they automatically disconnected, their long metal fueling gantry pivoting clear of the impending blast. Then the final data connection arm rotated back away from the base of the Soyuz rocket. Like rats leaping away from an endangered ship.

Their Soyuz was about to leave Earth, from the same launch pad where the first artificial satellite in history had been blasted into space—Sputnik, in 1957. Four years later, in 1961, Yuri Gagarin had also launched from here, the first human being to travel into the cosmos—the world's first cosmonaut.

And, in April 1975, a Soyuz crew had nearly died during ascent from here.

Svetlana thought about what had happened just three months earlier and reviewed what her actions were going to be if the cockpit indicators showed it might happen again.

A pulsing vibration shook her attention back into the moment as the engines exploded into flaming life and rapidly revved up to full power. Five rocket motors burning kerosene-oxygen were suddenly pushing the all-white 300-ton behemoth underneath them with a force of over 500 tons. A small smile curled her lips. Until this moment, the rocket had been supported from beneath on three metal arms, like an egg carefully balanced on three long spoons perched around the rim of a cup. As the engines now lifted more and more of the rocket's weight, the freed counterbalanced arms pivoted up with the Soyuz until it burst clear of the pad, pure power pushing it ever faster into the blue July sky.

"Pusk!" Alexei yelled from the center seat. *Launch!* The crew's eyes kept flicking across the instruments, watching for the unexpected, their heads being rattled against the headrests by the brutal thrust of the engines.

The g-force built steadily. Sir Isaac Newton had figured out that acceleration, force and mass were all related, and as the five engines voraciously burned the fuel, acceleration rose and the rocket's total mass rapidly dropped. Within a minute the crew was feeling two g's, and 45 seconds later they were pinned in their seats at four times their normal weight.

Bang! The four carrot-shaped booster rockets that had been bolted to the base of the Soyuz central rocket all simultaneously ran out of fuel and were jettisoned by explosive charges, sending vibrations up through the vehicle. With the instant loss of thrust, the g-force plummeted to a little more than one, and Svetlana felt like she was suddenly sitting in an easy chair instead of being crushed. As the remaining engine made small steering corrections to follow the computer-directed exact flight path, she thought, *Like I'm in a rocking chair.* She shook her head. *That is, if it were a fifty-meter-long rocking chair, forty kilometers above the ground, already going eight thousand kilometers per hour.*

And accelerating.

They were rapidly rising above Earth's air. After two and a half minutes, the air outside their ship was so thin that there was no longer a need for the streamlined shroud that surrounded the Soyuz, and in an explosion of sparks it split in half and fell away. Light instantly poured in through Svetlana's porthole window. This hadn't happened in the simulator, and she strained against the acceleration to catch sight of Earth below, but the shoulder straps of her five-point harness held her too solidly in place against her seat.

Nichivo, she thought. *No matter. I'll see it soon enough.*

She glanced at the clock. This was a critical moment. So far the rocket had been focused on getting them vertical, high above the air, into the near-vacuum that currently surrounded the ship. Now they could gradually tip over to align with the horizon and accelerate to the phenomenal speed needed to stay in orbit: eight kilometers per second. Over 28,000 kilometers per hour. A velocity that would take them around the world every 89 minutes.

But speed made them vulnerable. When you throw a stone across a pond with enough horizontal speed, it will skip and slide and enter the water gently as it slows. But throw that same stone steeply upwards, and it coasts and then falls almost vertically into the water, decelerating with great force when it hits.

That was what had happened to the crew in April. At 288 seconds into the flight, when the second-stage engine had burned all its fuel and was supposed to separate to allow the third stage to ignite, the explosives that were designed to fire to break the six mechanical locks that held the second stage in place failed; only three locks released. The third-stage engine ignited, but instead of blasting its exhaust into the emptiness of space behind the vehicle, it hit the still-attached metal upper structure of the second stage. The rocket plume acted as a blowtorch of monstrous power, melting the metal in its path. Without clean thrust, the vehicle lost speed and altitude. By the time enough flame had been directed onto the unreleased latches to liquefy them and let the second stage fall away, it was too late. The guidance system sensors felt the vehicle changing direction outside limits and initiated an emergency abort.

The Soyuz capsule's thrusters fired to yank it free from the doomed third stage. By then it had pivoted to point straight at Earth and was just like a rock falling straight down, gravity pulling it faster and faster, waiting for the air to thicken far below, near the surface.

The g-load was something no one had ever experienced before. The Soyuz and her crew were suddenly crushed at 21 times their normal weight, all the bolted-together avionics and plumbing and the crew's internal organs dangerously close to being torn loose. Somehow, the machinery and the cosmonauts survived the deceleration, the parachute opened properly, and the capsule landed on a steep, snow-covered slope in the Altai Mountains and began sliding and rolling downhill towards a cliff. Luckily, the tangled, dragging parachute snagged on some stunted trees and stopped the Soyuz just before it went over the precipice. The crew donned their cold-weather gear, climbed out into the chest-deep snow and collected enough wood to make a fire to combat the subzero temperatures until a rescue helicopter could retrieve them the next day.

The accident investigation team had assured the present crew that they had discovered and fixed what had gone wrong three months previously, but Svetlana knew this was the first real test. She intently watched the instruments and the clock to make sure the ship kept working.

At 288 seconds, just short of five minutes into ascent, the second-stage engine shut down on time. The automated system sent the separation command, a small electric current ran through the wires, and the five pyrotechnic charges ignited.

The third-stage engine erupted into life right on time, this time flawlessly. The empty second stage tumbled away as expected, to fall back to Earth and crash onto the sparsely populated Soviet territory below.

Alexei transmitted one word back to the keenly listening team in Launch Control. "Normalna." *All is nominal.* He then clarified, adding, "Third stage is stable, combustion chamber pressure within normal limits."

Svetlana realized she'd been holding her breath and exhaled slowly through her nose to keep from fogging up her visor. She glanced at the ascent checklist she was holding against her knee. Just a steady acceleration now, all the way up to final speed. She glanced at the pressure gauges, verifying that all seals were holding, keeping their precious atmosphere inside the ship. *A little metal bubble of air being pushed to incredible speed in the emptiness of space.*

Right on time, exactly 528 seconds after liftoff, the rocket engine shut down, the capsule separated from the final stage, solar arrays and antennas unlatched and sprang out into position, and the crew watched their checklists float up off their legs as they felt themselves in weightlessness.

Now how do I feel? Svetlana quickly considered and smiled again.

I feel like I'm safely home.

5

Apollo Command Module, Earth Orbit

"Man, I tell you, this is worth waiting sixteen years for!"

Deke Slayton, at 51 the oldest man ever to fly in space, was staring wide-eyed out through his right-side window of the Apollo capsule.

The blue glow of Earth reflected off his deeply lined face. He'd been one of America's first seven astronauts but had been grounded because of an irregular heartbeat discovered during a centrifuge training run. He'd taken years of medication and eventually undergone a cardiac catheterization at the Mayo Clinic to clear him with the NASA doctors, and today he was finally in orbit.

All that *Life* magazine and Kennedy hoopla in the early sixties, all those years helping other astronauts fly, but now he was undeniably *here*, in space! No one could ever take this away.

And his heart felt fine.

As Deke watched the coast of Newfoundland roll past at five miles per second, 90 miles below him, he twisted his spacesuit's red and blue wrist rings and pulled carefully on the black rubberized fingertips to slide off his heavy pressure gloves. He stripped off the soft white cotton gloves under them, stuffed those into the outer gloves to keep them from floating away and reached up to release his helmet's latches. He squeezed, pulled and slid the red handle of his neck-ring mechanism sideways, and heard the familiar metallic snicking noise as his helmet popped free. He maneuvered it up past his nose and the bulging ear cups of his comm cap and slid it into its mesh stowage bag.

Somehow, in the short time he'd been stowing his helmet, both gloves had disappeared. "Gonna have to get used to zero g," he muttered. He carefully moved his head and spotted one down by his right knee and the other floating almost out of reach above the helmet of Vance Brand, another spaceflight rookie, who was strapped in beside him in the center seat. Deke slapped Vance on the knee and gave him a thumbs-up, both men grinning at each other. He then retrieved the gloves, stuffed them into the helmet bag and settled in to listen to Houston talking to Tom Stafford, the mission commander. Tom had flown twice on Gemini and had orbited the Moon on Apollo 10.

The Houston CAPCOM, Kaz Zemeckis, a man Deke knew well from the tumultuous flight of Apollo 18, was speaking. "We've gone around the room and looked at all the data we had during the launch phase, and you're looking real fine. No problems."

"Super. Thanks, Kaz." Tom leaned forward in his reclined chair and twisted to smile broadly across the Apollo cockpit at Vance and Deke, raising his thumb in the air as well. "We're on our way, boys."

"We're going to be doing the TD&E in two minutes, Kaz. We're set up and counting."

Tom Stafford's voice, relayed through the communications ship *Vanguard* in the South Pacific, sounded tense.

No wonder, Kaz thought. TD&E meant transposition, docking and extraction. The crew had only been in space for an hour, and they were about to execute one of the trickiest maneuvers of the entire flight, including firing explosives.

Kaz glanced around Mission Control. He was seated at the CAPCOM console, working as the crew's capsule communicator — their trusted agent on the ground. To his left was Glynn Lunney, the flight director, and around the tiered room, staring at their displays, were experts in each of the spacecraft's systems. In front of them all was a large screen showing a blue-black map of the world. The small symbol of the Apollo ship was following a long, curved orange arc, currently passing 4,000 miles south of Hawaii.

Kaz twisted around and looked up through the tall glass windows behind him into the public viewing room, where Max Faget, the designer of every NASA spaceship since Mercury, was sitting next to George Low, NASA's Deputy Administrator. He'd heard that President Ford was also watching from Washington, alongside Soviet ambassador Anatoly Dobrynin and James Fletcher, NASA's Administrator.

Kaz turned back to face front, smiling wryly. *No pressure.*

The Apollo crew was about to push a button labeled CSM/LV Sep. It would send an electrical signal from their Command and Service Modules to a detonating cord, igniting it in a flash of sparks and light, explosively unzipping the ship into two sections, separating the crewed portion from the Lunar Vehicle adapter still attached to the Saturn IVB rocket. Four door-sized protective panels would tumble off into space, but the S-IVB would stay centered, motionless, waiting. Revealed at the end of it would be the prize that Tom Stafford needed to maneuver and grab — the Docking Module that would let them dock with the Soviet Soyuz spaceship that had launched eight hours before.

Despite the criticality of the event, there was no comm from the Apollo crew. Frowning, Glynn waved impatiently to get Kaz's attention. Mission Control always wanted to know everything that was happening, but Kaz's job was to let the crew do their work without constant interruption and distraction. Kaz shrugged and said, "They're busy, FLIGHT, sorry."

A full minute passed as they waited for confirmation. Engineers watched their telemetry, alert for malfunctions. Finally, Tom's voice crackled in their headsets. "We're off the IV-B."

"Roger, Tom," Kaz said, and fell quiet again. He'd spent months in the simulators with the crew and now visualized the intensity of what they were doing. Tom was moving his hand controllers to flip his ship around backwards, find the Docking Module against the blackness of space, and maneuver in precisely to stab it with Apollo's docking probe.

Tom's voice rasped with irritation from 3,500 miles away, over the Pacific. "Kaz, we got a problem. It's so bright in the background, I can't see my COAS." The COAS was the Crew Optical Alignment Sight, the aiming tube with crosshairs that Tom needed to use to accurately fly his ship in to dock.

At every console in Mission Control, engineers visibly tensed. "We got a problem" were the words the Apollo 13 crew had said after an oxygen tank explosion had crippled their ship, and it had taken three days of nonstop work to safely get the crew back to splashdown.

"Roger, copy," Kaz replied. He looked at the clocks at the front of the room. One of them showed the time until they lost signal over the horizon from the *Vanguard* comm ship. They had 90 seconds to try to help.

Rapid-fire questions and suggestions flowed into Kaz's earpiece from the engineers in the room. The simulator the crew had trained in had primitive optics and visual displays. Since this was the last mission of the Apollo program, there hadn't been money for upgrades. The crew hadn't experienced the actual brightness of the Earth or the Sun in the alignment sight.

What does Tom need right now? Kaz added up what everyone had said, glanced at Lunney and transmitted an idea. "Tom, suggest you move your head to compare your direct vision and the view through COAS, as well as make small attitude corrections to minimize the glare."

Then he shut up. Tom was an experienced fighter pilot and test pilot with three spaceflights under his belt. This was now his problem to solve.

A minute passed in silence. Then Kaz glanced at the clock and stepped on his foot switch to transmit something the crew needed to know. "Apollo, Houston, we're about thirty seconds from losing signal. I'll give you a call in twenty minutes via Rosman."

This is going to be a long twenty minutes, Kaz thought.

Just as Apollo was disappearing over the horizon from the *Vanguard*, Houston heard Tom's voice. "Kaz, I got the COAS back in. Finally. Thanks for the suggestions. Looking good for docking."

"Roger, Tom," Kaz said, as the whole room exhaled. By the time the spaceship had traveled far enough around the Earth that they could talk to them via the big antennas at Rosman, North Carolina, either Tom would have connected with the Docking Module or he wouldn't.

They'd burn that bridge when they got to it.

Kaz leaned back in his chair, feeling restless. Ever since going out for dinner with Laura, he'd been thinking about what they'd seen at the Chinese restaurant. The sense that something wasn't quite right niggled at the back of his brain. Why was the entrance guarded? Why had they treated the waitress so harshly?

He'd decided he wanted to take another look.

He twisted in his seat to catch JW McKinley's eye. Pulling the mic boom away from his mouth, he called, "Hey, Doc, what are you doing after we get off shift today?"

"Sorry, Kaz, I've already got a date," JW said. "It's my wife's birthday."

"Ah. Give her a hug from me," Kaz said. "No worries. I'm just curious about something and want to check it out, then grab some dinner afterwards."

The exchange had caught Jimmy Doi's attention, and he was looking Kaz's way. *Might be a better choice than JW.*

"Jimmy, what do you think—you free tonight?"

6

Chinatown, East Houston

"Just pull up here, Jimmy, under these trees."

At Kaz's request, they'd taken the doctor's black Chevy Monte Carlo. Less conspicuous than Kaz's white Thunderbird, in case anyone was paying attention.

On the drive up from the Johnson Space Center, the two had discussed Kaz's concerns about what might be going on at the restaurant. Jimmy told him he'd only been there once, had really loved the food and had seen nothing that made him uneasy. After they stopped, Kaz summarized the plan of action.

"Just an easy stroll around the neighborhood to see what's going on, and if all is quiet, we'll walk down the train tracks I saw in back so we can peek into the restaurant's rear lot."

Jimmy smiled. "Just a white guy and an Asian guy walking down the tracks in Chinatown after a typical day at work?"

Kaz smiled back and shrugged. "Yeah, but nothing dangerous. First sign of anything out of the ordinary and we beetle straight back here to your car."

By way of reply, Jimmy shut off the Monte Carlo's idling engine, opened the heavy door and climbed out onto the East Houston side street. The air felt hot and thick, especially after the cool of the car's air conditioning. Both men had taken off their ties but were still wearing the slacks and short-sleeved dress shirts they'd had on all day in Mission Control. They locked their doors and, with Kaz leading, walked towards the China Star restaurant.

The side street was quiet, but traffic was still heavy on I-10 just to the south, making a steady background roar of Doppler-shifting engines and rushing air.

"All look ordinary to you, boss?" Jimmy said, coming abreast of Kaz so he could be heard. "The place seemed pretty quiet when I was here."

"So far," Kaz responded.

They were deliberately walking at the pace of any two men stretching their legs after a long day at work. Acting is easiest when it's close to the truth.

As they came to the corner, Kaz looked hard up the restaurant road—no traffic was moving. They turned right and walked along the opposite shoulder from the raised strip of businesses that adjoined the China Star. Kaz moved to put Jimmy on his left so he could keep an eye on the storefronts while making conversation.

With his view blocked, Jimmy asked, "What are you seeing?"

"Almost every parking place in front of the restaurant is taken. Most of the other businesses are already closed." He kept his head tilted as if making conversation with Jimmy, but side-eyed the China Star's windows and entrance. "Restaurant's front deck looks pretty full. The entrance door is closed, just like last time."

He saw shadows shifting inside the entrance and started walking a bit faster. "Looks like someone's coming out. I want to be able to see inside."

Jimmy caught up, watching Kaz's face. "See anything?"

Kaz didn't answer until they were well past the restaurant. "Yeah, the same guy was behind the desk." He frowned, replaying what he'd just seen. "He definitely spotted us, but I'm not sure if he recognized me."

Jimmy thought about it. "Pretty normal for a couple of pedestrians in this neighborhood to catch his eye while the door is open, no?"

Kaz glanced at him. "Yeah, could be." He considered what he'd seen with Laura, though, and it reconfirmed his uneasiness. "I don't think he was just idly looking at people passing. The guy's whole job is face control, and to monitor what's happening out front."

He turned and looked back as they walked. "See any cameras?"

Jimmy did the same, squinting in the evening light.

"Seems like extra hardware and a jumble of wires above the entrance sign. So yeah, maybe."

Kaz nodded. Made sense.

Headlights were coming towards them, and each man raised a hand to shield their eyes from the sudden glare in the dusk. Before it reached them, the vehicle abruptly turned in at the far end of the strip mall and disappeared around the end of the last building.

Kaz angled across the road towards where it had gone out of sight, with Jimmy following his lead.

"Looked like a panel van to me, Kaz," Jimmy said. "I couldn't make out the signage. Some sort of delivery service, I think."

"Yeah, same."

They walked along the line of parked cars that were nosed into the strip, and slowed as they reached the far end to look down the alley. The van wasn't there. Kaz scanned the roofline for any closed-circuit television cameras and, seeing none, headed towards the back. Jimmy trailed him, keeping a lookout for anyone following.

As Kaz approached the rear corner of the asphalted alley, he slowed to listen, then crouched to lean forward for a quick peek. Seeing action, he rocked back on his heels. *Well, that's interesting*, he thought. He got up and came back to Jimmy.

"Let's find a way up onto those tracks."

The strip of businesses had originally been built to be resupplied by light rail, on tracks that spidered throughout Houston. But as cars and trucks had become more reliable and convenient, the rail lines had been abandoned one by one. Some had been converted to trails and bikeways, but this one was a dead end, amputated years ago by the multiple lanes of I-10.

Kaz guessed the closest place to access the rail line was where it crossed a side street, and he took a left out of the strip mall, looking for the nearest one.

Jimmy extended his stride to keep up. "Whadja see?"

"It's definitely a delivery van. The side and back doors are open and three or four guys are unloading bags and boxes. There are a few cars back there too, one with its trunk open."

"Could just be a restaurant delivery?" It was a Tuesday night. "Maybe they need a mid-week resupply of fish or something?"

"Yeah, it might well be." Kaz stopped abruptly. A worn footpath between two tall houses looked like it led to the tracks. He pointed at it. "Let's try here. I want to get a look before they finish."

There was no movement visible in the side windows of the two houses as they walked quietly up the path. Kaz paused briefly before they went past the back gardens, checking for people or dogs, then followed the path where it led, directly to the abandoned tracks. At the top of the short, sloped bank, he looked both ways, then waved for Jimmy to follow.

Switchgrass as tall as Kaz had sprouted up through the rusted tracks and creosote-gray railway ties, growing in thick clumps where it had found enough soil and water. Dense Texas sage had worked its way up the slopes, making an intermittent impenetrable wall almost as tall as the grasses.

Still, foot traffic had beaten a narrow path down the middle of the rails. A glance at the garbage on the ground showed what people came here for: countless cigarette butts, beer bottles, discarded hypodermics and occasional used condoms. A shortcut and a place for privacy in a rundown Houston neighborhood.

Kaz walked quickly along the path, dodging the occasional patch of gravel that might crunch loudly under his feet. He turned around briefly and held a finger up to his lips, cautioning Jimmy to do the same. In the places where the grass hadn't thrived, he hunkered over, making sure he couldn't be seen from the back of the strip mall. Counting steps, he stopped to listen when he thought he was getting close.

He heard muffled male voices ahead to the left. Screened by the sage and switchgrass, Kaz craned his neck but couldn't see anything, so he walked forward slowly, looking for a gap in the undergrowth. When he found one, he stopped and beckoned the doctor forward. Jimmy carefully and quietly picked his way to where Kaz now crouched, leaning to look too.

They were almost directly behind an open rear door, out of which a shaft of bright light spilled. Pulled in along the wall were three older, smaller vehicles. *The cooks and waitstaff*, Kaz thought. *Leaving all the room out front for the customers.*

Backed up towards the open door was a medium-sized panel van. Its headlights were off, but its interior lights poured through its open back and side doors. Parked at an angle next to it was a faded green Ford Galaxie 500 with the trunk open.

Both men watched for several seconds, then Jimmy whispered, "I count five men, four of them Asian."

Kaz nodded, staying quiet. Three of the Asian men were unloading heavy bags and lighter boxes, going in and out of the building's open door, partially blocking the light each time they passed. Kaz recognized one of them—the head waiter.

The fourth, distinctively broad-shouldered, was standing by the back of the van, holding a sheaf of papers and supervising the unloading. The fifth man, white and heavily bearded, was leaning on the Ford, smoking a cigarette. Waiting.

They watched as the man with the papers stopped the head waiter, checked the bag he was carrying and pointed at the green Ford. As the waiter carried it towards the car's trunk, the driver's door suddenly opened and a tall, brown-haired woman climbed out.

She walked around to join the bearded man, the two of them observing as the bag was loaded to one side of the large trunk, leaving room for several more that followed. Three boxes were loaded through a rear door into the back seat.

Once the load-out was complete, the head waiter and his helpers disappeared into the back of the restaurant, closing the door behind them. The parking lot instantly got darker. Still, Kaz could make out the strong-looking Asian man as he walked over to the Ford, holding out a page from his sheaf. Kaz strained to listen, Jimmy kneeling beside him.

"I show twelve bags and three boxes—that's all of them." His English was Chinese-accented, his words barely audible.

The woman took the page and looked at it, nodded and recounted the bags.

Beard tipped his head towards the restaurant's back door and said, "Now that the others are inside, I want to check what's in the boxes." He lifted the nearest box out of the car, set it on the ground and pulled something out of his pants pocket. *Jackknife*, Kaz thought. He watched as the man flicked the blade open and slit the tape holding the box closed. Carefully he rotated the cardboard flaps open, the Chinese man now leaning on the Ford, watching.

Beard looked up at the woman and said something. She opened the passenger door, reached in, rummaged around and emerged with a long black flashlight. She flicked it on and pointed it into the open box.

Beard reached in and, one at a time, pulled out smaller parcels and multicolored bundles, holding each one up to the light. He carefully opened one of the small boxes, then took the flashlight from the woman to study the contents, behaving as if he was inspecting something rare and valuable. Satisfied, he closed it up and put it back, then he tipped his head from side to side, shining the flashlight into the box, as if he was assessing the total number of items.

Finally he nodded and crisscrossed the box's flaps to close it, then returned it to the back seat and shut the car door.

He spoke to the Chinese man. "That looks like enough."

"Of course it is," the man replied, sounding impatient. "What time will you be there tomorrow?"

"We'll drive up before traffic gets heavy. We want to get there early to set up. You need to arrive by around ten."

Kaz saw the man shake his head but missed what he said. Beard shrugged and replied, his voice carrying, "Suit yourself."

No one shook hands. Beard lowered the lid of the trunk, carefully pushing it closed, and got into the car with the woman. She drove down the back alley, around the corner and out of sight. The broad-shouldered Chinese man watched them disappear, stood quietly for a minute longer, then closed the van doors, got in and maneuvered it neatly into the next slot by the parked cars, then went through the door into the back of the restaurant.

"Gotta be drugs."

Jimmy was talking around a big mouthful of cheeseburger. On the way back to NASA to drop Kaz at his car, he'd stopped at the first diner they saw. Both of them were glad for the quick service.

Kaz nodded, chewing, slowly reviewing all that they'd seen. "Maybe. Or just buying restaurant supplies off-market." He paused, considering. "Could have been stolen goods. Whatever the bearded guy was looking at so closely seemed expensive." Kaz glanced at Jimmy. "What do you think was in the bags?"

"Like I said, drugs." Jimmy took a pull on his chocolate milkshake, a rare treat after a long day. "What do you suppose he meant by 'That looks like enough'?"

Kaz looked away into the darkness outside the diner's plate-glass windows.

"Not sure." He sipped his black coffee. "They obviously made a deal in advance and this was just the delivery. No money changed hands. Maybe a regular distribution arrangement." He considered what he'd seen in the restaurant with Laura. "The head waiter was definitely in on it."

Jimmy took another big bite, chewed and swallowed, then said, "Whatever they're up to, sounded like it's going down tomorrow. What did the bearded one say? They'd drive up to beat the traffic?"

"Yeah." Kaz looked at his half-eaten burger and pushed it away, picking up a french fry. "Real question is, what do we do about what we saw?" He popped the fry into his mouth and chewed meditatively, glad it was still crispy.

Jimmy shrugged. "I'm not sure what the local cops could do with what we'd tell them. Raid the restaurant? Look for a green Ford?" He put the milkshake straw back between his lips, then pulled it out. "Sorry again that I didn't get the license plate." He smiled. "Heck, I'm the guy with two eyes."

Kaz smiled back. "We were at the wrong angle, and it was dark. But I'm going to call the Harris County Sheriff anyway when we get back."

He raised his coffee cup to Jimmy. "Thanks for coming with me, Doc. Been a while since the Great Wall. A little adventure to spice up the predictable day-to-day of Apollo-Soyuz." He shook his head ruefully. "We walked on the Moon, six times! And now all we're gonna do is dock, shake hands and undock. The Space Shuttle can't get here fast enough."

Jimmy touched the rim of his milkshake to Kaz's heavy porcelain cup.

"Cheers, man. Always glad to help add excitement to your boring life."

7

Soyuz Spacecraft, Earth Orbit, July 16

"What are you seeing, Svetlana?"

Alexei Leonov was talking loudly, knowing his voice would be muffled as it traveled up through the hatch from the Soyuz entry capsule into the cramped spherical living module where Svetlana floated. The fans and pumps that moved air and cooling water throughout the spaceship to keep the crew alive made a constant, low-level background din. Like riding on a bus. Or inside a womb.

On the other side of the Soyuz's thin aluminum hull, out in the vacuum of space, the air pressure was zero. An incomprehensibly empty nothingness. The metal on the sunlit side of the ship was hotter than boiling water, yet on the dark, shaded side it was far colder than dry ice. Almost cold enough to liquefy nitrogen.

Svetlana, Alexei and Valery were floating inside a tiny aluminum bubble of Earth's air, surrounded by instant death.

"Eight hundred and thirty-seven millimeters, exactly." Svetlana, holding onto a handrail with her left hand for stability, was staring at the outer scale of the large bronze pressure gauge. In her right hand she held a grease pencil and had carefully made a mark on the glass, aligned with the tip of the wire-thin pointer needle, between 830 and 840. That way, she could spot any pressure changes at a glance.

She pivoted her weightless body to the right and looked down so her voice would carry through the hatch. "What does the gas analyzer say?" She could see the top of Alexei's balding head as he turned a small black switch to select different pressure readings.

"Entry capsule pressure eight hundred forty, oxygen partial pressure two hundred nine."

Valery was loosely strapped into the flight engineer seat next to Alexei, following along in the checklist, ensuring no mistakes.

Svetlana nodded to herself. Air is mostly made of nitrogen, but about one-fifth is oxygen. The ground technicians had boosted the ship's internal air pressure to 840 millimeters of mercury before launch, higher than the air pressure on the ground in Baikonur, so they could check for leaks. And to give the crew a little extra oxygen boost in case a leak started during ascent.

"Ready for depress?" She said the words loudly and clearly, as it was an important step.

Alexei glanced at Valery, who nodded and gave a clear response. "Da, gatov." *Yes, ready.*

Svetlana flicked open two switch covers to the left of the pressure gauge. One was labeled 3AKP and the other OTKP, short for "zakreet" and "otkreet." *Closed* and *open.* Controlling the valve that opened a small hole out to the vacuum of space.

She stabilized her right hand with her fingertips, reached in with her thumb, as she knew it was a heavy, stiff valve, and threw the OTKP switch.

Immediately she felt her ears pop as the Soyuz started to lose pressure. Within seconds she heard a klaxon sound loudly and then stop, with Alexei calling "Normalna" from down in the entry capsule—he'd wanted to make sure the alarm sensor worked properly. Now he rotated the switch to reset it to a lower cabin pressure.

Svetlana was staring without blinking at the big pressure gauge, ready to instantly close the valve if they needed to. She pictured their air being sucked into the opened valve, flowing along the plumbing, racing around the many bends and finally out of their ship into the endless, pressureless void. The Soviet space engineers had long since learned to put a T-shaped fixture on the exhaust end of the pipe so the outrushing air would flow in two perfectly opposite directions and wouldn't act as a propulsive jet.

The long needle on the pressure gauge relentlessly rotated counterclockwise, like time going backwards.

"Syem sot!" she called loudly. Seven hundred. Nearly halfway there.

"Prinyata." Alexei's response was terse. *Transmission received.*

The Russian crew needed to drop their cabin pressure so they would be able to open the hatch after they docked with the American spaceship. Unlike the Soviets, NASA had decided years ago that it was simpler to have pure oxygen as the Apollo atmosphere. But high-pressure oxygen makes everything very flammable, so the Apollo ship operated at just five psi — one-third of normal Earth pressure. It had saved precious weight to land on the Moon without having to carry nitrogen tanks and extra plumbing. The lower pressure had also allowed the pressure seals and even the metal walls of the ship to be thinner. Weight had been everything. It had helped the United States win the race to the Moon.

When they docked with Apollo the following day, the two ships themselves wouldn't be in direct contact. The Americans had designed a Docking Module for the front of their ship that would mate with the Soyuz. The whole docked stack would look like a dumbbell, the two bulbous ends connected by a slender center. The Soyuz end would be at 500 millimeters of pressure, and the Apollo at 260. When the crews wanted to transfer to each other's ship they would float into the Docking Module, close their hatch and then use the tanks and valves to match the pressure of the other ship.

Svetlana heard the klaxon sound again as the pressure reached 600, and she decisively thumbed the switch labeled **3AKP**. *Closed.*

She pinched her nose between her thumb and forefinger and cleared her ears, waiting for the ship's pressure to stabilize, and then used the grease pencil to mark the new value of 600. They were targeting 500, but she wanted to make sure the valves worked properly, cycling closed and open. She paused until she was certain the needle had truly stopped and then reopened the OTKP valve.

The needle was moving more slowly now as the pressure pushing the air out continued to drop. She momentarily had a vision of her Soyuz as a sad deflating balloon.

"Five hundred fifty," Svetlana called.

Alexei's response floated back up. "Prinyata."

If they had left the Soyuz cabin at its original 840-millimeter launch pressure mixture of nitrogen and oxygen, the crew couldn't have instantly dropped to 260 to match the pressure in the Apollo ship. The sudden change would have affected their bodies like opening a can of Coke, causing the dissolved gases in their blood to fizz into small bubbles. Bubbles that would collect in their knees and elbows, doing vascular damage and causing instant pain, making the crew bend over to relieve the agony. The divers' nightmare literally known as "the bends."

And if the bubbles collected in the blood vessels of the brain, the damage could cause dizziness, seizures and loss of consciousness. Even death.

The needle crawled past 505, and just as it was reaching 500, Svetlana threw the 3AKP switch. There was a heavy metal cap floating in front of the panel on a short lanyard, and she screwed it back into position too—an extra off valve to protect from inadvertent depressurization.

Retrieving her grease pencil from where she'd tucked it under a bungee, she precisely marked the needle's new position.

"Four hundred ninety-nine, Alexei. Both valves closed," she called.

"Otleechna," he responded. *Outstanding*. "I'm showing five hundred exactly on my gauges." A short pause, and when he spoke next, she could hear the smile in his voice.

"Nice work, Sveta. We're ready for docking!"

Svetlana smiled to herself. She enjoyed working with Alexei, an accomplished yet humble man, quick with a kind word and accepting of her as a skilled crewmate.

Unlike most in the cosmonaut corps.

8

North Launch Complex LA-2B, Inner Mongolia, China

For millions of years, the chilled, dry air from China's Altai and Tian Shan Mountains had blown down into the highlands of the Gobi Desert. The lack of water had created a visibly empty land of weather extremes. In winter, it got as cold as minus 40, made much worse by the unending wind, driving the chill to the bone. Only a few hardy animals and tough plants could endure it.

But today was July 16, the middle of summer, with the sun high in the sky and the temperature nearing 100 degrees. The wind, equally searing, lifted and drove swirls of grit into the air, which rattled like dry rain on the metallic sides of the white-painted rocket, the volume rising and falling with each desert gust.

The buildings surrounding the LA-2B launch pad were designed to take it: low, rounded metal storage sheds, thick stone blockhouses with small windows, and covered circular fuel tanks protected by high bulldozed berms of rock and sand.

"Always the bloody sand," Fang muttered.

The periscope window of his spaceship was shielded for launch, blocking the brightness of the sunlight reflecting off the undulating pale brown, rocky land. He'd been born and raised well to the southeast, in Henan, on the humid, fertile flatlands along the Yellow River. Since he'd joined the People's Liberation Army at 15 to help support his family, the military had sent him to all corners of China, from the northeastern Korean border to the tropical southern island of Hainan. Fang had used his wits to rise from lowly teenage messenger and scribe to Air Force officer and pilot, flying the latest jet-powered fighters for 20 years.

But for the past four years, he'd been separated from his wife and family, living and training in total secrecy near Peking and up here in the desert as one of China's 19 astronauts.

And he, Fang Kuo-chun, son of a Henan schoolteacher and father of three young sons, had been chosen as the first Chinese citizen to fly in space.

It was risky as hell.

He was sitting on top of a CZ-2A rocket. "CZ" was short for Chang Zheng, the Long March, the year-long, death-filled retreat on foot of the Red Army 30 years earlier. Fang thought the name choice was oddly pessimistic; the only time the CZ-2A had previously launched, on its first test flight, a cable connecting the pitch-rate control gyroscope to the guidance system had apparently become disconnected. Hard to tell for sure when pieces of the wreckage were spread all over the Gobi Desert floor, but whatever the cause, the rocket had lost direction, tumbled and exploded just 20 seconds after liftoff.

The spaceship capsule he was strapped into, mounted on top of a new, improved CZ-2A rocket, had never flown before, but at least the designers had given it an upbeat name: Shuguang. It was to be the first of the new series of Chinese-piloted spaceships, so it was Shuguang-1.

Shuguang. First Dawn. Fang liked that.

Compared to the rockets the Soviets and Americans were flying, the CZ-2A was squatty. Just 30 meters tall, it was a lumpy 10-story building with a point on top. It was held solidly to the ground by the weight of its fuel and heavy metal launch mounts, but Fang could still feel a slight rocking from the wind gusts.

The rocket hadn't been designed to launch people. It was based on an intercontinental ballistic missile, with four brutal motors burning corrosive, highly explosive hypergolic fuel. An old Soviet design adapted for Chinese military needs. Fang knew he was about to go for a wild ride. The engineers predicted he'd be pinned in his seat at over eight times his normal weight, with potentially high vibration and extreme violence as the rocket's first stage burned out and the second stage ignited. There hadn't been time to build centrifuges to simulate it, as the Soviets and Americans had done. Fang had prepared by flying People's Liberation Army Air Force jets to the limit of their strength.

And his.

He glanced at his instrument panel as he listened to the voices of men he knew well, safe in their launch blockhouse 100 meters away. It was 30 seconds until ignition. He'd find out soon whether the previous problems had been fixed.

Fang was at peace with whatever was about to happen. He'd grown up during the floods and locust plagues that had killed so many in his province, and he had seen many fellow pilots die in their reverse-engineered homemade MiG fighters. It took sacrifice for China to advance. And of all the 900 million citizens in the People's Republic, he was the one who had been picked for this mission by Director Tsien. And by Chairman Mao himself.

Twenty seconds until launch.

Fang had been standing at attention on Tiananmen Square during the May Day parade five years previously when Chairman Mao, with Tsien beside him, had declared that the People's Republic would develop a manned spacecraft. The thought of it had sent a jolt of excitement through him, even as he stood rock-still in military formation.

Fifteen seconds.

That same excitement tingled now, and Fang flexed his fingers. An ancient proverb flitted through his thoughts: to smash the cooking pots and sink the boats. For victory, there could be no going back.

Ten.

His father had died just before Fang went into the military. He would have been so proud to know what his son was doing on this day.

Five.

Commands came from the computers on board, valves instantly pivoted open, and liquid fuel and oxidizer suddenly rushed from the safety of their separate tanks down multiple metal tubes to mix and explode in the inferno of the central combustion chambers. The CZ-2A lurched violently underneath him, a new beast rudely awakened, with a power far beyond anything Fang had ever felt before.

The countdown clock reached zero. Time to launch.

9

Jiuquan Launch Control, Inner Mongolia, China

Safely inside the launch control blockhouse, behind concrete walls thick enough to deflect rocket explosions, Director Tsien intently watched the TV screen. He didn't often travel all the way up from Peking to the missile site, but today's launch was historic. The first Chinese astronaut in space! As director of the Fifth Academy of the Ministry of National Defense, he had led all missile and nuclear weapons development under Chairman Mao. Today was a crowning glory!

As long as Shuguang, with Colonel Fang flying within, made it to orbit.

Director Tsien Hsue-shen was a small, thin man with thick, round glasses, and he had to lean forward to see the screen clearly. They'd made several design changes since the failure of the previous launch. As each second of launch ascent passed, he allowed himself a growing sense of relief, the operation's continuing success visible in the solid, stable flame under the rocket's first stage.

As it climbed into the air, the bright orange-yellow fire flickered smaller and smaller on the screen until it was barely visible. Tsien marveled at the improbability of it. He felt immense satisfaction at

China's amazing new ability to launch astronauts into orbit. World-class, as he'd promised Chairman Mao. Yet so unlikely after the crazy sequence of events that had taken him from his humble origins in Shanghai to being here, today, watching history being made.

Tsien leaned even closer to the screen, his eyes burning with intensity, willing the rocketship to succeed. He was stealing a prize from the Americans, an ambition that had driven him every day since the US government had so stupidly stolen his life and career from him.

The knock on the door, when it came 25 years ago, had been loud and authoritative. Four quick, strong raps evenly spaced, a pause, then identically repeated 10 seconds later.

"I'm coming!"

It was a Thursday, but Tsien was at home in Altadena, California. For the past three months, ever since Caltech had received a letter in June revoking his security clearance and the FBI had searched his office, he'd been instructed to stay away from the university.

An unsettling summer.

Tsien heard their two-month-old baby in the nursery start to cry at the noise, and his wife's comforting murmurs. As he got up from his chair, their toddler son, Yucon, looked up from where he was building with blocks in the corner of the living room. The knocks came a third time, along with muffled shouts from a male voice.

Tsien nodded reassuringly at Yucon, then went to answer the door.

It wasn't locked. Tsien took a deep breath and exhaled slowly to calm himself, reached for the knob and swung the door open.

Two men stood on the small porch, one short and one tall, both in uniform: shiny off-white cotton shirts, mustard-brown ties, dark-blue forage caps with matching trousers, and shiny black shoes. The badge of the Immigration and Naturalization Service was on each of their chests, and again on the caps. The shorter man was holding a clipboard with a sheaf of papers attached. He looked down to read the name.

"Are you Mister Hsue-shen Tsien?" The immigration agent

stumbled over the foreign words, but after 15 years in the United States, the Caltech professor was used to it.

Tsien was only 40 years old, but his wispy black hair had already receded from his broad, rounded forehead. He'd hoped to spend the rest of his life working with his colleagues in America, but the isolated summer had readied him for this knock on the door.

He answered quietly. "Yes, I am Professor Tsien Hsue-shen." He put his title and family name first, as was proper, especially for an official confrontation.

He looked past the men to their dark-blue sedan parked at the curb. The color matched the agents' caps and pants, and it had the same crest on the front door.

He heard his wife's voice calling, asking who it was, but he didn't respond because the man with the clipboard was speaking again, pronouncing each word distinctly, as if he was reading from a script.

"As agents of the United States Immigration and Naturalization Service," he intoned, "we have been instructed to place you under arrest on suspicion of being an alien communist agent, and to take you into federal custody." The man had a prominent nose, thick, dark eyebrows and a strong East Coast accent. *New York Italian*, Tsien decided. As he listened, his eyes flicked to the much larger man looming half a step behind. *Here in case I put up a struggle.* Despite the circumstances, Tsien smiled slightly at the absurdity.

"Do you understand what I am saying?" The agent was used to immigrants who didn't know how to speak American yet.

Tsien calmly replied, "Yes, I understand you. I need to tell my wife and to get some personal items to bring." He paused. "How long will I be in custody?"

The agent, only an inch taller than Tsien, straightened his back to be able to look down at him. "We're not at liberty to say. The duration of your incarceration will be decided by the courts, and a judge." His New York accent made "duration" and "incarceration" sound like a rhyme.

There was a pause as Tsien waited for the man to remember his implied question.

The agent glanced at his companion, then nodded. "Yeah, you can grab a few things. Agent Brubaker here will accompany you."

Despite his appearance of calm, Tsien felt both angry and sick. The accusation that he was some sort of communist spy was ridiculous. He'd come to America by invitation, as a Boxer Indemnity scholar, and had completed his master's and doctorate in record time at MIT and Caltech, where he was a respected scientist, researcher and professor. Both of his children had been born here and had US citizenship, and he and his wife, Ying, had applied to become American citizens the previous year.

Brubaker's heavy footsteps followed him as he walked back down the hall, through the living room and into the nursery. Ying looked up, worried and then alarmed when she caught sight of the oversized uniformed agent. The baby had stopped crying, and Ying was cradling the infant close to her chest.

Tsien felt a wave of embarrassment in front of his wife, but he controlled himself. They'd discussed the possibility that this could happen, and now that it had, strength was needed. "I'm being arrested, love. I need to get some clothes and identification and my briefcase." He frowned, thinking it through, and turned to look up at Brubaker. "Where are you taking me?"

The agent took his time deciding what he could tell the suspected communist, but eventually he said, "To the federal facility at Reservation Point. About an hour's drive from here." His accent was flat, middle America. He looked at Tsien's wife. "There are visiting hours."

Tears welled in Ying's eyes as she spoke to her husband in Mandarin. "How long will you be held?" She glanced down at the baby, then at the doorway, where Yucon was now standing, silently watching them. "What shall I do?"

Tsien answered in English, for the agent's benefit. "Before these men take me away, they will give you the address and phone number of where

I'll be, and the visiting times. I want you to call the dean at Caltech and Professor von Kármán to hire a lawyer, get them to organize my bail." Seeing the overwhelmed confusion in his wife's eyes, Tsien repeated himself in Mandarin as he hugged her and the baby. Then he turned back to Brubaker. "You and your partner will please clearly write out that information for my wife while I go upstairs and pack a bag."

Not waiting for objections, he turned, picked up his son and went out into the hallway and up the staircase.

Tsien's normally ordered thoughts were spinning. *Arrested!* That was for criminals. He had committed no crime! This was all the result of the witch hunt started back in February 1950 by Senator Joseph McCarthy, when he'd accused the State Department of employing over 200 men who were secretly members of the Communist Party. Tsien had already heard of other Chinese professors being blacklisted, arrested and even deported.

He set his son on the bed, bent to pull his overnight bag from underneath it and began filling it with underwear, socks and toiletries. *What is going to happen to me?* The thought hammered through his brain. He guessed it might take a few days to get bailed out, so he folded in a spare pair of trousers and a couple of shirts. *Will I be held in a jail cell?* He felt another wave of nausea as he put in a button-up sweater.

I was a full professor at 35 with a top-secret security clearance. The Americans trusted me to work on the Manhattan Project. How can this be happening?

As he picked up his son and his bag, he caught their combined reflection in the bedroom mirror. Tsien prided himself on his composure and tidiness, but the man he saw in the mirror looked uncharacteristically wild, with hair askew and jawline clenched in anger, his mouth a thin, hard line.

He stopped to look at himself head-on, his eyes burning with unaccustomed intensity, using the moment to center himself for what was about to happen. He was surprised to hear himself speaking out loud, the Mandarin words guttural with resolve.

"They will not get away with this!"

But they had, though it took another five long years of house arrest before President Eisenhower deported Tsien and his family to Hong Kong in exchange for China's release of some US prisoners from the Korean War. And now the Americans would pay for it—in more ways than one.

18

Near Houston, Texas

"Aaron, are you sure we're far enough away?" The tall woman sounded nervous.

Aaron glanced at his watch, stroked his thick beard and looked across at the old car parked on the floor of the quarry, deliberately ignoring her. He was the Weather Underground's bomb expert, and he found the incompetence of the other members as quaint as it was annoying. Self-declared revolutionaries with wild eyes and secret meetings and bandanas, but all pamphlets and posturing. Talking about class struggle to fight US imperialism, racism and sexism was inspiring, but it was the bombs that got noticed. He was the sole member they all counted on for actual action.

After 15 seconds of silence, he decided he'd made his point, looked at his watch again and calmly said, "We still have three minutes, Molly." He pointed to the rock outcropping to their left, high above the car, on the rim of the abandoned quarry. "At ninety seconds, we'll duck behind there."

He turned and looked Molly full in the face. She was a founder of the Weather Underground and defiantly pretty, with an oval face, unplucked eyebrows and long, dark-brown, unruly hair parted in the middle. She was wearing jeans and a black T-shirt, braless, with sandals.

Sandals, Aaron had thought when they'd met early that morning to drive to the quarry. *Figures*. He was wearing steel-toed construction boots.

One more glance at his watch. "Okay, let's move."

The two of them worked their way around the quarry's edge, Aaron leading. He wasn't fit and hadn't excelled at anything until a friend had invited him to join the Weathermen. Slightly breathless, he hunkered down behind the protruding rock and took Molly's hand, guiding her into place next to him, their backs against the thick, protective limestone. He felt his heart beating fast, mostly with excitement.

This was what he lived for.

He'd scouted the quarry using topographic maps at a Houston library. They were miles from the nearest farmhouse, and they'd already used the remote location for target practice for newly recruited Houston-based Weather Underground members. The presence of the rusted car was serendipitous. It had been abandoned in the quarry years before and was pockmarked with shotgun spray and bullet holes. Most of the glass was knocked out, the shards littering the hood and surrounding dirt.

While Molly kept watch, Aaron had loaded it with explosives.

He rechecked his watch, nodded to himself and stretched to take one last look. Squinting against the glare through his rimless glasses, he surveyed the view from the car out through the quarry entrance and down the long gravel track that led to the main road. He could just see a glint of light off the pickup truck with the Chinese sentry sitting inside. Ready to stop any lookie-loos.

Aaron saw no dust in the air, so no one was coming. He slumped back down behind the rock.

He was a self-taught and prideful bomb-maker. The explosion he'd engineered at the US State Department six months before had gone perfectly because he'd tested it. This next demonstration of power was going to be the Underground's biggest yet, and he didn't trust the materials they'd received from China. Verification was imperative.

The mistrust was mutual, which was why the Houston Chinese tong leadership had insisted on sending their man to protect their investment. Despite an aversion to including outsiders, Molly and Aaron had reluctantly agreed. They'd worked successfully with Chinatown gangs before, in New York City. An acceptable risk on the true road to revolution. China's class struggle had revolutionized people's vision of the possibilities of socialism. China was a worthy ally in the fight.

And China's agents had weapons and cash.

Aaron's bomb, loaded into the trunk of the junked car below, was simple. A battery provided the electric current, and an alarm clock closed the circuit to fire the blasting caps and ignite the explosive. Once he'd installed it, he'd tested the wiring with a light bulb. Satisfied, he'd carefully synchronized the clock with his watch, rerouted the wires and tightened the screws, forced the lid of the trunk down onto its broken latch, put his tools back into Molly's car, hidden on a side trail outside the quarry's entrance, and hiked with her up and around to the cliff's edge.

He'd never admit it, but he hadn't been sure how much explosive to use. He normally used dynamite sticks, which were readily available from construction suppliers. After two dozen Weather Underground bombings, he had a good feel for their destructive power. But this target was bigger. He'd read everything he could on the new chemical mixture, but data was sparse and there were more variables, so he'd had to guess.

Another reason to perform a test.

Molly grabbed at his arm, trying to see his watch. "How many more seconds?"

Aaron shook her off. He had been counting in his head, and it was time. Smiling, he raised his hand to his ears, his pointer fingers extended.

"Plug your ears, girl."

11

Mission Control, Houston

"Apollo, Houston, how do you read?" Kaz had been watching the large world map on the front wall of Mission Control, and the timer showed that the spaceship should have just moved back into radio contact.

Deke Slayton's voice crackled in his headset. "Loud and clear, Kaz."

"Hey, Deke, just before we get into the rendezvous phasing maneuver, we have some evening news, if you three are ready for that."

The NASA public affairs team had gathered clippings from the wire service, and Kaz was holding the flimsy teletype printout in his hand. The Apollo crews who had gone to the Moon had appreciated getting occasional updates on happenings on Earth, and NASA had carried on the tradition.

"Stand by just one minute, Kaz, and we'll get you on the squawk box."

Kaz pictured Deke throwing the communications switches and dragging the small portable speaker on its stiff wire to a place where he could Velcro it, so all three Apollo crewmembers could hear it.

"Okay, Houston, go ahead with the latest."

Kaz smiled. "As you might have guessed, you guys are dominating the news." Careful not to smudge the thermally printed ink, he read from the sheet: "Yesterday morning, President Ford and Soviet Ambassador Dobrynin watched and applauded the Russian Soyuz launch together at the State Department auditorium. President Ford said the launch marked the beginning of a very epic adventure into space and was blazing a brand-new trail."

Kaz paused. *Very epic adventure.* Unlike Nixon, the new president had a folksy way with words. He guessed that he and the crew would have a good laugh at that phrase over a beer when they got back. But not while the whole world was listening to their radio call.

He read the next paragraph. "Dobrynin then traveled to Florida with NASA Administrator Fletcher to view the Apollo launch in person, while President Ford watched the launch at the White House on television."

Tom Stafford responded. "We're looking forward to talking with President Ford after we dock tomorrow."

Kaz nodded. The president was planning to travel to Houston, to be in Mission Control to share in the historic international event. And the positive press coverage that went with it. He scanned ahead on the teletype, choosing what was worth transmitting. "Want to hear the sports scores?"

Deke, a Wisconsin native, answered. "Sure, how are my Brewers doing?"

Kaz mimicked a play-by-play announcer: "A two-run single broke a ninth inning tie and led Major League Baseball's National League All-Stars to a six–three victory over the American League last night. Secretary of State Henry A. Kissinger threw out the first ball in the game." He looked farther down the page for something interesting. "And Joe Namath, in a bargaining session, says he wants to play with the New York Jets for two more years."

Kaz glanced at the clock. Time for more serious work. The crew had to fire their engine to adjust their orbit to catch up with the Soyuz, and the engine burn would occur while their ship was out of radio coverage.

In his normal voice, he said, "Apollo, back to business. We see the correct final data loaded for the maneuver to burn attitude, but note that towards the end of this pass we'll lose comms, so we won't be able to watch you burn." He waited for a confirming nod from Lunney, next to him. "You have all the data on board and have a GO for the burn on time."

Tom's Oklahoma accent was clear. "Copy, Houston, GO for the burn. We'll start the maneuver now and see you on the other side."

Kaz looked again at the wall chart in front of him. "Talk to you then, Tom, through the *Vanguard* relay ship."

He leaned back in his chair. Tomorrow was going to be busy with docking and hatch opening, and with the disruption of the president visiting Mission Control. But what he and Jimmy had seen in the alley behind the Chinese restaurant had been bugging him all day. He would be getting off shift soon. He glanced at his watch, then turned and spoke to the flight activities officer at the console next to him.

"Hey, FAO, odd question, but do you know what time sunset is here tonight?"

12

Polly Ranch

The hot July evening sun was still well above the western horizon as Kaz accelerated down the narrow runway. At 70 miles per hour, he pulled back smoothly on the control wheel, eased the plane up off the tarmac and flicked the small switch to raise the landing gear. He saw the green DOWN light extinguish, watched the ammeter as the electric motor drove the wheels up and felt a pilot's satisfaction when the white UP light came on, confirming complete gear retraction. He grabbed the long floor-mounted handle to manually retract the flaps, and relished the familiar acceleration now that the airplane was cleaned up and flying.

Like a bird.

He glanced out the side window as the plane climbed past his house. His rear driveway led straight onto the runway at Polly Ranch Airpark, and after he moved in, he'd bought a 1959 Comanche 250, which he kept in his oversized garage. It was fun to fly locally, and he occasionally flew it east along the Gulf of Mexico and all the way across Florida to support NASA operations at the Kennedy Space Center on the Atlantic coast.

But tonight he just wanted to go look at things. Like many of his fellow pilots, he found that he often understood a place better when he saw it from above.

The Polly Ranch runway was aligned east-west, so Kaz turned left as he climbed, north towards Houston. He glanced at his watch, confirming that he had about an hour until sunset, at 8:23. After the day in Mission Control, he didn't want to talk to anyone on the radio, so he leveled off at 1,800 feet, below where air traffic control would notice him. He swung wide around the Ellington Field control zone and headed up along Galveston Bay.

The I-10 freeway cut Houston exactly in half, like a gray concrete belt across its bulging Texan waist. Kaz spotted the tall white column of the San Jacinto monument and cut inside it to fly along the north side of the freeway, then started looking ahead and out the pilot's-side window for his target. As he'd driven home from work, he'd been picturing what the Chinese restaurant would look like from the air, and now he scanned the north side of I-10.

He saw the angular cut of the abandoned railway first, standing out amongst the orderly, treed suburban streets. From there, the long, flat silver roof of the restaurant building was obvious. He turned the control wheel to bank to the left and circle for a good look. The airspace was pinched between Hobby Airport to the south and Intercontinental Airport to the north, but he knew that if he didn't stray too far south of I-10, he'd be okay. He tightened the turn and stared down along his left wing at the building.

The overhanging roof partially obscured the customers' cars parked in front, but the back lot was clearly visible, with the same neat line of cars by the rear door. A square van sat at the end of the row, and across the narrow lot, parked along the fence by the train tracks, was a green sedan.

Interesting. Last night I heard them say they were going to drive up and meet somewhere. As he turned the plane, he glanced to the north in the gathering darkness. *Where did you go? And why are you all back here now?*

The parking lot was already in shadow, and he saw a sudden angular shaft of light as someone opened the restaurant's back door. Three people walked out, took several steps towards the green car and then stopped to look up.

Must be my low-altitude noise. Kaz quickly rolled his wings level to keep them from reading the registration numbers painted on the side of the plane, and flew along I-10, westward towards the sun. He briefly considered turning back to follow them, but decided it was impractical at his speed. He'd need a helicopter to follow a car through city streets. And he wanted to pursue his second objective for the flight.

He judged there was still enough daylight and angled to the right to follow Highway 290. It was as good a guess as any as to what "drive up" meant, and the terrain north of Houston was all fairly similar. He just wanted to see it directly, in case it sparked an idea of where they might have gone. He pushed the throttle up to max continuous power of 24 inches of mercury and watched as the airspeed climbed.

Highway 290 was the main artery leading northwest to Austin, and it was mostly bordered by light industry as it led away from downtown Houston. As the urban sprawl thinned, Kaz pictured the three people he'd just seen, while they were fresh in his mind.

Two women and a man, he decided. *Likely the bearded guy and the woman I saw the night before, plus another woman.* But the glimpse had been too brief to be useful. He shrugged and looked ahead on either side of the highway. He was flying over a mix of small towns, squared-off farm lots and dark-green bush, spotted with occasional ponds and a few winding creeks. Population was sparse, and there were scars of what looked like oil drilling sites and spent quarries. Kaz pictured the van and the green car driving out here with purpose and stopping for . . . something. *Why did they have to come to the countryside?* he pondered. *If it was all about drugs or stolen goods, why bring them out here?* A thought niggled at the back of his brain but failed to take shape.

Kaz glanced at his watch. The runway back at Polly Ranch had edge lights, but it was only 22 feet wide, and with his 36-foot wingspan, he preferred to land in daylight. *Enough,* he decided, and turned south to skirt the edge of Hobby's airspace and get back on the ground before dark.

As the darkening Houston scrublands passed under him, he kept wondering, *What did they come out here for?*

13

Kettering Grammar School, 80 Miles North of London, England

The boy leaned forward, listening intently, his fingertips resting lightly on the frequency tuning knob.

The earphones he was wearing were heavy, an ancient pair supported by two metal straps that crisscrossed over his head and bunched his hair into a lump. They'd been worn by a generation of schoolboys before him, and the black leather ear cups were cracked and worn. The rustling noise they made in his ears was distracting, so he held his breath to try to hear better.

His name was Rupert, and it was his turn to detect the Soviets.

Looming on the tables in the classroom around him was a hodgepodge of radio and electronics gear, accumulated over the 15 years that Kettering's Satellite Tracking Group had existed. His physics teacher, Mr. Perry, had originally set it up to track the early Sputniks, but it had grown into an integral part of the school. This week, even though it was the end of summer term, there had been a buzz of activity at all hours with the Russian cosmonauts and American astronauts docking together.

In space.

Rupert was 14, a fourth-year, and had proven himself old enough to be trusted to work alone. He knew the exact time that the Soviets and Americans were scheduled to appear over the horizon, and had tuned in the Greenwich Time Signal pips, broadcast on BBC Radio at the top of the hour, to make sure the electric wall clock was correct. The Satellite Tracking Group logbook was open on the table in front of him, and he'd neatly written *17 July 1975* at the top left of the page.

There was a click and a hiss, and then the noise in his earphones resolved itself into the familiar warble of the beacon on the Soviet Soyuz. As his eyes flicked to the wall clock, he grabbed the Bic ballpoint on the table and carefully wrote the time in the leftmost column. Next to it he recorded, *Soyuz signal acquisition*, just as he'd been taught.

Maybe the cosmonauts are transmitting, he thought eagerly. He loved hearing the Russian words, as if they were being spoken just to him, like he was a British spy, here in this unlikely corner of Northamptonshire. He turned the dial to the different frequencies the Soviets used, waiting patiently on each for several seconds, ready to reach over to the large gray reel-to-reel tape recorder at the first hint of a human voice.

Nothing. Rupert sighed. Since the Russians had docked with the Americans, most of the communications had been through a NASA relay satellite. But sometimes they used their own radio to talk to Moscow directly. His town of Kettering was almost as far north as Moscow, so he was in the right place on Earth to eavesdrop.

Still nothing. His fingertips spun the dial towards another familiar frequency, but as it turned, he heard a brief burst of unexpected noise.

Rupert frowned. Who was transmitting on that frequency? He stopped and backed the dial up, carefully adjusting it to find the source of the noise.

There! He eased the dial precisely back and forth until he got maximum volume and clearest sound, and looked closely to note the specific frequency. He checked the time again and wrote it with the newly acquired signal in the book. He reached up and started the big tape recorder, just in case.

Who is it? Rupert's heart raced as he listened. It was the usual warbling carrier tone, but he'd never noticed the Russians using that frequency.

A thought struck him. Mr. Perry had glued a typed page with reference information into the back of the logbook. He flipped to the last page and held it open, running his finger down past the reminders about procedures and important phone numbers to a list of known frequencies.

He secretly hoped he'd found something that no one had ever heard before. He'd be the talk of the school!

But there it was, the exact frequency he was listening to, 19.995 MHz, already on the list. Rupert started to sigh as he scanned to the right, checking what they'd named this particular radio band. He stopped as he read the typed words.

```
24 April 1970, launch of China's first satellite,
Dong Fang Hong. Broadcast Chinese anthem, "The
East Is Red."
```

He listened in sudden wonder to the undulating sound coming through his headphones, then looked up, picturing what was above the ceiling of his grammar school.

The Chinese had launched another satellite! No one else had detected it yet!

Then Rupert thought of something else. *It's in the same part of the sky as Apollo-Soyuz!*

14

NORAD, Cheyenne Mountain, Colorado

In his office, buried 2,000 feet deep in the solid granite bedrock of Colorado Springs, at the end of miles of tunnels and behind a nuclear-blast-proof 25-ton door, Lieutenant General Richard Stovel had to make a decision.

His duty ops officer had taken the phone call from the school in England, alerting NORAD to an unseen satellite apparently launched from China. The British schoolteacher, speaking precise BBC Radio English, had passed along the specifics of what he and his students had calculated for the satellite's orbit, and North American Air Defense Command had swung their large tracking antennas to search the sky. They'd quickly found the new orbiter and added it to the roster of 245 active satellites they were already tracking.

At first, they assumed it was another scientific research satellite, like the first two that China had launched. But the Defense Intelligence Agency had indicated that the Chinese were working on heat shields and re-entry capsules that would allow them to send spy satellites with film canisters into orbit. So NORAD had been tracking it closely and had detected when the satellite's orbit changed slightly.

For the first time, a Chinese satellite was maneuvering.

The big mainframe computers in NORAD's underground complex did the math, backing out where the satellite had launched from and predicting where the new orbit would take it. Automated systems looked into the future, checking for any potential collisions with other satellites.

That triggered an alert flag, which had made it to Dick Stovel's desk.

Stovel carefully reviewed the briefing sheets, flicking the pages back and forth, visualizing what was going on high above his head.

Can that be right? Why would the Chinese be headed there? He stroked his trim mustache with his thumb and forefinger.

China was new at this. Did they even know what their maneuvers were doing to their orbit?

Stovel looked off to one side for several seconds, thinking. His job was aerospace defense, and this new satellite didn't look like that sort of threat. But it was definitely going to be of interest to the Pentagon, and maybe the State Department.

He thought further. *NASA too.*

Lieutenant General Richard Stovel grabbed his secure phone and started making calls.

15

Air Force One, Approaching Houston, July 17

"Ellington Tower, good morning, this is Air Force One. We'd like to make a pass at fifteen hundred feet over the Johnson Space Center on our way inbound, if that's okay."

"Copy, Air Force One, good morning, that's approved as requested. We see no unexpected traffic in your area. Call when you're inbound for landing at Ellington."

"Thanks, Tower, wilco."

The captain of the heavy Boeing VC-137C smiled across the cockpit at his first officer. They were about to undertake an unusual and fun bit of hand flying in what was normally a pretty boring duty. President Ford had his 23-year-old son, Jack, on board and had asked for a low flyby so they could see NASA's Mission Control together from the air. The airliner had already descended lower than its usual approach to Houston, east over Galveston Bay.

The captain keyed the intercom. "Mr. President, we're just passing south of the little seaside town of Seabrook, Texas, out your right-side window. In a minute you'll be able to see the large, open fields around the Johnson Space Center. Mission Control will be the square gray two-lobed building in the center, with a green quadrangle on one side and parking lots around the other three."

When he'd gotten word that morning that the president might make this request, the captain had called an Air Force buddy at NASA to make sure he had the facts right. He'd then contacted Houston Center air traffic control to give them a heads-up. Together, they'd also ginned up a little surprise for Jack.

Still, flying this close to the ground, he was wary of threats. After the recently foiled terrorist plot to fire shoulder-mounted surface-to-air missiles at Prime Minister Golda Meir's plane in Rome, Air Force One was equipped with missile-defeating chaff and flare dispensers. He'd briefed the detection and deployment procedures with his flight crew before takeoff. He hadn't gotten to be commander of the US president's plane, *Spirit of '76,* by being unprepared.

In his onboard stateroom, President Gerald Ford had his nose pressed against the square window. Seated facing him on a padded dark-blue leather chair, Jack was doing the same to his own window. Jack had just graduated from Utah State in forestry and was spending the summer at the White House while deciding what to do next. The president had invited him on today's trip to get a little father-and-son time.

Ford Senior mouthed aloud what the captain had just said. "Ahead on the right." He peered in that direction but saw only muddy brown lakes and dense olive-green bayous. "Can you spot it, Jack?"

"Yeah, there it is, just past that curvy road." Jack was used to his dad being a little slow on the uptake in new situations, and pointed ahead and down, craning his neck. He stuck a finger into his collar to loosen it; he was wearing a suit at his father's request. But he'd avoided a haircut—his long red-brown hair, parted in the middle, reached almost to his shoulders. "There's a bunch of buildings, and open ground beyond."

The president spoke. "I heard the captain say a two-lobed building next to parking and a quadrangle." Father and son scanned the ground as it rushed by at 250 miles per hour. The elder Ford pointed. "Think that's the one, just the other side of the long green square?"

"Yep, that taller one with the double flat roof has to be it." Jack had been a high school senior when Armstrong and Aldrin walked on the Moon during Apollo 11. He'd watched the events intently on television and couldn't deny the rush of excitement he felt on seeing Mission Control for the first time.

The plane banked to the right, giving both men a clearer view. Jack had brought his Polaroid SX-70 camera and took a picture, the mechanism whining and clunking as it dispensed the still-developing photo. Smiling, Jack removed it, then turned the camera quickly towards his dad, who was still looking out the window, and pushed the shutter again. "Mom will appreciate the photos. Stick them on the fridge."

The president smiled back at his son, grateful for this rare chance to do something fun together. His official duties had forced him and Betty to miss Jack's recent graduation and commencement—the pressures of the job were unrelenting, and mounting. The country was crawling out of recession at last, but unemployment was still climbing and he also had to deal with intense unrest across the country from the Vietnam War and Nixon's resignation—the circumstance that had thrust Ford into power. While he'd known taking over the top job in a crisis was a possibility when he'd become Nixon's vice president, he had never really believed it would happen. Now an election was coming that he wanted to win on his own merits.

But today would be fun.

"Look, Dad, a NASA jet!" Jack was pointing out the window, aft of their wingtip. The president leaned in, quickly spotting a nimble-looking white-and-blue jet against the darker ground, with NASA written on a yellow band across the tail. Jack took another noisy picture as the two crew in the jet waved with gloved hands, their white helmets and shiny dark visors glinting in the sunlight. "How neat is that?"

In the cockpit, the first officer had his neck twisted hard to the right, tracking the T-38 that was off their wing, glad to see the jet staying well clear. He watched as the smaller plane waggled its wings, applied power, accelerated and turned out in front of them, leading the way towards NASA's astronaut flying base at Ellington Field.

The captain eased his lumbering jet farther to the right to follow, keeping the flight smooth and g-forces very low for the VIP passengers in the back.

"Ellington Tower, Air Force One back with you. Thanks for the look-see and the escort. We're ten back for the straight-in full stop, airport in sight." The long runway and taxiways were clearly visible out the front windscreen.

"Air Force One, Ellington, glad to give the president a close-up of our pride and joy." The tower controller was playing it cool, but he would be telling everyone about this conversation once they safely got the big jet on the ground and parked. "The only traffic between you and the field is the NASA T-38, and he'll swing wide around to come in well behind you. Winds are three three zero at eleven, altimeter three zero zero three, you're number one and cleared to land, runway three five."

"Copy, Air Force One cleared to land on three five."

As the ponderous jet made its low, loud pass over the southern edge of the Johnson Space Center, thousands of NASA employees rushed outside to witness the unusual spectacle. The president of the United States only rarely came to visit, and word of the flyover had spread like wildfire. The sight of the white-and-blue Boeing with the presidential seal on its nose stopped productive space agency work for several minutes as everyone's attention turned skyward.

One observer was leaning on her car, shading her eyes with her hand as she watched the plane. She didn't work at NASA, but lots of south Houston locals were gathering with her, hoping to pay their respects to the new president. She had come early to get a parking spot on the city streets that crisscrossed the NASA center.

Once the jet had passed, she checked her outfit once more. A conservative off-white summer dress with a white bra underneath and sunflower-adorned sandals, all carefully chosen to match the image she wanted to portray. She'd also pinned up her newly washed hair and carefully applied her makeup—enough, but not too much, so that she appeared effortlessly feminine. She touched the reassuring bulk of the bag that hung heavily from a thin strap over her shoulder, picturing exactly what was inside it, and then she looked across to the angular double square blocks of Building 30. NASA's Mission Control, the nation's home of manned spaceflight. Her destination.

A few members of the general public were being permitted inside the building to watch the president speak with the crew, and she'd come early enough to make sure she was part of that select group. Now she walked from her car and joined the growing line of people waiting to get in.

Her name was Sally, and she prided herself on being calm and smart. And right in what she believed.

The people in the line with her were chattering with nervous excitement as they slowly moved forward towards the security check at the visitors' entrance. Sally was confident they would let her in. She was trained as a bookkeeper and worked for the wealthy Hearst family's People in Need organization to feed the poor. Ever since the heroic antiestablishment kidnapping of Patty Hearst by the Symbionese Liberation Army, the government had taken a special interest in the Hearsts and People in Need, and Sally had let herself be recruited as an FBI informant. She had saved a bureau letter and kept it in her purse in case she needed it to impress NASA security.

She would get in.

The security guard's voice was flat. "Driver's license." Sally watched him glance at the black-and-white picture on the paper she handed him. His eyes flicked from the photo up to her calmly smiling face. She could see him registering that she was pretty, just what she was going for with the hair, the shape-hugging dress, the matching bag and flowery sandals. Men were generally accommodating when it came to good-looking young women. He handed the license back, saying "G'wan in, ma'am—follow the stairs up to the viewing room. Restrooms are on the right when you get there." She returned his small smile with a broad, welcoming show of white teeth.

"Thank you, officer," she said, even though she knew he wasn't one. *Men are so simple. How the fuck do they get to run the world?* She tucked her license back in her bag and followed the line through the door and up the stairs.

When NASA had designed Mission Control 10 years earlier, they'd recognized the importance of public relations. Directly behind where all the flight controllers sat as they worked with astronaut crews on orbit, NASA had built a viewing room, with stepped rows of plush red chairs with lower halves that flipped down, like in a theater. Every seat had a good view, especially of the flight director and capsule communicator positions in the middle, and of the big screen across the front. To control distraction and noise, there was a three-piece glass wall between the two rooms, posted with signs forbidding flash photography lest it interrupt critical space operations at a key moment.

The front row of the viewing room was empty, roped off with Reserved signs for yet-to-arrive VIP guests. The next two rows were already filled, as the most eager visitors had wanted the closest view allowable. Sally had come a couple of weeks earlier on a normal visitors' day, dressed much less memorably, and had scoped out where she wanted to sit. She'd decided about five rows back, on the left side near the end, with room to stand up and not be immediately visible to the NASA escort at the front corner of the viewing room, but with the clearest direct view of the CAPCOM console. She knew the CAPCOM was the person who spoke with the crew on orbit and logically concluded that his station was where the president would be.

She stopped and stepped to the side as she entered the room, as if in awe, opening her eyes wide in visible amazement, waiting until the right moment to rejoin the shuffling line. As planned, she got just the right seat. She sat for a minute confirming the sight line, making sure the vertical metal window support frame wasn't in the way. She could see the rear left quarter of the flight director's head and had almost a full-body side view of the CAPCOM. Exactly as expected. After a minute she stood, asked the person next to her if they would please save her seat, excused herself as she squeezed past the people who had already filled the few chairs beside her, and, holding her purse, walked up towards the ladies' room.

She always emptied her bladder and double-checked her equipment before doing important things. It made her calmer. She might even go again, depending how long it took the president to get here from Ellington Field.

She was in position, was well-practiced, had everything she needed and was rock-sure that what she was doing was right.

All that was left was to properly execute.

16

*Office of Chairman Mao Tse-tung,
Peking, People's Republic of China*

"The United States is not reliable."

Chairman Mao's eyes flitted restlessly as he spoke, his mouth half open to allow for his labored breathing. He was 81 years old, and a life of chain-smoking unfiltered cigarettes had badly weakened his heart and lungs.

His eyes, puffy with age and poor circulation, narrowed to thin slits as he stared at his guest, then he mostly closed his mouth in a smile. "But you know that."

Tsien Hsue-shen held his country's leader's gaze and nodded. He knew that part of the reason Mao trusted him was the years of house arrest he and his family had been subjected to by the Americans and his ensuing decisive return to China. Mao carried—and Tsien had learned—the ancient, deep, unquestioning Chinese mistrust of other peoples and countries. Currently, the USA most of all.

Tsien wasn't certain why Mao had summoned him, so he kept quiet as he nodded.

They were seated in the darkly paneled room attached to the chairman's residence that had served as his office ever since Mao's health became too unreliable for unnecessary travel. Their chairs were plush and supportive, the side tables piled high with papers. The coffee table between them supported a half-filled ashtray and a water jug with stacked glasses beside it. Chairman Mao conducted most of the nation's business from this room and, during Tsien's weekly appointments, would often recline in his easy chair for brief naps.

This time the chairman had dismissed his assistant, so the two men were alone. He leaned forward stiffly and spoke again. "How is the space mission going?"

Which one? The question flicked briefly through Tsien's mind. As the head of China's space program, he was receiving regular detailed briefings on Apollo-Soyuz, through both official and spy channels. And Mao was too. But the reference to the US's unreliability had clarified Mao's meaning.

Tsien said, "The Soviets and Americans both launched on time, and initial reports are that the Apollo and Soyuz spacecraft are healthy and proceeding as planned with their rendezvous."

Mao listened impassively. Tsien took that as an encouraging sign. The mercurial nature of the country's leader made him nervous, even from the relative safety of his senior government position. He glanced at his watch. "The two ships are scheduled to dock in four hours."

Mao nodded, the flesh of his cheeks and neck jiggling slightly with the movement. He resumed glancing about the room.

So Tsien answered the other half of the question. "Our Shuguang vessel is a triumph. Launch of the improved CZ-2A rocket was flawless, and all initial communications and tracking show the spaceship on course in orbit." He glanced at his watch again. "Next pass over our Yuan Wang tracking ship will be within the hour."

Mao only blinked, rubbing the thumb and forefinger of his right hand together. Tsien knew the chairman was craving a cigarette, but he was under strict doctor's orders to refrain. If he asked for help getting one out of the pack on the low table and lighting it, Tsien would unquestioningly assist him. It was not his place to judge the man who had led the Long March.

Mao spoke, his voice thin and raspy. "And Fang Kuo-chun—how is he faring?"

The chairman had personally picked China's first astronaut. A lifetime of politics had taught him that putting hand-chosen people into key positions made all the difference. Along with decisively removing them when necessary.

"He is performing perfectly, as is expected of such a man," Tsien replied.

Of the many thousands of citizens he and his team had considered in early selection, and the thousand they had brought to Peking for examination and training, Fang had been a standout from the beginning. His loyalty was unquestioned, proven in both combat and personal conduct.

"I have spoken with him at every communications pass, and he sounds calm and strong."

Mao began to speak but was seized by a spasm that pitched his whole body forward. He coughed once, fighting it, and then repeatedly, with a wet, rattling, retching sound coming from deep within his lungs. His face went so red Tsien considered getting up to summon medical help, but Mao raised one hand to forestall him. Retrieving a linen napkin from his lap, he covered his mouth and, after more retching, spit up an unseen gob of mucus into the cloth. As the coughing subsided, he pinched the napkin closed and returned it to his lap, pointing to the water on the table. Tsien stood quickly and filled a glass halfway, mindful that Mao's hand would be shaky after such an episode and wishing to spare the man the ignominy of spilling it.

Eyes closed, Mao reached out with his fingers curled in the shape of a glass, and Tsien guided it into his hand, watching as he carefully brought it to his lips. Mao cautiously sipped and swallowed, the movement of his chin exaggerated to help clear the phlegm in his throat, and then took a second, slightly easier sip.

He paused, eyes still shut, and then took a long, smooth breath to regain control. He opened his eyes, held out the glass to Tsien, and relaxed back into his chair, his elbows seeking the solidity of the armrests.

Tsien set the glass on the table and took his seat again.

Mao waited for Tsien to stop averting his gaze and look him in the eye. When he did, Mao held Tsien's gaze for several seconds and then started glancing around the room, clearly indicating that the moment of extreme frailty had passed and was not to be acknowledged. With only a small further clearing of his throat, he asked, "And what of Fang's purpose?"

"Our monitoring teams confirm that the location and timing of our launch has yet to be detected. With every passing second, we gain advantage." There was pride in Tsien's voice. Almost a decade earlier, he had personally convinced Chairman Mao that China would soon be capable of human spaceflight, and he had stood at attention beside him at a May Day parade overlooking Tiananmen Square after they had successfully launched China's first orbital satellite.

A lifetime of study, work and tenacity had led to what was happening now. Tsien's personal version of a long march.

He was startled to realize he'd drifted off into a reverie for a moment, and that the chairman's eyes were once more upon him. He decided to offer up the final piece before he was asked.

"Our other plans are in place as well. They are just waiting for us to give the word."

Chairman Mao nodded several times, slowly. He would soon put the selfish Americans and the arrogant Soviets in their place, with minimal risk and maximum gain for his beloved China. The People's Republic. The oldest and greatest nation and people on Earth.

And now beyond it.

THE LONG MARCH

17

The Pentagon, Washington, DC

James Schlesinger was chewing on the stem of his pipe.

It helped him think.

His third-floor office was the biggest in the Pentagon. His broad mahogany desk was placed between two tall columns of curtained windows that looked out on the moored boats in the Pentagon Lagoon and, beyond them, towards the Potomac River. The top half of the Washington Monument was visible in the distance, rising above the trees along the river.

Schlesinger was the US Secretary of Defense, the appointed leader of the biggest military in the world, and the top-secret photographs he was holding were troubling him deeply.

The DIA intelligence analyst who had delivered the sheaf of photos to him had also brought a magnifying glass. The leather of Schlesinger's tall black chair squeaked as he leaned forward to use the lens, peering closely at each image.

The photographs had been taken by Air Force telescopes mounted in white domes on the top of Mount Haleakalā in Hawaii. They were

10,000 feet above sea level, where the air was clear and dry. The images were primarily infrared, resembling those from X-rays, with a few more familiar optical photos.

Definitely a capsule, he decided. That's what the analyst had suggested. The distinctive cone shape with a blunt end was unmistakable. *Like Al Shepard's Mercury ship.* A pointy end to push up through the air, a small cockpit for astronauts and a broad, flat bottom to absorb and deflect the heat of re-entry.

The Chinese have built a manned spaceship! Schlesinger grabbed the bowl of his pipe, the stem still clenched in his teeth, and pivoted in his chair to look out the window. *How did we miss this?*

His jaw tightened and his eyes narrowed under his bushy eyebrows. Why had the Chinese launched secretly? What advantage did this new capability give them? And why had they chosen this specific orbit?

Before Nixon had appointed him secretary of defense, a post President Ford had allowed him to keep, James Schlesinger had been director of the CIA, and before that, chair of the Atomic Energy Commission. Several classified projects threaded through all of those positions.

He frowned. *Can that be it? How could the Chinese have known?*

He spun his chair back towards the desk and pushed the intercom button on his phone to talk to his secretary in the adjoining small office.

"Get me General Phillips on a secure line."

18

Johnson Space Center, Houston, July 17

"What a beautiful day!"

Kaz laughed, realizing he'd said the words out loud, driving to work in his Thunderbird from his place at Polly Ranch. The normally hazy Texas Gulf Coast air was unusually clear under a cloudless blue sky. Although the temperature was forecast to reach 90, the humidity had dropped and there was zero percent chance of rain.

A perfect day for a convertible.

Even after two years of being detailed to NASA at the Johnson Space Center, Kaz felt an adolescent thrill driving in to work at the hub of manned spaceflight, the place where the moonwalkers had trained. And he was headed to the heart of it all—Mission Control.

Human spaceflight, he corrected himself, smiling. There was a Soviet woman on the Soyuz.

He turned left off NASA Road 1 onto Second Street and looked ahead to the uniform collection of hulking, flat-roofed government buildings. The tallest was Project Management Headquarters, appropriately named Building 1, nine stories of bureaucracy, with the center director's corner office on the ninth floor. Closer to him were several shorter blocks that housed simulators, test and development facilities, and astronaut classrooms. As he passed two parallel rows of buildings, the parking lots adjoining Mission Control, in Building 30, appeared on his right.

He noted far more cars than usual, and throngs of people walking the sidewalks and standing in the shade of the regularly planted live oaks. *Waiting to see the president arrive.*

NASA flight controllers came and went at all hours and were often in a hurry, so ever since he'd bought the T-Bird, he'd started parking it around back, in a distant, protected corner where there was less chance of it getting dinged. He turned right off Second Street into his regular lot, out of the way and still largely empty, saw that his favorite corner spot was open, turned the car around, and carefully backed it into place.

He'd dressed more formally than usual. Typically he wore the NASA standard—a short-sleeved shirt and tie—but as he was scheduled to stand next to President Ford while the country's leader spoke with the Apollo-Soyuz crew live on national television, Kaz had opted for a long-sleeved shirt, tie and blazer. He headed towards Building 30 with the jacket folded over his arm, not yet ready to put it on.

As he walked along the Second Street sidewalk, mulling the potential for problems during the upcoming key events, a car going the other way caught his eye. Years of combat and test pilot flying had taught him to pay attention to subliminal triggers, and he turned to look more closely. The traffic was heavy, partially blocking his view of the car, but he could see a square, faded green sedan moving away from him. He tipped his head to the side to try to see who was in it, but all he could make out through the dirty rear window was the shadow of a driver, plus maybe a passenger in the front seat.

Kaz stopped walking. *Where have I seen that car before?* Just as it disappeared from sight, he realized it was a Ford Galaxie 500, and the memory of the rear lot of the China Star restaurant flooded back.

Kaz frowned. Could it be the same car? Experience had taught him to mistrust coincidences.

When he'd called the sheriff's office to report the original sighting, the desk sergeant had been noncommittal about investigating, and no one had called him back. The Galaxie was a common model, but even if this was the same car, whoever it was had already driven away from Johnson Space Center.

He stood for a few more seconds, evaluating. *Likely nothing, and no discernible threat*, he decided. He checked his watch, noting that he was still early for his shift handover, and started walking again.

As usual, Kaz cut across the inner parking lot, past the throbbing hum of the long, low transformer blocks that provided electrical power to Mission Control and also housed the facility's backup diesel generators. They'd been built separate from the main building to allow for extra cooling, and for easy access when Houston Lighting and Power had to do maintenance. Like today. There was an HL&P van parked right beside the low structure, with a couple of technicians in coveralls and matching ball caps, their backs to him, bent over next to a transformer. Kaz walked along the side of the vehicle, cut left across the end of the parking lot, climbed the stairs of the rear loading dock and used his key to enter Building 30. Bypassing the crowds and extra security at the main front entrance.

Time to get to work. It was a big day for Apollo-Soyuz.

19

Apollo-Soyuz Docking, Earth Orbit

"Hey, Kaz, when we powered up that ATS, we got a horrendous background noise, and it seems to stay there."

Deke Slayton, voice beaming down into Houston Mission Control from on board Apollo via the Shoe Cove, Newfoundland, relay site, sounded annoyed. The powerful new Applications Technology Satellite was supposed to solve their communications problems. Its huge orbiting dish antenna was designed to relay transmissions from the Apollo capsule to multiple small receivers all around the world, providing nearly continuous voice and even TV signal. The mission plan had been built assuming it would work. But it didn't.

"Roger, Deke," Kaz responded in the customary even-keeled tone CAPCOMs had used since the start of the space program.

He looked across to the INCO console, where the integrated communications officer was talking intently through his headset to experts in his tech support back room. He turned while listening and caught Kaz's eye, holding up a finger to tell him to wait a second. He nodded a couple of times in response to what he was hearing, then reached to switch the communications loop he was talking on. His voice came over Kaz's headset. "FLIGHT, INCO, update on ATS."

The console next to Kaz's was the flight director's. Everyone reported to FLIGHT as the central point of knowledge and decision-making for Mission Control.

"Go ahead, INCO," Glynn Lunney said.

Kaz listened carefully too, so he could properly summarize to the crew on orbit.

"FLIGHT, we saw this same thing during ground testing down at the Cape. When locking up, ATS made a tremendously loud noise, but as soon as we got a good lock on the signal, it went away."

Glynn frowned. This would have been good information to have before the problem reared its head in space. He paused briefly to emphasize his displeasure, then glanced across at Kaz and nodded for him to tell the crew.

Kaz pushed his foot switch to transmit. "Apollo, Houston. Deke, that noise should settle down as soon as you get locked up on ATS."

There was a 30-second pause. Kaz pictured Deke making switch throws in the Apollo capsule, dropping the Newfoundland link and activating the orbiting ATS.

"Okay. Houston, how do you read through ATS?" Deke's voice sounded perfect.

"Loud and clear, Deke. How me?"

"Cleared up, no noise. It's amazing."

Kaz smiled. "How about that?"

Deke clarified. "We're getting an echo from you now, but it's workable."

"Roger, INCO's working on it."

As Kaz spoke, Glynn had already turned his furrowed brow towards INCO, who re-engaged with his back room. A persistent echo would be a mere annoyance for the crew at the moment, but a potential hazard during the upcoming mission-critical docking.

It would be even more complex once the two ships were docked and the Soviet Soyuz radios were directly tied through Apollo and relayed via the satellite back to Earth.

The flight director held the gaze of his communications officer. "Let's get this echo problem fixed, INCO."

"Roger, FLIGHT." INCO swallowed, and hoped his bobbing Adam's apple wasn't too visible. Everyone took communications for granted until they didn't work. And from experience, he knew that echoes were ethereal problems to solve.

He turned and reselected the communications loop with his back room. Like every other flight controller in Mission Control, he'd resolved that it wouldn't be his systems that derailed Apollo-Soyuz.

His turn to work the problem.

"Starting braking, Kaz." Apollo Commander Tom Stafford's voice was calm, almost clinical, in Kaz's headset. The transmission was scratchy, but clear enough.

"Roger." As Kaz spoke, he pictured what was happening in orbit, 140 miles above the Earth. The Apollo ship was just 3,000 feet from the Soyuz, closing at 20 feet per second. He did the math. Impact in 150 seconds if they didn't slow down—but Stafford would be moving his hand controllers to fire the forward thrusters, steadily decelerating. Kaz took a breath before he transmitted the key information that needed to be passed on. This call signified a major mission threshold, but he wanted to keep it easy and supportive for the crews facing the actual risk.

"Apollo, Houston. I've got two messages for you: Moscow is GO for docking; Houston is GO for docking. It's up to you guys. Have fun."

Tom's Oklahoma drawl was tinged with relief. "All right, it sounds good." He added an update for the Soyuz commander. "Half a mile, Alexei."

"Roger. Eight hundred meters." Alexei Leonov's Russian-accented English was clear, relayed through the Apollo and the orbiting ATS to

Houston. Kaz leaned forward to see past Glynn to the communications officer, who made eye contact and shrugged. No echo. So far, so good.

Tom spoke. "Soyuz, please tell us when you begin your maneuver."

Valery Kubasov, the Soyuz flight engineer, had been entering the command into his ship's attitude control system. "We're initiating rotation maneuver. You see?"

The three Apollo crewmembers intently watched the distant green Soyuz through their windows, waiting for it to turn away from its normal orientation, with solar panels pointed at the Sun, and point its docking mechanism at them.

Tom finally saw the Soyuz turning, the shadows and light reflections gradually changing. "Yes, very slowly."

Alexei transmitted another key piece of information. "Soyuz docking system is ready."

The two ships were about to ram into each other, and a complex mechanism of metal plates, springs, latches and dampening brakes was now fully extended, ready to take the blow.

"We are also ready," Tom responded.

Deke had extended and verified the Apollo docking system. Like two industrial-sized sets of robotic fingers, floating and reaching out for each other in space.

"I'm approaching Soyuz," Tom added.

The two ships flew towards impact. It was now a pure piloting task, Tom's hands dancing on the controls as he stared intently through his optical alignment sight at the cross-shaped target bolted on the side of the Soyuz.

"Less than five meters distance." He'd practiced the complex task hundreds of times in the simulators, and he knew the Soyuz crew wanted him to call the key ranges.

Kaz stayed quiet. Anything he said would be a distraction.

"Three meters."

Silence.

"One meter."

The ships' docking alignment plates were now close enough to overlap, ready to bang into each other and physically force the correct alignment to allow the more delicate restraining latches to click into place.

A light suddenly glowed brightly in Tom's peripheral vision. Small plungers on the Apollo docking ring surfaces had been pushed down as they bumped into the Soyuz, powering an electrical circuit to confirm what he could see out the window.

"Contact." Tom's voice was decisive. He'd done his job. Now the automated mechanism on the Soyuz had to work, using the contact electrical signal to drive latches and hooks to hold the ships together.

"We have capture!" Alexei's excitement was palpable. The latches had rotated over center, and the two ships were now mechanically joined in space.

Tom looked quickly at his panel lights and glanced at Deke and Vance, getting a thumbs-up from each. He responded, "We also have capture. We have succeeded! Everything is excellent."

A wide smile on his face, Kaz listened to the muffled congratulations and sighs of relief across the consoles in Mission Control. But the two ships were just loosely held by latches, and the force of the impact was causing them to tumble together slowly, like a bulbous, ungainly pinwheel. The docking systems now had to be carefully retracted and heavy hooks engaged to make the stacked spaceship structure sturdy enough to fire thrusters for attitude control, to get the solar arrays back pointing at the Sun to restart charging of the batteries. And to hold the hatch mating surfaces tightly enough against the seals to make the combined international ship airtight.

Kaz caught the tail end of a broken transmission from Moscow Mission Control: ". . . ready to mate." They were talking directly to their Soyuz crew, watching as they commanded the retraction.

On board Apollo, Tom reached out and gently squeezed the edge of the instrument panel between his fingers and thumb. He could feel the expected slight vibration as the retracting screw of the docking mechanism sent a high-frequency energy wave through the metal hull of the ship. Like a living thing. He reflected on what had just happened, then said with justifiable pride, "Kaz, I'd estimate my final closing velocity between zero point three and zero point four of a foot per second—on contact."

The entire weight of the mission had been riding on his shoulders, and he'd flown the docking perfectly. Good time for a compliment from Houston.

Kaz said, "Okay, Tom, I copy. It sure looked good down here, dead center." The equivalent of the copilot telling the captain "Nice landing."

Kaz and Glynn exchanged smiles. The relief in Mission Control was palpable. Flight controllers who had been leaning tensely forward in their chairs sprawled back, lighting cigarettes and taking sips of long-cold coffee.

Tom's voice broke in with an unusually urgent tone. "Houston, Apollo."

Kaz quickly set his coffee mug on the console, senses alert. Tom's transmissions weren't normally formal. "Apollo, Houston. Go ahead, Tom."

"Deke smells something pretty bad up in the Docking Module."

Now that they were docked, Deke would have opened the hatch to the tunnel-like Docking Module that linked them to Soyuz, exposing the Apollo capsule to a different air source.

New smells in the confines of a spaceship were bad news. There were air filters purifying the crew's exhaled carbon dioxide, but any smoke or contaminants mostly went directly to their lungs.

Not good.

Tom added, "We're going on the oxygen masks right now. And we're going to close that hatch. We don't know what it is yet."

Kaz glanced over his shoulder at JW McKinley, the crew flight surgeon, who was frowning in concern. Donning oxygen masks was the right next step, but what mattered was finding the source of the smell and stopping it before the air became unbreathable. An emergency undocking and re-entry to splashdown, all while wearing oxygen masks in a poisonous atmosphere, would be a mission-ending nightmare.

"Roger. Could you describe what you think the problem is?" Ask, don't assume.

Tom's voice was garbled by the mask. "... but we can smell it. It—it smells like—it's kind of weird. It smells something like cordite. But it might be, like, the flight glue or something like that."

"Okay, Tom, copy that it's a very bad odor. Was it a burning smell, or can you relate it to anything else that's familiar?"

The docking system had required high-current electrical power, and maybe some wires had burned up, leaving nasty chemicals in the air.

"Yes. It was a burning smell, something like burnt glue."

Shit, Kaz thought. Nasty stuff to breathe.

After a short pause, Tom spoke as if he'd been consulting with his crewmates. "It could smell something like acetate." A beat. "Yes, it smells like acetate."

Deke added clarification. "I've smelled that in new vehicles before. But it's really strong."

Tom said, "And it does have a tendency to burn your eyes."

Bad news.

"Roger. Copy." Kaz turned to look at Glynn. This could be something simple, or it might be a serious health risk. It required a decision.

Glynn spoke, selecting the communications loop that went into everyone's headsets, including all the technical back rooms. "EECOM, what are you seeing?"

The electrical, environmental and communications officer was ready. "We didn't see any current spikes, FLIGHT, so we don't think there was a short that would have melted anything. And nothing unusual on the atmospheric sensors." He clarified for everyone listening. "But we don't have great trace gas detectors. The crew's noses are way more sensitive."

Glynn nodded. No surprise. Good. He turned to look at JW, behind him on the right. "SURGEON, what do you recommend?"

"Stay on masks for now, FLIGHT. Give the air scrubbers a chance to do what they can for as long as the docked flight plan allows. Then have the crew do a quick sniff test, see if it's steady or worsening. If it diminishes, and the crew say the smell is tolerable, okay to proceed unmasked."

Not perfect, JW thought, *but acceptable.* The crew weren't in space to avoid risk; they were there to manage it.

Glynn held JW's gaze for a few seconds, then addressed the room. "Anyone else have any insights?"

Silence.

Glynn turned to Kaz and nodded.

Kaz glanced at the big screens at the front of the room showing where the docked ships were in relation to Earth, checking that they had a solid comm link. He pushed the button on the floor to transmit.

"Apollo, Houston." Good to get the whole crew's attention.

Tom's voice came back. "Kaz, we've been on the masks but doing sniff tests, and the smell is definitely going away. We think it was just the Velcro glue or something that built up in the Docking Module. It's pretty much dissipated now, and it's no longer hurting anyone's eyes."

Kaz smiled. Tom wanted to get on with the hatch opening and knew there was no way for Houston to judge how bad it was. *I'd do the same thing,* he thought.

"Copy, Tom. We've been discussing it down here, and with your description, you're cleared to go off masks and monitor for any reoccurrence of the smell."

"Thanks, Kaz. Concur. We'll pick back up in the timeline."

Kaz glanced at Glynn, who mouthed a yes.

"We're with you on page one dash twenty-two of the Active Docking Checklist."

He sat back in his chair again and took a deep, slow breath. The spaceships were safely docked and all problems dealt with. Soon they'd open the hatch between Apollo and Soyuz and take photos shaking hands, and President Ford would arrive to praise everyone. Then the crews would settle into two days of straightforward joint operations. It felt as if they'd just scaled the immensity of Everest and now only had to congratulate each other, plant flags and take pictures.

One more hurdle, to get the president's public relations event out of the way, and then everyone could relax into normal ops.

20

Building 1, Johnson Space Center

The NASA switchboard operator wished her office had a window.

It was a rectangular inner room on the second floor that she shared with three other operators. She'd tried to compensate for the lack of a view by hanging framed pictures on the wall beside her—snapshots of her son and daughter, her wedding photo, plus nature and space scenes she'd carefully cut from calendars—but it wasn't the same. Especially when she knew it was a clear, sunny Houston day outside.

The switchboard opened daily at 07:30. She and the other women had arrived at 07:00, as usual, to grab a coffee, get plugged in, listen to the overnight recorded messages, respond and be ready to route the steady stream of incoming calls to the 15,000 people who worked at the Johnson Space Center.

Partway through her shift, she glanced up at the round black-and-white government clock on the wall. The four of them took turns for coffee and lunch breaks, but she needed to pee. Two pregnancies hadn't been kind to her bladder, and sometimes she couldn't wait.

Just as she was going to lean across and ask the operator next to her to cover for her, her phone rang. Sighing, she picked up, hoping the call would be short.

"Good afternoon, NASA Johnson Space Center, how can I help you?" She squeezed her thighs together. Sometimes that helped.

Silence on the other end. The operator checked that the blinking light on her switchboard was steady, showing a good connection, and tried again. Sometimes people were nervous about calling NASA.

"Good afternoon, this is the NASA Johnson Space Center, can you hear me okay?"

A man's voice responded. "Yeah, I hear you fine. I need to talk to whoever's in charge there."

She frowned. Sounded like a crank call. Not her first. And the president was on-site today, which was bound to be stirring up the crazies. Some sort of Midwest accent. *Not a Texan*, she thought.

"Thank you, sir, can you tell me what your call is about, so I can put you through to the correct person?" She leaned forward to look at the square of paper taped to the top of her console, reminding herself of the emergency and security numbers. Just in case.

Another pause.

"Nah, I'm just going to give you a message, and you need to make sure you get it to whoever's in charge, ASAP. Can you do that?"

The man had spelled out the individual letters of "ASAP." *Definitely a crank*.

She made sure she kept her cheerful voice on. Hanging high on the office wall was a printed sign decorated with small American flags that reminded the four of them: You Are the First Voice of NASA to the Public.

"Yes, sir, I'll be glad to take a message and make sure it gets to the right person."

Christ, I've got to pee.

"Okay, listen carefully." His voice became formal, as if he was now reading aloud from a script. "I represent both the Weather Underground and the Symbionese Liberation Army. We have joined forces to plant a bomb at the Johnson Space Center. It is set to go off in fifteen minutes.

The bomb is in a location that won't harm any innocents, as we are opposed to violence, unlike the fascist military empire that NASA and their government rockets represent. This bomb has been set in support of the immigrant workers of Houston."

Startled, the operator scrambled to grab her steno pad and government-issue pen to write down what he'd said. She leaned left and looked at the emergency actions response page taped on the corner of her desk for how to deal with bomb threats. Instructions were in red block letters.

"Did you get that?" He sounded impatient now.

"Yes, sir." She read quickly from the page. "If you could please let me know, where is the bomb and what does it look like? Is it inside a building?" She scanned hurriedly down the list for key questions. "What is your name, sir?"

"Forget all that—did you get what I said?"

"Yes, sir." She glanced at her scrawled note and spoke louder to alert the other operators. "You are the Weather Underground and Symbionese Liberation Army, there's a bomb set to go off at JSC in fifteen minutes, in support of the immigrant workers of Houston."

The other three girls were all staring at her in shock. The most senior of them immediately pushed her console's red emergency button and hastily parroted what she'd just overheard, waving a hand in the air to let the others know what she was doing.

Urgently, the operator tried more questions from the list. "Sir, what kind of bomb is it? What will cause it to explode?" But as she was speaking, she heard a *clunk* and then the dial tone.

The threat had already been called in, but she followed the emergency checklist anyway and immediately dialed 3333, looking again at her hastily written notes, ready to pass on all the information she had. It was part of their training, and she wanted to make sure to do her part perfectly.

As she waited for Emergency to pick up, she thought, *Jesus, the president is here today! And I'm part of trying to protect him!*

She no longer had to pee.

21

Mission Control

It was as if Mission Control had been invaded.

President Ford entered Building 30 in the middle of a tight escort of Secret Service special agents in dark suits. They followed the NASA staff who greeted them to the elevator, up a floor and down the control center hallway. Two of the agents, a man and a woman, went into the visitors' viewing area to keep an eye on the crowd there, and two more entered Mission Control itself, doing a careful look around before stepping out of the way. Precleared press personnel followed them in, walking backwards with raised cameras and microphones. Once they were in position, the senior agent gave a signal and President Ford appeared in the doorway beside the center's director, Chris Kraft, the two of them followed by Jack.

Mission Control was arranged in three tiers so that all the console operators could see each other and everyone could see the information projected on the front screen. Stairs led up either side of the control room, and Kraft ushered the president up to the third tier.

Christopher Columbus Kraft Jr. may have risen to head the entire Johnson Space Center, but he had been NASA's very first flight director, and Mission Control was like home to him, one he had helped design and build. He turned to Ford, comfortable and authoritative, and directed the president's attention towards the big screen. "Sir, the up-and-down curves you see there, running across the map of the world, show the ground track of Apollo-Soyuz, tipped fifty-one point eight degrees from the equator—that cartoon spaceship following the curve is where they are right now."

Kraft was a slender man of medium height, his black hair graying at the temples. He took a moment to adjust his glasses to see the screen better. "The two spacecraft safely docked about an hour ago, and the combined crews are now flying over the South Pacific. They orbit the Earth every eighty-nine minutes. When you talk with them, you'll see on the curve that they'll be tracking nearly overhead of us here in Houston."

Ford stared at the screen, trying to take in everything Kraft had said. He had been an economics major and was a lawyer, but technology and science confused him. He turned to his son, saying, "Pretty amazing, huh, Jack?"

"Sure is, Dad." Jack turned to Kraft, smiling. "I read that your middle name is Columbus. Really?"

Kraft smiled back. "Yep. And I'm Chris Columbus Kraft *Junior*—it was my dad's middle name too." His smile grew wider. "I took a lot of ribbing for it in school."

Jack laughed. Being the president's son was bad enough. "I bet!"

President Ford was also smiling as he watched his son, aware that all the flight controllers behind their consoles were sneaking glances at them. He turned to the audience seated behind the glass partition and waved, knowing it was a friendly crowd. He made sure to hold the wave long enough for the press photographers to get a good shot. The upcoming election was going to be tough. To overcome Nixon's tainted legacy, he needed all the votes he could get. Vote-getting was a big part of why he'd traveled to Texas for an event he could have done by phone from the Oval Office. This was an opportunity to show his statesmanship and affability on NASA's popular stage, with his good-looking son next to him.

He noticed Kraft pointing across the consoles to the men in the center of the front row. "Mr. President, Jack, it's almost time to talk with the crew. Let me introduce you to the flight director and the CAPCOM."

Kaz was already standing, his one-eared headset's cord tucked out of the way so he could still listen to the crew as he greeted the president.

But before any introductions could be made, Ford reached out with his large, college football lineman's hand, and Kaz shook it. Both men were about six feet tall, but the president was much bulkier. Kaz was ready to hand him a headset and explain what was about to happen when Ford interrupted him, gesturing for his son to come forward. "Jack, here's someone I wanted you to meet."

Kaz was surprised. He'd been introduced to Nixon on a few occasions, but this was the first time he'd been in the same room as Ford.

The president's eyes were twinkling. "This is Captain Kazimieras Zemeckis—combat fighter pilot, Navy test pilot, astronaut selectee and someone who's served the country multiple times on special operations." He glanced at the cameras and microphones that were pointed at them, then back at his son. "I'll tell you some of the details of his service during our flight back to Washington."

Kaz hadn't expected the president to be so well-briefed on him and was feeling self-conscious as he shook the young man's hand.

Then Ford leaned in close and spoke directly into Kaz's uncovered ear. "Thanks for stepping up to be part of the DIA. We need men like you."

Startled, Kaz nodded, saying, "Thank you, sir," careful not to change his facial expression. His DIA involvement was meant to be kept quiet. A year earlier, he'd been approached to work for the Defense Intelligence Agency, the military equivalent of the CIA, which provided the president and senior military with analysis of the military intentions and capabilities of foreign governments and non-state actors. Kaz had accepted, but as far as NASA and his friends knew, he was still just on loan to NASA from the US Navy.

Kaz covered his discomfort by helping Ford put the spare headset on properly. He positioned the mic at the corner of the president's mouth and saw that Glynn had fitted Jack with a headset too, so he could listen in.

A voice spoke into Kaz's headset. "Two minutes out from the president's call with the crew, CAPCOM."

Kaz showed the president the toggle switch to push when he wanted to talk, and offered him his chair.

Ford shook his head, saying, "I'll stand." Standing would look better on camera. More youthful and vigorous.

Kaz pointed at a digital countdown clock in the upper corner of the front screen that was just clicking past 60 seconds. "You can see, sir, that we'll start in one minute. I'll cue you, and the crew will be waiting for you to begin."

President Ford pulled a folded page out of his inner jacket pocket, glanced at the names printed at the top to remind himself and set it on Kaz's console where he could see it easily. Then he smiled, glancing across at Jack. "I'm ready, Houston."

"Apollo-Soyuz, this is Houston. I have the president of the United States beside me. Are you ready for the event?" Kaz said.

As the American commander on board, Tom Stafford responded first. "Houston, everyone up here is listening, and we're ready."

To demonstrate the historic American–Soviet collaboration, Tom and Vance had joined Alexei in the Soyuz, and Valery, Svetlana and Deke were on the other side of a pressure hatch in the Apollo capsule.

Kaz nodded to cue the president. Ford looked down at his printed script, and then directly up at the camera of the television production crew in front of him. The senior technician raised a hand, counted down with five fingers and pointed at him.

Kaz tapped the headset cord as a last-minute reminder, and Ford pushed his transmit switch. "Gentlemen and gentle lady, let me call to express my very great admiration for your hard work, your total dedication in preparing for this first joint flight. All of us here in Houston, back in Washington, and across the United States send to you our very warmest congratulations for your successful rendezvous and for your docking, and we wish you the very best for a successful completion of the remainder of your mission."

His chief of staff, Dick Cheney, had written the script for him. The words felt stilted, but he was being broadcast live internationally and didn't want to make any gaffes. He continued reading, doing his best to look up occasionally.

"Your flight is a momentous event and a very great achievement, not only for the six of you but also for the thousands of American and Soviet scientists and technicians who have worked together for three years to ensure the success of this very historic and very successful experiment in international cooperation."

Ford winced. *Did I really just say "very" twice? I should have had my speechwriter do this, not Dick.*

On board the docked spaceships, the crews were clustered in their two groups, holding on to each other so they could share headsets to hear the president's words. Weightlessness and the confined space made them a jumble of arms and legs.

Tom answered. "Thank you, Mr. President. It certainly has been an honor to serve the country and work here." He mugged at Alexei Leonov, who laughed.

Enough, Ford decided. *Time to go off script.* After Nixon's ignominious resignation 11 months earlier, he'd been methodically attempting to show the American public a different kind of Republican leader, one who prided himself on his common touch.

He checked his script, where he'd written how to pronounce the Russian names. "I might like to say a word or two to Svetlana Gromova of the cosmonaut crew, as well as Colonel Leonov and Valery Kubasov. I remember the three of you on that enjoyable Saturday last September when both crews visited the White House and joined me in a picnic over in Virginia, just across the river. We had some crab specialties that I enjoyed, and I think you did. I am sure you are having a little different menu, somewhat different food on this occasion. What are you having over there out in space?"

That's better, he thought. *Everybody likes talking about food. And it'll be good to hear the woman's voice.*

Inside the Apollo capsule, Deke glanced at Svetlana. She shrugged and nodded, showing her readiness to reply, then pushed the transmit button on the long, thick cord connected to her borrowed comm cap.

"We get good space food, Mr. President. There are Russian dishes, some Russian music, some juice, some coffee and a lot of water." She decided to add a little humor. "But no beer, no crab." She pronounced it "kreb," rolling the "r."

The NASA technician in Houston who was controlling the communications link quickly moved a switch so the orbiting crew could hear Ford laughing.

The president was pleased. *That'll get some prime airtime.* He glanced back at the script and riffed from it.

"Now, Mr. Slayton, Deke, you've had a very, very long record of distinguished service preparing other astronaut crews for various space missions. As the world's oldest space rookie, do you have any advice for young people who hope to fly on future space missions?" *Two "verys" again, but that's okay.*

Deke said, "Well, yes, I have a lot of advice for young people, but I guess probably one of the most important bits is to, number one, decide what you really want to do and then, number two, never give up until you have done it."

Svetlana gave a small smile. *That's the standard cosmonaut answer to that question too.*

The president's voice was back in their headsets. "Well, you are a darn good example, Deke, of never giving up and continuing."

Time to wrap it up, Ford decided. "I congratulate everybody connected with the flight, and particularly the six of you, who are setting this outstanding example of what we have to do in the future to make it a better world."

Just in time, he remembered there was a key phrase he was supposed to include at the end, something important to Russian superstition. He read it verbatim off the page, smiling to get the right tone in his voice and looking up into the distance as if he could see the crew. "May I say, in signing off, here is to a soft landing." *Good TV.*

Ford was pulling the headset away from his ear when he heard Tom responding on behalf of the combined crew.

"Thank you, Mr. President. It certainly has been an honor to serve the country and work here."

Kaz took over. "Apollo-Soyuz, President Ford, this concludes the event." He glanced across at the integrated communications officer, who surreptitiously wiped the back of his hand across his forehead and flicked imaginary sweat towards the floor, then smiled at him.

No technical glitches made for successful public relations.

In the audience behind them, Sally had put her hand into her purse as the president had been speaking. Now there would be handshakes and people posing for photographs.

She watched the pig president take off his headset, hand it to the skinny, short-haired military killer next to him and start glad-handing everyone within reach. Some of the NASA people had brought their Instamatic cameras, and now that the main event was complete, the president's photographer was stage-managing specific photos. Each pose created a motionless vignette. A frozen moment, making targeting easier. Especially for someone who had practiced multiple times at the gravel pit with the weapon she carried in her bag. Someone who understood that doing nothing in a period of repressive violence is itself a form of violence.

Sally had looked around at the audience and the NASA people while the pig president was talking with the astronauts. Everyone so smug and self-congratulatory, so sure of themselves. And all the NASA people were white men. Not one female, Black or immigrant face to be seen!

She glanced at the dark-suited Secret Service people who were standing at the front corners of the viewing room where she sat. They were alternately surveying the audience and the distracting spectacle through the glass. No way would they be able to react fast enough.

And that buffoon Ford, with his stupid grin and spoiled son, had been the vice-president of the criminal Nixon! What had he said? "Distinguished service" and "advice for young people." Hypocrite! Every dollar should be taken from the Pentagon and NASA budgets and used to rebuild the people's cities, schools and hospitals!

So it was fitting that this was going to happen here, in Houston, where the wealthy, entitled Establishment rode on the obscene profits of the oil companies. A city named for its white, murdering founder. A city built on the backs of generations of abused workers.

The Weather Underground and the Symbionese Liberation Army had chosen their first joint action well.

And Sally was the trigger. Waiting for Ford to turn and wave at the audience.

22

Mission Control

Sally looked at her watch and double-checked the digital timers that were visible through the glass on the front wall of Mission Control.

Aaron should be making the call right now. She was curious how long it would take NASA and the pig president's flunkies to react. Would they lock down in place, or would they hustle to get people outside? Either way, it was about to get a lot more tense.

Time to act.

Inside her purse, she closed the thumb and fingers of her right hand around the short, knurled wooden stock of her .44-caliber Charter Arms Bulldog revolver. The cold weight of it felt good, familiar. She pressed her trigger finger along the curved metal guard, careful not to touch the trigger itself.

Not yet.

She wiggled the gun out of the purse into her lap, keeping her movements small, sliding the weapon under the bag to avoid alerting the people next to her for as long as she could. Her eyes remained fixed on the pig president. He was still posing for pictures and shaking hands.

Finally, he came up the stairs to meet with the NASA men behind the console just on the other side of the glass from her. *Perfect*, Sally thought. A short-range shot, maybe 30 feet.

What she'd practiced for.

She stood, letting the padded seat flip up behind her knees. She spread her feet and pointed her toes at the target in a stable stance. She cupped her left hand around the heel of her right hand and squeezed her right thumb and three fingers solidly around the grip, letting her pointer finger ease onto the trigger as she raised her arms to the sight line.

Classic firing stance, knees slightly bent, leaning comfortably forward at the waist, shoulders rounded and ready for the significant kickback of the .44. She tucked her chin into her neck as she lined up the sighting channel with the ramped blade sight at the end of the short, three-inch barrel. She'd already loaded a 200-grain hollow-point jacketed Smith & Wesson Special bullet in the correct chamber, along with one more in the chamber after it, just in case. She hadn't wanted the added weight, so she had left the remaining three chambers empty. Also, she'd figured, the team protecting the pig president wouldn't give her more than two shots.

When she got to her feet, she had caught the eye of the female Special Service agent at the front left corner of the room. The familiar metallic clicking noises of a pistol cylinder rotating into place snapped the other agent's head around. Both reached for their sidearms, yelling "Drop your weapon!" while gauging their shot. But with innocents all around her, collateral damage was highly probable, and they hesitated.

Sally had counted on it.

The woman was the closer of the two. She ran and then leapt, throwing her body into the narrow space between the front-row visitors' knees and the glass, trying to block the shot.

Sally and the Weathermen had discussed a center mass versus a head shot. Roosevelt had survived a bullet aimed at his heart—it had hit his glasses case and the thick papers of a speech he'd stuck in his breast pocket. There was a chance that Ford was wearing a bulletproof vest; he looked so bulky it was hard to tell.

As the trigger reached full throw, the pig president was standing still, listening to something the NASA guy in front of him was saying. Sally aimed directly at the middle of the balding, imperialist, racist warmonger's forehead.

The phone hanging on the console directly behind Glynn Lunney was ringing. The president and his son had also moved behind him and were chatting with the senior management console, so Glynn reached past them to pick up the handset.

His eyes widened as he listened to the hurried words coming through the receiver. Before NASA security had even completed relaying their urgent message, he yelled, "We have a bomb threat!" To make sure everyone heard him, he yelled again. "Listen up! We have a bomb threat! Set to go off in twelve minutes!"

23

Mission Control

Sally had purchased the 200-grain hollow points to get enough gunpowder for near maximum muzzle velocity with the heaviest bullet available. Never mind the recoil. The shot had to travel through a pane of plate glass and still inflict maximum damage when it reached its target.

As the firing pin hit the .44-caliber round, the shock-sensitive silver-colored primer instantly exploded into hot chemical gases and a shower of sparks, igniting the gunpowder. The ensuing explosion was contained by the tough stainless-steel body of the gun, which focused the force onto the flattened back of the lead bullet, accelerating it down the short barrel.

The bullet left the muzzle at a velocity of just under 1,000 feet per second. The spiral rifling grooves inside the barrel had set the bullet spinning, so it was gyroscopically stable and flew true, exactly where Sally was aiming.

The Secret Service agent, despite her heroic leap to fulfill her destiny and give her life in protection of a president, fell short. She landed heavily on the hard strip of floor at the base of the window, the bullet flying over her.

The plate glass that separated Mission Control from its viewing room had been chosen to block noise and allow clear viewing, not to stop bullets. The window shattered on impact, several large, jagged pieces slicing into the fallen agent and the visitors in the front rows, and a shower of small shards landing inside the control room.

Sally was already in position for her second shot as people began to scream around her. In case the glass had hampered her first attempt, this next round, fired through the broken window, would find its mark.

But the second Secret Service agent had anticipated her action and was scrambling diagonally across the rows of people to reach her. He and his partner hadn't stopped the first shot, but he was damned if there was going to be a second.

There wasn't nearly enough time for Gerald Ford to react. The combined sounds of the flight director yelling about a bomb threat, the gun firing and the glass breaking all reached him at the same moment as the small, hurtling piece of lead from Sally's gun.

It nearly missed. The deflection off the glass was just enough that, instead of hitting him squarely in the center of his forehead, the bullet glanced off the side of his skull, tearing its way messily through his scalp, causing instant ringing pain and a spray of flesh and blood. His right hand came up instinctively, and he grunted with surprise as he looked at the blood on his fingers. Then he was driven to the relative safety of the floor by the combined weight of the two Secret Service men near him.

Jack, standing to the president's right, heard a buzzing, whistling sound. Then his father's blood spattered onto his face and jacket and he was knocked down in the bodily rush to protect the president. It was Glynn Lunney, standing with the phone against his ear, who took the remaining force of the assassination attempt. The impact pushed him backwards and the phone flew from his hand on its coiled cord. A small, spinning bullet normally leaves a neat hole, but the lead had been deformed by breaking the glass, so the resulting wound in his forehead looked more like a keyhole. By the time his body hit the console and rebounded slackly onto the floor, Flight Director Glynn Lunney was dead.

The Secret Service agent, clambering over the rows of visitors to get to the shooter, yelled, "Get down!" But Sally stood her ground, shifting her aim to follow the president as his security detail brought him to the floor. Just as she reached full squeeze on the trigger, the agent stretched to slap the barrel up, and the bullet buried itself in the ceiling of Mission Control. His momentum carried him into Sally and knocked her violently onto the people to her left, who were scrambling to get away. Elbowing her in the face to keep her from firing a third shot, the agent wrenched the gun from her hands, and the shocked spectators joined in to help him hold the shooter down.

With the gun torn out of her hand, someone kneeling on the small of her back, and others pinning her limbs across several seats, Sally, a volunteer soldier of the Symbionese Liberation Army, formed to strike back at the misogynist, capitalist, racist government, was finished with her attempt to assassinate the president.

24

Soyuz Spaceship, 140 Miles above Earth

The equipment was brand-new, and that made it suspect. Spacecraft engineers prefer a proven pedigree.

When cosmonaut Yuri Gagarin became the first human to fly in space, on April 12, 1961, the Soviet engineers had to make a key decision: What air should be inside his spaceship? Should it be pure oxygen, which would keep things simple but carried the increased risk of fire? Or should it be standard air, mostly nitrogen with 21 percent oxygen, just like everybody was breathing in Moscow?

They opted for standard air, and rather than have the ship carry pressurized tanks of pure oxygen to replace what the crew breathed, they had installed a canister of a powdered chemical called potassium superoxide. It was as if it had been magically created just for spaceships: the moist used air the crew exhaled automatically reacted with the powder, which soaked up the unwanted humidity and carbon dioxide and released pure oxygen. Fans kept the refreshed air moving. The engineers installed tight seals at every hatch and potential leak point so the ship wouldn't lose any air during flight, avoiding the need to carry pressurized tanks of nitrogen.

Elegantly practical, until a dozen years later, when the bosses decided to dock Soyuz with Apollo.

As the crew raised and lowered cabin pressure to allow them to visit the US spaceship, they would occasionally need replacement nitrogen. So the Soviet engineers had to retrofit nitrogen tanks and valves somewhere into their proven and reliable Soyuz ship. They reluctantly decided to add two high-pressure tanks, one in the orbital compartment and one in the re-entry capsule. To keep things as simple as possible, they put valves on the tanks that the crew could turn manually. Nitrogen getting a little low? Open the valve, keep an eye on the gas pressure sensors and close the valve at the right moment.

But what if the crew was incapacitated in an emergency and couldn't operate the valve? Cosmonaut Valentin Bondarenko had burned to death in a low-pressure altitude simulator in Moscow, and the Soyuz 11 crew of three had died when a valve rattled open and depressurized their ship during re-entry. The design engineers had learned the hard way that they needed to include automated backup systems. So they attached the nitrogen tank in the re-entry capsule to the existing life support system and welded it into place with new plumbing and valves. If the cabin pressure dropped below 500 millimeters of mercury, a small electric motor would drive the valve open and nitrogen would hiss into the Soyuz capsule, mixing with oxygen until it got to an acceptable level.

Simple enough. And they'd tested it multiple times at the factory just outside Moscow, until they were sure it was acceptable as a one-time modification to their trusted Soyuz.

But they'd missed something.

"Wow, what a cool go-kart!" Vance Brand was delighted by his first tour of the Soyuz in orbit.

As soon as they'd finished speaking with the president, Vance had floated into the commander's center seat in the Soyuz re-entry capsule and had connected and tightened the straps enough to loosely hold him in place. He had his hands on the controls, and Alexei Leonov was hovering in the seat next to him, showing him how they worked.

Vance turned, chuckling, but saw that the Soviet commander was frowning, not understanding his words.

He clarified. "A go-kart is like a super-maneuverable small car, lots of power, very fun to drive."

Alexei's habitual smile returned. "Yes, very fun," he said. He struggled for a moment to recall an expression he'd learned, and his eyes twinkled when he remembered and delivered it. "Turns on a dime!"

They looked up when they heard Tom laugh. His head was poking down through the hatch above them. The two Americans were exploring the Soyuz while Deke Slayton was showing the Apollo to Svetlana and Valery. The hatch at the Apollo end of the Docking Module that joined the two ships was closed, keeping the higher-pressure Soyuz air out of the lower-pressure pure oxygen in the Apollo.

Alexei pointed at the control handle Vance held in his left hand. "For moving up-down, left-right, in-out."

Vance, a fellow pilot, nodded. "And the right one's for rotation?"

"Da. Up-down to pitch, left-right to yaw. Twist to roll." He made a small joke. "Rock 'n' roll."

Vance grinned. "Okay if I move them?"

Alexei reached past him and lightly tapped the unlit annunciator between the ivory-colored upper buttons on the command signal panel. "Light is off, so power is off. Go ahead. No problem."

With Tom watching, Vance pivoted the two joysticks, getting a feel for their stiffness and range of motion, imagining the vehicle responding to his touch. His eyes cast about inside the cockpit. "Where do you see the docking target?"

Alexei pointed at the large, dark, circular glass screen between Vance's knees. "Periscope," he explained. He pointed with his whole hand, his fingers aimed down and then forward. "With a mirror to see ahead." He shrugged and made another joke. "Soviet space engineers came from submarines."

"Foolproof," Vance observed. "Nice simple system, no electronics in the way."

"Astronaut-proof," Tom corrected. "Even better."

Alexei's eyes drifted up to the pressure gauge in the top-right corner of the instrument panel, and he frowned. He reached past Vance again and turned the small, pointed black knob next to the gauge, cycling through the different pressure sources.

Tom asked, "Whatcha seeing, Alexei?" Pilots don't like to see other pilots frowning.

"Azot is low," Alexei muttered. He glanced at Tom and spoke louder. "Azot—nitrogen. Little low."

Tom considered. "Want me to open the Docking Module valve, repressurize from the big tanks there?"

Alexei shook his head. "Maybe only my datchick—let me check it first."

Tom and Vance both nodded, knowing "datchick" meant "sensor." Hundreds of sensors on spaceships. They were often the first thing to fail.

"Excuse me," Alexei said, as he unstrapped and pivoted up around Vance to reach for valves buried deep in the structure behind the American's right shoulder. Tom pushed himself back up into the hatch as Alexei's feet floated past.

The cosmonaut checked that he had grabbed the correct valve handle, and then paused, visualizing the new system in his head. They hadn't bothered modifying the full-scale Soyuz simulator in Star City because of this one-time addition to the ship for the Apollo docking mission. All his training on the nitrogen system plumbing had been on partial mock-ups, and he wanted to be sure he got it right.

Satisfied that he knew what he was doing, Alexei nodded, then pivoted the handle 90 degrees, aligning it with the connected tubing—allowing the high-pressure nitrogen to flow from the tank, past the sensor and auto-regulator, into the Soyuz cabin. He kept his hand on the valve, ready to shut it off as soon as he saw the correct response on the pressure gauge.

Nothing to it. Just a quick squirt of nitrogen to verify that everything was working as expected.

The engineers at the Soyuz assembly plant, looking for the simplest routing for the nitrogen tubing, had predictably followed the existing plumbing tack-welded to the aluminum hull. Where they could, they'd also installed bracket clamps to more solidly hold the new tube to the parallel cooling water and oxygen tubes.

Finding a place for the pressure control regulator had required some ingenuity, and it had ended up buried under the right-side flight engineer's seat, out of sight but snugly welded against the hull. Not ideal, but good enough for one flight.

Installing the heaviest component, the nitrogen tank itself, was the hardest challenge. Once the tank was in place, there would be no easy way to fill it. So they needed to use an off-the-shelf tank that was prefilled and could be spun into location using its existing threads. They'd made room under the commander's seat to weld in a padded metal cradle with two metal locking straps. Before the rocket was towed to the launch pad by train and raised to vertical, a Baikonur technician had carefully carried the high-pressure tank into the re-entry capsule cockpit, fitted it into its cradle, spun it multiple times until it reached the prescribed torque, opened its pressure valve and watched the gauges to ensure there were no leaks. Confident that all was correct, he had closed the valve and locked the tank into place with the two latches. He'd then paused, pictured the vibrations and g-load accelerations of launch, touched the tank and traced its plumbing briefly with his fingertip for luck, gathered his installation paperwork and climbed out.

When Alexei Leonov, Soyuz commander and first human to perform a space walk out into the unending emptiness of the cosmos, turned the tank's valve, it started an unanticipated cascade of events.

A free-flying Soyuz in orbit spun slowly to ensure even heating and cooling of its metal hull, which was oriented towards the Sun to get power directly onto its solar arrays. But the engineering analysis team had calculated that it would be okay for Soyuz to stay put for the 47 hours it was scheduled to be docked with Apollo, even though it would be pointed in a non-standard direction and the hull heaters would be unpowered. They'd recognized that some parts of the hull, being always in the sunlight, might get too hot to touch, and had warned the crew. The shaded portions might get cold enough for humidity to condense on the internal walls like dew on a cold beer glass, but all the electrics were properly grounded, and as soon as they undocked, they would go back to normal.

Not ideal, but good enough. International cooperation required compromises. The Soyuz and her crew were tested and tough, and they could easily handle a little extra heat and cold.

But the tack welds couldn't.

When the Moscow technician had contorted himself to secure the pressure control regulator in place, he'd realized he could either reach it or see it, but not both. Not a big problem, as that often happened in the confines of spacecraft building, but it was a new system, so a new problem. First, he'd craned his neck to have a good hard look at where the regulator would go, then he'd stretched his shoulders to get his hands into place. After each quick weld, he'd leaned in to make sure it looked good, and when he was finished, he'd brushed each weld, pleased.

But the metal of the regulator and the hull hadn't melted together nearly as well as he'd thought. As the Soyuz, docked with the Apollo, went in and out of sunlight during each 89-minute orbit, the hull under the regulator got cold. Then wet. One by one, the welds developed tiny cracks as the dissimilar metals contracted in the cold. By the time Alexei opened the valve on the tank, the regulator was held by just one corner. When the small pulse of high-pressure nitrogen surged through the lines, the torque snapped the remaining weld, freeing the square, four-kilogram block that housed the electrics and valves of the add-on automated nitrogen system. Its plumbing should have held it in place. But the uneven heating had also affected the ship's metal tubes. Like dominoes, they rapidly released in sequence, allowing the regulator block to move. Sliding sideways to relieve the combined forces, it accelerated and slammed into the metal block next to it.

That housed the Soyuz vent relief valve.

To return to Earth, the Soyuz had to fall from the vacuum of space into thicker and thicker atmosphere, first slowing by friction and then by parachute. The entry capsule was strong when pressurized from the inside like a balloon, but as it neared the surface, it could easily be crushed by the surrounding squeeze of Earth's air pressure. It was a normal spaceship problem, and so the engineers had installed the vent relief valve, which automatically opened at an altitude of about five kilometers.

The sudden thwack of the nitrogen block hammered the side of the relief valve, and the instant pulse of vibration, unfortunately at just the right resonant frequency, tripped the valve open.

Suddenly there was an unexpected hole in the side of the Soyuz.

25

Mission Control

Every head was turned away from the big screen, trying to understand the turmoil. Glynn Lunney yelling about a bomb scare, the sounds of a gun firing and breaking glass, and voices yelling "Get down!" had sent several flight controllers out of their chairs onto the safety of the floor.

Some of them had also seen Glynn fall, and no one was paying attention to what was happening in orbit.

Dr. JW McKinley peeled off his headset and ran around the end of his console to get to the injured men, yelling, "I'm a doctor, let me through!"

But the Secret Service agents all had emergency medical training and had quickly assessed that the president wasn't badly hurt. Their prime directive was to get POTUS clear of the immediate danger, and then to his waiting car and away. When the two agents up in the visitors' area had secured the assassin, they called "Clear!" After a hurried scan for any other visible threats, the agents next to the president shouted "Up!" and lifted Ford back to his feet while frog-marching him along the consoles and down the staggered stairs towards the door.

"Where's Jack?" the president yelled, trying see past the agents.

"Here, Dad!" his son responded, coming after his father in a scared half-crouch.

Within seconds the cluster of men was through the door, and Mission Control was suddenly quiet.

In shock.

As JW knelt beside the fallen flight director, Kaz instinctively took over, speaking loudly enough for everyone within earshot, but also into his headset so the back rooms would know what was happening. They were a trained team, and now they needed facts and leadership.

"Everyone, listen up! The president is safe, the person with the gun has been subdued, and FLIGHT has been injured. Doctor McKinley is assessing him now." He took a deep breath. "There has also been some sort of bomb threat phoned in, but as of yet we have no details."

Kaz paused for a second, making sure everyone was looking at him and paying attention.

"NASA security will respond to the bomb threat and evacuate us if needed. That's their job. Our job is to focus on our crew in orbit. Everyone check in with your back rooms and look at your data. Until we get a replacement at the flight director console, let me know what you're seeing."

He pivoted to glance up into the visitors' area and saw that the Secret Service agents had already departed with the shooter and the NASA guides were shepherding all the guests out. *They'll be grabbing back rooms to get eyewitness accounts and statements. Not my top concern.*

He turned to JW, who was still on his knees next to Glynn. He looked up at Kaz, shaking his head. "He's dead," he said quietly.

Kaz nodded, keeping his eyes on his friend and away from Glynn's shattered forehead. Then he followed his own advice and looked at the data on the front screen. Still, his thoughts were churning. *FLIGHT's been killed. A bomb threat!*

Pieces of what he'd seen as he walked across the parking lot into work started clicking into place.

The electrical, environmental and communications officer's voice, loud and urgent in everyone's headset, overrode his racing thoughts. "Kaz, I'm seeing a rapid pressure drop in the Docking Module!"

While they'd all been distracted, Apollo-Soyuz had somehow developed an air leak.

Kaz reacted immediately. "Copy, EECOM, I'll direct the crew to follow docked ops emergency procedures."

EECOM nodded, both men adapting to not having a flight director in charge.

Kaz added, "Let me know ASAP how much time they have." It was the key question.

He yanked a checklist out of the pile at the end of his console and hurriedly flipped to the right page. He pushed his transmit button and spoke rapidly. "Apollo-Soyuz, you have a depressurization in the Docking Module–Soyuz stack. Go to page two-dash-one of the Joint Ops Emergency Procedures." He pictured the mayhem on board and decided on a reminder that he would have found helpful. "Oxygen masks are at panel eight twenty-eight."

EECOM came back with the answer to his question. "It's a fast leak, Kaz." He made a quick stab at a number. "Only about three minutes of useful air."

Christ! Kaz thought. Forget procedures. "Tom, get hatch four closed ASAP!"

They had to know immediately if the leak was in the Soyuz or the Docking Module between the ships, and get Tom, Alexei and Vance to the right side of the hatch.

"EECOM, how's the pressure in the Apollo Command Module?"

"Holding steady at five psi, Kaz." *At least that half of the crew is safe.*

Kaz leaned forward and punched a button on his communications panel. He didn't normally talk directly to Russia, but time was critically short. "Moscow FLIGHT, we see a very high leak rate in the Soyuz–Docking Module stack. The crew is working the depress procedure. Any Soyuz insights?"

He listened to the interpreter's rapid-fire Russian, the deeper responding voice of the flight director in Mission Control Moscow, and the translation back: "We have no telemetry right now and are listening to your communication calls. Have you heard Alexei reply?"

Kaz glanced at EECOM to make sure he hadn't missed a call-down in the confusion. EECOM was shaking his head no.

"No, nothing yet."

The Soyuz had to be flying above either Russia or a relay ship to be able to send data to Soviet Mission Control. A glance at the world map showed Apollo-Soyuz over the Indian Ocean. All Soyuz currently had was voice communications, relayed through Apollo. It would be several minutes before they were over a Soviet ground site.

Too long. He needed an update. He pressed his transmit button.

"Apollo-Soyuz, Tom, how do you read Houston?"

Just a low hiss of static. Then, at last, a voice.

"Houston, Apollo, Deke here in the Command Module, we read you loud and clear." A pause. "We're hearing nothing from the other three and see their pressure getting very low." Deke was keeping his tone flat, but the words were ominous. "Apollo pressure's normal, hatch two is holding." Hatch two was at the Apollo end of the Docking Module, and it opened away from Apollo, so a depressurization on the other side would be trying to pull it open. But it was designed to be airtight right down to vacuum.

Kaz responded, "Copy, Deke."

I need data! he thought. He turned to his left. "INCO, do we have any camera views?"

"No, Kaz, sorry, all cameras were off." Past tense.

"EECOM, any change?" Maybe the crew got a hatch closed but were too busy to call.

"No, FLIGHT. Hatch three's microswitches still show open, and the Docking Module's pressure's still dropping." A pause while he checked. "Showing just over three psi, no change in rate, and no flow into the oxygen masks."

Shit.

Kaz turned to the console behind him to the right. "SURGEON, what's minimum for consciousness?" A question no flight controller ever wants to ask.

Dr. Jimmy Doi had taken over the medical console when JW had gone to assist the president and Glynn. He already had a reference book open in front of him. "Kaz, time of useful consciousness at three psi is about forty-five seconds, max."

Kaz looked at Jimmy. That wasn't enough time.

EECOM had a suggestion. "Kaz, let's get Deke to command the Docking Module valves open, dump air in as fast as we can. Buy the crew some time."

Good idea. Kaz transmitted, "Deke, open the DM nitrogen and oxygen flow valves ASAP."

Inside the Apollo Command Module, with Svetlana and Valery watching, Deke threw the appropriate switches and checked gauges. "Valves are open, seeing DM tank pressures starting to drop."

On the other side of hatch two, inside the Docking Module, the twin hisses of inpouring gases were loud.

All eyes in Mission Control turned towards EECOM, who was staring intently at his screen. "Pressure drop has slowed, FLIGHT." A beat. "Leveled off now, holding at three psi." One more pause. "And climbing."

We're in a race, Kaz realized. *Can we flow enough air for the crew to function and solve the leak before the Docking Module tanks empty?*

JW stood up from where he'd been crouched next to Glynn, covering the man's face with a jacket he'd found hung on a nearby chair. "Kaz, they need oxygen more than nitrogen. Can we prioritize that?"

Kaz turned. "EECOM, will just oxygen flow alone be enough to hold pressure?"

EECOM had a hurried conversation with his back room. "Maybe, Kaz."

Worth a try. Kaz transmitted again. "Deke, you've reversed the depress, but we want to give the crew more oxygen. Please close the nitrogen valve but be ready to open it again ASAP."

"Copy." A pause. "Complete."

EECOM stared at his data. "Pressure has stopped increasing." Everyone waited, the room's tension palpable. "Looks like it might be holding at three point four." Ten seconds ticked by. "Looks steady, FLIGHT. And we have enough oxygen to flow at this rate for several minutes."

Is it enough? Time to try the crew again.

"Apollo-Soyuz, Houston." Kaz said. "Deke, that's holding pressure, no further action for now." He took a breath and spoke forcefully. "Tom, Vance, Alexei, this is Houston, how do you copy?"

As part of his pilot training, Kaz had been hypoxic, starved for oxygen, multiple times. Maybe the inflow of fresh oxygen would revive someone. And calling the crew by first names might cut through the fog if one of them was even barely conscious.

He waited.

Nothing.

He tried again. "Tom, Vance, Alexei, this is Houston. How do you copy?"

Just a low hiss of static.

In the back of his brain, reacting to the parallel urgencies of the situation, Kaz's subconscious had been replaying exactly what he'd noticed during his fast walk from his Thunderbird to the Mission Control building.

He was suddenly sure where the bomb was.

26

Soyuz Spaceship

All three men felt their ears popping.

As the Soyuz air rushed out through the failed valve into space, the pressure dropped rapidly. Unsure what was happening, Alexei immediately pivoted the nitrogen tank valve, still in his hand, back to the closed position, thinking maybe it had caused an overpressure.

They could all hear a loud hissing, and then came the blaring klaxon of the Soyuz pressure sensors alerting them to the new danger. Alexei's hands flew to the buttons on the control panels, cycling through systems and data to try to figure out what was happening. He watched the pressure gauge and the clock and did the quick math. He quickly typed the commands to shut the vent valve, but the valve didn't respond.

His ship was going to depressurize to vacuum, and he couldn't stop it. Time for action.

"We need to get out!" Alexei shouted above the noise as he physically pushed Vance and Tom up through the hatch into the Soyuz orbital module. He gauged the time remaining, grabbed the pressure suit bundled next to his seat and threw it up through the hatch. He'd need to wear it to get back into the unpressurized Soyuz re-entry capsule to fly it home.

There's lots of extra air in the Docking Module, he thought, scrabbling Svetlana's and Valery's suits out of their stowage spots and shoving them up through the hatch. He grabbed the needed checklists from the locker on the right and did a fast, hard look around for anything else they might need. He spotted two drink bags Velcroed to the wall and flicked them up through.

Communications, he realized. He pushed more buttons and selected the VHF radio frequency he'd need to talk directly with Moscow, unplugged the two headsets and stuffed the jumble of floating cables through the hatch, grateful that Tom was catching things as he threw them and getting them under control.

A quick glance at the pressure gauge.

"Chyort!" he shouted. He pivoted and launched himself up through the opening, twisting as he went to grab the hatch, release its hold-open mechanism and pull it closed.

But the design engineers hadn't built the hatch that way. They'd planned for what they viewed as the far higher probability of a leak being in the orbital compartment, with the crew in the re-entry capsule below. There were no solid handholds on the side of the hatch he faced, and the rush of air pouring past him through the hatch, drawn towards the leak, prevented him from pulling it closed. It was like trying to close a door with no handle in a high wind.

His entire spaceship was going to depress, not just the re-entry capsule.

Alexei made a rapid decision and yelled at Tom and Vance. "Everything into the Docking Module!" He grabbed the three pressure suits Tom had temporarily stowed under a bungee against the wall as Vance pulled himself through the hatch to receive them, and then pushed the suits up. Quickly, the two commanders grabbed everything Alexei had rescued from the lower capsule and flung them through the circular opening at Vance.

There was a large mechanical pressure gauge mounted on an angled shelf in the orbital module, and Alexei paused briefly to check it. His eyes opened wide at what he saw.

Human physiology originally evolved in the sea, with creatures using gills to extract oxygen from the surrounding water, flushing it steadily with repeated motion. Over millions of years some gills became lungs, with mouth and throat valves and abdominal muscles to pull in fresh air and expel used gases. Early lungfish, using a mix of gills and breathing cycles, were the first in the branch of animal life that climbed out of the oceans to live on land.

Our distant ancestors mostly stayed close to the water, where life was abundant, near sea level, with its corresponding high air pressure. But some animals moved to higher altitudes where there was less competition for food, developing bigger, more efficient lungs and hearts. Humans eventually joined them, living and hunting in the heights of Tibet and the Andes, genetic selection making for more efficient oxygen carrying in the blood and favoring smaller bodies and larger lungs.

But even the fittest mountain climber has a limit. At the top of Mount Everest, at the very limit of human capability, the air pressure is a third of that at sea level. And only 21 percent of that thin air is oxygen.

At the moment the leak began, the Soyuz pressure had been two-thirds of an atmosphere, lower than normal for the Soviets, a grudging engineering compromise so they could work with Apollo. In the precious time the three crewmen had been evacuating first the Soyuz re-entry capsule and then the upper orbital module, life-giving air had been rushing out into space. Pressure was now approaching critical levels.

The three men's bodies were responding the way human bodies had learned to do, over eons of evolution, when the delicate receptors in the carotid artery joining the heart and the brain sense low oxygen. With their hearts automatically beating faster to drive the blood through the lungs more quickly, they were gasping, hyperventilating to try to breathe in more air. They had all done pressure chamber hypoxia training as fighter pilots, and each now felt the familiar cues of oxygen starvation: dizziness, narrowed vision and increasing confusion.

"We have to hurry!" Tom yelled hoarsely, not recognizing his own voice. He knew that the Soviet hatch four, at the top of the Soyuz, was the same design as the hatch in the re-entry capsule and couldn't easily be pulled closed against the outrushing air. He'd decided it would be American hatch three, at the end of the Docking Module, that would save them; it pivoted towards the Soyuz, so it would slam shut and seal to stop the flowing air.

His responsibility.

"Help me, Vance!" Tom croaked—he could barely speak in the thinning air. He glanced over his shoulder to see Vance unconscious, floating motionless behind him against the curved wall of the Docking Module.

He felt Alexei bump into his side, and they both reached to release the hatch-locking mechanism. Tom repeatedly blinked and shook his head, trying to clear his vision and sharpen his focus, but everything was shimmering and weirdly lit. He felt his hands touch something, but he couldn't make his fingers and thumb pinch to undo the clasp holding the hatch. Muddily, he realized he had stopped feeling Alexei beside him. It was getting darker and darker, and he had a sudden overpowering urge to sleep, and couldn't remember why he shouldn't. With a last glimmer of reason, he turned to try to push off and float to the Docking Module's central control panel, to open the oxygen supply valve.

But denied oxygen, Tom's body did what evolution demanded: it prioritized survival. Like Vance and then Alexei, Tom lost consciousness, stopping all unnecessary use of what little oxygen was left, rolling the dice that if a new source of oxygen arrived within a few seconds, he'd live.

Three bodies floating weightless, gently pulled like flotsam towards a whirlpool, bumping together at the hatch mouth along the relentlessly flowing leak of air.

After a few long moments, Tom Stafford's limp body floated close to the air outlet valves. The ancient unconscious reflex of his lungs suddenly gulped the fresh, heavy flow of pure oxygen. His body spasmed in weightlessness, like a diver doing a jackknife, as the life-giving gas was carried through his blood.

Tom awakened as from a deep sleep, totally relaxed, still half dreaming. He couldn't see, but he was hearing a hissing noise.

Where am I? Tom felt weirdly lethargic and befuddled. *What is that noise?*

There was a klaxon of some sort honking above the hiss, and the familiar alarm urged him to wake up and think. He tried to open his eyes, but they felt like they were already open, and he still couldn't see anything.

Bad dream, he thought idly. He drifted past the air outlets in a back eddy of cabin atmosphere and floated into the far end of the Docking Module, where the fresh oxygen hadn't reached. The outrushing hole in the Soyuz kept pulling the fresh air away from him like a fountain into a drain, spewing it out into space.

The sudden wave of new oxygen in his blood subsided. Tom sighed contentedly as the noises faded. *Back to sleep,* he thought.

Just a dream.

27

Apollo Command Module

"Houston, Apollo, how do you read?"

Deke Slayton was deeply concerned. Tom, Vance and Alexei were still in the Docking Module on the other side of the hatch, where the pressure was near zero even though the DM's oxygen tanks had drained to nearly empty. He'd considered reopening the nitrogen tanks but had decided there was no point.

Nitrogen didn't keep people alive.

And now Houston had gone silent. He'd rechecked all his communications switches and verified the predicted contact times through the relay satellite. Apollo had three different voice radio frequencies, and he was cycling through them all, trying to raise someone on Earth.

Anyone.

Floating next to him, Valery and Svetlana were listening to his transmissions on borrowed headsets. She spoke the better English of the two.

"Why no answer from Houston?" Svetlana was thinking that maybe this American, Deke, knew something he hadn't told them yet. A pressure leak was the most serious spaceship emergency after fire. She and

Valery urgently needed to know the health of their commander, Alexei, on the other side of the closed Apollo hatch.

Deke's fleshy, deeply lined face was grave.

"I don't know, Svetlana." He pointed out the square side window next to her. "We're just over India and should still have a good link through the ATS communications relay. I don't know why no one is answering."

Valery spoke, his voice urgent. "How is Soyuz? Hatch closed?"

There was a chance that all the air had leaked out of the Docking Module but that the Soyuz and the three crew were still okay—safe within the ship's two small aluminum-walled bubbles of life-giving oxygen, separated by the vacuum of space.

Deke realized that the two Russians didn't know how to read all of the Apollo vehicle gauges, and he hadn't updated them. He shook his head as he pointed to a rectangular black indicator on the central instrument panel. "Our cabin pressure is holding fine." He leaned down and pointed at the differential pressure gauge on the forward hatch. "But the Docking Module pressure has fallen to near zero." He looked directly at Valery. "We don't have telemetry from Soyuz's orbital and re-entry capsules, but from what Houston said, I think the whole stack depressurized."

He could see Valery struggling with the English words, so he bluntly said, "I think Alexei, Tom and Vance are dead."

Saying it out loud caused the weight of it to hit Deke like an unseen wave. He'd just lost three of his closest friends, men he respected and loved. Three lifeless, helpless bodies in a defunct hulk of metal docked to his capsule's nose. And he was no longer just the Docking Module pilot. He was the Apollo commander, the lone American, with the two Russians in his ship completely counting on him.

And he couldn't raise anyone in Houston. *What the fuck is going on?*

Deke returned the round-eyed stares of Svetlana and Valery as they processed what he'd just said. He'd been chief astronaut for NASA for many years, dealing with the aggressive personalities of ex-fighter/test pilots and the complex intellects of engineers and former scientists.

He knew that astronauts needed facts and a plan of action. These two cosmonauts were now, suddenly, his crew. His only crew. Time to get them involved.

"Maybe whatever caused the depressurization knocked out our comm system. Any ideas?"

Valery frowned as he struggled to understand the English words, so Svetlana quickly translated for him. The two Russians remained silent for a long moment; Deke knew they were visualizing the Soyuz and Docking Module communication systems in their heads, trying to think of a common failure mode.

Svetlana broke the silence. "You said India. How soon are we over a Soviet ground site? They will receive Soyuz voice and data directly. Your Apollo ship can talk to them on 121.75 megahertz, yes?"

Deke nodded. "Yes, through the hatch bypass umbilical into the radio in the Docking Module, if it's still working." He reached with his left hand towards the upper right of the instrument panel and tapped on the top-right switch with his pointer finger. "Here's the communications master power." His finger moved down two rows. "And here's the VHF radio control. 'RCV' means receive only, and 'T/R' means both transmit and receive." He flicked the master power to Audio and the VHF to T/R, then set the small thumbwheels next to the switches to five, for medium volume.

With his left hand directly in front of her, Svetlana distractedly noticed for the first time that Deke was missing half of his ring finger and wore his wedding ring on his baby finger. *They would never have let him be a cosmonaut with a flaw like that,* she thought. Complete physical perfection was mandatory. *I'll ask him what happened, later.*

She looked out the window, saw the Himalayas and assessed their exact location and direction of travel over the Earth. "We should be over the Petropavlovsk antenna site soon—they will connect us to Moscow."

Valery raised a hand and spoke in English so the American would understand. "If Alexei dead, I was Flight Engineer Number One, so I am now Soyuz commander." He looked at Svetlana, expecting no objection and receiving none. Chain of command was necessary on a spaceship. He turned to Deke. "You are mission commander now, but I will talk to Moscow."

"Makes sense," Deke agreed. Clarity was good. He pointed again at the communications panel. "We're configured—give 'em a call."

Valery moved the comm cap's black microphone booms in front of his mouth and pressed the transmit button on the connecting cord. "Moskva, Moskva, kak sleeshetya?" *Moscow, Moscow, how do you hear?*

No response, but they weren't quite far enough north yet. Valery floated to the small, square window, looking for the familiar high brown plateau of Mongolia, and beyond it, the long, jagged finger of Sakhalin Island. Petropavlovsk, on the Kamchatka Peninsula, was just to the east.

"Moskva, Moskva, kak sleeshetya?"

Svetlana had moved to the forward hatch and began banging on the metal of the hatch with her flashlight, listening for any response. Just in case.

Deke nodded to himself. *Worth a try.*

All three of them heard the crackle of static in their headsets, and then a distorted voice speaking Russian.

"Soyuz-Apollon, Soyuz-Apollon, kak sleeshetya nas?" *Soyuz-Apollo, how do you hear us?*

"Shlooshayoo horoshow." *I hear you well.*

Continuing in rapid Russian, Valery summarized the situation and asked if Moscow was getting telemetry data from the Soyuz. If there was pressure in either compartment of his ship, the rest of the crew might still be alive.

There was a pause and then a blunt answer. Both the ship's orbital and re-entry modules showed zero pressure.

Valery closed his eyes at the confirmation. There was no longer any doubt. His commander and friend, Alexei Arkhipovich Leonov, was dead.

Deke was watching him intently. "Ask them why Houston isn't responding to my calls."

At their low orbital height of 140 miles, the Petropavlovsk site would disappear over the horizon quickly. Svetlana translated, and Valery asked Moscow the question.

Moscow's answer was puzzling. "We don't know. We have lost communications with Houston Mission Control also, both radio and telephone."

Svetlana pushed her mic button. "Do you think maybe an undersea cable has been cut?"

A pause while Moscow considered. "That might be. But there was some commotion there just before they stopped communicating. We heard something about a gunshot. All of our equipment is functioning normally. The problem is on their end."

Svetlana quickly translated for Deke. His eyes widened. *A gunshot!* The president had been there!

Moscow had a vital question. "Please verify the health of all crewmembers."

Valery answered, his voice heavy. "I, Valery Kubasov, am fine." He glanced at his crewmates. "Svetlana Gromova and Deke Slayton are also fine." He took a deep breath. "But with total depressurization of the Soyuz and the Docking Module, and the resupply oxygen tanks empty, it seems certain that the other three crewmembers are dead."

A pause, and then Moscow Mission Control asked, "What is the status of the Apollo ship?" The Soviet flight controllers needed all the information they could get before they lost contact.

Svetlana translated for Deke, and he pushed his transmit button. "The Apollo Command and Service Modules are both behaving normally, no issues."

Common words for him to use, but he was shaking his head in disbelief as he said them. Picturing the repercussions of what had just happened, and the complexity of what they were going to have to do to get safely back to Earth. What *he* was going to have to do.

But first things first. He pressed the transmit button again. "Moscow, you said there was a gunshot in Houston. Is the president okay?"

The voice of a translator in Moscow responded. "We don't know. We're calling alternative numbers for NASA in Florida and Washington. We will let you know as soon as we—" There was a crackling noise and then silence.

Svetlana looked out the window, picturing the arcing path of their orbit over the Pacific as they left Soviet territory. "We might pick them back up through Hawaii." She looked at Deke. "Do you have a flight plan with ground tracks?"

Deke nodded, reaching behind her to grab a thick book secured behind a bungee on the wall. It was Vance Brand's copy of the Joint Crew Activities Plan. *Now it's Svetlana's,* he thought. He flicked through pages, opened it to the right date and handed it to her. He pointed at the digital mission timer in the center of the Apollo instrument panel, and then at the left-hand column in the book, where it listed ground site communications opportunities.

Svetlana nodded. She and Valery had similar books, but they were in the Soyuz. She studied the list. "We should have Hawaii in five minutes. What frequency will they be on?" She needed to start learning Apollo systems, and fast.

Deke pointed to the forward hatch. "We'll need to disconnect from Soyuz comm, and it will revert to US frequencies." He pointed to a switch on the upper instrument panel. "We'll try VHF, and then S-band."

He looked at Svetlana and Valery. "Hopefully there'll be someone there to answer."

28

Mission Control

Kaz glanced hurriedly at his watch. Just before he'd been shot, Glynn had yelled that the bomb was due to go off in 12 minutes. *How long has it been?* With the president's exit and the depressurization on orbit, several vital minutes had passed. *Four?* Kaz decided five, to give himself margin.

That left seven minutes. He urgently needed to get out of Mission Control and clear the area around the bomb to protect any nearby innocents. But three men were dying on orbit, suffocating in a leaking spacecraft.

Next to him, Center Director Chris Kraft, who had recovered from being pushed to the ground by the Secret Service, now straddled Glynn's body. Grimly, he lifted the jacket and peeled the headset off the dead man's head, wiped off the spatter of blood, put the headset on and moved the microphone boom close to his lips. Straightening, he pressed the transmit button.

"Everyone, listen up. This is Chris Kraft. Until we get things sorted out, I'm now the acting flight director." He glanced at Kaz. "Thank you, CAPCOM, for stepping up. I want each console with an urgent problem to summarize it for me now, starting with EECOM." He hadn't been a flight director for several years, but the authority of the role flowed naturally back into him.

Kaz waved his hand urgently to get Kraft's attention. "FLIGHT, I'm certain I know where the bomb is, and we have six minutes. It's near the power transformer block out in the rear parking lot, so not a threat to Mission Control. Permission to go clear the area of any pedestrians."

He'd taken the best immediate actions available for the orbiting crew, and Kraft could take over comms with the surviving crew until he got back.

Kraft blinked, absorbing the rush of new information. No time to question how Kaz knew where the bomb was. It was an urgent threat, and Mission Control dealt in risk, facts and action. He nodded abruptly in approval and said, "Go—and get security to help you."

Kaz off peeled his headset, threw it on his console and sprinted for the exit at the front left corner of Mission Control.

Behind him, back at the SURGEON console, Dr. JW McKinley rapidly weighed his responsibilities. Three crewmembers were dying on orbit, but there might soon be casualties outside, at the Johnson Space Center. He turned to Jimmy Doi, next to him.

"Go help Kaz!"

Kaz raced down the stairs that led to the rear exit of Mission Control, leaping two and three at a time, pivoting around the corners, hanging on to the handrail. He slammed his hands into the metal bar that opened the exit door and burst through, out onto the loading dock. His eye scanned the parking lot.

The Houston Lighting and Power van was still parked next to the transformer block, but there were no men around it now. Multiple sirens were wailing from somewhere. Looking across Second Street, past the corner with Avenue C, he could see that the doors of the NASA fire station were open and a rotating red light was blinking brightly. A fire truck was moving, about to turn onto Second Street.

Pedestrians were on the sidewalks, and cars were driving on both Second Street and Avenue C, near the HL&P van. Kaz had no way to judge how big the blast would be, but he decided that his first priority was the people on foot.

He yelled as loudly as he could, running down the cement stairs and towards the sidewalk, pointing with an outstretched arm. "There's a bomb in that Houston Power van! Run! Run and take cover!"

Behind him, he heard a voice loudly repeating what he'd said, and glanced back to see Jimmy running diagonally away to his right, towards Avenue C.

Predictably, the pedestrians froze, trying to understand what was going on.

"Run and take cover!" Kaz yelled again, still pointing. "There's a bomb in that van!"

The people nearest him started running, and some dove into the shallow dry ditch next to the road. Kaz looked at his watch again. He didn't know whether he could trust the time, but it was all he had, so he yelled, "You have three minutes! Run and take cover!"

Kaz looked down Second Street and was relieved to see that the fire truck had turned in his direction. A plan quickly popped into his head, and he took off towards the truck, waving both arms, still yelling for the remaining pedestrians to get clear. In the distance he could hear Jimmy doing the same.

The fire truck, its siren on and lights flashing, cut diagonally across Second Street, towards Kaz, braking heavily as cars stopped in confusion or scattered to get out of the way. Kaz leapt and grabbed the truck's side mirror, swinging himself up onto the step by the driver's door. The firefighter wound his window down and Kaz hastily shared his plan, pointing to the van. The driver nodded. Shifting into low, he stepped on the gas, turning the truck to bounce through the shallow drainage ditch and across the low cement parking dividers, avoiding parked cars as he headed directly for the HL&P van.

Kaz yelled, "Get clear!" at the other firemen hanging on the outside of the truck. He leaned out to check if there were any pedestrians still in immediate danger.

Kaz yelled at the truck driver, "You got this?"

After the fireman nodded, his mouth set in a thin, flat line, concentrating on maneuvering his big vehicle, Kaz leapt off and ran towards the nearest cars on Second Street to get them to move clear, looking around to assess potential blast angles.

He spotted something unexpected in the distance. Something familiar. A faded green Ford Galaxie, stopped at an odd angle, well towards the back of the opposite lot. He realized it had a clear line of sight to the HL&P truck.

The clock in his head had been counting down. Kaz figured he had 90 seconds. He pounded urgently on the hood of the car pulled over on the street next to him and yelled, hoping the other drivers would hear too.

"There's a bomb by that fire truck! Get clear!"

The driver immediately lurched into gear and spun a quick U-turn, the car fishtailing slightly as, panicked, he stepped on the gas. In his peripheral vision, Kaz saw more cars doing the same as he ran across the road, away from the HL&P van.

Directly towards the green Galaxie.

29

Green Ford Galaxie, Johnson Space Center

It was going to be the biggest, most important explosion Aaron had ever created.

As with all the other bombs he'd built for the Weather Underground, he'd decided on a battery-powered alarm clock to close the circuit on time, sending an electrical current through wires to the blasting caps. It gave him more control of exactly when the bomb would go off and the freedom to be well clear of the blast site.

Aaron liked that. Time to make a phone call to get innocents out of the way and to maximize media coverage. Make a statement that people noticed.

The big difference with this bomb was what happened next. Instead of being attached to a few sticks of dynamite, these blasting caps were tightly wrapped with detonation cord and taped flush against a bundle of gel explosive Tovex tubes, all strapped securely to the top of five-gallon pails of fertilizer soaked with diesel fuel.

Once he'd received everything from the supplier in China, he'd read several mining instruction manuals at a Houston public library on how to put the bomb together. He'd also talked with a guy named Dwight from the SLA who had helped build the bomb that had stopped Army mathematicians from doing missile research at the University of Wisconsin a couple of years earlier. They'd made the mistake of using too much explosive, causing unnecessary collateral damage and killing a physics researcher who'd been working late.

Aaron was determined to get it right. Clean, accurate and reliable. His Weatherman reputation relied on it.

Still, in case the timer failed, the providers of the explosives had demanded a backup plan. Aaron objected, but they were adamant that it was a necessary part of the deal, so he'd added more det cord and Tovex tubes on the other side of the pails that could be set off by a bullet. If the planned explosion time came and went, one of the Chinese men would be in place with a rifle, his target marked on the van's exterior, to make sure they were successful.

Aaron had accepted it. Belt and suspenders. Not needed, but it wouldn't hurt either.

He hadn't admitted to anyone how nervous he'd been while mixing the diesel fuel into the fertilizer. Molly had watched as he'd used a bathroom scale and a kitchen measuring cup to get the ratio right, pouring the liquid onto the granulated powder and stirring it with a heavy wooden spoon, ensuring they were thoroughly blended. Even though he knew the mixture required an explosive shock to ignite, he'd eased in the spoon each time and stirred very slowly and smoothly. He'd made small talk with Molly to cover his unease, and both of them had visibly relaxed when he had all three five-gallon pails filled.

Their Chinese partners had provided the van, and Aaron didn't question where they'd gotten it. The HL&P paint scheme looked genuine, but the interior was bare. He guessed it was stolen, but it didn't matter. The van wasn't going to survive the blast.

The Chinese driver had parked it neatly at the Johnson Space Center location Aaron had chosen. Aaron had carefully hooked up the clock and set the time, tested it with a light bulb, as usual, and then securely wired it to the blasting cap leads. Both men got out, wearing what looked like real HL&P coveralls. The driver locked the vehicle, the circling green Ford pulled up, and they climbed in. They drove to a pre-chosen phone booth at a gas station on NASA Road 1, where Aaron made the phone call, and then they drove back to a spot at the far edge of the parking lot where they had a clear shot.

Just in case.

Inside the van, the small, round-faced electric clock robotically measured the passage of time. The glow-in-the-dark minute hand slowly tracked towards the fixed silver alarm arm, which Aaron had precisely set using the small, knurled knobs. Two wires protruded from the cut-open back of the clock, soldered into the place where the alarm bell would normally be activated.

Inside the Ford Galaxie, everyone was checking their watches, but they were counting on Aaron to have the correct time. He had called out five minutes, then four, then three, but when he got to two, he stepped up the frequency.

"Ninety seconds."

Molly was in the front passenger seat, nervously keeping an eye out for anyone coming close. Aaron sat in back, next to the shooter, who wound down his window. He lifted the rifle off the floor by his feet and checked that a round was in the chamber. He twisted and bumped into Aaron to get into a good firing position, using the window frame of the car to support the hand holding the forestock. He shifted to get comfortable, then leaned his face into the stock cheek rest, aligning his eye to see through the sight mounted on top.

A fire truck screeched to a stop near the van, blocking his view. The shooter said something in Chinese to the driver, who put the car in gear and pulled forward in the parking lot until they had a clear line of sight again.

"Sixty seconds." Aaron smiled to himself. This was NASA, and here he was doing a countdown. He decided that when he got to 10, he'd announce every second, just like he'd seen on TV.

Molly called out in a high, breathy voice, "I see someone coming across the street at us from behind the fire truck!"

The Chinese driver had been watching as well. He said something rapid-fire to the man in the back, who grunted and held his firing position.

"Forty-five seconds." Aaron was straining to see, being careful not to bump the shooter.

"I think he's looking at us!" Molly said, her voice intense.

They all saw the man shift from a fast walk to a jog.

The driver said something emphatic, and the shooter pulled the gun inside and cranked the window back up. All eyes were on the man, who was getting nearer.

"Thirty seconds—I think we need to move!" Aaron said. "We can come back around for a shot if it doesn't go off!"

The shooter spoke in Chinese and the driver answered, put the car into gear and stepped on the gas. Molly and Aaron's heads swiveled as they pulled away, watching the man slow to a stop and stare after them. As they turned around a parked car, the man pivoted and ran in the other direction. The driver turned right, back onto Second Street, ready to make a left onto Avenue B to circle back again.

Aaron glanced back at his wristwatch. He'd missed his 10-second countdown.

"Shit, it's time!" he yelled.

30

Explosion

Clockwork.

The alarm clock's electric current traveled up the wires and ignited the blasting caps. Their heat and pressure simultaneously set off the detonation cord and the Tovex tubes, punching a searing localized shock wave into the pails of diesel-soaked ammonium nitrate, which caused a cascade of vaporizing oxygen, nitrogen oxides and water trapped inside the fertilizer pellets.

The result was an instantaneous, enormous, explosive expansion of gases erupting from the center of the parked van. It burst like a metal balloon, with the thinner sheet-steel sides turning to ribbons and the heavier metal parts becoming projectiles blasting in all directions. The pressure wave drove downwards, bending and distorting the van's frame and axles into a crater in the asphalt while reflecting the energy back up and sideways.

Right next to the van, Mission Control's emergency power building took the brunt, instantly peeled of its metal covering, the explosion breaking and dislodging the complex electrical works and diesel generators within. The central section, closest to ground zero, blew completely open, sending heavy pieces of metal and wire flying and tumbling across the half-empty lot, slamming into parked cars and anything else in their path. The diesel fuel tank that fed the emergency power generators ruptured and caught fire, sending up a column of black smoke.

At the front of the van, the engine and some of the drive train cartwheeled violently across parked cars, coming to rest in the ditch next to Avenue C. The pressure wave pushed through the van's thin rear doors and raced across the open grass along the west side of Mission Control, knocking off large chunks of the building's cement facade.

The few remaining pedestrians and cars along Second Street would have been blasted by the shock wave and flying debris, but the hastily parked fire truck had contained them. Still, the explosion picked up all 46,000 pounds of the behemoth and pushed it sideways six feet before flipping it over onto its side.

The driver and firemen had leapt from the big vehicle and run hard to get clear, making it into the lee of their truck as the explosion began. Fortunately, the mass of the truck saved them, stopping the worst of the blast and deflecting it upwards into the sky.

Kaz had run across Second Street towards the green car, stopping when it sped off. He was running for his Thunderbird to give chase when the explosion hit. He, too, was protected by the big truck, but the noise of the blast echoing and rolling across the parked cars made him bring his hands to his ears, and instinctively he knelt, hoping any pressure wave or shrapnel would pass over him. As the sound died, he pulled his hands away and looked around as the firemen picked themselves up and pieces of metal kept striking the ground.

Kaz turned to the out-of-the-way spot where he'd parked his T-Bird, and was thankful to see it sitting there unharmed. He broke into a run, feeling for his keys in his pocket. He glanced back to see the green Ford stopped on the street, blocked by cars that had slammed on their brakes or had had their windows shattered by the explosion. As he watched, the

Ford's driver, cranking the wheel to get around a stopped car, drove up over the Second Street curb and accelerated along the edge, headed south, away from NASA and the blast site.

No NASA security or police car was chasing it. It was up to him.

With the Thunderbird's top down, Kaz vaulted directly into the driver's seat, turned the key, dropped the gearshift into first and accelerated hard along the rear of the parking lot, bumping up and over the dry ground of the open grass field that paralleled Second Street. He dodged onto the service road behind the Anechoic Test Facility, cut diagonally across its parking lot and spotted the green Ford in the distance, turning right onto NASA Road 1. Kaz glanced in his rearview mirror at the smoke and mayhem and looked forward along Second Street at the flashing lights of local emergency vehicles arriving to help. He kept his speed up as he took the diagonal entry onto NASA Road 1, tires squealing, fishtailing through the turn and accelerating, scanning the road ahead.

The green Ford Galaxie was nowhere to be seen.

He twisted his head to look at the passing side streets into Nassau Bay: nothing. He stared down NASA 1 but saw no commotion of a car going fast.

Shit! How did I lose them?

He had a thought and pulled a hard U-turn into oncoming traffic, car horns blaring, and searched the parking lots and gas stations along the south edge to see if the Ford had pulled in somewhere to hide.

Nothing.

They saw me giving chase. How long were they out of my sight? Thirty seconds? What would I do in their shoes?

The King's Inn, he suddenly realized. It was nearby and had multiple parking lots, so many places to quickly hide. Cursing, Kaz U-turned again and raced back up NASA 1, turning into the sprawling hotel on the north side.

There were deep lots on both sides of the marquee-covered entrance. He chose the one on the right, as it was nearer. Assuming the Ford's occupants were armed, he cruised quietly along the near edge of the lot, scanning each alley of cars, ready to instantly accelerate if he needed to. *Nothing*. He turned into the farthest row and carefully picked up speed, trying to spot the familiar faded green of his prey.

Nothing.

Kaz felt the passage of time like an urgency of emotion about to spill over. He pounded the steering wheel with the heel of his hand as he wove through the maze of cars, pivoting his head to check the entrance as he went. As he reached the farthest corner of the lot, he glimpsed a flash of metallic green in the distance pulling back out onto NASA 1. He cursed and was turning back through the nearest row of parked cars when a blue sedan abruptly backed out in front of him, the driver not looking. Kaz slammed on his brakes, stopping just inches from impact, the squeal of his tires causing the other driver's head to whip around in shock. He stalled, blocking the way.

Kaz slammed into reverse and grabbed the seat next to him to twist around as he backed up, spinning the wheel and maneuvering to get into the parallel exit row. He accelerated hard out of the lot and down the hotel's long driveway and raced back onto NASA 1, but the green car was gone. He drove fast to the west—past the U-Joint and all the way to Highway 3 at Webster—but he had lost the Ford. It might have turned up El Camino Real, or it could have just outrun him.

"Shit!" he yelled, pounding his steering wheel again. He used the traffic light to U-turn and headed back east, fast, aiming for the tall column of smoke at the Johnson Space Center.

31

Johnson Space Center

Kaz squirmed in his seat, reaching to fish his access badge out of his back pocket. Ahead, he could see that the pillar of smoke was dissipating.

Nothing left to burn, he guessed.

He slowed on NASA Road 1 to turn onto Second Street, but a pale-blue Houston Police car was blocking the road, lights flashing. Two uniformed cops stood next to it, directing traffic away. One waved his arms impatiently at Kaz, yelling as he pulled up closer and stopped, "Road's closed. Turn your car around, please, sir."

Kaz held out his badge. "I'm Navy Commander Kazimieras Zemeckis, NASA astronaut support, working the Apollo-Soyuz flight. I'm needed in Mission Control."

Keep the decision the cop has to make simple.

The patrolman frowned as he read the badge, then studied Kaz's face and short haircut. His eyes flicked across the length of the white Thunderbird.

"All right, you can pass. Stay out of the way of the emergency vehicles and park this pretty car well clear." He handed Kaz's badge back and stepped to the side as Kaz pulled around the end of the patrol car.

Ahead of him was mayhem. A Nassau Bay fire truck was spraying the last of the fire, and several ambulances and multiple police cars, all with lights flashing, were parked near the scene. Several private cars had been damaged by the blast and were abandoned on the road. Beside some of them, medics knelt to help wounded passengers. The damage to Mission Control looked more cosmetic than structural.

Power was the problem. The bombers had targeted the main electrical building, which also housed the backup diesel generators. At best, Mission Control would have battery-run emergency lighting and no functioning communications. But with the spaceship depressurizing on orbit, he had to get inside and see what he could do.

The Apollo-Soyuz crews were in serious trouble.

He turned left off Second Street, retracing his hasty exit route behind the Anechoic Test Facility and through its parking lot, clear of the blast area. He parked, leapt out and jogged his way through the emergency response teams, badge in hand. NASA security was at the door of Mission Control. Kaz recognized the man, thought for a second and came up with the name.

"Hell of a day, Ted. They letting essential personnel in?"

"Hi, Commander Zemeckis, not yet. Power's completely down, and they're worried about building damage. I've been told to direct all Mission Control personnel to Building 2." He pointed south, past the adjoining buildings. "That's where everybody is."

Kaz thanked him, turned and jogged straight across the parking lot and grass quadrangle to Building 2, the Public Affairs Auditorium.

Chris Kraft was standing at the podium on the auditorium stage, speaking to about 100 people from Mission Control watching from the theater-style seating. Everyone here played a key role in supporting the astronauts in orbit, and they needed leadership. They needed a plan. Most urgently, they needed a way to reestablish communications with Apollo.

Chris Kraft noticed Kaz come in and waved for him to join him onstage. As Kaz climbed the steps at the side, Kraft asked, "Any updates about what's going on outside?"

Kaz spoke loudly, so everyone could hear. "The fire from the explosion is out, and paramedics are here, helping the injured. The bombers got away for now."

Kraft nodded. A telephone had been set up on a low table next to him, along with a couple of hastily positioned chairs. "Thanks. We're patching in calls now from the operators at the antenna sites that Apollo is going to pass over, until we can get an emergency generator running to power up Mission Control. We'll be purely audio until then." He looked down at a man sitting in the front row. "INCO, how long until we pick them up over Hawaii, and what is the next ground site after that?"

The integrated communications officer looked from the mission planning papers he'd brought with him to his wristwatch.

"Should have Hawaii in three minutes, FLIGHT." He flipped a couple of pages in his lap. "Then it's a long arc around South America and up over central Africa. If we can't reestablish comms through the ATS relay satellite, we won't be able to talk with the crew until they're over the Russian ground site at Ulan-Ude, near Lake Baikal." He did the math. "About sixty minutes. Unlucky geometry."

Chris Kraft nodded and pointed at the phone. "CAPCOM, we'll put that phone on speaker so everyone can hear. Hopefully Hawaii can patch you through directly. We need a detailed situation report from the crew, and I want you to summarize our situation here for them too." He considered what else they could do. "INCO, how long is the Hawaii pass, and when exactly will they acquire Ulan-Ude? We'll need to sort that piece out directly with the Russians."

INCO was ready this time. "Hawaii pass will last a little under five minutes. Expect Ulan-Ude sixty-five minutes later, at twenty-one thirty Greenwich." He looked again at his watch. "That's four thirty here, FLIGHT."

On the table, the phone rang.

At the top of the Kōkeʻe mountain ridge in Hawaii, Shaun Akana's heart was racing. Outside of his blockhouse, a hot, humid wind was blowing hard, trying to shake his 30-foot-wide tracking antenna. But the huge white dish was solidly bolted into Kauai's volcanic bedrock and smoothly pivoted on its heavy base to point patiently at the horizon to the northwest.

Waiting for Apollo-Soyuz to appear.

The phone call had completely unnerved him. Shaun had set all the switches on his control panel to be ready, as normal, when someone from NASA in Houston had called to say there'd been an explosion and power failure there, and as a temporary fix, he, Shaun, was going to have to manually patch crew audio through a phone line.

He'd never done that before. And it sure wasn't in his standard operating procedures manual. The voice on the other end of the phone had said, "You've got five minutes. Can you do it?" And Shaun had said yes.

But how? When the NASA person had hung up, Shaun looked at the telephone receiver in his hand and then at the small, round speaker built into the upper-right side of his panel. A heavy silver microphone on a squat base sat on the far-right corner of his console, gathering dust. He'd never actually used the microphone! Who would he talk to? He was just an audio technician, making sure to patch all signals from the antenna through to the customer. Normally NASA.

The astronauts were going to transmit to him on 296.8 megahertz, so he'd set the receiver to the right frequency and adjusted the speaker to maximum volume. He didn't want to miss their call.

He thought to pull the phone handset closer to the speaker, but the cord was too short. *Shit!* He ran into the storeroom and scrambled around in the spare cables locker until he managed to find a decent-length phone cord with what looked like two good ends. He hunted around in the dark shadow under the console table to unplug the short line, then used the longer cord to reconnect the phone, lifted the receiver to his ear and was relieved to hear a steady dial tone.

Okay, he thought. *This might work.*

He slid his rolling chair close to the panel speaker, lifted the heavy microphone and set it where he could talk into it, and set the phone, with its new cord, just to his left. He checked the clock to the left of his analog phase meters, set to Hawaiian Standard Time, and looked at his clipboard to double-check the predicted rise time of Apollo over the horizon. He had 90 seconds.

The phone rang. He fumbled as he picked it up and answered. "Kauai Tracking Station, Shaun Akana." Cripes, his voice had cracked. *Get a hold of yourself!*

"Kauai, this is Houston, how do you read?"

"Loud and clear, Houston." *Better.* He could feel his voice grow calmer and deeper with the familiar words.

There was a pause, then a few clicking noises, and the Houston voice changed, sounding like the person was in a big hall. "Kauai, this is NASA CAPCOM, how do you read?"

"Uh, I have you loud and clear, NASA CAPCOM." As Shaun spoke, there was a squeal of feedback, and he yanked the handset away from his ear. He waited a few seconds and cautiously brought it back to his head. "Uh, I heard feedback, Houston, how do you read me now?" No squeal this time. He glanced at the clock. Forty-five seconds to get this sorted out.

"Kauai, sorry for that—we've got things set here now. Waiting on you to patch through the call from the crew."

"Copy, Houston."

Shaun took a deep breath. He pulled the desktop microphone close, leaned in on his chair to make sure it was near enough to his mouth and reached up to double-check that he'd maxed the speaker volume knob. Right on cue, he heard a loud crackle and turned the knob down a bit.

"Houston, this is Apollo-Soyuz through Hawaii, how do you read?"

Shaun pushed the transmit rocker switch on his microphone to respond to the voice from orbit. "Apollo-Soyuz, this is Hawaii, acting as a voice relay through to Houston. Stand by."

He turned the phone handset upside down, pointing its talking end towards the speaker and its listening end towards the microphone. He leaned into the mic, pushed the toggle and spoke again. "Houston, Apollo-Soyuz is listening, if you want to try a voice check."

As he heard the CAPCOM start to talk, he pushed the transmit toggle. *Please, God, let this work.*

"Apollo-Soyuz, this is Houston, how do you read?"

Kaz had set the phone on speaker and was holding the stage microphone close to where the sound came out. He'd adjusted the volume quickly when they'd had the feedback, and now the whole room waited to hear from orbit.

"Houston, Apollo, loud and clear, how do you hear us?"

Deke Slayton's voice echoed through the hall. Kaz tapped the button to drop the volume a couple of notches and leaned close to the phone to talk.

"Deke, we hear you loud and clear."

Floating in the confines of the Apollo capsule, Deke nodded in relief, looking at his Soviet crewmates. Direct contact with Houston was what he needed.

"Glad to hear your voice, Kaz. I'm here in the Command Module with Svetlana and Valery. Are you getting any data downlink from Apollo or Soyuz?" Deke knew time was short over Hawaii and prioritized the question to quickly understand the situation.

"Negative, Deke, just voice. We've had multiple problems here, but the biggie is an explosion that knocked out power to the Mission Control building. Not sure how long it'll take to come back online, but for now we're talking through a phone patch from inside Building 2. The flight control team is all here listening, and Chris Kraft is acting as flight director." Kaz glanced at Kraft, who nodded. *Good summary.*

Kaz continued, "Before we lost power, we saw a Soyuz–Docking Module depressurization, with oxygen flowing for the crew on that side of the hatch. We're standing by for an update."

The entire room held their breath.

"Bad news, Kaz. The oxygen tanks are depleted and the pressure in the Docking Module shows zero. We've been tapping on the hatch, but no response from the crew. We talked a few minutes ago with Moscow, and they said the Soyuz was depressurized as well." Deke was deliberately blunt, to make it clear. "Tom, Alexei and Vance are dead."

Kaz closed his eyes and slumped, feeling like everything had suddenly drained out of his body. The room was silent with shock. Three crewmembers had died on their watch. Everyone's worst nightmare.

Chris Kraft spoke. "CAPCOM, let's get an Apollo status."

Kaz opened his eyes. He spoke, and the Hawaii technician pushed the microphone button again for him, listening incredulously.

"Apollo-Soyuz—Deke, Svetlana, Valery—that is truly terrible news. We're all reacting here and will sort out a forward plan. What is your vehicle and crew health assessment?"

Kraft pointed at INCO in the front row, and Kaz saw him holding up three fingers. He hastily added, "We have three minutes in this comm pass, Deke, and then may not have you again until you talk to Moscow in an hour."

"Copy, Kaz. Crew health for the three of us is fine, and no snags with Apollo." Deke had been thinking. "But the only way we can talk with Moscow is through the Docking Module and Soyuz radios. Not sure how long they'll last in vacuum. And we'll need to sort out a plan for undock and re-entry." He looked at his crewmates. "We have Tom's and Vance's spacesuits here in Apollo. I'm sure we can make them fit Valery and Svetlana well enough."

Kaz nodded. There was a rising buzz of urgent conversations amongst the team seated in front of him as everyone started reacting to the news. Kraft was talking directly to individual flight controllers, starting to prioritize actions.

Kaz had a thought. "Deke, as soon as we're done talking with you, we'll give Moscow a call and sort out the first steps of a joint plan. They should be able to update you through Ulan-Ude at twenty-one thirty

Greenwich time. Meanwhile, we're scrambling to get temporary power to reactivate Mission Control."

He paused and looked at Kraft, who thought for a second and shrugged.

Kaz nodded, and transmitted, "You have any questions?"

INCO was holding up two fingers.

"Yeah, Kaz, Moscow said something about a gunshot as well." Deke paused. "Is everyone okay?"

Kaz decided to be clear but nonspecific. No need to overburden the crew.

"The explosion was some sort of bomb, out by the power transformer building, and it looks like a few people might have gotten hurt in the blast. Also, someone in the MCC viewing room fired a gun that badly injured a flight controller. Fortunately, the president got away safely."

Inside Apollo, Deke nodded and looked at Svetlana, who was translating for Valery. "You two have any questions?" he asked her.

Svetlana pushed her mic button to transmit. "Is it possible for us to put on the Apollo pressure suits, depressurize the cabin, open the hatch, get our crewmates' bodies and bring them home?"

Damn good question, Kaz thought.

Kraft immediately shook his head no, but he looked to his senior flight controllers in the front row for confirmation. Several spoke simultaneously.

"Likely too much loose weight in the cabin for re-entry, FLIGHT, we'd need to work the numbers."

"We should have enough oxygen reserve, FLIGHT, but not sure we could count on the suit fit."

"It would give us a chance to retrieve other key items also, FLIGHT."

"Don't want to risk damaging the hatch seal, FLIGHT."

Kraft held up his hand, palm towards them. "CAPCOM, tell them we're looking into it."

INCO held up one finger.

"Apollo, Houston, good question, Svetlana. We're checking if that's possible and will discuss with Moscow ASAP. We have less than a minute left in this pass." Kaz looked around the room, seeing no one trying to catch his eye.

He had one final thought, just in case Apollo ran into further problems while they were out of communications range. "Deke, suggest you brief emergency procedures and sort out revised crew roles, and let us know your plan when we next speak at twenty-one thirty."

Deke looked at the Russians floating on either side of him in the Apollo capsule.

"Wilco, Houston. Talk to you then."

In his blockhouse on the Kauai mountaintop, Shaun watched as the signal strength faded and fell to zero. He flipped the phone handset around and put it against his ear.

"Houston, Kauai Tracking Station here. They're out of range now."

"Copy, Kauai, thanks for the help," Kaz responded.

Shaun hung up the phone, leaned back heavily in his chair and realized he'd been sweating profusely. He felt totally drained. And no wonder.

Holy shit.

32

Johnson Space Center

The large glass doors of the Public Affairs building were thrown open, and a fit-looking man with a flattop brush cut came hurrying into the auditorium, taking the steps towards the stage at a run. The room was noisy with multiple discussions, and Chris Kraft was sitting and talking on the phone, a finger in his ear so he could hear.

The man with the brush cut spotted his target and shuffled quickly across a row to get close to Kaz.

"Commander Zemeckis, there's an urgent call for you in Building 1."

Kaz looked up at him, frowning. He had been talking with the flight activities officer in the front row, trying to hammer out a preliminary set of changes to the flight plan to discuss with Deke when they got communications back. He didn't need an interruption.

The man kept quiet, staring at him. Kaz didn't recognize him, but the haircut and the way he stood made it obvious he was military.

An urgent call in Building 1. Right. Kaz excused himself from FAO, saying he'd be back soon. With nearly an hour until the crew would be talking with Moscow, Kaz had time.

Especially for this sort of call.

Kaz lowered himself onto the hard government chair in the secure room in Building 1. Ever since the Air Force had been deeply involved in the near catastrophe of Apollo 18, the Department of Defense had maintained a shielded communications room at NASA. The man who had fetched him—a junior military liaison to NASA, responsible for security—quickly reminded him how the specific buttons on the phone worked, then left the room, closing the heavy padded door behind him. Kaz picked up the oversized handset, held it next to his ear, pushed the blinking yellow button, waited for the green light to come on and said, "Hello, Commander Kazimieras Zemeckis here."

Kaz was still breathing heavily. The two of them had jogged all the way over and up the stairs—no time to wait for an elevator. On the way, the man had explained that a very senior officer from Washington was calling him, but he didn't know who. It wasn't his place to ask.

But the voice on the other end of the secure line was familiar.

"Kaz, Sam Phillips here. The news is full of the assassination attempt on the president, and I'm also hearing there was a bombing? What's the situation there?"

Kaz summarized the details in Houston and quickly updated Phillips on the depressurization and deaths on orbit.

The general gave a long, low whistle. "Wow, that's terrible, Kaz. I hadn't heard yet. Tom and Vance were longtime friends of mine, and I met Alexei once and liked him. What a horrible loss."

Both of them sat quietly, holding the heavy handsets next to their ears. Two military men, contemplating the reality of sudden death.

The general broke the silence. "The other three okay?"

"Yes, and Deke is working closely with us to sort out new roles. Our comms are intermittent until we get power back up."

"Yes, that makes sense," Phillips said. He knew the layout of the space center well. "Probably take half a day or more to get something working," he said, mostly to himself.

Phillips paused, shifting gears. "Kaz, I'm not calling about the bombing or the attempt on the president's life," he said, "but about an interesting phone call I just got. Our friends at NORAD are tracking a new satellite, launched a couple of days ago. From China."

Kaz waited. His MIT PhD was in electro-optics, and he'd been doing analyses of Chinese construction in the high desert south of Mongolia ever since their first suborbital launches there. His expertise in this area was why Phillips had sent him to China with Nixon.

"We turned the big cameras in Hawaii to have a look, and this is a different design than their two previous orbital satellites. I'll get you pictures as soon as I can, but it's a classic elongated capsule shape, designed to withstand re-entry."

Kaz pictured it. "A spy camera, able to bring the film back and land under parachute?"

Both the Americans and the Soviets had versions of the same technology, though they were transitioning now to digital images that could be beamed back to Earth.

"Maybe, Kaz. But you know as well as I that it's a small step from there to scale up and man-rate a ship to start flying astronauts." He paused. "Or cosmonauts, or whatever the Chinese will call them."

Surprised, Kaz asked, "You think this ship has someone aboard, General?" *That'd be nuts!* "They would have had to leapfrog several technologies and accept considerable risk."

"I agree, but it's the trajectory of this satellite that's making us consider it. They launched into 51.6-degree inclination and are at two hundred and thirty-two miles altitude."

He waited for Kaz to figure it out.

"Skylab?" Kaz frowned deeply. Seventeen months ago, the American Skylab space station had been abandoned, and it was now orbiting Earth uncontrolled. He knew it was being monitored by Houston, with NASA techs regularly checking its health status, but unless the Space Shuttle program got going soon, Skylab's orbit was going to keep decaying, and it would eventually burn up in the atmosphere. It had no engines to re-boost itself.

His mind was running through possibilities, and he asked the question out loud. "Why would they launch co-orbital with Skylab?"

"Not just co-orbital, Kaz. The ship has recently maneuvered to place it on an unmistakable intercept trajectory. That has lots of folks scratching their heads here in Washington too."

Kaz leapt ahead. "Must be one of two things, sir. Mao wants to upstage Apollo-Soyuz, demonstrating new Chinese capability. Or there's something on Skylab that China wants." He thought further. "Could even be both."

In his office at Andrews Air Force Base, just south of Washington, General Sam Phillips nodded. Kaz was quick.

"But there's something else, Kaz. A high-security program I don't think you've ever been in-briefed on, called Project Seesaw. Heard of it?"

Kaz had heard rumors. "Wasn't that an ARPA program in the nineteen fifties? Something to do with laser weapons that didn't pan out and got shut down in the sixties?"

The general snorted. Even with top-secret programs, word eventually seeped out. "Yes, something like that. But it showed some promise, and it got resurrected. As I was finishing up as Apollo director, the Air Force asked me if there was any way NASA could test it secretly in space. They needed an orbital platform with lots of room and enough continuous power to recharge a bank of capacitors to drive the laser. So we scarred it into Skylab's design."

Kaz's eyes opened wide, realizing what the general was saying. Somehow, the astronauts and necessary ground control personnel had kept this a secret. A secret with hardware too large to have been brought back to Earth in the last Apollo capsule that had undocked.

Amazed, Kaz blurted out, "There's an energy weapon on Skylab?"

"There is, and I was calling to ask you a question. It's an even longer shot now, given what's just happened. Still, I have to ask. You've worked directly with these folks, Kaz. Do you think, considering the health of the Apollo ship and its remaining fuel and oxygen reserves, that Deke and the two surviving cosmonauts could change orbit and dock with Skylab before the Chinese get there?"

Kaz pushed open the exit doors of Building 1 and walked slowly down the steps and across the lawn towards the pond, his head buzzing with questions. Trees shimmered in the July heat along both sides of the long, grassy quadrangle at the center of the Johnson Space Center. He stopped in the shade at the water's edge, watching the ducks swimming next to the central aerating fountain. He didn't have long, but he wanted to think.

He'd told General Phillips that Apollo likely had enough fuel and oxygen to get to Skylab. But everything else was in turmoil. Would Deke be able to handle it? Now that he was the sole American on board, everything would be on his shoulders, and he hadn't trained for all of the tasks he'd have to perform.

Kaz looked to his right at Building 4, the Astronaut Office. The chief astronaut, John Young, would be breaking the news of the deaths of Tom and Vance to their wives. Both women had been there in the viewing room, dressed to meet the president, when the shooting and then the bombing had happened. A nightmare ending to what should have been a day of triumph.

And now Marge Slayton was going to have to live with the added risks they were about to ask her husband, Deke, to take.

Two ducks were quacking loudly, chasing each other in the water. An unwanted thought flashed through Kaz's head. Deke had been grounded for over a decade with a heart problem, some sort of arrhythmia. It had cleared up enough for the NASA doctors to approve him as one crewmember in three on the relatively simple Apollo-Soyuz mission, but the mission was suddenly on a whole different level. Could Deke's heart be trusted?

Kaz needed to ask JW.

He was also going to have to talk with Chris Kraft—he'd gotten clearance from General Phillips to in-brief him on the Chinese spaceship. Kraft already knew about Project Seesaw on Skylab, Phillips said.

But what were they going to tell the rest of the control team, and for that matter the American public? How would they explain why they were suddenly heading for Skylab?

A duck paddled by with three small, fuzzy yellow ducklings in close trail formation, counting on her. Something Svetlana had said echoed in Kaz's head.

Yes, he thought. *That might work.*

He turned and started walking quickly towards Building 2.

33

Building 2, Johnson Space Center

Chris Kraft looked at his wristwatch and closed the door.

"Gentlemen, we have nine minutes until we can talk with the crew through Moscow, but something urgent has come up, affecting what we might say."

There were five people standing in the small room adjacent to the central hall. Kraft had chosen his key controllers for this conversation, and now looked to Kaz to explain the situation and his idea.

Kaz made eye contact with each man as he spoke. "I've just been talking with Washington. They don't want us to abandon Tom's and Vance's bodies in orbit, and the Soviets are bound to feel the same about Alexei Leonov's. But I don't think we can safely deorbit the Apollo capsule with the weight of six crewmembers aboard."

He waited for a response from the small group. The flight dynamics officer nodded. "Yeah, Kaz, three stiff bodies would make a mess of gross weight and center of gravity, especially during deorbit burn, piloted flight and parachute opening. Not a good idea. But I'm going to need to run the numbers to be sure."

Kaz nodded. "That's what I figured." He glanced at the electrical, environmental and communications officer. "Can we do an internal spacewalk to retrieve the bodies?"

EECOM had already been thinking about it. "Yes, we have the oxygen margin. If we just put Deke on the long umbilical through the hatch, keeping the Russians inside the Apollo capsule, it should work. Unless the bodies are too deep inside Soyuz to reach. But I think we have enough length to get them. And if we only send Deke, he's the only one who'll need a good suit fit."

Dr. JW McKinley spoke directly to Kraft, without being asked. "The three men's bodies will be ugly, FLIGHT. The rapid depressurization will have bloated their guts, and there will be vomit, shit and piss—all liquids will have evacuated in vacuum. Repressurizing the bodies inside Apollo will release lots of stink, and decomposition will accelerate. Depending how quickly we retrieve them, they'll also be in some state of rigor mortis, so they may be hard to get through narrow hatchways." He shook his head. "Not pretty, and we don't want them with the crew inside Apollo for long."

Kraft nodded and turned back to EECOM. "A mechanical systems question. Once we retrieve the bodies and jettison the Docking Module and Soyuz, will the docking system be fully compatible with Skylab?"

EECOM took a step back in surprise. "Skylab?" He blinked several times behind his thick glasses, and then slowly spoke. "Right—a potential place to store the bodies in case we can't bring them back?"

Kraft nodded. "That way, we optimize for mission safety but don't abandon anyone. When the Space Shuttle eventually docks with Skylab in a few years, it'll have room to bring the three of them home. And Skylab has an airlock to better store their bodies."

EECOM visualized his docking systems, and those of Skylab. "Yes, FLIGHT, our cameras and probe are the same we used for the three Skylab missions. They should all work fine for Deke to fly, if needed."

Kraft glanced again at his watch. "Right, go get your back rooms thinking about all this. Once we've talked with the crew, we'll start putting together a plan." He turned to Kaz as the men filed out. "You're talking to Deke in five minutes, Kaz, but only for as long as the Russians let us."

He waited until the room was empty except for the two of them.

"Here's what I want you to say."

34

Apollo Command Module, Earth Orbit

"Moskva, Moskva, kak sleeshetya?" Valery was floating inside Apollo, repeating the call to Earth every 15 seconds.

Deke had asked Valery to make first contact with Moscow Mission Control. As soon as they patched communications through to Houston, he would take over again.

Svetlana glanced through the window, verifying that the Apollo-Soyuz combined spaceship was passing over Iran, south of the Caspian Sea. "Should be soon," she said.

A distorted, crackling voice sounded in their headsets.

"Soyuz-Apollon, kak sleeshetya nas?" *How do you hear us?*

Valery responded in rapid-fire Russian, while Svetlana translated for Deke.

"He's telling them about the depressurization, and that Alexei is dead." She paused, listening. "Moscow is asking are we sure. Valery said yes."

Deke grabbed Valery's arm to get his attention and pointed to his watch. Valery nodded, spoke to Moscow and listened to the answer. "We have nineteen minutes," he said in English. "Maybe some breaks."

Svetlana clarified. "Moscow says nineteen minutes total on this communications pass, maybe intermittent through some of the ground relay sites."

Deke checked his watch. *Nineteen minutes! Russia is a big country.* "Tell Valery I need the last ten minutes to talk to Houston."

Valery checked his watch, looked at the list of Cyrillic notes he'd been taking and nodded to Deke to take over comms.

Deke transmitted, "Houston, Apollo, how do you read?"

Kaz was sitting next to the speakerphone on the stage in Building 2. Again he held the microphone up to it so all the flight controllers in the auditorium could hear Deke. Kaz leaned in to speak.

"Loud and clear, Apollo. We've been listening to the translation of Valery's conversation with Moscow. Do you need a summary?" Kaz knew Deke's Russian was rudimentary.

"Yeah, Kaz, that'd help, though Svetlana translated most of it."

"Copy. The Russians want Alexei Leonov's body brought back to Earth, if possible. They discussed potentially strapping him, and maybe all three bodies, into Soyuz and closing the hatches so they could command undocking and re-entry from Moscow. They also talked about retrieving the Soviet pressure suits and finding a way for Valery and Svetlana to fly the Soyuz home unpressurized, but that didn't sound likely. No way to safely get them from Apollo through the Docking Module and into Soyuz without being on umbilicals, and no way to adapt the American equipment to plug into the Russian." He paused. "Regardless, the Russians want to fly their Soyuz and Alexei's body back."

Kaz glanced at Chris Kraft, who nodded at the summary.

"Copy, Kaz." Deke looked at his new crewmates. "Valery and Svetlana are looking closely at the suit hoses here now." Deke's primary job was to get the three of them safely back to Earth. Everything else was secondary. He considered the risks for several seconds, then said, "I'm not sure it's worth taking a chance on an internal spacewalk just to retrieve bodies. And I sure don't like the idea of sending Tom and Vance back to Earth in an unpiloted Russian ship."

Kaz was nodding. "Roger that, Deke. We'll be talking directly with Moscow to make a good joint plan. Fortunately, Apollo is healthy, and you've got deep oxygen and maneuvering fuel reserves. We'd like you to start resizing Tom and Vance's pressure suits for the cosmonauts, since they'll need to wear them for re-entry. And I've got two other things, when you're ready." Kaz had heard some static while he was talking and wanted to be sure Deke could hear him clearly.

"Copy all, we'll get the suits resized as best we can. Go ahead with your other points."

"Center maintenance gave us an update. They're patching a big diesel generator directly into the Mission Control power circuit. The damage to the building is cosmetic, not structural. Hopefully we'll be back with more normal comms and data within an hour or two."

"Roger, glad—" Deke's voice cut off abruptly.

Kaz waited a few seconds and then called, "Apollo, Houston, how do you hear?"

A Russian interpreter's voice came through the speaker. "The Kolpashevo ground station is offline, we'll have comms again in ninety seconds through Ulan-Ude."

Kaz looked at his watch. Another five minutes or so to talk after that, he figured. Should be enough. He looked out at the controllers in the auditorium. They had arranged themselves into subgroups by technical discipline, and the small knots of expertise were all talking quietly and intently, only pausing to listen when the crew transmitted from orbit. One man was waving, trying to catch his eye.

Chris Kraft noticed and loudly said, "Go ahead, FAO." He wanted everyone to listen to the flight activities officer, the main crew scheduler.

FAO said, "FLIGHT, after this pass, it's going to be a long period with no comms, as we'll miss Hawaii, swing south of Chile, and miss Ascension Island. Next signal won't be for fifty-five minutes, when we're back with the Russians." He shrugged in apology, adding, "Orbital mechanics."

Kraft nodded and made eye contact around the room. "Anyone got anything the crew needs to know or do in the next hour?"

There was a pause as each controller weighed the urgency of their concerns. No one spoke up—they had lots of upcoming replanning and changed procedures, but communicating it all could wait.

The Moscow-based interpreter's voice spoke again through the phone. "Houston, you should be able to reach the crew again now."

As Kaz spoke, the room quieted. "Apollo, Houston, how do you read?"

"Got you loud and clear again, Houston. Last we heard was you're within an hour or two of getting back into Mission Control, and you had another thing you wanted to say."

"Roger, Deke, and just a heads-up that when we lose you over the Pacific in five minutes or so, we won't have comms again for about an hour."

The FAO held up a hastily handwritten sign that said *AOS 23:10 UTC*.

Kaz confirmed for Deke. "Acquisition of signal should be about twenty-three ten Greenwich time."

"Copy, Kaz, twenty-three ten."

Floating beside Deke, Svetlana tracked ahead and penciled in a note in her borrowed flight plan.

"Apollo, the other thing I wanted to mention is forward plans. We have several options under discussion to get the three of you safely home, and we are reprioritizing secondary objectives. But here's the current best guess, when you're ready."

Deke saw that both Valery and Svetlana had heard the tone in Kaz's voice and were listening. "Go ahead, Houston."

"Once you've got the suits resized, we want to step towards an Apollo depressurization and internal spacewalk, to retrieve key items and reposition the three bodies. By then we'll have an undock plan to either separate the Soyuz and then the Docking Module in sequence or jettison the two of them together. After undocking, we're working up a plan to raise your orbit and have you dock with Skylab as a holding place for the bodies until the Space Shuttle can come and retrieve them."

Inside Apollo, Deke blinked several times. *Skylab!* he thought. He'd trained multiple times as a backup docking pilot, but this was a whole new level of complexity, especially with no American crewmate to help him. He started shaking his head. He'd been NASA's chief astronaut and director of flight operations for a decade and was used to making decisions, and this one was a no.

He said, "I don't like the risk trade-off of Skylab at all, Kaz. We need to talk a lot of details before I'd agree to do that."

Kaz looked at Kraft, who gave a small shrug. Only he and Kaz knew about the Chinese spacecraft, and only a couple of the flight controllers had the security clearance to have been involved with Project Seesaw. Explaining the rationale to Deke needed to wait until they had secure communications, without the Soviets listening, on board and in Moscow.

Kaz kept it light and vague. "Roger that, Deke, we agree with you. We're just looking at all options at this point."

INCO was holding up two fingers.

"We have a couple minutes of comms left in this pass. Do you or your crew have any last questions?"

On board Apollo, Svetlana translated Kaz's words into Russian for Valery. Deke watched him frown and recoil in weightlessness when she mentioned Skylab, then start speaking rapidly in Russian. As she started to summarize for Deke, he gestured for her to transmit instead so Houston and Moscow could hear before their time was up.

She pushed her mic button. "Several years ago, when America and Russia were planning our mission, they originally considered docking with Skylab or with the Soviet Salyut station. But the idea was rejected as being too complex. We agree with Deke that adding it in now increases the risk. Our remaining flight plan must be discussed and agreed to between our countries."

Kaz glanced at Kraft, who turned his palms up briefly in a gesture of agreement.

"Houston copies, Svetlana. We're about to lose you as you head out over the Pacific. Good luck with the suit-fitting, and we'll talk to you again at twenty-three ten."

Deke responded, "See you then."

Svetlana kept her face an unemotional mask, but her heart had leapt at the mention of Skylab. This had been planned as a simple flight, just docking Soyuz and Apollo together. Especially compared with her first spaceflight, which had stretched her skills to the limit and taken her to the surface of the Moon and back.

The loss of Alexei Leonov and the two Americans was a tragedy, but the mission itself had just gotten much more complex and challenging.

She didn't want to let it show, but for the first time during all of Soyuz-Apollo, she was excited.

35

Building 2

Standing onstage, Chris Kraft raised a hand to address the crowd of flight controllers.

His face was drawn and his expression serious. "Folks," he said, "it's been a long, terrible day in spaceflight. We've lost multiple lives in orbit and the life of a valued colleague and friend, Glynn Lunney, here on the ground. There's going to be a thorough investigation into what happened today, not just by the Soviet space agency and NASA, but by other US government agencies as well. And that's going to be a necessary but real distraction for us as we go about our primary business of supporting the remainder of the Apollo-Soyuz mission."

He stopped, his attention caught by the doors at the back of the auditorium opening and closing repeatedly as new people entered.

"I see the oncoming Mission Control shift personnel arriving. I need each of you who are going off shift to do a thorough handover briefing with them and then go home to get some much-needed sleep. Tomorrow is going to be a complex day of replanning and executing new crew activities, and I need you sharp and rested. Fortunately, as Kaz mentioned, it looks like we'll be able to move ops back into Building 30 overnight, which will help improve our efficiency."

He made slow, deliberate eye contact with individual team members as he continued to speak. "The events of today—the assassination attempt, the bombing and the sudden depressurization of Soyuz—none of them were things we, as the flight control team, could have prevented. The most important thing to take comfort and pride in is that our reaction to each of these events has been swift, logical and competent. The remaining three crewmembers are safe. Tomorrow we'll have clear plans of what to do with the bodies of the three who died and how we will work towards bringing Deke, Valery and Svetlana home."

As the oncoming flight director and CAPCOM joined Kraft and Kaz on the stage, Kraft delivered a reminder. "There's going to be a lot of media interest in what happened here, but that's not your job, especially with the non-space-related events. When we regain communications with the crew in"—he glanced at his watch—"fifty-one minutes, I expect everyone who's arriving to be fully up to speed and the off-going shift to be home getting ready for bed, or headed that way."

Kraft paused, looking around at all the weary faces, then summarized, "An awful day, but we reacted well. I'll see you all bright and early tomorrow morning on console." He scanned the expectant faces. "Any last questions for me?"

The room was quiet, but Kaz could see that everyone was thinking about Kraft's words.

The new shift's flight director nodded to Kraft as he stepped up to the mic. "Okay, for the oncoming team, you heard Mr. Kraft. Let's get at it."

A buzz of voices erupted in response.

Kaz had already found the time to brief astronaut Bob Crippen, his replacement CAPCOM. But he wasn't sure whether Crip had the security clearance on Seesaw, so he'd kept that part quiet. As Kaz was about to say goodbye to Crip and Kraft, he noticed that the brush-cut military man had reappeared at the edge of the stage and was staring at him intently.

Kaz was tired, and irritated to see him again. Tersely he asked, "What?"

"Sir, there's a meeting in Building 1 you've been requested to attend." When Kaz didn't move, he clarified, "With the FBI." Then he added, sotto voce, "And the Secret Service."

Kaz nodded and turned to Crip. "You good for now, Crip? I'll swing back by when they're done with me."

Crip nodded. "Yep, all set. And Kaz, you should take Chris's advice and just head home afterwards. You're more tired than you think, and we can sort things out from here."

Building 1's eighth-floor conference room was full, and smoky. Suited men sat around the long, oval table with cups of coffee and ashtrays in front of them, listening to a man wearing a dark-blue suit and tie who was standing at the head of the table with a flip chart beside him. As Kaz came in, the man stopped and spoke to him directly, his voice flat.

"And you are?"

FBI, Kaz concluded. *But I'll be polite.*

"Navy Commander Kazimieras Zemeckis, detailed to mission support here at NASA."

No reason to mention his Defense Intelligence Agency affiliation, at least not yet.

The man nodded. "We've been expecting you." He pointed to the back of the room. "Dr. Jimmy Doi here told us that you were outside with him at the time of the bombing, and you might have had interaction with the bombers themselves."

The man waited.

Kaz hadn't noticed Jimmy when he came in, but it made sense that he was there. Jimmy had also been an eyewitness, and Kaz hadn't seen him in the Building 2 auditorium for a while.

Kaz said, "I've been busy speaking directly with the surviving astronaut crew on orbit as they deal with the dead bodies there, so if I'm late, I'm sorry." He let the word hang, looking quickly around the table, recognizing a couple of faces, and then back at the FBI man. "I don't know who you are, or most of the people here."

Kaz waited.

The man made him wait for a few moments in silence, then said, "Richard Dancey, special agent in charge of the FBI Houston field office." He gestured with his chin at the other men in the room. "We have several other FBI personnel here, as well as DIA and Secret Service." A beat. "And the local Harris County Sheriff, Jack Heard," he added, nodding to a square-jawed, jowly man at the far end of the table. Kaz knew Heard.

Dancey looked back at Kaz. "FBI has jurisdiction here, and I'm leading the initial investigation. Time is important, so I'd appreciate it if you could let us know what you saw today."

Dick Dancey. Kaz thought. *Perfect.* He looked at the flip chart. "Do you have a map of the bomb site yet?"

Dancey nodded, flipping back a couple of pages to a hand-drawn overview of the area beside Mission Control.

Kaz went to stand beside Dancey and indicated points on the map as he described his actions and those of Jimmy Doi, including his pursuit of what he believed was the bombers' car up NASA Road 1.

He looked at Dancey. "I'm pretty sure I've seen that car before." He quickly described his first dinner at the China Star restaurant with Laura, his ensuing reconnaissance with Jimmy and his later Comanche flight overhead. He pointed at Sheriff Heard. "I called your office with a description of what I'd seen, and specifically the vehicles, but never heard anything back."

The sheriff shifted in his chair and frowned.

Dancey had fished a small notebook out of his suit breast pocket and was making notes. He asked for the spelling of Kaz's, Laura's and Jimmy's names, and the exact dates and times of the events Kaz had described. He glanced at the room.

"Any questions for Commander Zemeckis?" *A promotion*, Kaz noted.

A broad-shouldered man with close-cropped hair raised a finger.

"Agent Clint Hill, Secret Service," he said. "Thanks for all your actions today, Commander."

Kaz nodded.

"I was in the room during the assassination attempt," Hill said, "and we'll need accounts from everyone who was in Mission Control today as soon as your pace of operations allows. But for now, could you give us a summary of what you saw?"

Christ, was that also today? Kaz felt a sudden wave of fatigue. His false eye felt gritty, and he rubbed the cheek near it as he recounted what he remembered: Glynn's phone ringing, Glynn yelling a warning about the bomb, a gunshot with glass breaking, another gunshot and then the commotion of bodies next to his console.

Followed by the rapid, deadly decompression on orbit.

There was a moment's quiet after he finished. Then Agent Hill said, "Thanks, Commander. That's clear and matches the sequence we've established."

Kaz looked at Jimmy, who nodded and shrugged.

Helluva day.

Special Agent Dancey reasserted himself. "Commander Zemeckis, we require that you stay in the area. We may need to talk further with you tomorrow and subsequently. For now, though, you're free to go."

Truly a Dick, Kaz thought. He turned and left the room, finally ready to take Chris Kraft's advice to get home ASAP.

To sleep.

But as he walked down the hallway towards the stairs, he heard the conference room door open and close behind him, and then a man's deep voice. "Hey, Kaz, got another minute?"

Kaz turned and saw one of the faces he'd recognized in the room. He smiled. "Hey, Roof, I was wondering if you were going to say anything."

Rufus Youngblood was also smiling as he stepped up to shake Kaz's hand. He glanced up and down the hallway and said, "Let's talk through there," gesturing ahead at the stairwell entrance door.

Once the door had closed behind them, Rufus stopped on the landing and said, "So you enjoyed meeting Special Agent Dancey?"

Kaz snorted. "Yeah, a special kinda guy." He raised his eyebrows. "But he seems to be warming to me."

Rufus was a civilian analyst with the DIA, based in Houston and working out of the Air Force facilities at Ellington Field. When General Phillips had recruited Kaz to be part of the DIA, Rufus had been his local point of contact. Kaz had been unsurprised to see him at the table—the only Black man in the room.

Rufus said, "You want a quick summary of my part in this?"

Kaz nodded. "Sure do."

"Today's combined bombing and assassination attempt immediately got the attention of General Graham back at DIA HQ in Washington, and he called me directly to come and be part of what the FBI and Secret Service are doing." He smiled. "And to report back on what they're up to." Rivalry between the FBI and the DIA, the military equivalent of the CIA, was strong, and their relations not exactly trustful.

A door opened on a floor somewhere below them, followed by the receding clatter of someone descending the stairs. Rufus waited until he heard another door open and then silence.

"Given the warning phone call that came in before the bombing, the Feebs are all over the Weather Underground angle. They even have an internal thing called the Special Target Information Development group that's supposed to be infiltrating and curtailing them." He shook his head. "But they completely failed to predict today." He looked away and then back at Kaz. "So far, the shooter isn't talking, so no one knows what the link is between the Weathermen bombings and the attempt to kill the president. But we all think there has to be one."

"So someone's escalating operations?"

Rufus shrugged. "Yeah, maybe. Eventually they'll squeeze information out of her. Might just be an alliance of convenience, with NASA a symbolic government establishment target and an opportunity for close access to the president. That he was coming here, down to the time he'd be on-site, was well publicized."

Kaz looked sharply at the DIA man. "But does what I saw at the Chinese restaurant fit in? That green car that was in both places? Maybe the Weathermen are getting resources from organized crime?"

Rufus returned Kaz's stare. "One of the main reasons the DIA posted me here is to keep an eye on the influx of immigrants, especially from China, and the non-state-actor criminal problems they bring." He tipped his head in the direction of the conference room and frowned. "You only gave a quick summary of what you saw. Anything you didn't mention?"

"Maybe a couple relevant things. The restaurant has a guy on the door making sure no one gets in unless he permits it. And the man with the papers I saw out back had a lot of muscle for a wholesale food delivery guy. Made me extra suspicious."

Rufus nodded.

"One other thing. The people I overheard behind the restaurant said they were going to meet somewhere the next morning." Kaz paused to remember the exact words. "They said they were planning to 'drive up before traffic.' So after I flew over the restaurant, I headed sorta north to look around, guessing that's where they meant. But now that there's been a bombing, my guess is they went somewhere to run a test. Lots of abandoned oil sites and gravel pits out there—empty and not far from the city."

Rufus's dark-brown eyes were watching Kaz intently. "Yeah, could well be. I'll mention it to Dancey when I go back in. They've got the manpower to go look."

After a short silence, Kaz asked, "What security clearance level are you, Roof?"

"Top Secret, why?"

"There's some stuff going on with Apollo-Soyuz that has a military component. I think I should get you in-briefed, but I need to check who's allowed to know first."

Rufus was starting to speak when the door next to them suddenly opened and Jimmy Doi walked through. He pulled up abruptly, surprised.

"Hey, Kaz." He nodded at Rufus, then said to Kaz, "I'm heading back to Building 2 and then home. Was thinking of maybe a quick beer and a burger to let the day settle." He looked briefly across at Rufus, not sure who he was, and then back at Kaz. "JW might want to come as well."

Kaz decided not to make an introduction—it was too complicated to explain why they were talking in a stairwell. Instead he said, "Sure. I should eat, and a beer would go down well."

Rufus took the cue and excused himself, ducking past Jimmy and back through the door into the hallway.

Kaz called after him, "I'll be in touch tomorrow." He glanced at his watch and started down the stairs, with Jimmy behind him. "U-Joint in twenty minutes?"

36

The Universal Joint, Houston

Kaz hadn't realized how hungry he was until he walked through the swinging Naugahyde doors of the U-Joint and smelled grilling meat. He went straight to the bar, where he opted for whisky instead of beer and ordered a double cheeseburger. With fries. Not good for him, but tonight it sounded perfect.

The ponytailed waitress had been working at the U-Joint for years. "You want that Scotch neat, Kaz?"

"That'd be great, thanks, Janie." He rubbed the flesh next to his gritty false eye and grimaced.

Janie had been watching him. "I think you should have a double."

He lowered his hand and smiled tiredly. "You're the expert."

Janie poured a healthy three fingers of Scotch into one of the cut crystal glasses she kept below the counter and slid it over. Her expression was unusually serious. "Sounds like it was the bitch of all days at NASA."

He took the glass, raised it to her and took a sip. "Sure was."

She nodded in commiseration. "I'll bring that burger over in a minute."

Kaz took his whisky and walked to the jukebox, looking for something that matched his mood. He put in a quarter, pushed the buttons and watched as a record got slotted into position. The opening chords of "Black Water" by the Doobie Brothers sounded just right as he carried his glass to one of the small, square tables. The room was mostly empty. Looked like most of the NASA folks had taken Chris Kraft's advice and gone home to bed.

He'd just sat down when Jimmy and JW came through the doors. JW took note of Kaz's whisky, asked Jimmy what he wanted and went directly to the counter to order. Jimmy sat down heavily across from Kaz, his expression solemn for once. He glanced around at the aerospace memorabilia tacked to the ceiling and walls of the U-Joint, his mind elsewhere, and then back at Kaz.

"Awful day," he said at last.

Kaz nodded. The Doobies were singing, "Mississippi Moon, won't you keep on shinin' on me?"

Jimmy leaned his elbows on the table and rested his chin on interlocked fingers. "Whadja think of that FBI meeting?"

No mention of running into Kaz with a stranger in the stairwell. *Good,* Kaz thought. He shrugged. "They're doing what they need to do. The interagency rivalries will be a pain, but they'll work it out. We just need to keep them from disrupting the rest of Apollo-Soyuz."

JW arrived with his hands full, and Jimmy removed his elbows from the table. JW set down a tall mug of draft beer and a cup of coffee. He sat, raised his coffee and said, "I'll drink to that." He took a sip of the hot black liquid and sighed. "The rest of Apollo-Soyuz is going to be quite a handful."

Kaz sipped his whisky and sat back, looking at the doctors. "What do you two think we should do with the bodies on Skylab?"

Jimmy deferred to JW, who set his cup down on its saucer. "The ten space walks we did on Skylab were all done in the suits the crew wore to return home, so we obviously can't put the bodies in those. Years ago we talked about keeping a few body bags on board, but that got nixed—we thought that one of our crew dying up there was a low probability." He pursed his lips and shook his head. "No one imagined a scenario like this one." He took another sip of his coffee. "I think our best bet is to put them into the Skylab airlock, close the hatch and then vent the airlock to vacuum. That'll keep the bodies from decomposing, which will give the Shuttle crew a much nicer task when they eventually bring them back." He looked at Kaz through his thick glasses and grimaced. "They'll be like frozen mummies."

Jimmy was frowning. "I don't get why we're going to Skylab at all. I know having extra bodies aboard is beyond normal planned limits, but surely the Apollo capsule and its parachutes are strong enough to handle a bit of added weight?"

Kaz knew everyone was going to be asking that question, and he'd been thinking about a credible answer. Watching Jimmy to gauge how it went down, he said, "Three main things. One, as you say, is weight. The most rocks we ever brought back from the Moon was on Apollo 17." Kaz glanced along the photos stapled to the U-Joint wall until he found the crew's faces, and pointed at them. "Gene and Jack outdid themselves, collecting a record two hundred and fifty pounds' worth, but these bodies would exceed that by a hundred pounds or more. Plus, the moonrocks were stowed in preplanned containers in specific locations inside the Command Module. And that's the second thing—precisely knowing the center of gravity."

Kaz picked up his whisky glass, holding it between his thumb and fingertips, and all three men looked at it.

"The Apollo capsule has a broad, flat bottom like this glass here. It's not very aerodynamic, but it does fly well down through the atmosphere. The air rushes up evenly around all sides of it, with the center of the air's resistance aligned with the middle of the ship."

He tipped the glass slightly.

"But if we load the cargo so that the weight is off-center, the ship will fly crooked. That actually helps us, as the crookedness drags the ship to one side or the other, depending on which way we roll." He turned the glass in his fingers and moved it across and down towards the table in an arc. "And we can control roll with just the little thrusters that are built into the outside of the capsule. That way, we can steer and even flatten our entry into the atmosphere, controlling g-load and choosing exactly where we're going to splash down."

He looked back at Jimmy. "Make sense so far?"

Jimmy nodded. "I see your point. If we can't be sure exactly where the bodies are or how much they weigh after several hours in vacuum, we won't know the center of gravity of the capsule."

Kaz looked back at the glass in his hand and tipped it to demonstrate as he spoke. "You got it. It means we can't steer the vehicle accurately. If we enter too shallow, we'll skip off the atmosphere, which slows us down, and then fall in more steeply. And if the ship enters too steep, it digs in, can't handle all that air friction at once, overloads the heat shield and burns up."

He took a sip and set his glass down. "Brings me to the third thing, and that's having decomposing bodies inside the capsule with our crew. You medicos know better than I do how bad that can get. It could easily be several days before re-entry if any more problems arise, or if there's bad weather in the splashdown zone. The sooner we can safely off-load the bodies, the better for crew health. And when the Space Shuttle eventually flies, they can bring body bags up with them and hermetically seal the remains for their return home."

Kaz thought the words had sounded convincing coming out of his mouth. When absorbing a new idea, people needed a credible story to tell themselves and others.

And Jimmy was nodding again. "Yeah, when you add all those factors up, it makes way more sense."

JW said, "Tom's and Vance's families sure won't like it."

Kaz nodded. "Yeah, no doubt." He sipped his whisky again, watching Janie heading their way balancing three plates of burgers. "But it's the three living astronauts that we have to focus on."

Janie set a loaded plate in front of each man.

"Everything else comes second." Kaz picked up his cheeseburger with both hands and took a large bite in case his face betrayed what he was thinking.

Some of what I just said is true.

The evening was still warm, with humid air blowing in from the Gulf of Mexico and up across Galveston, so Kaz left the Thunderbird's ragtop down. He started the car, drove carefully across the grass parking lot out onto NASA Road 1 and turned west into the fading orange light of the sunset.

Jimmy's comment echoed in his head. *Awful day.*

Got that right.

As he drove, he worked his way through the next day's timeline, reviewing the important events that could go wrong—what all pilots focus on. The internal space walk to retrieve the bodies would be unusual but straightforward. The Soviets would most likely ask that Leonov's body be returned in their Soyuz, so that left the surviving crew with only Tom's and Vance's corpses to deal with. Next, they needed to let the Soyuz undock, jettison the Docking Module and start maneuvering the cleaned-up Apollo towards Skylab, orbiting 90 miles above them.

Each step had its own complexities, but they were all things that Deke should be able to handle.

The big question was what they would find when they got to Skylab. Speed was critical. They absolutely had to get docked ASAP, to deny any potential Chinese access to the Skylab space station. At the very start of his shift, he needed to find a way to talk privately with Deke and fully brief him on what was happening.

As he crossed under I-45, the businesses and streetlights of NASA and Webster ended and the road narrowed to two lanes. It was part of the reason he'd bought his place at Polly Ranch: he liked the solitude of the countryside. Kaz leaned back, looking up through the haze at the stars. He could feel the headlong rush of the day flowing out of him like a long mental sigh. A sudden bone-weary tiredness took its place.

The small sign announcing Polly Ranch Airpark loomed up out of the darkness in his headlights, and he turned left onto the crushed-shell side road. The T-Bird's wheels thrummed briefly as they crossed the cow grid built into the road, and Kaz followed the curve around the end of the runway, turned up his driveway, opened the garage door remotely and tucked the car inside, next to his airplane. He turned the key and listened for a few seconds to the quiet ticking of the cooling engine, breathing in the familiar hangar smell of avgas and machinery.

As he opened the car door and stepped onto the smooth cement of the garage floor, a thought that had been niggling at the back of his head all day forced its way to the front.

If the Chinese intended to dock with Skylab, where had they gotten detailed drawings and specifications of the American docking system? He pictured the *Life* magazine close-up pictures and press package articles he'd seen—nothing there that would be useful to them. But it had been almost a year and a half since the final crew had undocked and abandoned Skylab, so it was old news now. Had enough time passed that the key information was out in the public domain?

He opened the connecting door to the house and turned reflexively to look at his car and plane before shutting off the light, his thoughts elsewhere.

He sighed. He faced a huge day tomorrow, figuring everything out. But for now, sleep.

37

Apollo Command Module, Earth Orbit

Why do the Americans choose such tall astronauts?

The Apollo spacesuit that had been Vance Brand's fit Svetlana poorly. As it pressurized around her body, it had lifted the helmet so high that she couldn't see properly, and as the arms elongated, they pulled her fingers out of the gloves. She pushed her arms down like a bird tucking in its wings, forcing her head as far into the helmet as she could manage so she could see how Valery was doing. He was taller than she was, but in Tom Stafford's suit, the lower part of his face was obscured by the helmet's neck ring. He caught her eye and shook his head, disgusted.

To resize the suits, they'd removed the metal lengthening rings in the arms and legs and pulled the inner adjusting laces as tight as they would go. There was also a long strap that pulled up between their legs to a buckle on their chests, which Deke had helped them cinch all the way, but it wasn't enough to adapt the suits to the cosmonauts' smaller stature. The technicians had built these suits for two men who were around six feet. Not for Valery at five-nine, and definitely not for Svetlana at five-six.

But as a woman in a man's world, she'd worn ill-fitting flight gear her entire life. *Don't complain about it*, she reminded herself. *Just make it work.*

"How are you two doing?" Deke asked.

"Fine," Valery answered flatly. He wasn't going to complain either.

"Copy," Deke responded.

They were hot mic, meaning the two Russians could hear the American's labored breathing as he worked down by their feet, jammed into the small space in his pressurized suit, straining to reach and turn the latch mechanism and open the hatch to the Docking Module. Svetlana and Valery each raised an arm to deflect Deke's legs and feet as he twisted and kicked near their helmets, concentrating on his work.

Deke had vented all of the oxygen out of the Apollo spaceship, depressurizing down to the empty vacuum of space, so he could open the hatch and retrieve the bodies on the other side. Their suits were bulging, holding a pressure of 3.7 psi around their bodies against the eternal emptiness of the universe.

Three small, cloth-covered bubbles of life.

"Houston, Apollo, I've got the latches retracted." At his console at the Johnson Space Center, Kaz listened as Deke took a couple of breaths. "I'm pushing hatch two open now, into the Docking Module."

"Copy, Deke."

Kaz was relieved to be back in his CAPCOM chair in Mission Control. During the night, the facilities teams had restored power and reestablished communications with the Apollo crew. Behind him, they'd installed two sheets of plywood over the viewing room glass where the assassin's bullet had shattered it. And someone had had the unenviable task of removing Glynn Lunney's body and wiping and mopping to clean up all traces of his killing.

The room looked almost normal. But coming into Mission Control had felt strange. Like he was entering a holy place that had been violated.

Kaz spoke again. "Just a reminder, Deke, to please take photos as you go." Fatal accidents were rare in spaceflight, and several flight controllers, especially the flight surgeon, had asked for detailed imagery so they could learn from this one and prevent it from happening again.

"Roger, I've got the Nikon with me." Deke raised his arm to look at the floating 35 mm camera tethered to his left wrist, then reached down with his right hand to get some slack on the long umbilical connected to his spacesuit. He took a deep breath, grabbed the curve of the open hatch with both hands and started to pull himself through.

"I'm going into the Docking Module now."

Two fluorescent floodlights were installed opposite each other midway up the Docking Module, but there was a large shape right in front of Deke, blocking the light. Trying to see, he looked up inside his fishbowl-like helmet, fighting the stiffness of the suit and the narrowness of the hatch. No luck. He pushed harder with his hands, moving farther inside.

Suddenly a face was pressed against the clear plastic of his helmet.

"Mother of Christ!" Deke yelled, recoiling, trying to pull himself clear, back into the Apollo hatch. But the stiff suit and the umbilical held him in place, with the bulging face directly in front of him. He turned his head and closed his eyes, trying to shield himself from the horrific sight.

He knew it was Tom Stafford, but a nightmare version. Tom's face was swollen and discolored, the skin pale as ivory across his forehead and chin, blotchy and blue on his bloated cheeks. His mouth was half open, and there was a wide stain of red where something had dried on the skin below his nose.

The worst part was the eyes. They were wide open and had turned from blue to opaque white as the liquid inside them had bubbled and boiled away into the vacuum.

Deke felt himself starting to be sick and swallowed hard to control it, keeping his face turned away.

"Apollo, Houston, did you call?"

Kaz had heard Deke swear, and had guessed why. He hoped his familiar words would help Deke gather himself.

"Significant heart rate spike, FLIGHT." JW was watching the telemetry from the sensors Deke wore on his chest.

Kaz looked across the consoles at JW, and the doctor frowned back. He didn't like Deke stressing his heart any more than necessary.

Deke's voice came back, sounding shaky. "Roger, Houston, I'm inside the Docking Module, and Tom's body is right here by the Apollo hatch."

Deke steeled himself, opened his eyes and turned to look his friend in the face, past the rust-colored smear on his own visor. Tom's sightless, milky eyes were still right in front of Deke. "I can confirm that Tom's dead, and I'm moving his body up beside the oxygen purge system so I can get farther into the DM."

But the body was stiff, bent slightly at the waist, and both arms were sticking out as if reaching to give Deke a hug, the elbows slightly bent. Tom's knees were bent as well, all of his joints locked in position by rigor mortis.

Deke carefully pivoted the body and pushed it along the curve of the hull and into the narrow gap between the purge system boxes and the end of the main control panel. Then he grabbed a handrail with his left hand and pushed hard on Tom's belly with his right to get him securely wedged.

"Sorry, buddy," he muttered.

The camera floated into view on its tether. Deke grabbed it and held it up in front of his visor, pointed it at Tom, and fumbled to press the shutter with his pressurized gloves. He wound the frame forward with his thumb, hoping the plastic film would work properly and the emulsion coating wouldn't dry out too quickly in vacuum.

With Tom stuck in place, his arms still reaching out, Deke turned and looked farther down the Docking Module.

Another floating body blocked the hatch to the Soyuz. It was facing away but was wearing the same orange-brown flight suit that Deke and the NASA crew had chosen for the mission, so he knew it was Vance Brand.

To transit the length of the module, Deke pulled on his umbilical with one hand and grabbed successive handholds with the other. When he reached the body, he gently pivoted it, grimacing as Vance's face came into view. Dried blood was crusted where it had flowed and bubbled away out of his ears. Vance's body was also in rigor, and his empty eyes seemed to stare at Deke as he wedged Vance up between the hatch and the square box of the furnace control experiment. As Deke paused to take the requested photos, he noticed a TV camera mounted above Vance and a video camera floating on its cable.

"Houston, are you watching this?"

Kaz responded, "We've got good keep-alive signal from the video camera, Deke, but no image. When you get a chance, we'd like you to power cycle it."

"Copy." Deke pulled himself along the handrail, grabbed the floating camera and flicked its toggle switch off and then on.

"I see a good power light on the camera now, Kaz."

In Mission Control, INCO spoke. "FLIGHT, we're getting a video signal." He paused. "Do you want it on the main screen?"

Chris Kraft nodded. There was no one behind them in the viewing room, and he'd ordered all live voice and video to outside television feeds cut. Including to Moscow. His team needed to see the reality of what they were dealing with, but he wanted to control the situation for as long as possible.

"Yes, INCO, let's have a look."

He spoke to the room. "Folks, this isn't going to be pretty, but I want each of you to look closely for any details that affect your systems." Kraft figured that the task focus would help everyone deal with the gruesomeness of dead bodies.

Kaz transmitted, "Deke, we're seeing your video feed now. If you can, please give us a pan around."

On the big screen in Mission Control, there was sudden haphazard movement as Deke grabbed the video camera's pistol grip and started pointing and narrating.

"Okay, that's aft in the Docking Module, and you should be able to see Tom up against the side wall."

The images of angular white and gray control panels and storage boxes gave way to the hatch of the Apollo capsule at the end. The orange-clad body of Tom Stafford curved up the side of the image, like a posed mannequin hanging on the wall.

A helmeted head suddenly appeared in the hatch. The face inside the helmet turned, revealing Valery, craning his neck to see.

With Deke on the one long umbilical extension on board, Valery and Svetlana had had to make do with much shorter leashes. Still, Valery had managed to twist around, and now had pulled his umbilical to its maximum length. As Soyuz commander, he needed to see what was happening.

He looked up at Tom's body and then at Deke. "Where is Alexei?" he asked.

Deke held the video camera steady as he answered. "That's Tom beside you, and Vance is back here to my left." He pushed away from the console to let Valery see past him. "I haven't been into the Soyuz yet. That must be where Alexei is."

From inside the Apollo capsule, Svetlana asked, "Houston, can Moscow see the video you're sending?"

In Mission Control, Kaz glanced at Chris Kraft, who said, "CAPCOM, tell them we have voice with Moscow and are working to send them video ASAP."

Kaz repeated the small lie. On board, Svetlana translated Kaz's words for Valery.

The cosmonaut thought for a second and said, in Russian, "Moscow, Soyuz-Apollo, how do you hear us?"

Kraft immediately pushed a button on his console to select the correct communication loop and spoke quickly. "INCO, is Moscow enabled to respond?"

"No, FLIGHT. They can hear the crew and the Mission Control common loop, but they can't transmit through our assets."

Kraft nodded. Given the potential upcoming operation to Skylab, with its secrets—and potentially even Chinese involvement—he needed to establish and maintain clear control.

He leaned forward and pushed the button to speak again on MCC common. "Moscow, this is Chris Kraft. Would you like to talk to your crewmembers?"

The Moscow flight director's voice rasped back in a thick Russian accent. "Da. Yes. And we are ready for video also."

Kraft turned to Kaz and nodded for him to reply to the crew.

Kaz pushed his transmit button. "Valery, we're enabling Moscow comms now. Just give us a sec while we get the interpreter hooked in."

In a back room, the duty interpreter leaned forward. She was slightly puzzled by what Kaz meant, as she was always ready, but she pushed her transmit switch to respond.

"Translation console is ready."

Valery started speaking and the translator's voice came into everyone's headsets in Mission Control, as well as to Deke on orbit, louder and slightly lagging, a cacophony that required concentration.

"Moscow, Kubasov here. Have you been listening to all our comms? Do you have video yet?"

The Soviet flight director in Moscow Mission Control was on his feet, looking at his forward screens.

"Yes, we've heard all voice transmissions, but no video yet."

"Copy. Any change on the plan for Alexei's body and the Soyuz configuration?" Valery knew Moscow could speak with Houston directly, but as the Soyuz commander on board, he wanted to be sure he understood what they wanted.

"No change. Strap cosmonaut Leonov into the center seat, tie down loose items, set switches for ground-controlled undock and automated re-entry, and close hatches."

Valery nodded. He'd briefed Deke on the Soyuz buttons he needed to push and how to use the hatch tools, and Svetlana had used a grease pencil to draw a diagram on the blank back page of a checklist, which was now folded and tucked into Deke's spacesuit leg pocket.

Svetlana spoke from inside Apollo. "How much longer do we have on this communications pass?"

In both Moscow and Houston, the flight directors looked at the digital timers on their front screens. Since she had asked in Russian, Moscow answered. "On the American relay satellite, we have another twelve minutes. Then there will be a gap of . . ." A pause while he consulted his team. ". . . fourteen minutes when we will have you radio-only via the American *Vanguard* relay ship."

Kaz interrupted. "Moscow, we concur, and with only twelve minutes left in this pass, we need to get our crewmember to work doing what you just outlined." He glanced at Chris, who nodded. They needed to hurry.

Both men knew they had to get the Apollo ship docked to Skylab so they could deal with the wild card of the Chinese ship.

And the clock was ticking.

38

Soyuz Spaceship, Earth Orbit

As Alexei Leonov was dying, weightless and unconscious, the last outflow of air from the Docking Module tanks had nudged him back through the Soyuz hatch like a piece of flotsam in a sluggish stream. The mixture of gases had been oxygen-rich, but too thin and low-pressure to feed his lungs and brain enough to revive him. He had died as a captain should, exhaling his final rattling breath inside the darkened confines of his wounded ship. He now floated in the spherical upper section of the spaceship he had commanded.

Deke paused at the hatch of the Soyuz to take still pictures, aware that both Soviet and American specialists would study them closely to reconstruct what had happened when he got the film back to Earth.

But they also wanted real-time video, and time was running out on this comm pass. Contorting himself to pull enough slack on both his suit umbilical and the video camera cable, he got himself through the hatch. It was smaller than the ones in the Apollo — a tight squeeze barely wide enough for his pressure-suited shoulders. He squirmed and twisted, inching the cloth of the suit along the hard, curved metal of the hatch. Like a baby being born, suddenly he was through.

Alexei's body floated as a shadow in the darkness in front of him. Deke pictured his training in the simulator in Star City to remember where the light switch was. He nudged the corpse aside, reached blindly for the control panel and flicked the toggle switch to ON.

The wall-mounted recessed bulbs blinked a couple of times and then steadied into bright light, casting harsh shadows. Deke squinted at the sudden glare. With the video camera in his right hand, he grabbed a curved handrail with his left to steady himself and move back against the wall in the confined sphere.

"Houston, I'm inside Soyuz now." He was surprised how reedy and breathless he sounded. *Took more effort than I thought to get in here.* He pointed the video camera at the pale-yellow felt-covered wall until Houston and Moscow confirmed they were ready to see the third body.

Kaz responded, "Copy, Deke, we see your video of the Soyuz interior, and everyone's watching." He glanced at the wall clock. "We have eight minutes left in this pass, and Moscow would like to monitor your actions if you can get everything done in time."

"Copy." Deke aimed the camera towards Alexei, using his other hand to turn the stiff body towards the light. As he filmed the slack, blotchy blue-and-white face, stained with rusty remnants of blood, Deke realized it was one of the rare times he had seen Alexei when he wasn't smiling.

"Houston, let me know when you've seen enough." His tone was bitter as he felt a surge of frustrated anger. His three friends shouldn't have died this way. He'd lost many squadron mates flying B-25s in Italy during World War II, and he'd been director of flight crew operations, working in the Florida launch-control blockhouse, when the Apollo 1 crew burned to death in their spacecraft. He'd learned to accept death as an inevitable part of his dangerous professions, but it still made him both sad and furious, every time.

"Thanks, Deke, that's enough video," Kaz said. "If you could, move now to strap Alexei into the entry capsule."

Moscow hadn't said they'd seen all that they wanted, but Kaz knew time was getting tight.

To maneuver Alexei's stiffened body, with its outstretched arms, down through the narrow hatch into the Soyuz re-entry module, Deke realized he was going to have to force it. He floated the legs through first, turned Alexei 90 degrees until his arms were reaching back up towards Deke, and then pushed on his chest, grinding the back of his friend's head against the bare metal to bend his rigid neck and pivot him through. He tried to ignore the scalp that peeled off, becoming a waving flap, as the body bent barely enough and popped clear. *Just a dead body*, he reminded himself. But it sickened him, and he swallowed several times as he retrieved the video camera from where he'd tucked it under a wall-mounted bungee.

Again Deke wormed his bulky shoulders through the narrowness of a Soviet hatch, and with his legs still sticking out into the orbital module, he floated Alexei into his central commander's seat and loosely connected the shoulder, waist and crotch straps. Alexei's legs were rigid, bent slightly at the waist and knees, and Deke couldn't get enough leverage to tuck them into the desired fully bent position on their metal footrest. He let them splay into the space under the instrument console, grateful that Alexei was only five-foot-four. Deke grunted as he pulled on the straps, cinching the body solidly into place in the contoured seat.

A voice came into his headset, speaking Russian, followed immediately by the English translation. "We need all loose items removed from the re-entry module."

"Wilco." Deke knew it made sense. Moscow was going to fire the small capsule's engines and then fly it automatically, down through the Earth's atmosphere. Having multiple articles floating randomly inside could affect how the ship would fly. He retrieved all the small items he could find and pushed them up through the hatch into the orbital module. That part would be jettisoned and burn up in the atmosphere.

From his spot out of sight at the other end of the Docking Module, Valery asked, "Deke, you have questions?"

Deke pulled Svetlana's note out of his pocket and compared it to the Soyuz instrument panel. She had circled switches and numbered them in the sequence he had to follow. He'd studied enough Russian to recognize and be able to pronounce the Cyrillic characters.

"Okay for now, Valery, thanks."

The panel was already powered on, with arrays of small, square buttons, some glowing, showing they were active. Soviet Mission Control had selected most of them correctly, and he only had to push a few to match Svetlana's diagram.

Kaz's voice was back in his helmet. "Deke, Moscow is asking that you get a clear video of the control panels so they can verify configuration. We have 90 seconds left in this comm pass."

"Copy." Deke wanted to float fully into the capsule so that the panel would be easier to see, but his suit's umbilical was stretched to its full length. Instead, he stretched his arm as best he could and flipped the video camera in his hand so the panel would appear right side up, then slowly scanned across it, pausing at each quadrant. When he judged there was about 30 seconds left, he said, "That enough, Kaz?"

In Houston, Kaz had been listening to the Russian back-room chatter. "Yep, all switches look correct. Good work, Deke. Please just take close-out still photos and then close the hatches, with Valery's instruction as needed. We'll talk to you again through CONUS sites in about thirty-five minutes."

"Roger, Houston, talk to you then."

Deke found the hatch closing tool nestled in a metal clip mounted on the curved wall of the orbital module. He'd trained on it in Star City, and its shape felt familiar in his hands as he turned the selector to the closed position and inserted the square metal tip of the tool into the matching recessed location on the hatch. He started to swing the hatch closed, but he caught sight of Alexei in his commander's seat and grabbed the camera for one last photo. Alexei had two daughters, and Deke figured they might appreciate the photo one day.

Honoring his final orbit.

Deke pivoted the re-entry module hatch into place, nestling it smoothly against its seals, and then cranked the ratchet on the closing tool until it had reached the needed torque and started ratcheting instead of driving. Satisfied, he pulled the tool out, floated back and looked at the jumble of loose items floating in the orbital module. He decided to push everything through into the Docking Module, which would be jettisoned and slowly decay in orbit until it burned up. When he was done, he took one last look around the Soyuz module, then squirmed his way through the upper hatch, feet first to avoid tangling his umbilical. He used the tool to close that hatch as well, and then clam-shelled the matching hatch to the Docking Module closed.

He glanced up to where Vance Brand was pinned to the wall. *How are we going to fit these two bodies in with us in the Apollo capsule?* Rigor mortis was temporary, so they would soon be more maneuverable, but the blank, staring eyes unnerved him.

Deke had an idea. In his suit leg pocket was a bag he used to protect his helmet when he de-suited. He undid the pocket zipper, took the bag out and grabbed the console edge to pull himself close to Vance's upper body. Working with one hand while he steadied himself with the other, he clumsily slid the bag down over Vance's head and pulled the drawstring tight around his friend's neck. He floated back to inspect his work and nodded.

"Lootcha," Valery said, watching from the hatch at the other end of the module. *Better.* Neither man was squeamish, but covering the face somehow felt more respectful.

"Svetlana, I'm about to start moving Vance's and Tom's bodies up into the Apollo Command Module. You ready for them?" Deke asked.

"Yes." She had been picturing what to do with them and had a plan.

39

Mission Control

"Apollo, Houston, for Deke." Kaz kept his tone even but would be choosing his words carefully.

"Kaz, Deke here. Go ahead."

"Deke, we'd like a private medical conference with you, please. Recommend you have Valery and Svetlana get off headset so we can talk with only you." He glanced at Chris Kraft. "Nothing urgent or life-threatening, just private."

Kraft gave Kaz a thumbs-up. He and Kaz were in a small room, up one floor from Mission Control, that was normally used for private biomedical monitoring, with a separate link from the broader communications loop. The room was empty except for Kaz and Kraft.

On board Apollo, Deke looked at Svetlana and shrugged. Astronauts and doctors had a traditionally adversarial relationship, given that a medical issue could lead to grounding, and often did. Deke assumed it was the same for cosmonauts.

Svetlana frowned. "No problem, Deke, but is it something we should know about?"

Valery watched the two of them, understanding enough English to realize what was going on.

Deke raised both palms and shook his head. "Not that I know of. Just take your headsets off and give me a minute to talk to them, so we can sort it out."

Svetlana translated for Valery, who made a dismissive face. "Vrachee!" he said, spitting out the word. *Doctors!* He'd been grounded from a previous spaceflight when staff at the Institute of Biomedical Problems had detected a swelling on his right lung. They'd said it was tuberculosis, but it turned out to be an allergic reaction to an insecticide they were spraying on the trees in Moscow. The backup crew had flown in Valery's place.

Valery and Svetlana peeled off their comm caps and looked out the windows away from Deke, giving him as much privacy as the small craft allowed.

Deke moved down into the transfer tunnel, as far from Russian ears as possible, and turned his back to them.

"Okay, Kaz, I'm the only one listening. What's up?" He paused, but before Kaz could reply, quietly asked, "Are you seeing something on my heart monitor?" Though he'd felt nothing abnormal, he was always aware that his fibrillation might recur.

"Thanks, Deke, and no, your ticker is doing fine, as expected. We just needed an excuse to talk to you about something else. I'm here alone in the biomed back room with Chris Kraft, on a secure comm loop, and this is for your ears only."

Deke frowned. He sure didn't need more mission complications. "I'm listening."

"Deke, back in seventy-one, while you were head of flight crew operations, there was a classified experiment built into Skylab. Records show you were in-briefed on it."

"Yeah, Kaz, I'm aware of Seesaw. One ex-military crewmember from each Skylab crew with a high enough security clearance ran operations on it." He thought back. "As I recall, Jerry Carr did a lot of good work on it, and then it got mothballed at the end of Skylab 4."

Kraft nodded as Kaz replied, "Yep, that's right. But we think the secret got out somehow, and Seesaw is the real reason we need you to dock with Skylab."

He described NORAD's detection of the Chinese spacecraft, its trajectory to intercept Skylab and the assumption that there might be crew on board.

"Holy shit, Kaz!" Deke glanced over his shoulder up the tunnel, making sure the cosmonauts hadn't noticed his outburst. His mind raced. "I'm up here with two Soviets, and now you're telling me I need to head off a potential Chinese Skylab docking?" He thought further. "And keep my cosmonaut crewmates from seeing Seesaw as well?"

Kaz and Kraft made eye contact. "That's exactly right, Deke," Kaz said. "It's why we've been hustling you along so quickly with the body retrieval and Docking Module jettison, and the upcoming orbital maneuvering. Assuming the Chinese have reverse-engineered a docking mechanism, you're our only way to keep them from getting aboard."

Deke asked the obvious questions. "Where is the Chinese ship now, and how much time have I got?"

"We're tracking it closely, along with the rendezvous trajectory they're using. As far as we know, it's the first time they've flown a profile like this. It looks like they're calculating all orbit adjust burns from their domestic tracking sites and two deployed ships, so they're being extra conservative. We're confident you'll get into proximity an hour or two before they do. And they won't have cooperative communications with Skylab for onboard distance and speed, so their approach will have to be visual. Which means it'll be slower."

"An hour or two is cutting it mighty fine, Kaz." Deke considered something that fighter pilots, given their planes' small gas tanks, always thought about. "How are my fuel reserves?"

"We've run the numbers multiple times, and we think you'll be fine. The revised profile is just like we described it on the open comms—rendezvous, dock, transfer bodies, wait for good orbital alignment, then undock and deorbit to the waiting recovery ship off Hawaii."

Chris Kraft said something to Kaz, and he summarized it for Deke. "We're bringing all Skylab systems back online now, after Jerry and his crew shut it down seventeen months ago. It's got some aging ship problems, but we think it'll be fine for your short stay and out through a Space Shuttle docking in a few years."

Deke had been thinking. "What do the Soviets know of the Chinese spaceship?"

Kaz looked at Kraft, who shrugged.

"We don't know, Deke, but we assume the Russian tracking systems have detected the launch from China, and probably the orbiting ship itself. They haven't yet asked for any special communications with your crew, but my guess is, as soon as they get their Soyuz deorbited, they will. As far as we can tell, for now they believe us—that we're just docking with Skylab to optimize safe return of the bodies, and of you and their cosmonauts."

Kaz glanced at his watch. "Deke, this comm pass is about to end. Any other questions for now?"

Deke closed his eyes for a few seconds, calming his whirling thoughts. "Confirm we're using my heart fibrillation history as a continuing excuse for private comms?"

"Yeah, we think that's simplest."

Deke nodded and then reopened his eyes. "But the real question we need to answer is what to do when the Chinese get to Skylab."

Kaz and Kraft nodded too. "Agreed. We're working on a plan." Kaz rechecked his watch. "Talk to you again through Guam in twenty-five minutes."

"Copy that. And Kaz?"

"Yeah, go ahead, Deke."

The voice from orbit was grave.

"Holy shit, man."

48

Skylab

A relic.

Hurtling through space at 17,000 miles per hour, forever trapped in Earth's orbit by gravity. An 80-foot-long cylinder, 20 feet across—80 tons of mostly aluminum going 5 miles per second.

Skylab. America's first space station.

Abandoned.

It had been built at the tail end of NASA's Apollo program, after President Nixon had canceled the last three Moon landings, afraid of another Apollo 13 accident or deadly fire. But the huge Saturn V launch rockets meant for the next missions had already been assembled and paid for, and begged for a purpose. And so NASA convinced a stingy, Vietnam-plagued Congress that an orbiting laboratory would be good for science, and that the planned Space Shuttle would be able to dock with it as a research destination in space.

But space missions rarely go according to plan.

During Skylab's 1973 launch from Florida, the giant rocket's vibration and forces tore off a thermal shield and one of the solar arrays. The first astronauts to visit Skylab had to do emergency space walks to deploy the remaining solar array and rig a space blanket to shade it from the relentless heat of the Sun. Skylab ended up looking like a backyard project, with one wing missing and an orange tarpaulin pulled loosely across it.

But it did its job. Three separate trios of astronauts lived and worked on Skylab, for 28 days, then 59 days, and finally for a world-record 84 days. They ran nearly 300 scientific and technical experiments, some public, some less so. And when the final crew closed the hatch on February 8, 1974, they left a duffel bag full of food handy, as a welcoming gift for the next crew to arrive.

But Apollo was done, and the Space Shuttle's first flight kept being delayed, so no one ever came.

Until now.

41

Apollo Command Module, Earth Orbit

"Apollo, Houston, you ready for Soyuz undock?" Kaz had been listening to the Russian voices on the communications loops from Moscow, and they had asked him to relay the question.

Inside the Apollo capsule, Deke looked across at his two Russian crewmates. They were loosely strapped into their seats, wearing their blue serge flight suits with the large red Soviet flag and CCCP across their left shoulders. They had their headsets on, and both raised a thumb in response to Kaz's question.

Deke was back in his orange flight suit, happy to be out of the pressure suit with the space walk completed. Svetlana had rotated the seats up out of the way when she and Valery had floated the bodies in, and now Tom and Vance, both with bags over their heads, were tucked underneath the seats. For now, their arms reached up through the gaps, zombie-like, but soon rigor mortis would fade and they could tuck the arms down and out of sight.

"Houston, Apollo, yes, we're ready for Soyuz undock."

Deke had the checklist open on his right knee and had decided that

Svetlana would take the seat beside him because of her English skills. He didn't want to miss any steps and knew he needed all the help he could get. She already had her right pointer finger on the checklist, tracking where they were in the undock procedure.

"Copy, Apollo, we show you in a good config, you have a GO for undock. On panel one eighty-one, we would like the three TV camera switches—the power switches—in the on position."

Deke spun in his seat to reach down into the lower equipment bay and threw the switches. "You got it."

In Houston, Kaz looked up at Mission Control's blank front wall TV screen, waiting. With the Soyuz unmanned, both Houston and Moscow wanted to watch the post-undock maneuvers carefully. If something went awry, they would be counting on Deke to move the Apollo ship clear.

A burst of light lit the screen, and then it settled into a steady image from the Apollo internal video camera that showed the view of Soyuz through the window.

"Apollo, Houston. We have a good TV picture now, thanks."

"Okay," Deke responded.

His two crewmates were craning their necks, looking along the length of the Docking Module at the Soyuz at the far end. Deke stared at his instrument panel, reminding himself which switches to throw if he had to activate his hand controllers and visually steer clear.

A Russian voice came into the three crewmembers' headsets, saying, "Rastikovka," followed immediately by the interpreter's translation: "Undocking." Her voice continued as the Soyuz undocking springs pushed the ships apart. "Seal compress off. Indicator off. Intersection compress off."

The TV image was blossoming as the Sun moved into the field of view. Kaz said, "Apollo, Houston. The internal camera is getting reflections from the window. Can you move it down a little, so we won't see the Sun?"

"Roger," Deke responded.

Svetlana reached up, loosened the camera mounting arm and pivoted it slightly.

All eyes watched the Soyuz moving away, with Deke looking through his alignment sight, gauging distance. "Houston, I see about fifteen meters."

The interpreter's voice responded. "Twenty meters. Soyuz is initiating orbital rate attitude."

Now that the Soviet ship was undocked, it needed to take control of its own attitude, firing its small thrusters to pitch slowly and follow the Earth's curve as they flew across the horizon.

On the screen at Mission Control, the receding Soyuz looked reassuringly stable, but the Sun was moving back into the picture, overpowering the image.

"Apollo, any way you can shift the camera again to avoid the bright sunlight?"

Deke and his crewmates all had a hand up, shading their eyes against the unfiltered intensity of the Sun as it passed directly behind the Soyuz. "Sorry, Houston, it's burning our eyes out here too. Just need to wait until the angles change."

Deke was very uncomfortable with not being able to see the Russian ship. "What range and rate are they seeing?"

Svetlana asked, "Deke, want me to ask Moscow directly?"

Deke nodded, squinting hard out the window.

In Russian, she said, "Moscow, Apollo, give us continuous range and speed. No need to interpret."

There was a short pause, and then a clear Russian voice announced, "Thirty meters, opening at point one meter per second."

"Copy," Svetlana replied, and translated for Deke. She asked, "Moscow, how do the angles look?"

"Right in the center, we have a clear image looking down-sun."

Deke nodded as she translated, exhaling in relief. Pilots hate not being able to see.

Kaz transmitted, "Apollo, Houston, big picture, when Soyuz gets to one hundred meters, they will fire their first separation burn. Once they're safely clear, we'll be asking you to jettison the Docking Module, and then as soon as we've got the new orbit vector numbers, you'll see the uplink to accept for your first burn to adjust orbit to intercept Skylab."

Intercept Skylab. The words echoed in Deke's ears. He'd had the simulator training to enable him to do it, but he had never expected it to be part of Apollo-Soyuz. Especially not with him in sole command. And with a Chinese ship nearby.

He kept his voice flat. "Roger, Houston, we'll be ready."

But he was thinking something else entirely.

42

Shuguang Spaceship, 270 Miles above Earth

Fang's spaceship had no windows.

The Chinese aerospace engineers had been in a race to meet Director Tsien and Chairman Mao's stringent deadline. To be ready to launch on schedule, anything that added unneeded complexity had been discarded. The Shuguang spacecraft's design was stripped to the bone, light and ruggedly purpose-built, with all the customer-focused elegance of a hammer.

Fang Kuo-chun was the first person to orbit the Earth with no way to look directly outside.

But his task was going to require all his piloting skill, and a clear view of the target was mandatory. So the engineers had improved upon the Soviet Soyuz's periscope design. Like a submariner under the sea, Fang's sole visual link with the outside world was through a series of lenses and mirrors in a tube. Mounted in the center of his one-man cockpit, facing him low on the instrument panel between his knees, was a large, circular, glass-covered display. It showed the peripheral image of the reflected horizon, so he would be able to control orientation, and a large central view of the intended target.

What Fang was seeing was mostly blackness: the unending emptiness of the universe, with a scattering of stars moving across it as Shuguang orbited the Earth. But the sign he was looking for had just appeared in the middle of the screen—the object the simulators at the secret training facility near Peking had trained him for.

A star that wasn't moving.

He'd had help. After Mao's 1970 decision to fund a Chinese astronaut program, two Yuan Wang–class space tracking ships had been built. They'd sailed and positioned themselves, one in the Atlantic and the other in the South Pacific, and had been following Fang's ship. They had done the calculations and uplinked targeting information to fire the Shuguang's engine, maneuvering the ship closer to the target.

Once the ship was in visual range, the rest was up to Fang.

Initially, the light in the center of Fang's periscope display was fuzzy, too far beyond the system's optical range to bring into focus. But as the distance decreased, his objective was becoming clearer. His vision was perfect, but still he squinted to make out the details of the sunlit shape against the darkness.

Fang glanced at his checklist, then double-checked the small clock mounted above the periscope display. The Sun would set soon, and he would lose sight of his target. Uncooperative spacecraft near each other in the darkness were dangerous. Per his flight plan, an upcoming maneuver would raise his orbit to the same height as his prey. Two objects going in the same direction at the same altitude orbiting Earth don't get closer to each other. His instructors had called it a "parking orbit," which his ship would maintain until the next sunrise, in 45 minutes.

He entered the command data that had been sent up from the Yuan Wang ship, enabled his engines, watched as the ship turned, and listened to the brief pulse of the main engine firing as it nudged him to the desired orbital height. When the burn was complete and the Shuguang pivoted back to its original attitude, Fang was relieved to see the glowing light of the target reappear in the periscope view.

Distance and closing speed were vital pieces of information. The Shuguang had a small radar mounted off-center from its nose that pinged out pulses of energy, timing and tracking the reflected signals as they bounced off the target. Fang checked what the radar showed: 12 kilometers distant, and zero relative rate. Exactly as desired. Two small artificial moons, one quietly chasing the other around the world.

Mounted at the front tip of his ship was a complex mechanism that needed activation. During the 45 minutes of darkness, he was scheduled to power up the new system, check that it was functioning as planned and deploy it into the desired position. Carefully following his checklist, Fang worked methodically in the dim light inside his cockpit, listening as the mechanical systems came to life and extended out, away from his ship.

Like a beast baring its teeth, readying for impending contact with the enemy.

43

Chairman Mao's Residence, July 18

Mao's senior staff all stood up as the weekly status meeting concluded, and then they slowly left the darkened room, talking quietly. Mao had asked two men to stay behind, and they moved to the chairs closest to him to accommodate the weakness of his voice.

Mao was seemingly frailer every day. And bright lights bothered him.

Teng Hsiao-ping, Mao's military Chief of General Staff, lingered when he was halfway to the door, trying to judge why Mao was excluding him from a meeting with these two. But the chairman sat with his eyes closed, waiting until his personal secretary assured him the room was empty of those he wanted gone. Mao mumbled something, and the aide responded quietly and then also left, deferentially ushering Teng ahead of him. The sound of the heavy door closing at the far end of Mao's wood-paneled private office was distinct, echoing slightly.

The truth was, Mao no longer trusted Teng. After a lifetime of service and sacrifice together, of building China to a restored greatness, Teng was becoming too capitalistic, openly defying the Great Proletarian

Cultural Revolution. Defying the very essence of the socialism that Mao so passionately loved and believed in.

This three-man meeting was in support of current operations that would undeniably show the world the power and glory of Mao's China.

Tsien Hsue-shen, the director of China's space program, silently nodded at the man in the seat opposite him as Chairman Mao cleared his throat to speak.

"Class struggle is the key link."

A truth, but a non sequitur. The two men were used to such statements from their elderly leader. They waited.

"It was Stalin's big mistake." Mao had partially opened his eyes but was looking straight ahead, not at the two men, as he spoke. "There is always need for revolution. The American labor unions are reactionary and must be supported. And support from within is the true path." There was an echo of his former fire in the words.

Mao slowly turned his head and looked at Tsien. "How have events unfolded?"

The previous day's bombing and assassination attempt in America had been summarized for all as part of the staff meeting, but the China-relevant specifics had been left out. Secrets needed to be kept if they were to remain effective.

"They have proceeded well," Tsien said. "The foreign space operations were disrupted at key moments, and our mission is going smoothly." He glanced at his wristwatch. "Fang Kuo-chun is getting close to Skylab, and there has been no apparent detection of his spaceflight."

Mao's eyes opened wider, and he stared intently at Tsien from under his swollen eyelids. "What of the assassination attempt?"

To Mao's right, the other man spoke. "That required very little support from our contacts, Honored Chairman. There is much unrest and dissatisfaction amongst the American working people." He paused. "With their upcoming election, it will likely not be the last attempt."

Mao nodded slowly. This man—Wang Tung-sing—had once been his bodyguard, but he had risen to become Minister of Public Security.

Wang's tentacles reached deep inside China, and out through the extended arms of organized crime that were spreading across the world with loosened immigration for Chinese nationals. Wang was a useful tool for the leader of the Chinese Communist Party.

Mao stared at the man. "What further action do you have planned?"

Wang, who found the scrutiny uncomfortable, was glad to have an answer. "We are going to continue to disrupt operations there in an untraceable way." He glanced across at Tsien, considering how much to say. "Americans rely too much on unprotected key individuals. We have identified one such person who is crucial to their operation, and we are moving to remove him."

Mao sat motionless, unblinking. He'd devoted a lifetime to making decisions that shaped China and its people to match his vision. The two men allowed him the silence he needed as he pondered. At last, he slowly turned back to Tsien.

"How much more time is required until completion?"

Tsien didn't want to over-promise. "One full day, Revered Chairman. Maybe less."

Mao closed his eyes, settling back into the supporting comfort of his chair. In a thin, wavering voice, he said, "When time is short, decisive action is critical."

The room filled with the low, wet sound of his labored breathing.

The two men looked at each other, realizing approval had been given and the meeting was over. They rose without speaking, quietly walked the length of the room, opened the heavy door and left.

44

Apollo Capsule, 232 Miles above Earth

"Apollo, Houston, we show terminal phase final maneuver complete. You're looking right on the money, range fifty-three hundred feet, closing speed thirty feet per second."

Astronaut Bob Crippen had the CAPCOM night shift and had guided Deke through the maneuvering burns to raise Apollo's orbit to match Skylab's.

"Copy, Crip, we show the same and are waiting on sunrise for Skylab to appear."

Floating above his crew couch, Deke felt tired. And undeniably nervous. Houston had given the crew as much downtime as possible to sleep between engine firings, but he'd only napped fitfully. He closed both eyes tight and rubbed his face with his open palm, hard. That always helped him get more alert when he was flying jets. And he sure needed it now.

Next to him, loosely strapped into the center couch, Svetlana watched Deke rub his face. She still found that amputated finger jarring. She had grabbed enough catnaps to feel alert, though she had a dull headache. Valery, beside her, was breathing through his nose, frustrated at having nothing to do.

She peered through the forward window, trying to see Skylab in the darkness, ink on black velvet, a silhouette against the unblinking stars.

Valery leaned forward to do the same, and after several seconds, cursed in disgust. "I see nothing!" he muttered in Russian.

Svetlana pushed the transmit button. "Houston, what time is sunrise?"

At his console, Crip heard the flight activities officer answer the question in his headset, and he parroted it up to the crew.

"Sunrise in four minutes, forty seconds, Svetlana."

"Copy." She translated for Valery, and looked ahead to the sweeping dark curve of the horizon for the brightening purple glow that would herald the Sun's reappearance.

Deke glanced at her. He'd given her permission to talk directly to Houston as needed. So far she'd made no mistakes, but he fundamentally didn't trust her. In a lifetime of flying in combat, as a test pilot and with NASA, he'd never flown with a woman.

But so far, so good.

And she was what he had to work with.

During the short night, the corpses' arms had relaxed, and the two Russians had used heavy gray tape to bind Tom's and Vance's hands to their thighs, elbows tucked in. Moving the bodies to do so had released a lingering smell of shit, but it was tolerable.

They were coming up on Skylab from slightly below, catching up to it. Deke was watching through his alignment sight, waiting for it to appear so he could judge its size relative to the glowing reticle and calculate how far away they really were. They were getting range and speed displayed on the instrument panel, calculated by measuring the Doppler shift and time delay of their radio signals. But all pilots prefer direct visual confirmation to relying on instruments.

"Deke, Valery, are you hungry?" Svetlana had used the short pause to reach back between the seats and open a stowage locker, and she was now studying the food cue card. "Maybe nuts or crackers?" She rummaged with one hand, careful not to dislodge items as she searched.

Deke's first reaction was to say no, but then he realized he couldn't remember the last time he'd eaten. "Yeah, that'd be great, thanks."

"Blue Velcro, that's you, right?"

Each crewmember's food had color-coded Velcro dots on the package.

"Yep." A pause while he considered their new circumstances. "We may as well keep things straight. Why don't you be white and eat Vance's food. Valery can be red and have Tom's."

"Okay, will do." She was reaching across his lower legs now to fill a drink bag. She recognized that these men would be comforted by the normality of a woman preparing them something to eat. The upcoming docking was going to be demanding.

She stuck the filled bag and two packages onto the Velcro square in front of Deke. "Tea with lemon, peanuts and dried apricots."

Deke thanked her as she stuck items next to Valery, describing them in Russian to him.

"You're welcome." She'd chosen dark chocolate, almonds and cocoa for herself. She took a bite of the hard bar, opened the straw to sip the cocoa and looked out the forward window.

"Sunrise," she said. It happened fast, the glow lighting up her face and the interior of the ship. She pointed. "And Skylab!" The small, insect-like shape of the laboratory was dark against the bright backlighting.

Valery saw something else in the sunlight out his side window. His voice was urgent. "Deke! I see . . ." He struggled unsuccessfully for the English word, then said it in Russian for Svetlana to translate.

"Sparks, Deke! Valery is seeing sparks outside." She twisted to look over his shoulder.

"Sparks? What the—" Deke closed the straw's valve on his tea and leaned across, catching a glimpse of sparkles in the sunlight, some drifting by the window slowly, some moving fast.

He checked his propulsion system pressure gauges while pushing the comm button to transmit. "Houston, we're seeing what look like fireflies out the starboard window. Maybe a propellant leak."

He looked ahead at Skylab, still a mile distant. It was close to alignment with his optical sight. *Good*, he thought. Whatever was leaking wasn't affecting their attitude control. Yet.

Crip's voice came into their comm caps. "Copy, Deke, we're looking at the data."

There was a 20-second pause while the experts in the technical back rooms rapidly compared updated pressures and quantities. The front-room controller listened and summarized, and Crip repeated it for the crew. "We're seeing what looks like a small leak from the thrusters in service module quad B. We should have time to troubleshoot which one, but for now please work the SM RCS quad B secure procedure."

"Copy, in work." Deke peeled the systems checklist off the Velcro beside him, flipped to the right page and leaned forward to throw switches, closing the valves that were feeding the leak.

"Complete," he reported. He turned to Valery. "The sparks should slow down and stop soon."

The cosmonaut watched intently, with Svetlana looking over his shoulder. "Da, tyepir myensche." He looked back at Deke. "Less."

The experts in Houston had been watching as well, and Crip transmitted, "Good config, Deke, pressures are stabilizing. Let us know if you see continued leaking."

"Wilco." Deke gave a thumbs-up to Valery. Maybe he had two crewmates he could count on.

He no longer felt tired.

45

Apollo Capsule

"Apollo, Houston, we show you at three hundred feet, all systems nominal."

Crip made the transmission to reassure the crew, but also to offer a regular cadence of voice contact. The final stages of docking were tense, and critical.

Deke responded, "Copy, Crip, we're receiving solid range and range rate. Skylab's getting big in the windows."

Deke glanced across the cockpit, out the window to his right. No more fireflies. They'd troubleshot the leak to a single forward-firing jet that had been partially stuck open, and had sent commands to isolate it. The ship had 28 thrusters total and could easily compensate for one failure. But it would burn a little more fuel.

Deke looked at the rendezvous checklist in his hand. It had been written for the Apollo-Soyuz mission profile, but with Houston calling up the differences for him, it was good enough to get them docked to Skylab.

He hoped.

BAM! There was a sudden echoing sound of metal on metal, like a hammer striking steel, and then a grinding, scraping noise. Their vehicle lurched sideways, tugging the straps of the weightless crew, and they could hear thrusters automatically firing to restabilize.

"What the hell!" Deke hurriedly scanned the instrument panel. Apollo 13 had had an oxygen tank explode, with similar symptoms and dire results. That crew had barely made it home. But no alarms were ringing, and the pressures all looked normal.

"Deke! Look!" Valery was pointing at Deke's side window, wide-eyed.

Deke snapped his head around to the left and leaned forward to see. Bits of debris tumbled past the window—white shards and shiny strips of metal. But what transfixed all three Apollo crewmembers was the large, smooth shape beyond the debris.

Drifting past them, glinting in the newly risen sunlight, was another spacecraft. It had a long black nose and capsule section joined to a white cylindrical base. They could see a long, deep gouge along the nose that ended in a peeled-up section on the white portion. The ship was tumbling slightly, its thrusters firing.

"We've been hit!" Deke felt his heart lurch. Houston had said the Chinese ship was at least an hour or two behind!

Svetlana looked closely as the other ship moved out of view of the side window, drifting into Deke's forward rendezvous window. Painted against the black of the ship's hull was a large red rectangle with a gold star and an arc of four smaller stars in the top-left corner.

"China!" she said, her mind racing. *Is it a threat—a bomb?* No, she quickly realized. The capsule shape meant it was designed not only to get to space but also to survive re-entry. And it had blundered into them, not targeted them. She'd read classified Soviet reports about the Chinese developing a recoverable spy satellite. *Are they spying on us?* She quickly shook her head, rejecting the idea. There hadn't been enough time since NASA had made the decision to dock with Skylab for the Chinese to respond and launch a vehicle.

So this ship had been independently headed for Skylab. As if the Chinese and Americans were in some sort of secret race to get there.

But why?

Deke was urgently transmitting. "Houston, Apollo, we have a problem." He kept the wording vague, not wanting to transmit anything classified.

No response. He transmitted again. Nothing. He checked the switch config, verifying that they should be relaying everything through their large, high-gain antenna and the ATS-6 satellite.

But there was no answer from Houston.

Valery pointed towards Deke's side and forward windows, his finger moving slowly to track the small pieces still floating by. "I think China hit big antenna." He was picturing the aft end of the Apollo ship. There were protruding thruster blocks, and the big, exposed engine nozzle they'd need for their deorbit burn. "Maybe hit more too," he warned.

Deke considered that briefly and then gathered himself. *Fly the plane!* he thought. *Aviate, navigate, communicate* was the pilot's mantra, in that order. He looked through his sighting reticle and was relieved to see Skylab still centered and getting closer. A glance to the side confirmed that the Chinese ship was drifting away, not on course to dock and jam them up. He looked at his speed and distance indicators—they had gone blank. *Makes sense if we lost the antenna.* He looked through all the windows and saw no sparkles to indicate a new fuel leak.

He made a rapid decision. And he needed help.

"We're going to continue docking. Svetlana, I'm gonna call estimated distances using my reticle, and I want you to set up a timer to calculate closing speed. Valery, use all the windows to keep an eye on the Chinese ship. Let me know ASAP if it looks like it's maneuvering back towards us. Okay?"

"Yes, okay." Svetlana flipped her checklist to a blank page and hastily drew a table with five columns as she translated for Valery. He floated clear of his crew couch and moved up and behind Deke so he could see better out the port side window but stay out of the way.

"One hundred and eighty feet!" Deke called out.

During the night, he and Crip had discussed the size of the Skylab solar panels and fuselage length, and he'd drawn a quick reference table versus the glowing rings on his reticle so he could rapidly estimate distance as a backup to the radar data. Not perfect, but the best he had.

Svetlana was staring at the digital timer on the instrument panel while writing, and decided to repeat what Deke said, to ensure no mistake. "One hundred and eighty feet." It wasn't meters, as she was used to, but it didn't matter. Numbers were numbers.

She figured she'd need three or maybe four distance calls before she'd trust that her math was accurate enough to give Deke a speed. From her rendezvous training at Star City, she knew how critical closing speed was. By the time Skylab got big enough for them to visually assess when to fire braking pulses, it would be too late to do so, and they would crash into it.

"One hundred and fifty feet." *Damn, this isn't very accurate*, Deke realized. *But it's all we've got.*

Svetlana repeated the number and wrote it in her table, next to the time.

"What's our speed?" Deke demanded.

"I need one more range to be sure, Deke. I don't want to give you bad information."

She's right. He squinted hard to get an accurate sighting. "One hundred and thirty feet."

"Copy, one hundred and thirty feet." Svetlana figured out the delta distance, converted the time to seconds and quickly did the math. "Rate is . . . four feet per second."

"Shit, that's too fast!" Deke pulled several times on the T-shaped controller in his left hand, counting firings of the thrusters he needed to slow him down.

He took another sighting. "One hundred and ten feet."

Svetlana drew a line below her previous numbers. Now that Deke had braked, she had to recalculate the speed. "One hundred and ten feet, copy."

"We're closing slower now," he said, relief in his voice, then called, "One hundred feet."

She quickly did the calculation. "Copy, one hundred feet, looks like about two feet per second now."

Deke considered that. *Two feet per second, a hundred feet, so fifty seconds if I do nothing. Good.* He noticed they were drifting off-center and moved the controller down a couple of times to correct. "Ninety feet now."

"Copy, ninety feet." A pause. "Two point two feet per second." The third data point, written tidily in her table, made her more accurate.

"Great, we're under control for now. Let's ride this in to twenty-five feet and then slow some more." Deke looked for the Chinese ship. "What are you seeing, Valery?"

The cosmonaut had been keeping quiet, understanding the criticality of docking speed and distance, waiting for Deke to ask. In halting English, he said, "I am seeing China ship moving away. No change."

"Copy. Eighty feet now, Svetlana."

"Eighty feet." She calculated. "Two point three feet per second."

Deke leaned over and checked the docking mechanism status. He'd already set it up and saw no change. He mentally reviewed his actions at the moment of contact and what to do if he missed. *God forbid.*

When he looked back through the reticle, Skylab was really starting to grow in size. Soon he'd have to use the laboratory's diameter as his reference.

"Sixty-five feet."

Svetlana frowned slightly. Fives were harder math. "Copy, sixty-five feet . . . still two point three feet per second."

They were rising too high again, and Deke pulsed down to center Skylab in his reticle. He spotted the small target he'd use for fine alignment at docking—a cross mounted on a standoff post, with a matching painted cross on a plate at its base. By visually lining up the two crosses, he could ensure the docking mechanism would hit dead center.

"Deke, what's the new range?" Svetlana prompted.

He refocused. "Forty-five feet."

"Copy, forty-five feet. Speed is . . . two point five feet per second."

She pictured her Soyuz docking training, and knew what she would want to hear when given that information. "Recommend braking."

Not yet, Deke thought. The sooner they got docked, the more time they'd have to deal with the Chinese ship. Better to hurry in and brake late.

"Thirty-five feet, Svetlana."

She noted that he hadn't followed her advice and accepted it. *Maybe if we'd trained together*. She made the new calculation. "Two point six feet per second. Almost at twenty-five feet."

"Roger that, thanks." Deke was amazed at how quickly he'd come to trust this woman with critical information. He counted seconds until he guessed they were at twenty-five feet and pulled the hand controller several times to brake. Then he recentered Skylab in the reticle and measured the distance. "Twenty feet." Alignment looked good.

"Copy, twenty feet." She'd drawn a new horizontal line.

"Eighteen feet." *Time to get serious*.

"I see two feet per second." No need to repeat distances now. Just quickly get the math right.

"Fifteen feet."

A slight pause. "Still two feet per second." She decided to ask. "What is design docking speed?"

Deke had one eye closed, focused on the docking target. "Twelve feet. We wanna dock at zero point two feet per second."

"Copy. Still two feet per second." Just as she was going to recommend braking, she saw him pull several times on the hand controller.

"No need for speeds now, Svetlana. I'm visual from here." Deke watched the growth rate of the target, comparing it to the ideal he'd practiced in the Houston simulator.

"Five feet," he muttered to himself. "Slightly low and left, correcting." His fingers danced on the two hand controllers.

"Three feet." He assessed. "Speed looks good." The crosses appeared perfectly aligned.

"Two feet, contact next."

Svetlana realized she was holding her breath.

"One foot!" Deke's voice was loud and had risen half an octave.

There was a metallic sliding noise, and then a thump, and several lights on the instrument panel changed. Deke checked each of them to make sure the docking mechanism was holding and the Apollo attitude control system had shut itself off, so the two ships wouldn't fight each other.

A broad, relieved smile creased his leathery face, and Deke looked triumphantly at Svetlana. "We did it! We're docked!"

Deke felt his 51-year-old heart stutter.

46

Polly Ranch

A noise woke Kaz up.

He didn't generally move while he was asleep, and was still lying on his back, the same position he'd been in when he'd fallen into exhausted slumber. He blinked hard into the darkness a few times to clear both his good and his glass eye, and he turned his head on the pillow to see 3:00 glowing on his bedside clock.

Three a.m., he thought. The deepest hour of sleep. *What woke me up?* He listened intently, hearing nothing.

His house was a long, three-bedroom bungalow, brick on a concrete pad, with the oversized hangar garage at the far end. He kept his bedroom door closed at night to help deaden any sounds.

All quiet. Kaz frowned. He didn't normally wake up in the middle of the night.

His bedroom door suddenly burst open like it had been kicked, crashing into the Sheetrock wall, and men were yelling and shining bright flashlights into Kaz's face. He spun and kicked his legs to get clear of the bedding and dive into the relative protection of the far side of the bed, but hands were already grabbing at him. He lashed out blindly and felt the blow connect before the heavy weight of two men was on top of him on the bed, pinning his arms and legs. He twisted his head and was starting to yell to wake his nearest neighbor when he felt a gloved hand clamp his nose and mouth shut, blocking his breathing.

Kaz twisted violently and kicked and pulled hard with his arms, but he couldn't budge his captors, and his struggles only accelerated his urgent need for more oxygen. *I need a change of plan*, he realized. He gave one last surge of motion and then went limp.

The two men straddling him didn't move, waiting to see if he was faking. After 15 long seconds with no air, Kaz heard the man on his chest say something guttural, and then a light was bright in his eyes and he felt fingers release his nose, the rough-gloved palm still heavy across his mouth, with the thumb locked under his chin.

Kaz took a surging, grateful breath through his nose, and then several more.

Suddenly the gloved hand pulled clear, but as Kaz opened his mouth to yell, it was stuffed full of wadded cloth and the hand clamped down again, holding it in place. Kaz fought the instantaneous gag reflex and then worked to relax, breathing through his nostrils, recognizing what this meant.

These men weren't trying to kill him, just render him immobile and silent. But why?

He rejected the idea of theft, as there was little in his house of value to anyone but him. This was purposeful, and personal. *They're either warning me or kidnapping me, or both*, he decided. For what? It had to be connected to the bombing and the people he'd seen at the restaurant. The bulky weight on his chest made him think of the muscular Asian man with the sheaf of papers.

The hand pulled away again and was immediately replaced with something taut and thick and braided that pushed the wad of cloth solidly into his mouth. Unseen hands pulled his head up and tied a knot tightly behind his skull. Then they blindfolded him. He breathed as deeply and evenly through his nose as he could, replenishing his oxygen. If there was a chance to escape, he wanted it to be here, on his home turf, rather than wherever they were planning to take him.

The man who'd been pinning his legs let go a little, quickly tying a thin rope around his ankles and drawing them together tightly. Then he tied Kaz's knees.

Trussed, Kaz thought. Escape was looking less likely. But no reason to give up. As the man on his chest shifted his weight to tie Kaz's hands, Kaz wrested his right fist free and jabbed a punch with all his might at where he guessed the man's chin and neck would be. His blow glanced off something hard and into softer flesh, but the man just grunted. Kaz felt the weight shift away from him slightly, and then he was hit with a powerful slap that twisted his neck fully to the stops, stunning him.

As he shook his head to clear his thoughts, the men lashed his arms tight to the sides of his body. Both men got off. Strong hands picked him up, turned him and hefted him belly down over a heavily muscled shoulder. He was carried out of his room and down the hall. He sensed a left turn towards the back of the house and felt the change of temperature and humidity against his bare flesh as they stepped outside through the sliding glass rear doors. Kaz heard glass crunch under their feet and guessed that the sound of them breaking the patio door was what had woken him.

He heard and felt the change as they walked on the grass around the end of his house, then heard the rattle of keys in a lock, followed by the unmistakable creak of a car trunk being opened. The man carrying him leaned forward, pivoted Kaz like a large sack and dumped him in, banging his hips and neck on the trunk's hard curves. Then came the creak and slam of the trunk being closed, and the muffled sound of doors opening and slamming, the engine starting and the car rolling down the drive.

He'd been neatly, efficiently abducted.

Almost naked and bound in the trunk, Kaz tried to keep track of the sound and motion to figure out where they were going. He heard the tires on the cattle grid as the car drove north out of Polly Ranch, and then felt the car turn to the right onto FM 528. He counted seconds in his head, picturing the curve in the country road as they headed east. As he got to 600, he felt the car slow, turn left and then accelerate hard, the tire noise shifting from the rumble of country road blacktop to the rhythmic, repeated slabs of highway concrete.

They were on I-45, headed north towards Houston.

Kaz took stock. He had nothing on but the underwear he'd slept in. The ropes were secure and tight. He slid the right side of his face along the rough carpet of the trunk floor and felt the cloth blindfold shift. He repeated the motion, ignoring the rug burn on his cheek, until the cloth had cleared his good eye, but when he opened it, he could see nothing. The trunk was as dark as if his eye wasn't open at all. He thought for a second and worked to roll the blindfold back into place. Not being able to identify their faces might keep him alive.

Awkwardly, he wiggled onto his back, bent his hips to get his bare feet up against the trunk lid and pushed hard. Then he tried kicking, but the lock held tight.

Worth a try, but he wasn't getting out until they let him out.

He considered. Who would raise an alarm? The two men had broken into his house through the sliding back door, facing the runway. The neighbors were unlikely to notice that. And his Thunderbird was tucked inside his closed garage as usual. Nothing to raise suspicion.

He was expected back on shift in Mission Control at 08:00. When he didn't arrive, someone would call his house, thinking he'd overslept, but there'd be no answer. Bob Crippen would stay on as CAPCOM until they could find a replacement, and eventually someone would drive out to Polly Ranch to check on him. But not for hours.

He was on his own. He found the thought clarifying and thus comforting. Whatever was going to happen, it was up to him alone to solve it.

47

Mission Control

"Apollo, Houston, how do you read?" Crip had repeated the call five times already, but there was still no answer. They had lost all voice and data communications with the crew at a critical moment during docking, and all he could do was transmit into the void. He felt helpless.

The flight director spoke urgently. "INCO, any idea yet why we lost contact?"

"FLIGHT, the signal being relayed through ATS-6 just suddenly stopped, unknown why. ATS-6 itself checks normal, so it's gotta be some sort of failure of the high-gain system on board Apollo. To troubleshoot, we need to get back over a ground site to pick up the crew again through the omni antennas." A short pause. "If it's worst case and the S-band system is down, we should get voice through the VHF antennas."

The flight director looked up at the front screens. "How soon will we pick them back up?"

"In about twenty-five minutes, FLIGHT, at three nineteen Central, via Goldstone." INCO's voice was apologetic. Everyone in the room knew that was past the planned docking time.

The makeshift crew of one American and two Russians on board Apollo were on their own.

FLIGHT took another tack. "EECOM, what's Skylab's attitude control and comm status?"

The physical impact of the Apollo docking would be detectable in Skylab's data, and maybe they could use its communications system as a backup relay.

"FLIGHT, Skylab is ready for docking, holding attitude, ready to automatically go free drift at first contact. Comms haven't been used in a while but should be good." He paused and decided to voice the obvious for the whole room. "But we won't have comms until we're over that same ground site in twenty-five minutes."

The flight director summarized for the room. "Okay, people, let's be ready for when we get acquisition of signal. The crew should be docked by then and will be waiting for our help with next steps and to work the communications problem."

And maybe more than that, he thought. He ran his finger down the phone numbers list under the plastic sheet on his console, picked up the telephone receiver and dialed his counterpart at NORAD.

48

Shuguang Spaceship

His spaceship had been wounded.

Fang Kuo-chun had followed his procedures meticulously. He'd waited in the parking orbit during orbital darkness, and on time, slightly before the moment of sunrise, he'd fired the thrusters to maneuver closer, towards docking. He'd been intensely focused, watching the orbiting laboratory getting bigger in the reflected periscope image. The visual ranging system of scaled circles that they'd devised at the Institute of Space Medico-Engineering in Peking had worked well.

And yet, when he was still 100 meters away, there had been a collision. His ship had reacted well to the unexpected violence, going into free drift and shutting off all thrusters, ringing multiple alarms to get his attention. He had opened the periscope lens to maximum field of view and spotted the edge of Skylab still in the upper-right corner. He'd followed the emergency abort procedure, reengaging thrusters to maneuver and ensure safe clearance. The prescribed plan was to back away, reestablish visual contact and then attempt another approach and docking.

But what did I hit? Fang wondered. Was there unexpected debris *orbiting close to Skylab? Maybe a solar panel or radiator that came loose?* He glanced at the Earth globe display on his control panel. His next communications period with Peking was still many hours away, though he would have a brief linkup via the Atlantic relay ship in 45 minutes.

He needed to make several key decisions before then.

What damage did I incur?

One of the reasons that Chairman Mao and Director Tsien had picked Fang as China's first astronaut was that, 10 years earlier, he had collided with an American AQM-34 intelligence-gathering drone while flying in cloud, knocking it out of the sky. The collision had damaged his J-5 fighter, but he had stayed calm, kept control and landed safely, gaining the rare honor of a merit citation, first class.

And now, calmly, he checked the Shuguang's pressure gauges for his reaction control and thermal systems tanks. He flipped back in the notebook strapped to his knee, compared readings and was relieved to see that everything was holding. The air pressure in the cabin hadn't dropped either, or he would have felt his ears popping.

He nodded. It was a tough ship, well built. He just needed to keep trusting it, maneuver clear, reacquire visual and set up for a second docking attempt. Hopefully he'd be able to spot what he had hit and avoid it this time.

Fang watched the clock on his instrument panel, using it to estimate the distance where he could safely turn his craft to once more point directly at Skylab. He knew they'd built some margin for added precaution into the procedures, and he decided to shave a few minutes off. The last thing he wanted was to run out of daylight—the next sunset was in 35 minutes—or fuel reserves before he got docked.

It would be shameful, a mission failure. He wouldn't accept that. He'd been a military man since he'd joined the People's Liberation Army at 15 years old, and he'd lived his life with purpose. The chairman himself had handpicked him for this historic first spaceflight.

Fang was going to succeed.

Now, he decided, and he moved his rotational hand controller to turn the Shuguang ship. He'd been using the periscope to orient with the Earth's horizon, but now he leaned forward and twisted the knob to turn the prism that would allow him to see out the front of his ship again. He was gratified to see the brightness of Skylab pivot into view. Fang didn't see any debris he might hit this time. *Maybe I knocked it out of the way.* He manually pointed his ship to hold the target in the center, adjusted the lens to a more magnified setting and pushed on the translational hand controller to recommence approach. He turned his checklist back to the approach and docking page and began filling in the table to once again calculate distance and speed.

Glancing again at the image in his periscope, he realized something was different. Fang frowned and leaned close. He found himself squinting hard to force himself to accept what he was seeing.

Where previously there had been a waiting docking port and a small visual target, now he was looking at a dark circle surrounded by a larger silver circle. His flight path was still slightly off-center, and as a result he could see a curved length of silver beyond the concentric circles.

Fang was looking at the gray-black engine bell and silver aluminum body of a spaceship, newly docked to Skylab.

He shook his head to try to clear it. *How can this be?* he wondered. Doggedly he kept following the approach procedure, moving closer to Skylab as his mind raced. *That must be what I hit!*

He checked the clock. Still 30 minutes until radio contact with the relay and tracking ship. But they couldn't guarantee him real-time communications with the decision-makers on the other side of the world in Peking, so they wouldn't be much use.

Could it be the Soviets? The thought alarmed him. Could the Russians somehow have used Apollo-Soyuz as a decoy and usurped the Chinese plan by docking with Skylab first? He pictured the Soviet Soyuz spaceship and compared it to what he was seeing. No, he decided. The Russians used green external insulation, not silver, and the Soyuz was more bulbous and bug-like. Not smooth like the ship growing in size in front of him.

This is an American Apollo ship. He snorted. *How can that be?* They had publicly ended their Skylab program 17 months ago, abandoning this laboratory. The Apollo-Soyuz mission had been announced as the very last Apollo flight. Had that been a deception?

Fang knew his window to decide was only open for the next few minutes. Did he abort the rendezvous, maneuver clear and wait many hours for Peking's decision? By then, his fuel reserves would be very tight. He'd already used up most of his margin in making this second attempt.

Or should he press on? The Americans had built Skylab with two docking ports, and Fang and the team of mission designers had built procedures for him to use the second if the first docking attempt was unsuccessful.

Like all fighter pilots, Fang was comfortable making instant decisions based on whatever information was currently available, counting on his skill and the capabilities of his craft to emerge victorious.

He would continue. He pulled several times on the hand controller to slow his closing speed and then raised it several times to start his fly-around. He turned the pages in his checklist to the backup docking port procedure and picked it up at step one.

He found great pride and comfort in deciding a thing of such consequence, and in having the skills to back it up.

He had come this far and had a clear mission.

He would dock with Skylab. And then deal with whoever was on board.

49

North of Houston

Kaz felt the car slow, turn and then stop.

He was cold. And battered. He could feel the hot area of bruising on his face from the hard slap he'd received, and he ached from the awkward position in which he was tied. The stink of exhaust had filled the trunk, nauseating him, and Kaz had squirmed blindly on the floor until he'd found a small gap that allowed an inrush of fresh air. He'd breathed deeply to stay oxygenated. And ready.

They'd been on the highway long enough that Kaz had given up counting to try to gauge distance. Instead, he navigated by road type. He'd felt it when they eventually left the repetitive thumping over the highway's concrete slabs for smoother asphalt, with occasional stops and starts. Traffic lights, Kaz figured. Then later, after a turn, they drove onto a gravel road, the rattle of small stones loud against the wheel wells next to him.

The final part of the drive had been rough, jostling over a long, potholed gravel road of some sort. A private laneway north of Houston, he guessed, curling his trussed body as best he could to hold his head off the hard, bouncing floor of the trunk.

And now, stillness. After the low vibration of the motor stopped, he heard muffled male voices and doors opening, and felt the shifting weight of bodies climbing out of the car. He heard and felt three doors slam closed.

Three of them, not just two. Then, after a few seconds spent picturing men getting out of a car, he amended that. *At least three. Underestimating the enemy can be deadly.*

During the drive, he'd formed several plans, depending on what his abductors' actions might be. He guessed the drive had taken about an hour total, and he knew sunrise was at about 6:30, so it was still going to be fully dark for at least 90 minutes. That might even the playing field, with him blindfolded.

The sound of the key in the lock, the double creak of the trunk opening, then a wash of cool air. Through the cloth of the blindfold, Kaz saw a sudden brightening as they shone a flashlight on him, and then strong hands grabbed him around the chest and waist and lifted him up and over a broad, muscular shoulder again. No one spoke.

The man carried Kaz face down, head and torso hanging over his broad back, his thighs clamped firmly under one beefy arm. Still bound, Kaz decided there was no point in resisting. Even if he kicked himself free, he'd still be trussed. And there were at least three of them.

He could feel the man climbing, changing direction as if following a path. The pace slowed and the sound suddenly deadened as if they'd entered a building. Kaz hadn't heard a door opening. There was a short, low conversation in what Kaz assumed was Chinese, and he was suddenly pivoted off and dumped onto the ground.

He landed face up and felt a gritty, hard floor under him. The men were talking, and Kaz was able to pick out three distinct voices. Then he heard the unmistakable metallic clicking sound of a large folding knife opening.

Kaz tensed.

Hands rolled him onto his side, and he felt the knife tugging and sawing at the cord that bound his arms to the sides of his body. With the constriction released, Kaz flexed his fingers to get rid of the numbness as blood flowed back through his arms.

He hadn't seen any sustained light filtering through the blindfold to indicate that they'd turned room lights on. He guessed they were still working by flashlight.

Good, Kaz thought. *I've been passive long enough.*

He could feel the man's breath on his chest as he leaned to cut the cord around his right wrist. As soon as it was free, Kaz twisted hard and swung for the man's chin, leading with the heel of his hand. The unarmed combat training he'd done with the Navy had stressed that punching with a closed fist, while effective, often led to a damaged hand. The heel of the palm was tougher.

Solid contact. As he followed through, Kaz felt the man's teeth banging together and the jaw joint shifting sideways where it attached to the man's skull.

The man's weight fell away, and he swore loudly. Kaz didn't hear the knife hit the ground and braced himself for another retaliatory slap. Or worse.

Worth it, he thought. These people had shot at the president and bombed Mission Control.

But instead of retaliation, one of the other men started to laugh, jibing in Chinese, likely at the man he'd hit. He heard a growl, then a hand closed around Kaz's left wrist and yanked his arm out sideways, pulling hard at his shoulder socket. Someone then grabbed Kaz's right wrist, dragged him roughly onto his side and lashed both wrists together. Kaz could feel jerky motions through the rope as if the other end was being attached to something, and then he felt himself being drawn upwards, his hands over his head. Someone kept pulling until Kaz was vertical enough to get onto his tied knees to take some of the weight off his extended arms and shoulders.

After a rapid, muted conversation in Chinese, Kaz heard another laugh, then a slight rushing noise of air. A crashing blow landed on his exposed rib cage, and he felt the familiar searing pain of broken bones.

Coughing involuntarily, he arched, bracing for the inevitability of another kick.

But . . . nothing.

As his coughing and retching subsided, he gingerly took quick, shallow breaths against the agony. In the distance, he heard the car's engine start and then the crunch of its tires as it began moving. He yelled against the gag in his mouth, but the sound of the car was already starting to recede. With both arms, he yanked down hard against the suspending rope, but the pain from his broken ribs was excruciating, and whatever was holding him up didn't give.

Kaz hadn't expected to be abandoned. He was nearly naked, cold, trussed like a turkey, gagged and blindfolded, at least one rib was broken, and he didn't know where he was.

Time for a new plan.

FIRE DRAGON

50

Pearl River Delta, China, March 1279

It was Heng's secret weapon, and he was about to fire it.

The core was a thick bamboo tube as long as Heng was tall, though he wasn't very tall. He'd hollowed out several of the bamboo's internal dividers and carved one end open like the mouth of a dragon. Next, he'd securely lashed four smaller tubes to the sides with layers of fine cord, tightly knotted and daubed with fish glue, angling them back and down like stiff legs. Then he'd partially filled all five tubes—the big central one and the four canted legs—with a powder that he'd mixed himself.

A powder of three colors: black, yellow and white.

The gray-black charcoal was common enough, used in medicines, paint and ink. Vendors took the densest pieces from the embers of fires that burned everywhere across China and pounded them into dust.

Rough yellow crystals of sulfur, which had been dug out of the rock in Hanzhong for a thousand years, were always in demand for their ability to fight skin diseases and malnutrition. The alchemists called the crystals brimstone, and ground them into a sparkling, pale sun-colored sand.

But the main ingredient was snow-white saltpeter. Potassium nitrate, mined in the soil of caves in western Szechuan. The ancient name was solve-stone, as it readily dissolved with many things, and to be rendered pure, it needed to be boiled and dried.

Heng had carefully poured from his three jars of bone-dry colored powders, tapping the sides to get small, exact heaps on his weigh scale of 75 parts saltpeter, 15 parts sulfur and 10 parts charcoal. As he mixed them in a ceramic bowl with a wooden spoon and filled the bamboo tubes, he knew he was creating something of unprecedented power.

Huo yao. Fire chemical. An explosion just waiting for a spark.

But Heng's bamboo creation wasn't a typical firework. The true secret of his weapon lay in the mouth of the tubular dragon. Waxed fuses from the front two legs ran up into the corners of the carved mouth, to ensure a desired time delay.

Heng had privately tested and improved his design for months. After he'd fired a successful demonstration for a senior armaments officer in Kublai Khan's navy, he had received approval to trial the new weapon in battle. When asked what it was called, Heng had answered with a name that had occurred to him while he'd been carving the bamboo.

Fire Dragon.

It was now early dawn on the morning of war, the light just starting to illuminate the many ships and the surrounding low hills. Heng was exhausted. Working without sleep, he had built 10 Fire Dragons, now sitting on the central mid-deck of the Yuan warship, carefully covered with oiled cloth to keep the dew off.

The ship's captain had grudgingly given him permission to lash a launch mount to each of the low side rails, ahead of the heavy oarlocks. Heng had double-checked everything and now was squatting in the darkness with his back against the central mast, staying out of the way of the ship's crew and waiting for the order to fire. The armorer's firepot was secured centrally ahead of the mast, and Heng checked his breast pocket again for the pinewood sulfur matches that would carry the flame to his weapons.

A blaring trumpet sounded across the water, followed by the reverberating booms of repeated drumbeats. Ships' captains across the Yuan fleet yelled in response to the signal, and the oarsmen began pulling at full strength, accelerating the ships towards the line of Song ships silhouetted in the distance.

The captain shouted Heng's name, pointing at him and then at the launch mount on the port rail, making eye contact for emphasis. Heng nodded in reply and hurriedly peeled back the oiled cloth to reveal the first of his creations. He grunted as he cradled and lifted the tube—its size limited by what one man could carry—balancing it carefully as he moved across the deck.

The launch mount was simple: a three-foot-long section of bamboo narrow enough to fit between the downwards-protruding legs of the Fire Dragon and split lengthwise to cradle it. Heng had mounted the support on a post that could swivel, and after he gently placed the Fire Dragon in its cradle, he turned it to face forward along the curve of the ship's hull, directly aimed at a Song ship.

Heng hurried to the firepot, pulled a long match up out of his chest pocket, stuck it through a hole into the pot's embers and lit it. He shielded the small pitch and sulfur flame with his hand as he raced back to his weapon. He faced the captain, sneaking glances forward to judge distance. From testing, he knew he needed to be inside three li—each li the length of a village—to reach the target.

No other weapon in the world could reach that far with any accuracy. Arrows were limited by the strength of the bow and archer, and the heavy trebuchet catapults were only accurate enough to lob their ceramic bombs at nearby forts and buildings, not distant moving ships.

Heng peered forward in the predawn light, gauging that they were about four li away from the nearest enemy ship. The oarsmen were pulling hard, keeping pace with the wave of Yuan ships surging forward in a wide line. The captain was bawling orders for the archers to be ready, and then he paused, looked directly at Heng, raised his arm and chopped it down.

Heng gave an exaggerated nod, trying to look confident. He pivoted the mount directly towards the dark shape of a distant ship, muttered a short prayer and, with his hand trembling, brought the still-flaming match to the tar-soaked fuse at the back of the weapon.

It caught immediately, and the flame spread to its destinations in four lines along the sides of the Fire Dragon, leading to a central fuse, which simultaneously lit the four legs and main tube, all packed with huo yao fire chemical.

With more of a whoosh than a bang, the four legs thrust upwards and forward to support the weight, while the fifth and biggest tube blasted a focused, burning torch of central thrust. In a blaze of sparks, the Fire Dragon was suddenly gone from its bamboo cradle and racing level across the water.

Through his many failures, Heng had learned how important balance was, and he had glued and lashed an iron weight onto each weapon to keep it from climbing or descending while in flight. To help it fly straight, he'd mimicked the fletching of arrows and the tail feathers of birds and fitted his weapon with a three-piece wooden tail.

The captain's eyes followed the trailing sparks as the odd device raced away from his ship, then stole a glance at Heng. The small man's eyes were on his creation, his lips moving as if he was mumbling a prayer.

The captain spat in disgust. It was a time for strength, not favors from gods. He turned back to his trusted oarsmen and archers and roared encouragement, urging them onward to battle.

But Heng wasn't praying. He was rhythmically counting the time since ignition, breath by breath. He knew that there was about 30 breaths' worth of powder in each tube, and as he reached 28 shi, he leaned forward, trying to will his invention into action. Like the fireworks that had inspired it, the Fire Dragon had a delayed surprise, a dormant component waiting for the right moment.

As the fire burned to the end of the front legs, it reached another set of fuses, setting the small flammable cords alight. These fuses burned quickly up the sides of the main tube to the weapon's carved bamboo mouth, then turned the hard corner and disappeared into its maw.

This was the secret of the Fire Dragon. When the fuses reached their destination, they set off the black powder packed into the base of a bundle of rocket arrows. In an instant, a flock of iron-tipped arrows burst forth from the dragon's mouth, accelerating at the unsuspecting Song ship and its crew, spreading out as they flew.

It was as if 30 archers had suddenly appeared at point-blank range and all fired together. The lower arrows in the formation hit the sides of the ship, from the waterline up to the rail. But most struck at deck height, matching the level they'd been launched from. This unexpected rain of destruction slammed into the crew, who were standing on deck, staring at the enemy ships in the distance, believing they were still beyond normal firing range.

Heng was jubilant. *Fire Dragon works!* He looked at the captain for affirmation, but the man had missed the second flash of light.

Obeying his own instincts, Heng ran across the deck to grab another rocket. He hastily mounted it onto the launch cradle, lit another long match, turned the mount towards a ship of appropriate distance and ignited the fuse. As soon as that Fire Dragon raced out across the water, he fired another one. These were standoff weapons, no use once they got too close to the enemy; he had seven more chances to wreak early havoc and help win the battle.

By the time the last Fire Dragon had flown and Heng slumped exhausted against the mast, the captain had caught on to the damage the inventor's new weapon had inflicted. The Fire Dragons had helped turn the tide of battle. Damaged Song ships were burning, being boarded or sinking, with only a few being rowed away at maximum speed to fight another day. And already the captain was thinking of the next battle. Perhaps the little man could modify the weapon so that the arrows not only struck down the enemy but carried fire to wreak extra havoc—a tactical advantage to help win the war with less risk to his men. A technology to perfect and jealously protect.

A single weapon performing like two waves of archers, magically accelerating arrows to their impossibly distant target.

A two-stage rocket.

51

Jiuquan Launch Site, Northern China, July 18, 1975

It looks like a beached whale, the missile engineer thought, not for the first time. *A great white whale.* He glanced around at the surrounding brown hills and allowed himself a small smile. *Not many whales out here.*

His name was Song Chang, but Chang was so commonplace that everyone just called him by his family name, Song. He didn't really care. In fact, as a senior engineer, he liked the simplicity. To his team, he was Song, a man to be listened to and respected.

But the task Song had been given, his orders coming from the very highest level, was anything but simple.

He walked along the length of the heavy, multi-wheeled truck, looking up at the long white missile nestled in its dark-green metal cradle. It was nearly 30 meters from tip to base, with flush black fins and four squatty engine bells at one end and a pointy black cone at the other.

The business end.

The missile was called Dong Feng, which meant East Wind. It was China's first intercontinental ballistic missile, and this model was a modified Dong Feng 4. After several early failures, version four had been successfully launched more than five years ago.

It was a giant leap forward for China—technology on a par with the best in the world. Now they were able to attack potential enemies as far away as Moscow and Guam, providing the deterrent security of mutual destruction.

Song loved that he was a vital part of it.

The massive carrier was parked next to the mouth of a cave laboriously carved into the bedrock of the Jiuquan Launch Site. Not only was storing and loading the missile's corrosive fuels simpler and safer inside the protection of a cave, but their operations were secure from the prying eyes of the Soviet and American spy satellites that regularly passed overhead.

Song had spent the past several hours overseeing the fueling of this Dong Feng 4. The missile was built in two sections: the big, lower first stage to push it up through the air, and the smaller second stage, attached to the conical black tip, to accelerate the missile to its final speed.

And target.

The fuels were truly nasty and demanded respect. Song and his team had pumped 65 tonnes of nitric acid and hydrazine into the missile's smooth metal tanks. Both were extremely toxic and corrosive on their own, and immensely explosive and powerful when mixed together. They were using a specific type of hydrazine called UDMH, unsymmetrical dimethylhydrazine, because it was stable at normal temperatures and, as a result, could be stored for a long time. The colorless nitric acid kept well too, though it would chemically burn any skin it accidentally touched. They kept emergency tanks of water in the cave and on the truck, with hoses handy to rapidly flush any spillage.

Song made a joke of the danger with his team of men. To get high, he told them, rockets drink rocket fuel and men drink baijiu, so don't confuse the two. And he made sure the men had plenty of baijiu liquor here at the remote launch site for their time off.

Now that the carrier had hauled the missile out of the low cave, they needed to cover it with the full-length desert-camouflage tarpaulin. He watched as an oversized forklift lifted the rolled tarp up and over the prone missile's base, and supervised as his men methodically unrolled it along the full length, tying it securely into place.

They would be a convoy of three trucks. Handpicked personnel, kept to a minimum, and so far kept in the dark. Song had chosen his most trusted and competent men to travel with him, but he was the only one fully briefed on what they were about to do. He'd ensured that the other two trucks were already loaded with all the gear they needed, and he glanced across at them sitting in the sunshine, set to go. Heavy-duty off-road SX250 transports built at the Shaanxi Automobile Manufacturing Plant, with rugged square frames and tall, high-traction tires. The best technology the new might of China had created, entrusted to him.

Standing now beside the front of the missile, where the black cone enclosed the most fragile and mission-critical components, Song watched with satisfaction as his men carefully finished with the heavy tarpaulin. When they were done, he made a point of checking the heavy knots, then complimented them on their work.

He glanced up at the endless blue of the Gobi Desert sky. With the missile well camouflaged, they'd be three trucks traveling the long, straight roads, raising a small cloud of trailing dust. Unremarkable, like heavy transport vehicles everywhere.

He checked his wristwatch. His men had been efficient, which meant he was several minutes ahead of schedule. *Good*, he thought. There were bound to be problems on the road, and every extra minute saved was an added margin for success.

Song glanced around one last time. The men had all clambered down off the missile transport and were waiting near him. He smiled, thanked them loudly and then called the names of the individuals who would be traveling with him. He raised one hand in the air and made a circling motion, and then pointed at the trucks. The universal signal to gather together and go.

Song walked to the front of the missile carrier, swung himself up into the cab and started the big, rumbling diesel engine. They had a long way to travel, and he was taking the first shift driving.

As a leader should.

52

North of Houston

First things first, Kaz thought. *Get the blindfold off.*

He only had one eye, but he needed it to see what he was up against. It would be dawn soon.

Kaz had heard the car drive off but suspected they'd left one of the men behind to stand guard. As he rubbed the side of his face against his raised bicep to work the cloth up off his good eye, he listened intently for the sound of nearby movement or breathing.

Nothing. *Maybe he's gone outside to take a leak*, Kaz guessed. *Or he's just being quiet, watching me in the half-light.*

But no one came to stop him, so Kaz kept working. Eventually he manipulated the blindfold up and over his eyebrow ridge, and it slipped up off his head and fell to the ground.

The pressure of it rolling over his eyeball had made him see stars, and Kaz blinked repeatedly to clear his vision, then opened both eyes wide and looked around.

It was still dark. *Good*, Kaz thought. *If I can't see him, he can't see me.*

Kaz tentatively pulled with both arms to lift his full body weight, but the tension on his damaged ribs made him gasp in agony, automatically flinching and twisting to the side.

He grimaced and caught his breath. *Am I about to puncture a lung? Or are the ribs just broken in place?* Visualizing that part of his skeleton, he slowly filled his lungs as far as they would go and then held his breath, mentally probing the stabbing sensation below his heart. He twisted and flexed, the pain barely tolerable. *But steady,* he thought, with some relief. *Likely just cracked, maybe with some tearing of the muscles that hold them together.*

Painful as hell. But livable.

Kaz twisted slowly from his suspended wrists to look around the room, leaning sideways on his knees as he pivoted. There was an angular change in the darkness ahead of him to the left. *The door. And it's open.* A barely perceptible lightening outside as the first tendrils of dawn lit the upper atmosphere.

Soon he'd be able to see. And his captor would be able to see him.

Time to think quickly.

Why did they kidnap me? It was the most important question. *Are they planning to interrogate me?* Kaz had extensive knowledge of how Mission Control worked, but so did lots of other people. And very little of that knowledge was classified. *So what do I know that is worth them doing this?* Project Seesaw, he realized. But how had the Chinese heard about a top-secret program like that when he had just learned of it himself?

Kaz listened intently, hearing nothing. It was still so dark inside he couldn't make out any details of the room. He twisted his trussed body and got some weight onto his knees, easing the fire in his shoulders and ribs.

He reviewed the recent events: the shooting, the bombing and the detection of a Chinese spacecraft near Skylab. He felt sure that his abductors had been speaking Chinese. A thought popped into his head, and he blinked several times, initially rejecting it and then considering it.

Shit, Kaz thought. *That might be why.*

He glanced up and saw that enough light had crept into the room that he could dimly make out what was above his head.

Time for action.

The white cord around his wrists was looped up and over what looked like a square structural beam. Above it, the structure was open to the roof. *What is this building?*

Out the doorway, he could now make out vague shapes, but no straight lines indicating another building. He blinked hard and opened his eye wide to let in as much light as possible. He'd sensed that the man had carried him up a small hill. In the distance, he saw what looked like a stone wall with vegetation on top, and maybe trees behind it.

Kaz considered. *A quarry?* He looked around inside the brightening room. *That would make this some sort of utility building. Maybe a pump house? Don't quarries flood?*

The lack of a door was a sign that it had been abandoned, and the overgrowth outside meant the quarry was probably defunct. *A good place to come if you don't want to be noticed—or even to set off an occasional explosion and not raise any eyebrows.*

He looked back up at the beam and then around him. The hulking shapes of jumbled machinery loomed. The floor was rough-poured concrete and the walls were of stone, irregularly laid. *Constructed from the loose rocks of the early blasting.*

Kaz reevaluated. *Likely to keep tools and equipment out of the rain.* He looked back up. *Old enough to be unstable?*

The dawn was coming faster now, and Kaz once again listened hard and looked carefully for any sign of a captor. His only chance at escape was to somehow get free and surprise whoever was standing guard. He took a deep breath and pulled with both arms to lift himself off his knees and onto his bound feet.

He couldn't believe how much it hurt. *They're just fucking ribs! Why so many nerve endings?* He grimaced and kept pulling until his feet were under him. Cautiously, painfully, he stood.

Being able to lower his arms decreased the torsion on his rib cage and instantly reduced the pain. He gasped a few times as it subsided, balancing carefully. With his ankles and knees bound together, he teetered, so he kept a slight tension on the rope to keep from falling.

But he was standing. *Progress.*

He could now clearly see a jumble of sand and stones outside, with sickly-looking weeds and a curved rock wall in the distance.

No sign of anyone else.

He tipped his head back and studied the dark beam above him. A couple of feet away from where the cord was looped over it, he spotted a rusty nail that someone had hammered into the wood long ago. Kaz took half a breath and held it to stabilize his rib cage as best he could, then raised his arms to get some slack in the rope. He got the cord between his hands, then pivoted his bound wrists in a jerking motion and found he could inch the rope along the beam towards the nail. When the rope was about halfway to the nail, he took a fresh half-breath, pulled with his arms to support his weight and hopped forward, fighting for his balance. The searing pain made him groan, and he held his new position to see if anyone had heard him.

Still quiet. *Did they leave me here alone?* Smarter to assume someone was there, beyond the door. They could just be napping after a long night.

Kaz steeled himself and worked the rope closer to the nail. This time, as he hopped forward, he fought to stay silent. He paused to let the pain subside, and with one concerted final tug, he slid the cord against the nail. He took his weight on his arms again, clenched his teeth and swung himself to stand beneath the nail.

Now, how to use it? It was hand-forged, the top oblong and flattened where it had been pounded in. But the shaft was still four-sided and solid, with sharp-looking edges running its full length. He straightened to get as much slack as possible, spread his palms as wide as he could with his wrists still tied together, and stretched a section of rope between them. Leaning forward, he forced the rope hard against the nail and started to saw it against the sharp edge.

The cord was thin, white and braided, and looked new; Kaz figured his captors had bought it especially for this purpose. *But they intended to tie me up, not suspend me*, he guessed, thankful it wasn't too thick to saw through.

The pain from his ribs was worse when he pulled with his left arm, but Kaz fought the agony to keep the sawing motion firm and even against the nail. If the cord slipped, it would shift to a new section and he'd lose ground. By focusing hard on what he was doing, he could ignore the agony, at least somewhat, and he was soon rewarded as the rope began to fray. He pushed forward with his left shoulder to apply even more torque, but the pain made him gasp and he stopped, breathing heavily, standing as still as possible to keep the rope in place.

He took another half-breath, leaned into it and twisted the rope back and forth. He found himself imagining that he was underwater, free diving, feeling the familiar increasing burn in his lungs as his body used up its oxygen and enlisting his self-control to override the natural panic and urge to take a breath. He'd used the same technique flying jets when the oxygen bottle feeding his mask was getting low and he needed to wring the most time out of each breath. As the telltale creeping grayout and flashes of light told him he was truly out of air, he stopped, held his position, refilled his lungs to clear his vision and started sawing again.

Stupid way to cut a rope, he thought, and suddenly he was through, the white cord giving way. Overbalanced, he fell forward, turning just before he hit the floor to take the impact on his right shoulder, trying to protect his ribs. But the pain shot through him more sharply then ever, and he couldn't help but yell "Fuck!"

Kaz lay on the hard floor, dazed. *How loud did I just shout?* He waited to hear the rush of heavy feet as someone came to investigate.

But . . . nothing. Just him, lying on a concrete floor in nothing but his underwear, trussed at ankles, knees and wrists, breathing in the dust he'd kicked up.

He smiled wryly through the grimace.

Time for part two of the great escape.

In the early-morning light, Kaz spotted a wooden workbench along the wall with a heavy vise bolted to one corner. He inchwormed his way across the gritty floor, rolled onto his knees and reached his bound wrists up and over the open jaws of the vise. The serrated steel provided a much more efficient cutting surface, and he cut the cord with just a few passes back and forth, using his body weight like a pendulum. His hands were numb, but they were finally free.

Kaz shook them out, then grabbed the vice and pulled himself to his feet, exhaling sharply at the jab from his ribs. Benches meant tools, and he still had ropes to cut.

And he needed a weapon.

Whoever had abandoned the place had taken all the good stuff with them. Kaz looked for familiar shapes among the workbench's scattered jumble of rusted metal, heavy with dust, and spotted one. As the feeling returned to his arms and hands, he reached for the knurled handle of a long screwdriver. The slot tip had broken, creating a jagged end.

He also found a broken hacksaw blade. Transferring both weapons into his left hand, Kaz lowered himself with his right until he was sitting, his knees bent in front of him. Using the saw blade, he quickly cut through the cord around his knees and then leaned, sucking up the pain, to free his ankles. Next, he carefully slid the blade under the ropes on his wrists and cut through them. Using the vise again as a crutch, Kaz hauled himself to his feet, clutching the broken screwdriver.

Free and slightly dangerous, he thought.

And cold.

Another look around the room revealed a length of cloth hanging from a nail against the far wall. His legs and feet still coming painfully to life, Kaz hobbled over to grab it. He lifted it off the nail and shook it, happy to find it was an old set of blue cotton coveralls. He grunted as he twisted his legs and arms into them, then worked the stiff, stained cloth up and over his shoulders. After a few tries, the heavy front zipper worked.

Boots would be too much to hope for, he thought, scanning the floor and the low open cupboards and seeing none. He did another search along the workbench and found a hammer with one claw broken off. *Better than a skinny saw blade.*

Dressed and clutching his two makeshift weapons, barefoot, Kaz moved painfully towards the morning light shining through the open door.

53

Northern China

Song squinted ahead through his transport truck's thick windshield. His headlights revealed little, just a dead-straight gravel road descending slightly through the monotonous regularity of rectangular farm fields. Spread on the broad bench seat next to him was a large topographic map, folded to show him this part of China—the country's very northern edge, in the broad river valley of the Irtysh, which carried melted glacier waters down from the Altai Mountains.

Waters that flowed from China into the Soviet Union.

A railroad and a main highway ran parallel to each other directly to the border, but Song and his small convoy of three trucks had turned off onto a side road several kilometers back, as planned. They had driven due north for an hour, and then west again, and were now moving through the night across the stepped fields of the Yibawu Tuanchang agricultural community.

Song had been carefully briefed using high-resolution aerial photographs of the region. He had a clear picture in his head of what to expect, and he and his navigator were both staring hard ahead, occasionally double-checking the map.

They were looking for a little-used one-lane bridge. The local farmers had tilled the soil on both sides of a small tributary of the Irtysh River for thousands of years, and they needed a way for their animals and machinery to cross. They didn't think much about the distant boundary concerns of Peking or Moscow. What mattered to them was meeting their agricultural production quotas. But the tributary whose banks they farmed defined the Chinese border with Soviet Kazakhstan, a border with the combined USSR that was 7,600 kilometers long.

A border that was hard to monitor everywhere.

Song glanced up at the clear night sky, thankful for the dry July weather. The road under his wheels was narrow, crowned and thinly graveled. It would have been more challenging if it was wet.

They moved slowly but steadily, easing down the shallow grade so the big diesel engines would make as little noise as possible. He had his headlights on low beams and had ordered the two transports behind him to turn their lights off completely until they were crossing the bridge. It was easy enough for them to follow his taillights, and it was good tactics to make it more difficult for an observer to count trucks.

Song's headlights bounced up and down as he crossed a culvert, and at last, in the distance, he caught a glimpse of the bridge rising slightly above the flatness of the fields.

Weight was his big concern. Even though its heft was distributed across the multiple wheels of his long truck, the missile was heavy. When he'd asked his higher-ups, he'd been assured that the bridge was deceptively sturdy and regularly stood the test of grain wagons and trucks. He'd pressed the point, and they'd sent a lone driver on the long trek to get photographs, which revealed that the bridge was old, heavy and stone; it had looked solid.

But amongst all the worries of his mission, this was the one that had been weighing most on Song's mind. He felt his heart beating faster as he approached.

He'd decided the best plan was to cross quickly. One truck at a time, of course. The photos had shown that the approach was flat, and that the bridge had only a slight rise in the center of its span. Just like he'd briefed, he reached out and turned on his flashers for 10 seconds to warn the other trucks that it was time.

Yet Song couldn't help the cartoonish image in his head of the bridge crumbling away beneath him, stone by stone, as he sped across, and on the approach he had to resist the urge to push the accelerator pedal to the floor. Instead, he checked his speed, cranked his window open so he could lean out for a side look if needed, and concentrated on steering exactly down the center of the narrow bridge, keeping a steady distance from the low stone wall next to him on the driver's side.

The sound of the wheels changed as they came off the gravel road onto the bridge's approach, shifting from a growling chatter to a smoother whine, and then to a lower rumble as the truck drove onto the bridge itself. Song felt his butt cheeks clenching involuntarily, and his knuckles went white as he gripped the wheel, imagining the sudden collapse that would send his irreplaceable cargo into the river, its volatile fuels mixing and exploding as they spread across crumbling stone and water.

He felt slightly lighter in his seat as the transport crested the rise at the bridge's center, and he concentrated on steering exactly down the center towards the far side. Once he was safely across, he knew there was only a short distance before the turn onto the road that paralleled the river. He kept his left foot poised over the clutch, and as the cab passed the end of the bridge's stone wall, he moved his right foot off the accelerator and onto the brake, steadily applying force, looking ahead for the T-junction. It came up sooner than he expected, and he braked hard, all the tires digging in to slow his momentum. Not sure he would make it, he wrestled with the wheel as he slowed and turned the massive machine. The surface had changed from stone back to gravel, and he could feel the front wheels sliding towards the perpendicular ditch at the far side of the crossroad. He leaned even harder on the wheel, demanding that the truck do his bidding, and at last it responded, digging in, turning and shuddering to a halt just as his right front tire was about to leave the graveled edge.

Song gasped, realizing he'd been hyperventilating, and shook his head as he deliberately unclenched his hands from the wheel. The navigator started laughing, bending to retrieve the map from where it had slid onto the floor of the cab.

"Nice driving, Song laoban!"

"Laoban" meant "boss," a term of respect, and the man meant it.

A broad smile of undeniable relief spread across Song's face as he shifted the truck into the lowest gear and moved forward, out of the way of the two smaller trucks behind him. He hit his flashers again for 10 seconds to let them know when he was clear, and turned to look out his open window as the first and then the second truck flicked on their low beams, crossed the bridge, extinguished their lights and turned to join him.

They were across! A wave of energy surged through him as Song accelerated and shifted up through the gears. He took a deep breath and let it out slowly, refocusing on the tasks that lay ahead. His navigator had turned on his red-filtered flashlight and was double-checking the map, readying for the next turns—first to the right, to head west, and then another right. Following the side roads, staying out of sight.

Traveling north, out of Soviet Kazakhstan and into the motherland of Russia itself.

54

Mission Control

"Okay, everyone, I need your attention. Give me a green when you're listening." Chris Kraft's voice was deadly serious in the headsets of every console operator in Mission Control.

Side conversations ceased as each man reached to push a square plastic button on the lower part of their console under a label reading Status Report. They could choose red, amber or green. In a moment, the rectangular grid at the top of Flight Director Kraft's console rapidly populated with green lights. As soon as he saw that everyone had responded, he spoke.

"The outgoing flight director and I have just been on the horn with our friends at NORAD, and we have a significant new development for the Apollo-Soyuz mission." Kraft turned his head and looked briefly at Crip, at the CAPCOM console. They held eye contact for a moment, recognizing the significance of what Kraft was about to say. "Two days ago, the Chinese secretly launched a spaceship from north central China, and we think it may be manned. This is a brand-new capability for them. We're unsure of the ship design, and more importantly, we don't know their purpose. But recent events are making it clearer."

He glanced at the front screens. Still several minutes until the next communications with the Apollo crew.

"NORAD's been tracking the Chinese ship and found that they launched it into a coplanar orbit with Skylab. With the last tracking update, they were surprised to find that the Chinese ship was maneuvering aggressively and rapidly to intercept Skylab. It's now crystal clear that that is the purpose of China's first manned spaceflight—to approach Skylab. They may even be intending to dock. We don't know. The State Department is in urgent contact with the Chinese, but so far, no word."

Kraft paused, seeing expressions of amazement and concern on the faces turned towards him. *Now for the real kicker.*

"Final NORAD trajectory data showed the Chinese spacecraft in close proximity to Skylab unexpectedly early, just as the Apollo crew was commencing approach to docking. We'll know better once we talk to Deke in a few minutes, but it looks possible that the reason we lost high-gain communications may be due to some sort of contact between the two ships."

He let that sink in, understanding the alarming implications the news had for several of the console operators. Time to wrap it up and give clear direction.

"I want everyone's back rooms to be thinking about potential damage from a collision, and about immediate actions to recommend when we regain communications in"—he glanced at the timer on the wall at the front of the room—"seven minutes. We need to look at the Skylab data too, to see if Apollo got docked. And I want every console to consider the strong possibility that the Chinese ship may be attempting to dock as well. But for now, our top priorities are the health and safety of our Apollo crew, their ship and getting our revised mission objectives complete ASAP: dock to Skylab, transfer the bodies, undock and get Deke and the two cosmonauts safely back home to Earth."

He looked around and saw that most of the console officers were already talking to their back rooms.

"Any urgent questions?" he asked.

Silence on the comm loops. All of these people had worked Apollo Moon landings and Skylab flights and were highly experienced. Time to let them work their technical specialties at speed.

"Right, let's be ready when we reacquire comms."

Kraft and the others had just completed a handover from their counterparts on the night shift, and he hadn't expected Crip to still be on console as CAPCOM.

"Where's Kaz?"

Crip shrugged. "Don't know, FLIGHT. It's unlike him, but maybe he slept in." He frowned. "Or maybe that old car of his had a flat on the way in. I've called the Astronaut Office to go check on Kaz and to get me a sub as soon as they can. But I'm fine to cover for a while."

Chris nodded. Ordinary shit happened, even on critical flight days.

He knew Crip was ex-Navy and had supported all three Skylab missions, and had even done a 56-day simulation in a hypobaric chamber with two other astronauts to develop Skylab procedures and equipment. But Kraft wasn't certain if Crip had been in-briefed on Seesaw, and hesitated to mention it now.

Crip beat him to it. "We need a plan to keep the cosmonauts away from the more sensitive equipment on Skylab." He accentuated the word "sensitive" to make his point clear, glancing around the room. Since Kraft was the space center's director, Crip had assumed he knew of Seesaw. "And now, with the possibility of Chinese astronauts being thrown into the mix, it's even more urgent."

Kraft nodded. "Kaz and I already had a private conference with Deke to get him up to speed, but that was before this accelerated Chinese presence." He'd been thinking about it. "I've asked the Skylab Program Office for a list of everyone who worked the classified payload, and for a straw man ops plan for how to proceed once docked. We'll be having a side meeting as soon as they're ready. But for now, assuming we reacquire comms shortly, I need you to keep that in mind when you're talking to Deke."

Crip chewed the inside of his lower lip, thinking. "You think it's possible that's why the Chinese are there?"

Kraft held Crip's gaze for several seconds, then said, "We have to accept that it's not just possible, but probable. Why else would they have given themselves such a complex mission profile for their first flight? What else would be worth it?" He looked around the room and dropped his voice so just Crip could hear. "I'm also thinking that they must have had significant inside information on details of our operations and hardware."

He frowned. "It may come to direct physical conflict on board Skylab. You ready to help Deke with that?"

Crip looked at the timer. Ninety seconds until acquisition of signal for communications. He said, "Deke fought in Africa and Italy during World War II, as well as in air combat over Japan. He did stall-spin at Edwards in that bitch of a plane, the F-105. And he sure as hell fought NASA and the doctors to get assigned to Apollo-Soyuz."

Crip gave a small, deliberate nod. "We can count on Deke."

55

Chairman Mao's Residence

George H.W. Bush was nervous.

He'd been in Peking for nine months, as the new chief of the US Liaison Office, and he and his wife, Barbara, usually bicycled everywhere. He'd found it gave them a rare chance to meet regular Chinese citizens. But an urgent request for a private meeting with Chairman Mao was highly unusual, and so he'd asked the Liaison Office driver to take him across Peking's downtown to Mao's residence, just west of the Forbidden City. It had turned out to be an unusually hot July day, peaking at 95 degrees, and Bush was glad for the big American car's air conditioning.

Mao's staff had instructed Bush to come alone, without an interpreter, which added to his nerves. He climbed out of the back of the dark-blue Plymouth, walked briefly in the direct sunlight and stifling humidity across a courtyard to join an escort waiting for him in the shade, and then followed the man into the relative cool of Chairman Mao's home. His escort led him up some stairs and down a short corridor, and then silently showed him into a darkened inner room, the air thick with cigarette smoke.

This was Bush's first private audience with Charman Mao. He'd chosen his best suit, a dark-blue single-breasted with wide pinstripes, and a cross-hatched tie over a crisp white shirt. The United States hadn't had an embassy in mainland China since Mao had thrown them out in 1949, but thawing relations since Nixon's visit in 1972 had allowed the new Liaison Office to open. As its chief, Bush was the ambassador to the People's Republic of China in all but name, and he wanted to dress the part.

And now he was sweating.

There were two men in the shadowed room. Mao, unmistakable, was seated in a high-backed chair at the center, and remained where he was as a small, lean, oval-faced man with a receding hairline stood to greet Bush. The man tipped his head back to look up at the much taller American and said, in almost unaccented English, "Ambassador, the chairman has asked me to attend our meeting today in a technical function, and also to act as interpreter." The small man spoke quickly and decisively, as if waiting for Bush to keep up.

I know this guy, Bush thought. He scanned his memory, reviewing the endless in-briefings he'd had on senior Chinese personnel when he'd taken over the Liaison job. *He was a prof at Cal Tech!* But no name popped into his head.

The man watched Bush think, as if evaluating him, and then said, "My name is Tsien Hsue-shen. I am Director of the Fifth Academy." Seeing no recognition in Bush's facial expression, he explained further: "And Director of the National Defense Science Committee on Space."

This is the guy we deported! George suddenly realized, sketchy details rushing back into his head. In the 1950s Bush had been preoccupied with running an oil company in Texas, but he had read about the case—a cautionary tale of American stupidity—when he'd gotten into politics in the early 1960s.

Bush glanced at Mao, who appeared to be sleeping, and then back at the expressionless Tsien. "It is an honor to meet you, Director Tsien." He decided to try standard Texan self-deprecation, and smiled wryly as he said, "I'm just the new guy they appointed to run the Liaison Office."

Tsien nodded, unsmilingly, and turned towards Mao. "May I present our revered leader, Chairman Mao Tse-tung."

No one was shaking hands, so George stayed where he was, bowed slightly and then tried out some of the rudimentary Mandarin he had been taught, speaking loudly in case Mao was hard of hearing. "Hen rongxìng neng jiandao ni." *It is an honor to meet you.* Bush knew his pronunciation was terrible, made even worse by his blend of New England and Texan accents. But it was worth a try.

Chairman Mao's eyes opened and he smiled lopsidedly, nodding in response, and then said something Bush didn't understand, his voice weak. He spoke from the right side of his mouth, and his left eye didn't open fully, as if that side was partially paralyzed. Bush had heard he'd had a stroke.

"The chairman says your Chinese is very good. He thanks you for coming on short notice and invites you to sit."

Bush was pretty sure that Mao hadn't said all that, but he was used to smart interpreters filling in the blanks. He took a seat to the chairman's right, on his good side. Tsien sat on the left, facing Bush. There was a small table in the center, with a jug of water and three glasses. And a partially full ashtray.

"It is a warm day. Would you like a drink, Mr. Bush?"

Bush could feel sweat on his forehead and an unwelcome trickle running down the center of his back. He envied the simple light cotton pants and open-necked shirts the other two men were wearing, and for the thousandth time in his life, silently cursed the American requirement to wear a suit and tie.

"Yes, that'd be great, thanks."

Tsien poured three glasses and carefully held one up for Mao, who shook his head no. Bush took the proffered glass with thanks and drank half of it at a gulp, wishing there were ice in it. Still holding his glass, he decided to follow protocol to open conversation at the right level and looked directly at Chairman Mao.

"I have spoken to President Ford and Secretary Kissinger this morning, and both of them specifically asked me to pass their greetings to you." Not entirely true, as there had been only an exchange of secure telexes, but it established who knew about the meeting.

Mao smiled again, then spoke, Tsien translating. "I have met Henry Kissinger many times and look forward to meeting President Ford at the first opportunity." Then the smile faded. "But what we have to tell you today is urgent and extremely sensitive." Mao winced as if in sudden pain, his eyes closed, and he suppressed a cough. He made a slight gesture with his good hand, and Tsien continued for him.

"The reason we wished to speak with you is because of some information that our intelligence services have recently uncovered. It concerns China and the Fifth Academy greatly, but we also realize that it may concern the United States of America even more. As the alliance and trust between our two great nations strengthen, we wanted to let your president know immediately."

Tsien spoke the words without emotion, his expression placid. *Odd duck*, Bush thought, followed by *Peking duck*, a brain blip he ignored. Any sharing of intelligence from China was extremely unusual. He couldn't think of anything to say, so he set his glass on the table, glanced at Mao and focused his full attention back on Tsien.

"We have solid intelligence that the Soviet Union has developed a mobile anti-satellite weapon, a missile, and that they are planning a test in the near future." Tsien paused, looking at Bush to make sure he fully understood the import of what he'd just said. Bush had been a combat pilot in World War II against the hated Japanese, but he wasn't sure that Bush had any space-related experience or insight. "We are unsure of specific location or date—just that it will launch in the east of the USSR, near China, and soon." He paused again, and then said, "We also do not know their target, but based on previous anti-satellite operations, we suspect it will be one of their defunct older satellites."

Holy shit, Bush thought, his mind racing. He knew the United States had detonated a nuclear weapon in Earth orbit during the early 1960s that had caused widespread satellite damage, and he had heard of a more recent classified program to launch a rocket from a high-flying

F-106 fighter aircraft that could target specific orbital satellites. But as far as he knew, what Tsien was describing was an all-new Soviet capability. *Why are they telling me this?* he wondered. *And what should I ask for? What would Washington need?*

"That is extremely interesting intelligence," he responded. "New Soviet missile technology that can target valuable satellites would be destabilizing for the world. Has your intelligence gathered any specifics on the mobile launch platform? And is the platform based on an existing missile? If so, we'd have some sense of the limits of its altitude and range."

Tsien glanced at Mao. Seeing no response, he turned back to Bush.

"We are sorry, but the answer to both your questions is no. Our intelligence is solid, but preliminary. And since, as you know, China now has domestically important satellite launch capability, this new Soviet threat is worrisome to us as well."

Mao coughed and made a small waving motion with his right hand, the arm supported by the chair's armrest. Both men waited for him to speak.

"Mr. Bush, please tell my friend Henry Kissinger about this threat, with the necessity for absolute secrecy as to the source of the information." He paused as Tsien translated, and then said, "He will give good counsel to President Ford as to what to do, just as Fifth Academy Chairman Tsien wisely counsels me."

Mao's good eye had only opened slightly as he spoke, and it closed again as he finished, his chin slumping into the folds of his neck.

Tsien looked away from Mao, whose breathing had become labored, and finished the translation. Then he stood, in a clear signal that the meeting was ending.

As he got to his feet, Bush said, "I will pass this information personally and immediately to Secretary Kissinger and President Ford. If they have urgent communiqués in reply, I will contact your office directly."

Tsien walked with Bush to the door, opened it and ensured that the escort conducted the tall American down the hallway towards his waiting car. Tsien re-entered the room, closed the door, and sat next to Mao.

He was used to being patient as he waited for the chairman's failing body to catch up to his still razor-sharp mind. After a minute, Mao's eyes opened. He glanced at Tsien and raised a finger to point at the table.

"Would you like water, or a cigarette?" Tsien asked. The doctor had strictly forbidden smoking, but it wasn't Tsien's decision to make.

A ghost of a smile softened Mao's face. "Water, for now."

Tsien picked up the glass he'd poured and carefully guided it into his chairman's wavering hand. He looked away as some dribbled out the left side of his mouth, and quickly retrieved the glass when Mao held it out.

Mao spoke, looking straight ahead, his voice slightly stronger. "That planted the seed deeply. The Americans will do as we expect."

He looked directly at Tsien. "Your plan is working well."

56

Situation Room, the White House

It was a smallish room, created out of necessity.

A completely secure island in the tumultuous sea of the White House, protected from eavesdropping, interruption and unwanted visitors. President Kennedy had demanded that it be built after the disaster of the Bay of Pigs invasion, and every president since had used it in times of national crisis.

In the center of the room was a square wooden table that could seat up to 10, surrounded by dark, wood-paneled walls. Thick, muffling carpet covered the floor, and three rows of fluorescent lights hung in a low ceiling made of cheap-looking sound-absorbing tiles. A black-and-white television was recessed high into the paneling on one side of the room, and heavy pale curtains covered a wall unit that housed a pull-down projection screen and a surface where large maps could be pinned. Above the curtains, a small, rectangular sign said No Smoking.

Everyone ignored it.

President Gerald Ford sat at the head of the table, his back to the curtains. His head was neatly bandaged, a long rectangle of pink-brown

Elastoplast stretching from above his right temple to behind his ear. To his right was Henry Kissinger, Secretary of State and National Security Advisor, sprawled back in his chair. To Ford's left sat James Schlesinger, Secretary of Defense, smoking his ever-present pipe. Ford had also asked the head of the CIA, William Colby, to attend, and he'd taken the seat next to Kissinger.

Four men of immense global power, hastily gathered to decide what the United States should do faced with this new, vital piece of intelligence.

Ford didn't like using the Situation Room. It reminded him too much of the satirical movie *Dr. Strangelove*. He always felt like he was in a comic opera when seated at the table; the whole room struck him as self-important. He much preferred conducting business from the Oval Office. That felt more legitimate—especially important to him since he'd never been elected president. He'd been handed the vice-presidency after Spiro Agnew resigned in a corruption scandal, and had inherited the presidency when Nixon left office in post-Watergate disgrace.

But they couldn't meet there because it had so many windows and doors, and the information that had been relayed from China by George Bush demanded the highest level of security. Ford turned first to Colby, the CIA man.

"Bill, do you think this Chinese intelligence is credible?"

Colby was gaunt, his hair slicked back above wire-rimmed round glasses, his mouth set in a perpetual frown. "Credible—hard to say. But possible, yes." He frowned more deeply; as the head of the CIA, he intensely disliked being surprised. "Hard to believe the Chinese uncovered something outside their own borders that we didn't already know about, but they've got a long history with the Russians." He ran his tongue across his front teeth like he'd eaten something sour and swallowed, his large Adam's apple bobbing. He nodded, then grudgingly admitted, "The Russians could have developed a mobile anti-satellite weapon. We've seen no indication of a new ASAT, but yes, it's possible."

Henry Kissinger stirred in his seat and interjected, his deep, authoritative voice raspy. "A new ASAT would very likely violate the Anti-Ballistic

Missile Treaty. But the Soviets might be weaseling on the edge of the agreement by modifying an existing missile. We'll need to see images of the hardware to decide."

Ford nodded. He didn't totally trust Kissinger, feeling that Nixon had given this man, born in Germany, too much power. But Kissinger had been key in negotiating the détente with the Soviets, as well as bringing about the warming of relations with China, and Ford made a point of listening carefully to him.

Across the table from Kissinger, James Schlesinger took his pipe out of his mouth and said, "Space warfare is for real, and a growing threat. The Soviets have had kamikaze satellites for over a decade that can maneuver close to ours and detonate in a hail of shrapnel, causing mutual destruction." Schlesinger had been the CIA director before Nixon appointed him to run Defense. "The ABM Treaty has stopped such orbital tests, but this new capability the Chinese have uncovered, if it's real, would be a game-changing technology for the Soviets." He clamped the pipe back between his teeth, took a long pull and spoke with his jaw clenched, exhaling white smoke. "A launch would very likely violate the treaty."

Kissinger, still leaning back, pivoted in his chair to look at Colby. "We need better intelligence. Do you have any people on the ground? Or can our reconnaissance assets find this mobile missile and photograph it?"

Colby was the fourth most important man in the room, and he knew it—he'd been appointed to head the CIA by his predecessor, Schlesinger, and was definitely not on a par with Kissinger or Ford. Defensively, he said, "I have asked our Moscow assets for corroboration, but they haven't had enough time to investigate and respond." He pushed his chair back, got up and walked around behind Ford, pulling the curtains back to reveal a large map of Asia. Ford shifted his chair beside Schlesinger's so he could see.

Colby pointed at the curving northern border of China. "George Bush was told that the test will be in the east of the USSR, somewhere near Chinese territory. The main part of the border is about fifty degrees north." He pointed to his right, where the mainland ended at the Sea of Japan. "The farthest southern point is here by Vladivostok, but that's likely too close to Korea and Japan for the Soviets to conduct tests they want to keep secret."

He suddenly realized that he was enjoying himself, standing here instructing these three men. Time to show his depth of operational experience and insight. He reached and pointed north of Mongolia at the long blue crescent of Lake Baikal. "The Soviets would need rail access to transport the components of a new missile system from the factories in Moscow to eastern Russia. The Trans-Siberian Railway parallels much of the Chinese border, and it could haul and off-load such components at any of the major cities along the way. But for the test, they'd need military radar and communications-monitoring infrastructure, so my guess is the Belaya aviation base complex, near Irkutsk."

He leaned in and looked through his glasses to find it, then put his finger on the Angara River, just north of the city. "No guarantees, of course, but a good place to start looking. I've already tasked the new Keyhole-9 satellite, launched by the National Reconnaissance Office in June, to target the region, and Belaya specifically. We should be getting film back down in a day or two for our analysts to look at."

Schlesinger took the pipe out of his mouth again. "That may well be too late. And the Soviets are probably launching out there in the middle of nowhere so we don't detect them. An anti-satellite launch won't take all that long, and we don't want to miss it. Can you get better coverage using SR-71s out of Kadena in Japan?"

Colby was ready for the question about using the high-altitude reconnaissance planes. "We have three Blackbirds permanently based at Kadena and can deploy more from stateside if we need them. The Soviets will likely launch their first test of this missile in the daytime to better observe it, which will help us too." He looked directly at Kissinger. "I'm thinking that since the Chinese told us about this and are interested in the results, maybe we can get clearance to fly into their airspace along the border."

Kissinger nodded. The SR-71 Blackbirds were the highest-flying, fastest jet aircraft in the world and had been a prime source of US intelligence for over a decade. He looked at Ford as he spoke. "It will be a reasonable thing for Bush to ask, so long as we promise to share what we find. If they say yes, we're bound to learn more about that part of China too."

Ford turned to Schlesinger. "I'll task Bush with seeking approval from the Chinese, but let's start readying enough SR-71 assets for this mission. The fact that Mao personally briefed Bush shows that they're keeping this close to the vest internally, so that should speed up approval."

He glanced at Colby and then back at Schlesinger. "There's one more thing I wanted to mention that may or may not be related. You've all been briefed on the Chinese spaceship that's apparently in the same orbit as Skylab. And you also know that because of the tragic events of Apollo-Soyuz, our own ship is now going to be docking with the space station. The Chinese ship may be manned, but we have no confirmation of that yet, nor do we know their intent. I will be directing Bush to ask Mao and Tsien for details on their new spaceship and their intended mission profile and objectives."

Kissinger nodded. "Getting surprised by a new Soviet missile is bad enough. We don't need more surprises from the Chinese." He pointed at Ford's bandage. "And you don't need any more surprises either, Mr. President."

After a short silence, in which every man kept any further thoughts to himself, Ford decided to wrap up. "We need more information on both issues and have decided on actions to get it ASAP. As soon as we hear back from George Bush, we'll meet again."

57

Southern Siberia, USSR

Song and his three-truck convoy had driven north for nearly two days, rotating drivers. Before they'd left, they'd repainted the vehicles the correct shade of dark green and added the external markings of the Soviet Strategic Rocket Forces—the golden shield, arrow and sword emblem—to the doors. The license plates were in Cyrillic, and every truck had someone riding in the cab who could speak some Russian if needed. This close to the Kazakh border, the Asian faces of the crew wouldn't be too unusual.

Just in case, there was a Type 56 submachine gun strapped into a rack in each cab for ready access, and every crewman was armed with a Type 54 pistol.

But the emptiness of the rolling Altai foothills, and now the southern edge of the Krasnoyarsk Krai, had worked in their favor. There were no internal borders to cross, and no curious local militsiya had dared stop them. They were just another military transport convoy, to be feared and respected, rolling through the endless beech forests and small subsistence agricultural towns of the vast Soviet Russian hinterland.

The site they'd chosen for the launch, after much poring over topographic maps and high-altitude photographs, was a tapped-out and abandoned logging zone. Song and his navigator had led the convoy there, only stopping to refuel from the tanker truck and for the men to eat and shit. They were exactly on schedule, and now it was time.

They turned onto the logging road and followed it until they were well off the main highway. Song pulled into a dry, open and flat location and parked. The drivers of the other two trucks pulled up next to him, and all of the men dismounted, happy to be able to stretch their legs and get to work on what they were trained for.

The orientation, solidity and levelness of the launching vehicle was critical. Song had parked on the precise heading, using the built-in compass on the dashboard, and now the launch crew pivoted the braces and pads down from the frame, extending and jacking them into place against the hard soil. Song walked amongst them as they worked, double-checking the floating-bubble level indicators, both fore-aft and left-right. They'd need to reset them when the missile was erected prelaunch, but experience showed that taking care now meant only fine-tuning then.

A second work crew set up a temporary mess tent and dug a slit latrine downhill and downwind from the site. They weren't going to be there long, but long enough that they needed to take care of basic amenities. Sleeping quarters were cots and hammocks in the trucks, the same ones they'd been using in shifts during the drive.

Song had a notebook containing the most critical procedures and information: exact time, azimuth and elevation of launch. He had no way to securely communicate with home base at Jiuquan, but it wasn't necessary. Because of their speed, objects in orbit had extremely high inertia and, as a result, their location was predictable unless they fired thrusters to maneuver.

When it came to targeting such an object, time was the most critical factor. Satellites passing over southern Russia were traveling at nearly five miles per second; just a few seconds' error in launch time would mean a significant miss. And the Earth was spinning on its axis. Where Song and his team stood, they were traveling at nearly 650 miles per hour towards the east, thanks to the Earth's rotation. The mission trajectory experts at Jiuquan had done the math and set the exact parameters that Song would need to meet the objective, which he now double-checked in his notebook.

The other challenge was how to ensure precision on a portable launch platform so far from a reliable source of timekeeping. Most of the crewmen wore standard mechanical Shuangling wristwatches, which required regular winding and readjustment every few weeks. But in 1972, the Shanghai Watch Factory had begun experimenting with timepieces that used quartz crystals, based on Japanese Seiko technology. Running electric current through a small fragment of quartz caused it to vibrate at a frequency a microchip could count. The chip then generated an electric pulse every second, which drove a motor to turn the hands on the digital watch. Song and his navigator had early versions on their wrists, and the technology had been integrated into the launch circuitry of the missile itself.

They had the time, the location and the targeting information. They had gotten precisely into position on schedule, and Song had posted two armed men on the logging road near the highway to ensure they wouldn't be disturbed.

As the leader of the clandestine detachment, Song kept his movements slow and deliberate and his face a mask of calm. But inside, he was burning with excitement. This would be the first operational test of the missile, at the direction of Chairman Tsien Hsue-shen himself. And there was a strong rumor that Chairman Mao was also watching closely.

To get to this moment had required great leadership, technological advances, clear vision of execution and audacity. That's what thrilled Song the most. They had made it this far despite the odds against them. Audacity was on their side.

Now they just had to wait for the Earth to turn.

58

Kadena Air Base, Okinawa, Japan

Blackbird. Pretty good name for a stealthy jet, Frank Bergnach thought.

Walking towards the SR-71, parked inside a hangar with its big doors open to the afternoon sun, he could barely make out the plane's charcoal-colored curves and angular streamlined edges. It was like he was looking into a dark hole.

The SR-71 Blackbird strategic reconnaissance aircraft had another name—a nickname, really—that Bergnach preferred. Habu. A Japanese pit viper whose neck and head resembled the long, pointed nose and cockpit bulge of the jet.

Both kinds of Habu were deadly with purpose.

Habu took two men to fly: the pilot, to get it off the ground and coax it up over 80,000 feet, at paint-blistering velocities more than three times the speed of sound; and the back-seater, the RSO, or reconnaissance systems officer, to navigate the fastest jet ever made. The standard RSO joke was "You've never been lost until you're lost at Mach 3."

The RSO also ran the ever-changing suite of sensors and communications gear that allowed Habu to do its job: to spy on the enemy while flying so high and fast that no missile could touch it.

Frank Bergnach was the pilot, and his RSO was Rick B. Darlington, call sign RB. They'd been paired for 18 months. As they stood next to the jet, they could see that it was leaking fuel. As usual. The Habu was a flying fuel tank, with its 80,280 pounds of gas weighing far more than the plane itself. There was no way to completely seal the high-temperature titanium structure, and so, when the tanks were full, a steady slow drip of jet propellant JP-7 hit the ramp.

Frank and RB liked the smell. It meant they were going flying.

Habu normally flew in the morning, but today's mission required takeoff at 16:00 and a return near sunset, so the two had woken up later than usual. They'd eaten brunch and done medical checks, and then climbed into their bulky orange S1030 pressure suits, which caused them to waddle slightly as they approached the cockpit access stairs.

They climbed the stairs in turn, taking care not to catch the stirrups on their boots; the stirrups would click into place in the cockpit to keep their legs from flailing if they had to trigger a high-speed ejection.

Hopefully not today. Especially not today, given where they'd be flying.

Frank and RB each stepped over the aircraft's sill into their separate cockpits, and the groundcrew climbed up after them to help them click their stirrups into place, hook up pressure hoses and tighten ejection seat straps. A physical joining of man and machine.

The two closed their canopies, listening to the low electric whine and mechanical thunk that verified the heavy quartz-glass structures had locked into place. After the stairs were pulled away, Frank and RB confirmed the positions of the critical switches and knobs in their cockpits, and then it was time to start the engines.

It took tremendous power to crank the giant J58 turbojets. The groundcrew wheeled over a monstrosity they called the Buick, a trailer with two big V8 Buick Wildcat engines that drove a starting shaft that hooked directly to the bottom of the J58. Using his intercom, Frank said to the crew chief, "Take rotation on the left," and the groundcrew revved the Buick up to max, all 16 exhaust stacks roaring and spitting unmuffled fire. The J58 slowly responded, spinning up relentlessly until Frank moved his left throttle ahead to IDLE to start flowing fuel.

But that still wasn't enough.

The JP-7 jet fuel was hard to ignite, so the next step was squirting highly explosive triethylborane into the combustion chamber, where it mixed with the air's oxygen and burst into flame, setting the fuel ablaze. When the left engine started running on its own, Frank said, "Disconnect," and they repeated the process for the right. When both were running, the engine-mounted generators started making electricity, and RB and Frank methodically powered up and checked all systems. Then Frank engaged nose-wheel steering, signaled for the crew chief to pull the heavy chocks away from the main wheels under each wing, moved his throttles forward a titch and began taxiing out of the hangar, headed for runway 23 right.

The control tower had been given their classified taxi and takeoff time and had restricted all other movement on the taxiways and runways of Kadena Air Base. Frank recognized the privilege and took pride in being the very pointed tip of the spear that was the US Air Force.

He taxied and turned into position on the runway, exactly on the white-painted centerline.

In the back seat, RB was watching the clock and gave Frank a heads-up via intercom. "Thirty seconds."

Frank tensed his left hand on the throttles as he held position with his toe brakes. At fifteen seconds, he started pushing the throttles smoothly forward, giving time for the big engines to spool up, moving the two levers towards MIL: military power.

"Five, four . . ."

At the familiar pacing of RB's countdown, Frank got ready to lift the throttles over the MIL stop to go into afterburner.

". . . three, two, one, hack!"

RB started the navigation clock and Frank rotated his ankles back to release the toe brakes and pushed the throttles towards maximum.

A shot of triethylborane squirted into the afterburners at the back of the engines, both huge blowtorches ignited, and the men felt the quick twist and pulse of heavy new thrust against their backs. Satisfied that everything was working, Frank pushed both throttles all the way forward to their hard stop.

Maximum thrust. Twenty-five tons of force accelerating them down the 12,000-foot runway on the southwestern coast of Japan's Okinawa Island.

Facing the East China Sea.

Frank made small corrections to the nose wheel to keep the plane on the centerline and flicked his eyes occasionally to the airspeed indicator. At 180 knots, he steadily pulled the control stick aft, watching the nose rise and feeling the sudden smoothness as Habu's main wheels left the ground at 210 knots. He brought the nose higher and reached to flick up the wheel-shaped lever that raised the landing gear. He cross-checked the artificial horizon in front of him to set 25 degrees nose up.

Habu climbed fast.

As the airspeed rose to 400 knots, Frank raised the nose to 35 degrees. In two minutes they were at 20,000 feet and nearing the speed of sound. He eased the nose down slightly to help the jet break through the extra drag of the sound barrier, watched his Mach meter go supersonic to 1.05 and then brought the nose back up.

They were racing away from the surface of the Earth, accelerating as they climbed.

He made small corrections to make sure they were steering exactly on the black navigation line and then engaged the pitch and roll axis of the autopilot. That gave him finer control, adjusting small wheels under the gloved fingertips of his right hand. He engaged HEADING HOLD for one last check of the nav system and, satisfied, threw the AUTO NAV switch. Every pound of fuel was precious, and the computer would fly the jet as efficiently as possible.

As they approached Mach 2, more and more of the air flowing into the engines went directly to the afterburners. The thinning air poured in, mixed with raw fuel in the afterburners and exploded out the exhaust, pushing Habu ever faster.

All around the world, air traffic control had the responsibility of helping airplanes safely fly up to the maximum altitude possible—60,000 feet, about 11 miles above the surface. But the SR-71 easily exceeded that. As the digital altitude indicator clicked past flight level 600, RB shut off all normal communications and airplane identification and activated the sensing systems that they would need for today's mission. Converting Habu from a normal plane into a one-of-a-kind.

Just 14 minutes after Frank had released the brakes, now 200 miles out over the sea, they were in the final cruise climb to 80,000 feet and Mach 3. Up where no one could touch them.

But this time, instead of heading north over Korea's DMZ or southwest towards Vietnam, as they usually did, they were on a heading that no Okinawa Habu had ever followed. A little bit north of due west, set to fly exactly overhead of the city of Shanghai and directly into the heart of China.

59

Apollo Capsule, 232 Miles above Earth

"Valery, can you see the Chinese ship out any of the windows?"

Deke yelled the question from down in the Apollo Command Module's nose, where he was working in the tunnel adapter with Svetlana's help. Once the structural hooks had solidly connected Apollo with Skylab, he'd pressurized the short tunnel between the two ships, opened Apollo's forward hatch and thrown the switches to retract the docking mechanism, and he was now undoing the connectors to remove it so he could open the hatch that led into Skylab.

"No, Deke. But night now."

During the few remaining minutes of daylight after they'd docked, Valery had floated between each of the Apollo capsule's five windows, keeping a lookout, careful to avoid kicking the bodies under the seats as he moved. He was now peering out into the darkness. The angular shapes of Skylab were barely visible, occasionally illuminated by the passing lights of Earth's cities below.

Svetlana was holding a flashlight for Deke and reading him the steps. Picturing what she'd seen during docking, she floated up for a quick check through the forward rendezvous windows. "Deke, none of our windows point at the second docking port, right?"

Deke paused for a moment to visualize the Skylab design. She was right—all of the Apollo windows pointed sideways or up.

"Yeah, good point. The second port is under our nose, on the other side of the docking adapter." He turned back to his work. The connectors were finicky and hard to see, even through his reading glasses, and he was trying to hurry. At least the heart arrythmias he'd felt had settled down. He said, "Can you give Houston another call? We should be over a ground site soon."

Svetlana, half wearing her comm cap, pushed the transmit button. "Houston, Apollo, how do you read?"

No response.

Valery said, "Maybe communications soon." He tried to remember the right English words, gave up and spoke in Russian, and Svetlana translated. "Valery says we're almost across the Pacific Ocean, and our ground track should take us past Cuba and up over the east coast of America."

Deke nodded as the docking mechanism finally came free in his hands. He pulled it clear and stowed it behind the opened hatch.

"Okay, thanks. I'm sure they'll give us a call as soon as we appear over the horizon. For now, I'm gonna equalize the pressure with Skylab so we can open this hatch. Tell Valery to be ready to clear his ears."

The air that flowed from Skylab through the equalization valve into Apollo smelled stale and metallic, like the hot, sharp smell when the sun shines on a tin roof, briefly reminding Deke of being up in the rafters of his family's tobacco barn in Wisconsin. The two ships' pressures were already close to equal, at around five psi pure oxygen; he licked his fingertips and held them close to the valve until he could feel that the airflow had stopped, then squeezed his nose shut and blew to pop his ears. He only needed to do it once.

The Skylab hatch facing him was simple: a long handle that rotated a set of gears that would retract the five latches around the perimeter, and a central locking mechanism. Deke smiled wryly when he saw that the final Skylab crew had left the hatch unlocked. Welcoming all who made it there. Then a thought wiped the smile off his face. *Is the backup docking port unlocked too, ready for a Chinese visitor?*

He grabbed the gray rubber hatch handle and pulled on it to turn it clockwise. It didn't budge. He looked through his glasses again at the central lock.

"Svetlana, can you bring that light closer?"

She floated into the confined space next to him, shining the flashlight directly where he was looking.

Deke put his finger on the lock and mumbled, "Yep, unlocked, and clockwise. Just need more armstrong."

As he braced his feet against opposite sides of the hatch structure, he felt Svetlana floating clear to give him room. Grabbing the handle with both hands, he pulled and twisted, trying to free it without damaging the mechanism.

Still no movement.

"Shit!" he muttered.

"Need oil?" Svetlana suggested.

"Yeah, maybe."

Whatever lubricant had been on the latches might have been eroded away by atomic oxygen in the vacuum of space. He thought through everything that was stowed in the capsule. Petroleum-based products were generally banned because they were so flammable in the pure oxygen atmosphere and also released a toxic off-gassing, but he remembered that there was a small tube of O-ring grease stowed on board for the furnace experiment.

But where? He had a sudden thought. "Svetlana, do you see beside you, by my right hip, the stowage racks marked with an 'R'?"

Svetlana swung around in the tight space and shone her light, spotting several long, latched white doors with R1 through R5 stenciled on them.

"Yes, I see them." She looked closer. "There are . . ." She hunted for the word. ". . . labels on them."

"Great. Look for Furnace."

"I see it, Furnace, in R4." She squeezed the R4 door latch levers together and swung the door open. Inside, a maze of partitions held things in place in weightlessness. "What are you looking for?"

"A small silver squeeze tube with a cap. Should have 'Grease' written on it."

She probed, the flashlight clenched between her teeth, careful to not let the myriad stowed contents float free. A glint of silver caught her eye, and with her fingertips she retrieved the small tube. "I've got it."

Deke's head was still buried in the tunnel adapter, so she placed the tube in his outstretched hand.

"Great, thanks!"

She closed the locker and refocused the flashlight for Deke as he carefully squirted the contents of the tube into each joint of the hatch mechanism, wiggling everything that would move to work the grease in.

He floated the empty tube back to her, grabbed the handle again, jiggled it forcefully in both directions several times and then braced himself again for a full-strength clockwise heave.

With a squeaking sound, it suddenly gave. He turned the handle until he saw that all five outer latches had rotated clear. Then he pounded on the flat exposed outer metal of the hatch, and it pivoted away from him.

Into Skylab.

60

Southern Siberia

Song had his men raise the heavy missile slowly. No need to rush after coming all this way, he'd decided. A stripped gear in the transmission or a blown hydraulic line would spell disaster. He watched, frowning, when the missile swayed slightly in its supporting cradle as it was jacked up to near vertical above the carrier truck. Song was glad for the calm morning—he didn't want to push his luck by waiting any longer, and a high wind would have forced them to delay until the Earth-orbiting target appeared overhead again.

And Director Tsien was expecting the launch to happen today.

As the missile pivoted skyward, its exhaust bells swung closer to the ground behind the aft end of the truck. Song's men used shovels, rakes, saws and their hands to clear the heavier branches and loose rocks from the expected blast zone. They didn't want any ricocheting debris to damage the rocket or the carrier. They'd already parked the other two trucks well clear of danger.

With a thunk and a sudden increase in the pitch of the whining pump, the missile reached launch attitude. Song walked close to double-check the angle of the pivoting mechanism against the protractor etched into the metal. He nodded, then yelled for the operator to shut down the motor.

Song's missile was in the right location on Earth, pointed correctly and tipped at the needed elevation. A giant malevolent robot waiting to be brought to life. He checked his watch against the checklist and ordered his men to shelter in the bulky shadow of the other trucks. He watched as they laughed and jostled past him, excited for what was about to happen, and called after them to remember their ear protectors. What was about to happen would be loud. Once he was sure everyone was clear, Song and his navigator climbed up into the cab of the transport, which the Dong Feng design engineers had adapted and reinforced. Song twisted two wing nuts to release a fiberglass cover below the center of the dashboard. He pivoted it open, revealing the switches, knobs, small keyboard and push buttons of the launch control panel. And the two key slots in the center. The truck's idling engine would provide the electrical power.

Song had helped write the prelaunch procedures, but for security he handed his navigator the checklist to read him each step. It was too easy to forget things when one was anxious and excited. The two men worked methodically through the list, calmed by the familiar steps, activating and pressurizing the systems inside the missile that loomed above and behind them.

The checklist called for a time check, and both men compared the time on their wristwatches to the control panel's digital display. All three agreed to within a fraction of a second.

As the exact launch time approached, Song imagined the missile's target racing around the Earth towards them, certain that its supreme speed and extreme height made it immune to threats from the ground. He felt like the ultimate predator, concealed and powerful, awaiting the approach of unsuspecting, vulnerable prey.

The navigator confirmed that all data had been entered and that the switch configuration was correct, then reminded Song of a vital remaining step. Both men fished below the collar of their shirts for the thin metal necklaces they were wearing and pulled them up over their heads. Suspended from each was a small brass key. A final safeguard to ensure control of the launch and the irreversible unleashing of the awesome power of the Dong Feng missile. The two men leaned forward and inserted the keys, and Song counted down.

"Three, two, one, now." He pronounced the final Chinese word, "fa-sheu," extra clearly, and as he said it, they turned their keys in the slots.

The system was now active, armed to launch according to its internal timer. Song and his navigator sat back against the wide bench seat of the truck, feeling nervous relief. They had done all they could. Now it was up to the missile itself.

Thirty seconds before launch time, following the final steps in the checklist, Song gave three long blasts on the truck horn, warning his men. With 20 seconds remaining, he and his navigator donned their ear protectors. At 10 seconds, with a final glance at each other, they leaned forward in the cab until their chests met their thighs, and clasped their hands over the backs of their heads.

Ready for launch.

61

80,000 feet over Northern China

In the front seat of the SR-71 Habu, Frank was staring through the visor of his pressure suit at the projected map between his legs, cross-checking it against the paper map and mission plan clipped to his right thigh. "RB, I show us exactly on track, with the first control point in one minute." One minute to the real kickoff of this clandestine high-altitude mission.

"Copy, concur, Frank." RB double-checked his sensor controls in the back cockpit, including the small sensors behind his cockpit that were tracking the stars in the black sky above them. They were exactly on course, crossing northwestern China at 33 miles a minute—covering more than a mile every two seconds. "We're all set."

With both huge afterburners pushing them along supersonically through the thin upper air, the Habu jet was burning fuel at 1,000 pounds per minute—2.5 gallons per second. As soon as they'd finished the data-gathering pass, they'd need to descend to the waiting aerial refueling tankers, 10 miles below them, flying a racetrack pattern over western China at 25,000 feet, ready to give them enough fuel to make it back to base.

Unless Habu was in a turn, RB couldn't see anything but sky through his cockpit's two rectangular windows. To compensate, a small TV repeater screen in front of him allowed him to "see" forward, but it was like watching a movie of what was happening rather than the real thing. Between his knees was his projected navigation map, and squarely in front of him was the radar primary display—his real focus.

RB said, "Turn in thirty seconds."

The autopilot would make the precise turn from a northwesterly heading to pure west, exactly on track with the Chinese side of the border. That would allow the side-looking radar mounted in Habu's nose to see hundreds of miles to the north.

RB glanced again at the nav map and called, "Three, two, one, turn."

The standard joke was that the Habu pilot just drove the RSO to work. RB was now in charge.

In the thin air of extreme altitude, the SR-71 turned gingerly to avoid airflow disruption into the engines and a possible loss of thrust. The sustained high speed and friction had also heated the titanium skin to over 600 degrees and the airframe was less rigid; the pilot was limited to 45 degrees bank and 1.5 g to keep from bending the aircraft.

As Habu rolled out, RB felt the familiar tingling excitement of secret operations. In the mission briefings, he and Frank had been given a specific time to be on target, and they were there now. The amount of data pouring in through the radar returns took time to process, which meant the gray-tones image RB saw on his central screen was delayed by up to a minute. He twisted in his pressure suit and stretched to try to see the horizon to his right through the high, slanted window.

In the front seat, Frank had a slightly better side view. "The weather guessers were right, RB. No clouds," he said with relief. There was blue sky below and blackness above, all the way to the horizon, hundreds of miles away.

RB glanced at his timer and voiced another countdown. "Three, two, one, now." If it was going to happen, this was the exact predicted moment. They could hold this westerly heading for only another minute before they had to turn south to stay clear of the Kazakh Republic border.

Nothing. Both sets of eyes urgently scanned left and right, from the distant horizon to as close as they could see under the plane's right side.

Frank spotted it first. "There!" he shouted into his headset. "Right at four o'clock, halfway to the horizon!"

A smudge of white had suddenly appeared and was growing as Frank watched, drawing a thin vertical line into the sky, clearly visible against the darkness of the terrain beyond and then the blue of the sky.

A rocket launch. Unmistakable. From a previously unused location in the Soviet Union.

RB's view was impeded by the canopy, so he looked back at his radar return, willing the processor to go faster and show him something.

"It's high enough now, you should be able to see it, RB." Frank wanted his RSO's eyes on the smoke trail as well, to get as accurate a description of what they'd seen as possible.

"Yep, I see it!" RB couldn't keep the excitement out of his voice. The mission had been hastily assembled, with unprecedented cooperation from the Chinese and a first-time flight path for the SR-71 program, and it had worked! His mental clock had been ticking, and he glanced again at the timer. "Turn in ten seconds, Frank."

"Yep, I see it. You get good data?"

RB stared at the radar image on his screen, and just as the jet started its left turn, the visual spike of the rocket launch appeared. He smiled broadly. "We sure did. Medals all around." He glanced at his dwindling fuel gauges. "Now let's find the tankers and go get some gas."

RB and Frank understood the importance of what they had just seen, and verbally reported using the high-frequency HF antenna mounted into the long pitot tube protruding out the jet's nose. Word would be rapidly passed to Washington, up through the USAF chain to the Joint Chiefs, and on to the secretary of defense and the president. They were the ones who would need to decide what to do about this new Soviet capability.

That was not Frank and RB's problem. All they needed to do was get home to base and celebrate.

Once again, Habu had done its job.

Like no other jet in the world.

62

North of Houston

Kaz stopped just inside the open doorway, peering out and listening. He saw nothing moving and heard only the chirping of morning birds. Otherwise, dead quiet.

He glanced at the weapons in his hands and transferred the hammer to his right, thinking he could throw it if he needed to. The screwdriver was more suited for close-in fighting. Better than nothing, but surprise was his greatest advantage.

Left or right? The path sloped down to the left. *If I were standing guard, I'd take the high ground to the right.*

Time to move.

With the hammer raised above his shoulder and the screwdriver at waist height, Kaz took three barefoot strides through the doorway, pivoting hard to his right, all muscles tensed and ready to strike.

A man dozing in a chair was leaning back against the stone wall of the building. His hands, crossed in his lap, loosely cradled a pistol. Black hair, broad Asian face, bulky-looking shoulders. Kaz recognized him from behind the restaurant.

Run or fight?

The pistol decided it for him. If he ran, barefoot in a rock quarry, and the man woke up, he'd be an easy target. So Kaz quietly stepped forward, placing his feet carefully and shifting the screwdriver in his hand so he could reach out to grab the pistol.

The man's eyes snapped open, and he dropped the chair onto four legs and scrambled to get a secure grip on the gun.

Now! Toes digging into the dirt, Kaz closed the distance and swung the broken hammer down hard, hitting the man solidly on the parietal ridge of his head. With his left hand, he stabbed at the man's hands to keep him from raising the pistol, and then crashed into him, knocking both the man and his chair over. They rolled in a jumble along the wall and onto the weedy gravel and exposed stone of the quarry floor. Kaz swung the hammer again as they tumbled, hitting flesh, and flailed with the screwdriver to do more damage as the man tried to push clear, shaking off the hammer blow, freeing a hand so he could use his pistol. Ignoring the searing pain in his ribs, Kaz stayed close, gouging with the screwdriver and dragging the broken hammer claw across whatever flesh he could reach.

"Aaaahhh!" the man yelled, grabbing the cloth of Kaz's coveralls and using all his strength to throw Kaz off him.

Landing hard on his back, his ribs screaming, Kaz rolled fast onto his stomach so he could use both hands to push himself up. His right hand landed on a stone, and he grabbed it as he twisted to throw the hammer at the man's head. Then he rose and turned to face his adversary.

They were only feet apart. One of his tools had damaged the Chinese man, who was bleeding profusely from his forehead, a loose flap of skin hanging down. But he was smiling as he raised his pistol.

Kaz figured he had one chance. Yelling, he raised the screwdriver high—a decoy—and launched himself, swinging the rock he'd grabbed in a hard, upwards arc towards his opponent. Instinctively, the man leaned left to avoid the screwdriver, and the sharp edge of the stone caught him squarely on the jaw. He staggered, and Kaz pressed his advantage, bowling the man over, swiping at the pistol with his left hand while he again raised the rock. Kaz was on top when they hit the ground, and he smashed the heavy stone down, this time onto the man's temple. There was a fleshy, crunching sound, and the man was still.

Kaz raised the rock again, breathing heavily, not believing it was finished. When the man remained motionless, he dropped the screwdriver and poked him hard in the eye.

No reaction. The man was definitely out.

Maybe dead.

The rock slipped from Kaz's fingers and he fell onto his good side in the dirt next to his opponent, exhausted, gasping painfully for breath and suddenly nauseated. He felt his stomach lurch, and he lifted himself to dry heave, the spasms bringing searing new agony from his ribs. He collapsed again, curling into the fetal position, letting his body's reaction subside and mentally taking inventory of any new pains. He brought his right hand up in front of his face and noted that it was bleeding. But the cuts weren't deep. Then he took a small breath, laboriously rolled onto his hands and knees and shakily stood.

The man's pistol was lying beside him. Kaz bent, swore at the jab from his broken bones, picked it up, checked that the safety was on and slipped it into his coveralls pocket. He frisked the man, found a folding knife and tucked that into his coveralls as well. He noticed that the man was wearing slip-on leather shoes, and he yanked one off. He tried it on and was disappointed to find it too small and narrow for him to use.

Barefoot it was.

He glanced at the sun across the crater of the gravel pit and realized with disbelief that the fight had only taken a few minutes. He took another breath, a little deeper this time, and winced.

Time to go.

He found a path to the quarry's entrance and started moving along it, grunting at the stabbing pain in his side with every step. The path's surface, a mixture of dirt and gravel, poked into his bare soles, and he slowed his pace a bit to try to pick the smoothest spots for each step.

As he clumsily hopscotched towards the road, he realized that the man's job had been to guard him until the car came back. Which it was bound to do. Lurching into a half run, ignoring the jabs to his feet, he made it to the quarry road, which curved to the left. Towards the main highway, Kaz figured. There was no car in sight as of yet, but he had to hustle. He glanced at the road's rough gravel surface. *Shit.* It had been left to degrade, likely for years, in the hot, wet Houston weather.

The shoulder next to the growth of tall weeds was smoothest, so he stayed to the side, only walk-running on the road where the rains had deposited enough mud and dirt to cover the sharpness of the crushed stone. As he cleared the edge of the quarry, the curve of the road straightened out and he could see ahead to the public road in the distance.

He'd hoped for a nearby farmhouse, with a phone and maybe footwear he could borrow, but he saw nothing except open, poorly tended fields. He guessed the land had been bought by speculators waiting for the inevitable profitable northward expansion of Houston.

I'm gonna have to hitchhike.

As he reached the main road, he looked left and right for approaching vehicles. He thought back to the turns he'd sensed while riding in the trunk and turned right. The shoulder was broader and mostly smooth dirt, and he picked up his pace to a halting jog, checking ahead and back over his shoulder for a ride.

The July sun was well above the horizon now, and Kaz was thankful for the coveralls. He'd ridden in the trunk on this road for a few minutes, so he had some distance to cover. He was thirsty, in pain and hungry, but he had urgent information for NASA and the DIA, so he kept up as quick a pace as his feet and ribs allowed.

He saw a car coming towards him in the distance. Kaz was about to step out into the road to flag it down when an alarm sounded in his head. He crouched and then dropped quickly into the weed-filled ditch, peering through the tall windmill grass, waiting for the car to pass. His reaction puzzled him, but he honored it. Years of air combat and test flying in high-performance jets had taught him to trust his lizard brain when it tried to protect him.

He could hear the car now, the rising Doppler sound of an engine being pushed hard and tires crunching on gravel, and then it flashed past. It was a green sedan with a black-haired driver, and maybe someone in the back. As Kaz leaned out to watch the car recede, the red brake lights came on.

Shit, did they see me? Kaz felt for the bulge of the knife and the gun in his pockets, but they'd be of uncertain use against a pursuing car with armed men inside. *Run or hide?* The weeds and grasses in the adjoining field were too short for any real concealment. The ditch was too tangled for speed, and if he ran down the road, he'd be in a losing race against a car.

So hide. He looked back towards the car and saw that it was out of sight, maybe doing a three-point turn. He scurried low across the road and down into the ditch on the other side, where they'd be less likely to look for him. He found decent cover in a thick clump of fescue and leaned out again to watch the car return.

But it didn't.

Kaz considered the facts. Was it the same car he'd seen at the restaurant and after the bombing? *Yes.* Was the distance about right that it had turned onto the quarry road? *Yes again.* Which meant that the occupants of the green sedan were about to discover their friend's inert body. And Kaz's escape.

Like a mirage, another vehicle appeared, coming from the same direction. *All or nothing.* Kaz clambered quickly up out of the ditch, stood in the middle of the road and fanned his arms over his head, ignoring his ribs, waving in the universal signal of distress.

Ford F-150 pickup, dark blue and well used. He hoped his coveralls would tip the balance enough in his favor for a local to not just speed past him.

With relief, he watched as the truck slowed, pulled up abreast of him and stopped. The driver, his unshaven tanned face partially covered by a faded Exxon baseball cap, leaned across and rolled down the passenger window.

"Y'all look like you could use a lift."

63

Situation Room, the White House

"What the fuck are those Commies up to!" James Schlesinger spat out the words.

As the secretary of defense, he was responsible for the Army, Navy, Marines and Air Force, second only to the president in terms of responsibility. His core purpose was to protect the security of the United States. The radar images from the SR-71 showed a whole new capability to worry about. A whole new threat.

An Air Force colonel had put several photographs on the table and set up the TV screen to show the video that had been transmitted from Kadena after the SR-71 had landed. The men in the room had watched it twice and then had asked the colonel to leave.

Schlesinger now held one of the blown-up photographs in his hand, his pipe in the other, and swore again. "Conniving bastards! Why would the Soviets do this?" He threw the picture down and looked angrily at President Ford, then answered his own question. "They're trying to derail the arms limitations talks. Make you look ineffectual for the next election."

Ford nodded, the long bandage on his head reflecting the fluorescent overhead lights. "Maybe. Brezhnev would be much happier with a Democrat in charge, someone who would weaken our military."

From the end of the table, Henry Kissinger rumbled, "Does NORAD know what the missile was targeting? And whether it was successful?"

Schlesinger glanced at the head of the CIA, Bill Colby, and said, "Our surveillance assets around the world are staring at that part of the sky, trying to answer your question. NORAD says the only satellite that lined up with the missile's trajectory was a dead one—an old Soviet rocket body in an eccentric orbit."

Ford asked, "Any threat to our Apollo crew on orbit?"

Schlesinger clenched his pipe between his teeth and talked around it. "Doesn't look like it. Different altitude, and they were on the other side of the world at the time." He took a puff and realized his pipe had gone out. "If the missile hit its mark, Apollo might run into the debris field, depending on how big it is."

Colby asked, "Why would they do this during Apollo-Soyuz, a joint US–USSR exercise?"

Kissinger answered. "Apollo-Soyuz is the object of much public attention, both here and in the USSR. Maybe they thought we would miss it." He considered. "Without the Chinese alerting us, we might have."

A distorted voice suddenly blared out of the beige phone speaker in the center of the table. "Gentlemen, George Bush here. I've been listening but haven't seen the SR-71 imagery. Can you hear me okay?"

"Yes, we hear you," the president said.

"I've been wondering how the Chinese not only knew that this launch was coming, but also the precise timing. Their intelligence apparatus within the Soviet Union must be better than I've been led to believe."

Colby nodded. "We're having a hard look at that now. But it seems like a clear power play by Mao, especially on top of them launching their first manned spaceship. Mao wants to disrupt our relationship with the Soviets and to show the vultures angling for his job his strength and reach." He glanced at Kissinger, who was slowly nodding.

Kissinger spoke loudly, knowing speakerphones sometimes had trouble transmitting his basso voice. "George, you said that Professor Tsien Hsue-shen was with Mao when you met him. At that time, we didn't know that they were aiming to dock with Skylab. Have you had any luck getting another meeting?"

"No, they've been saying the chairman isn't feeling well enough." Bush paused. "Might be true—he looked like he'd had a recent stroke. But the other guy, Tsien, he was as sharp as a tack. My guess is, he's pulling a lot of these strings." He paused again. "I think it might be a while before I get another meeting."

Ford had been listening intently to the conversation. Schlesinger might be Sec Def, but Ford was commander in chief. "We'll need to deal with this Soviet launch in the medium-long term," he said, "but for now, we've got to protect our crew and our assets on Skylab."

He looked at Kissinger. "Henry, I want you to use your back channels into the Soviet Union to see if we can get any better insight into this new ASAT weapon."

To the phone, he said, "George, let us know ASAP what you hear over there in China. I'll be getting regular updates from NORAD and NASA, so let's plan to meet again as soon as we have something concrete."

64

Mission Control

Kaz strode into Mission Control, unwashed and unshaven, but in his own clothes and wearing shoes. Following him through the door was Dr. JW McKinley.

The pickup truck driver had listened, amazed, to Kaz's abduction story, shaking his head, and offered to turn around and drive him as far south as he needed to go. They'd stopped at the first gas station with a pay phone, and Kaz had borrowed a dime and called JW, already on console, to tell him what had happened and ask him to meet him en route to the space center with clean clothes, shoes and Kaz's wallet and NASA badge. JW had swung by Kaz's house to pick up his stuff and then met him in a Red Barn restaurant parking lot just south of downtown Houston. Climbing awkwardly out of the pickup, Kaz had thanked the driver, who refused the $20 bill he offered.

With no time to waste, Kaz clumsily changed clothes in the back seat of JW's car on the drive to NASA. Watching his friend in the rearview mirror and seeing him wince as he dressed, JW asked, "Ribs or shoulder?"

"Ribs. Got kicked low on the left side, but it's not too bad."

"Sure," JW responded. "Buddy, before you go on console, I'm going to take a few minutes and tape you up, whether you like it or not. And bandage that hand."

Inside Mission Control, Kaz quickly climbed the tiered steps and crossed behind the flight director, headed for the CAPCOM console.

"Sorry I'm late, FLIGHT," he said.

Chris Kraft turned to look at him. "Doc McKinley gave me a quick heads-up before he left. Christ, Kaz! What the hell? Glad you're okay."

Crip looked at Kaz's bandaged hand and up at his face as he retrieved his headset from the drawer. "Y'all right? You look like shit."

Kaz shrugged. "Tough night, but I'm okay. I'll tell you the details later. More importantly, what's going on here?"

He needed to call NASA security to watch his house, and call his DIA contact to debrief the abduction, but for now the orbiting crew took priority.

Crip gestured with his chin at the front screen. "Apollo is just south of Panama on an ascending track. We'll have comms through Merritt Island in a couple of minutes. But some serious shit has happened since you went off shift." He quickly briefed Kaz on the loss of communications and the unexpected proximity of the Chinese ship.

"So how long has it been since we last had comms with Deke?"

"More than an orbit—about a hundred minutes. We were unlucky with the ground track."

Kaz pictured all the things that could have happened in that time. "Any confirmation from Skylab telemetry that they've docked?" He considered his own question. "Or that anyone has docked?"

Crip shook his head. "Nothing, but we're about to regain comms—you want me to stay on for a bit, or do you have enough detail?" Looking again at Kaz's bandaged hand and the contusions and dirt on his face, he added, "You sure you're up for this?"

As Kaz nodded, JW appeared at his elbow with two packets of Dad's cookies, two Tylenols and a steaming mug of black coffee.

"Thanks, Doc, you're a lifesaver." He turned back to Crip. "Yeah, I'm ready."

"Apollo, Houston, how do you read?" Kaz could see from the map on the front screen that they weren't quite within predicted comm range yet, but he didn't want to miss a second of it. Deke was sure to be needing help.

He tried again. "Apollo, Houston, via Merritt Island. How do you read?"

A crackle in his headset, some unintelligible static and then a female voice. "Houston, Apollo, loud and clear, how do you read us?"

"Loud and clear, Apollo. Good to hear your voice, Svetlana. Houston is standing by for a status report."

There was a pause, and then Deke's voice. "Kaz! Man, am I happy to be talking to you. Svetlana said you want a status report. Let me see . . . Last we talked was pre-docking. Since then, we had a collision with another spaceship that wiped off our high-gain antenna, but we still got docked with Skylab. I've removed the docking mechanism and equalized pressures, and we've just gotten the Skylab hatch open—it was sticking, and we had to grease it. We're about ready to ingress."

"Copy all, Deke." Kaz glanced at Kraft, who was holding up both hands, palms forward, signaling him to wait. "Please standby on the ingress until we've had a quick chance to look at all your data."

Kraft polled the room, asking every console to check their systems, then turned back to Kaz. "Let's get an update on the Chinese spacecraft, CAPCOM."

Kaz transmitted the question on everyone's mind. "Apollo, about the collision you mentioned, any details on the other spacecraft, and where it is now?"

"We took a glancing blow on our port side, Kaz, and saw some fresh gouges on the side of their hull, so I assume we have some too. But all our systems look good. There was floating debris, we guess from our high-gain antenna. The ship looked to be about the size and shape of a Mercury capsule, with a Chinese flag on the side. Valery's been scanning nonstop, but he's seen nothing out the windows since it drifted off to Skylab's port side during our docking. We're not sure where it is now."

"Copy." Kaz turned to Kraft and spoke on the Mission Control voice loop. "FLIGHT, all okay for Skylab ingress?"

If the Chinese ship was maneuvering to dock to Skylab's secondary port, the situation was urgent.

Kraft waited a few seconds, listening to the final feedback from the room, then nodded. "Let's have Deke ingress Skylab alone, while the cosmonauts ready the bodies for transfer." He leaned close to Kaz and said quietly, "And remind Deke to cover anything the Soviets shouldn't see."

Kaz looked back at Kraft for a moment, thinking about what he would say, and then stepped on the transmit switch. "Apollo, Houston, all stations here report that your vehicle is healthy. Deke, you have a GO for solo ingress to Skylab. Recommend you cover any fragile equipment to protect it, and meanwhile have Svetlana and Valery prep Tom's and Vance's bodies for transfer."

Deke replied, "Copy all, Houston, wilco. I'm headed into Skylab now."

Deke had floated back up into the Apollo capsule while he was talking with Kaz. When Svetlana finished translating for Valery, she looked at Deke.

"The Chinese ship might have docked too. We need weapons."

Deke stared at her for a couple of seconds and then nodded. "Good idea."

He pulled himself across his couch and reached down behind the headrest, careful to avoid Tom Stafford's blue-wrapped head as he retrieved a bulky white canvas roll from the aft stowage cupboard. He peeled back the Velcro and unrolled the bag, revealing a tool kit. From a central restraining pouch, he pulled out a large metal adjustable wrench and gripped it.

"There are a few more tools in here that you can use, but for now,

I'm going into Skylab alone. I want you two to pull Tom's and Vance's bodies out, ready for transfer. If I see that the Chinese ship has docked, I'll call for help."

Svetlana looked through the kit as she translated for Valery. She pulled out a ratchet wrench and a metal ratchet extender as their best options, handing Valery the extender. She looked at the wrench in her hand. "This is too small." She considered what they had carried in the Soyuz. "For an emergency landing, do you have a pistol or . . ." She searched for the word. ". . . a gun that makes a bright light in the night?"

"A pistol or a flare gun? No." Deke's eyes opened wide. "But you've reminded me of something!"

He ducked down towards the forward hatch and opened a side locker, pulling out two bulky square cloth bags. He floated them back up to where Valery and Svetlana could see, unzipped the lid on the nearer one and slid out a heavy silver knife in a metal sheath. "Survival kits," he explained. "I forgot we had them. There are small flares in there, but these machetes are better." He floated the adjustable wrench he'd been holding to Svetlana and pointed at the unopened bag. "You grab that other knife and put these kits away."

He slid the knife out of its tethered Teflon-lined sheath. It was 17 inches end to end. The blade extending from the knurled metal handle was long, curved and sharp, with a pointed tip and a serrated opposing edge for sawing.

"That'll do," Deke said, carefully sliding the blade back into its sheath. He unzipped the lower right leg pocket of his flight suit and slid the sheathed knife inside, tightening the zipper to leave the handle protruding for quick access.

He looked at Svetlana and Valery. "See you in a couple of minutes."

Deke pivoted in the small space below the seats, pulled himself down and forward into the tunnel adapter and floated out of sight.

65

Skylab

Deke pushed on the Skylab hatch. It creaked slightly on its hinges as it swung fully open and then hit the full stop with a metallic bang.

Pitch-black in there. Deke pulled his flashlight from his thigh pocket and flicked it on.

"Need a damn light switch," he mumbled to himself. He played his flashlight beam around the jumbled interior and then across the nearest curved wall. He found four long fluorescent lights and a small protruding switch. He flicked it on. After a quick snapping noise, some flashes and a rising hum, the lights started flickering. He reached out and tapped hard on the closest tube, and it settled into steady, increasing brilliance. A second light lit up farther down the module, casting harsh shadows. Old bulbs, he figured. But good enough. He tucked his flashlight away.

Okay, first things first. Deke grabbed an air duct tube and pulled himself fully through the hatch, orienting with what he remembered from training. Stowage and experiments up to the left, big experiment control panel up to the right, and ahead of him, mounted in the floor, the Seesaw experiment. And the circular entrance to the second docking port.

That hatch was closed and latched.

All right! he thought with relief. *We're ahead of the Chinese ship.* He paused. *But maybe they've gotten docked.* He tried to picture where the Skylab windows were and hunted in the shadows until he found a hinged metal cover next to the hatch. He undid the latch and rotated the cover back, revealing a square of glass with the blackness of space beyond. He pivoted to shut off the wavering lights so his eyes could readjust to darkness.

As his night vision returned, Deke began to see the faint purple glow of Earth's horizon and the lights of cities rolling past below him. With a start, he spotted the distinctive shape of New York City's harbor as they moved up the east coast of the US. But as his eyes adjusted more fully, he saw something he'd hoped he wouldn't see. At the edge of the window, partially blocking his view, was a smooth, bulbous white curve reflecting the city lights below it.

The Chinese spaceship. Close and motionless.

"Fuck!" Deke spat out the word.

He spun to turn the lights back on, tapped again on the nearest flickering bulb and rechecked the second hatch. It was flush in place, with all the latches tight.

Okay. They haven't gotten into Skylab yet. I need to bar the hatch.

He moved to study the center of the hatch mechanism. There was a toggle switch labeled Lock/Unlock, set in the UNLOCK position, just as his docking hatch had been.

Deke slid the switch to LOCK. He tried to remember whether there was any way to override it from the other side, or to overpower it, but he wasn't sure.

He searched around until he spotted a square metal box mounted on the far curve of the wall, beyond the main control panel. He pushed off and floated up to it, reminding himself how the four dials and three switches worked, hoping the system had been left powered. He selected ON for comm channel A, turned a second knob to PTT for Press to Talk, cranked the SPK VOLUME to max, leaned close to the built-in microphone and pushed the XMIT toggle switch.

"Houston, it's Deke, inside the Skylab Multiple Docking Adapter on comm channel A. How do you read?"

"Deke, Houston has you loud and clear from the MDA. How us?" Kaz's heavily distorted voice blared through the small speaker.

Deke winced and turned the volume down, then pressed XMIT again. "Loud and clear, Kaz. I've only ingressed as far as the MDA, but can confirm that the second hatch is closed and latched. I just locked it too, because out the window I can see that the Chinese ship has docked."

In Mission Control, all conversation stopped. Kaz recovered first.

"Copy, Deke, good news that the radial hatch is closed and locked, and Houston concurs with your actions." Kaz pictured what would be most concerning if he were in Deke's shoes. "We'll get EECOM to confirm the hatch locking mechanism details and will look through Skylab inventory for a way to further bar the hatch."

He glanced at Chris Kraft, who nodded and said to Kaz, "Tell him to get on with transferring the bodies and keeping Skylab secure."

Kaz chose his words carefully. "Deke, while we're checking that, we'd like you to ingress farther into the Skylab airlock and through to the main workshop. We'd like an update on the status of the station in general, and we'll need to cover experiments and set airlock hatches and switches for transfer and storage of the bodies as soon as possible." He glanced at the forward screen. "We have solid comms for the next few minutes through CONUS sites and then Newfoundland. Then a gap until Madrid, and then a long gap after that."

Deke pictured the ground track. After Madrid, there would be no comms until the other side of the world, through Guam. *Good to know.* "Copy, Kaz."

A thought occurred to him. He pushed off, floated back to the second hatch and pressed his ear against it. No metallic sounds of attempted ingress. All he could hear was the beating of his heart.

Good.

He pulled himself farther into the module to look at the Seesaw hardware, a long box covered with a hinged panel. It was unlabeled and he'd need a screwdriver to open it. Nothing much for the cosmonauts to see.

Also good.

He floated back to the comm panel and pushed the toggle. "All quiet here in the MDA, Kaz. Moving now into the airlock."

66

Skylab

Deke floated forward towards the hatch that led to the airlock module.

Skylab had been built as cheaply as possible. The main workshop habitat had been converted from an unused S-IVB rocket, with the crew living inside its big hydrogen fuel tank, modified for the purpose. A grid of internal bulkheads had been welded into place as makeshift rooms. The airlock, needed so that the crew could do space walks to repair broken exterior equipment and retrieve experiments, was an old design, the hardware recycled from the 1960s Gemini program. The resulting cobbled-together vehicle vaguely resembled an insect, with the Apollo capsule now in the place of the head, the docking adapter and airlock as the slender central thorax, and the main living workshop as the fat trailing abdomen.

Deke stopped at the airlock entrance, noting that the hatch was free on its hinges, and he clicked it securely into the clips that would hold it open. He guessed the last Skylab crew had missed latching it in the rush of leaving. He grabbed both sides of the open hatch and pulled himself into the darkened airlock.

The air tasted stale. *I'll need to get some recirculation going*, he decided as he hunted in the half-light for another light switch. He spotted two small oval windows, but the light coming through them was reflected and diffuse. He pulled out his flashlight again, found the switch, turned it on and was rewarded with fluorescents blinking on along the tunnel of the airlock. At the far end was another hatch, open to the deep blackness of the main part of Skylab.

He spotted another comm panel, set the switches, floated close to the mic and said, "Houston, I'm inside the airlock." He looked around. "We'll need bungees or something to strap the bodies in here."

"Copy, Deke, agreed. We'll go through the inventory list to find you a location. And we're working up procedures for you to depressurize the airlock once the bodies are inside." Kaz reflected momentarily on the words he was using: the two were no longer Tom Stafford and Vance Brand. They were becoming "the bodies."

"Houston, rather than take time to do a main workshop look-see now, I should go help Svetlana and Valery. We can do the tour once the bodies are in place."

Kaz looked at Kraft, who asked the room, "Anyone object to Deke's plan, or have any suggestions?"

EECOM spoke up. "FLIGHT, there are two extra crew restraints in the R5 locker in the Command Module, and we think there are some bungees in the Skylab workshop lockers. We'll have an exact location soon."

"Copy, EECOM." Kraft nodded at Kaz, who passed the information to Deke.

Deke replied, "Roger, Kaz, we'll grab those on the way by, thanks. I'm headed back to the Command Module now."

As Deke entered, the Apollo capsule was crammed with people, alive and dead. Valery had released and rotated the crew couches up out of the way, and Svetlana was floating the first of the two bodies down towards the hatch.

Deke quickly updated the Russians on the Chinese ship and hatch status, and then said, "Hang on a sec." He reached past the wrapped head to get at locker R5. He flipped through the stowage folds until he found the Restraints label, then pulled out two bundles of webbing, held with elastic. He stuffed them into his left leg pocket, floated backwards towards the hatch and said, "Okay, I'll guide this end."

Holding one leg, Svetlana pushed the body along as she moved from handhold to handhold. Deke eased the corpse's shoulders through the hatch, the rigor mortis mostly gone now. Like some weird, horrific birth, the entire body slid through into the larger open space inside the Multiple Docking Adapter section of Skylab.

Svetlana looked around, still holding the body by an ankle. The tubular layout with angular workstations and covered metal stowage boxes reminded her of the Soviet Almaz spy station she had served on. *I bet Skylab took lots of detailed pictures of the Soviet Union when it was operational.* As they floated the body past a large box labeled Film Vault, she nodded to herself. She wasn't sure what "vault" meant, but she knew that the high radiation in orbit would rapidly expose film, which needed to be stored in lead-lined containers. *We spy, they spy, what's new.*

Valery floated into the MDA behind the first body, and Deke updated them, with Svetlana translating. "This is the docking adapter section of Skylab. This hatch here"—he pointed to the locked hatch—"is where the Chinese ship is docked. You can see it through that window." He pointed.

Svetlana studied the hatch, picturing possible timing and sequence of events. "Any chance the Chinese crew already got in?"

"Nope," Deke replied. "The hatch was still sealed when I ingressed, and I locked it. The Chinese crew is stuck inside their ship, and I intend for it to stay that way."

Valery had his face close to the window, peering out into the darkness. Then he inspected the hatch, touching the latches with his fingertips. He said something in Russian, and Svetlana nodded.

"Deke, Valery says we should take the bolts out of the latch linkages so there's no way for the Chinese to open it from the other side."

Good idea, Deke thought. "I'll suggest that to Houston—they're working on a plan." He tugged again to start the body moving, and realized that with the head covered, he didn't know whether it was Tom or Vance. That bothered him, and he turned the body so he could read the name tag on the suit: Brand.

"Sorry, buddy," he muttered as he reached back to move through the airlock hatch.

Svetlana spotted the communications panel high on the wall. "Deke, we need to talk to Moscow."

He'd been thinking about that too, and looked down the length of Vance's body at the cosmonauts. "I agree, but the Skylab frequencies are preset and won't work directly with yours. As soon as we can, we'll patch you through via Houston." He pointed over his shoulder. "That's the airlock where we'll stow the two of them, and beyond it is the main living and working area of Skylab. Let's get Vance here strapped down, and then we'll go have a quick look."

He pulled the bundle of restraints out of his leg pocket and floated it to Valery. "You go on ahead and find a place for the clips to connect."

The switch panels and lights inside the airlock had metal grid covers to protect them from the clumsiness of spacewalking astronauts, and Valery easily found several locations to secure the straps. When Deke and Svetlana had the body in position, he pulled the restraints tight across Vance's chest and legs, the body bending to conform to the curved walls. Deke gave a few tugs to make sure it was secure, then turned towards the gaping black opening at the far end of the airlock.

"Do you two have flashlights?"

Svetlana nodded. "Yes, part of the Soviet flight suit kit." She reached into a leg pocket, pulled out a stubby black cylinder, looped the tether around her wrist and pushed a button twice, turning it on and off. Valery followed suit.

"Great. Come with me." Deke grabbed the rim of the hatch and eased through, then grabbed a handhold and pivoted himself out of the way.

Svetlana and Valery followed him into the darkness.

67

Skylab

The narrow beam from Deke's flashlight shone into the void.

He had a sudden feeling of vertigo, like he was perched on the rim of a deep, dark cave, overbalancing and holding on with just one hand. Reflexively, he tightened his grip on the thin handrail, feeling his heart beat rapidly.

"Turn your flashlights on!" he urged. A single pencil beam in the blackness wasn't enough for him to get his bearings.

He heard two small clicks, and twin pools of light joined his own. The added illumination revealed the scale of the module they'd entered. Deke hadn't realized during his training just how big the Skylab orbital workshop was, and how it would feel to float into it from the narrow confines of the airlock. He realized he was going to have to push off and float across the void, down to the shadowed gridded floor of the first-level bulkhead.

He turned and shone his light around the hatch entrance and behind Svetlana, looking for a light switch, but spotted another comm panel instead. He reached past her, configured the switches and pushed XMIT.

"Houston, we've transferred Vance's body to the airlock, and all three of us have just ingressed into the workshop for a quick inspection." His voice echoed like he was in an auditorium.

"Copy, Deke, thanks for the update. We have about two minutes left in this pass, and then we'll lose you for five minutes or so as you cross the Atlantic. Then we'll have you through Madrid."

"Roger." Deke glanced at his watch. The normal communication with Kaz had calmed him, and he took a deep breath, settling his heartbeat. "We'll have a quick look around, and we should have Tom's body transferred before we lose you after Madrid." He released the XMIT switch, told the others to follow him and pushed off.

Svetlana waited until Deke's feet were clear, watching his light as he tumbled and floated away, then gently pushed off the handrail. She was used to moving gracefully in weightlessness. Deke was pointed the wrong way when he ran into the grid structure of the mid flooring, and he floundered to get a handhold. Valery, who had only flown within the restricted confines of a Soyuz, scrabbled to a stop on the bulkhead several feet away. Svetlana stopped right where she had aimed, next to the six-sided hole in the gridded floor that opened to the next level. Not waiting, she pivoted and nudged herself through and down.

Valery was shining his lights through the grid of the flooring when he swore loudly. "Chyort, shto etta!" *Shit, what's that!* Deke and Svetlana turned to see what he was illuminating.

Off to one side, against the curved wall below, three white-faced people in orange flight suits were holding handrails, looking up into Valery's light.

"Christ!" Deke yelled.

Svetlana pushed off and floated directly at the three motionless figures, shining her light ahead. There was something weird about their faces. As she neared, she realized their heads weren't heads at all, but white bags tucked in at the neck of the zipped-up flight suits. The hands were smaller white bags, gray-taped; large safety pins held the mock hands in place. She poked a body, and it moved easily. "Mannequins!"

she said, incredulous. She looked closely at the flight suits. "The name tags say Carr, Gibson and . . ." She floated across to the last. ". . . Pogue."

"Those assholes!" Deke's heart was thumping wildly in his chest again, to the point of pain—something he hadn't felt before. He gasped slightly as he explained, "The last Skylab crew. They must have set them up as a joke on the next crew to arrive." He took a deep breath until his chest was full and held it, willing his heartbeat to settle into a normal rhythm.

"A joke?" Valery said. "Not so funny."

Men, Svetlana thought. That crew had been in space for over 80 days. So they'd pulled a prank—no real harm. She turned and shone her light around the lower bulkhead level of Skylab, seeing exercise equipment, experiment hardware, a toilet and small sleeping rooms.

By now the two men had floated down through the central opening, and Valery was shining his light on a bulbous red structure semi-submerged in the middle of the floor. He read the label aloud. "Trash Disposal Airlock?" He pronounced it "tresh," with a rolled "r."

"Yeah," Deke confirmed. "Anything that might spoil or stink goes in there and gets sucked into the old empty oxygen tank under the floor that's depressurized to vacuum. Kills the bugs." He was rubbing the left side of his chest and grimacing as he spoke.

Valery nodded appreciatively. "Good idea."

Suddenly, from above their heads came the creaking of door hinges, followed by the unmistakable centering rattle of a hatch settling into place and the squeaking of metal on metal under load. All three flashlights pointed up through the bulkhead grid above their heads to the center of the workshop dome.

The hatch they had left open was now closed.

Someone had just locked them in.

68

Mission Control

Kaz looked up sharply. Deke's voice in his headset was urgent, breathless.

"Houston, someone just shut the hatch to the airlock from the other side!"

"Copy." Kaz looked at the front screen. "We have thirty seconds, then no comms for five minutes, until Madrid." He glanced at Kraft, who was already speaking staccato to the room. "Anyone have immediate suggestions for the crew?"

EECOM spoke up instantly. "FLIGHT, it's an old Gemini hatch that uses a cable system they could cut if needed. There's a full toolbox in stowage locker . . ." He listened briefly to his back room. ". . . E623, in the aft compartment."

Kaz rapidly parroted the words to Deke, picturing what was happening on orbit. The Chinese crew had somehow gotten out of their docked ship and were now alone inside the docking adapter, with unrestricted access to Seesaw. And to the Apollo capsule.

"Copy, Kaz, we'll—"

Deke's voice was cut off as Skylab arced across the Atlantic, beyond the horizon from the Newfoundland antennas.

Kraft spoke loudly. "Listen up, people. We have a foreign crew on their own inside both Skylab and Apollo. I need ideas on how we can monitor them and slow them down or stop them from doing anything to harm our crew or the United States of America."

Kaz had an idea and spoke on the Mission Control comm loop. "FLIGHT, we can trigger the caution and warning alarms to distract and misdirect them."

Kraft nodded. There was a panel of lights inside the docking adapter that would illuminate and sound various loud alerts for emergencies like depressurization and electrical malfunction. "EECOM, get on that ASAP. The more realistic, the better."

At the communications console, INCO said, "FLIGHT, I think Deke left the speaker box on inside the docking adapter. So whatever Kaz says can be heard by the Chinese crew in there."

Kraft thought for a second, then scanned the room. "Who in here speaks Chinese?"

Seated beside JW at the SURGEON console, Jimmy raised his hand. "I do, FLIGHT."

Kraft said, "Hustle up here and get plugged in next to CAPCOM, Doctor." He glanced at the timer at the front of the room. "We have under four minutes to work up a plan."

Svetlana had been searching the bulkhead walls of the Skylab workshop with her flashlight, and she finally found what she was looking for. She threw the switch, and lights sizzled and blinked on all around the interior, making her squint at the brightness. Deke was near her, hurriedly opening toolbox drawers inside a wall panel, and Valery had launched himself up to the overhead hatch, his fingers now tracing the mechanism, looking for ways to open it. He grabbed the central blue handle and shook it hard, but it didn't budge. He peered more closely at a small circle on the hatch covered by a metal lattice, and turned to yell at Svetlana.

"*Yest okno!*" *There's a window!* He leaned close, trying to see through the small, thick-glassed porthole down the tunnel of the airlock and into the docking adapter. "I see someone!" he yelled in Russian. "One crewman, doing something near the Apollo hatch."

Svetlana floated next to Deke and translated Valery's words as the American kept rifling through the toolkit. He handed her a pair of small side-cutting pliers, then pulled open the bottommost drawer. "Bingo," he said. He slid long-handled heavy wire cutters out of their slot, then floated over to the central trash airlock, bent his legs and pushed off, launching himself up through the hexagonal opening. Tumbling as he floated, he yelled, "Valery!" The Russian turned, caught him and then pointed at the small window.

Deke handed Valery the wire cutters and stabilized himself to look through the window. The Chinese astronaut was over 25 feet away, and the view of him was distorted and poorly lit, but there was no doubt about what he was doing: unscrewing the bolts holding the cover on Seesaw.

Christ, we need to hurry, Deke thought. His chest was hurting constantly now.

Svetlana flew up and landed next to them, and asked, "Deke, do they have weapons?"

Good question. "I've only seen one guy, and that Chinese ship looked pretty small, so I think he's probably alone. I can't tell about a weapon. My eyes are old—you have a look."

Svetlana leaned in and squinted, trying one eye and then the other, then shook her head. "I don't see one, but his suit has many pockets, so he might."

Valery had hooked his toes under a nearby handrail to stabilize his body and free up both hands. He said something quickly, and Svetlana translated.

"He wants to know if you're ready for him to cut the main hatch cable."

Deke leaned back to get out of the way, grateful that Valery was doing the cutting. He felt a weird wave of weakness, like he suddenly needed to sleep. He shook his head to clear it. "Yeah, go ahead. The cable will be under tension, so be ready for it to snap back."

Svetlana passed Valery the warning. Then she asked, "What is the plan after Valery cuts the hatch open?"

Deke looked at her. *Shit, she's right. I need to get on top of this!* He grabbed Valery's arm to stop him for a second, and said, "You have the other knife, right?"

Svetlana answered for him, pointing at Valery's leg pocket. "Yes, he does."

"Okay. As soon as the cable's cut and the hatch opens, I want Valery to hustle through with his knife out and take the Chinese intruder prisoner. You and I will follow right behind to help."

Svetlana quickly pictured how it would work. Only one person could go through the narrow hatch at a time, so it limited their options. She retrieved the heavy adjustable wrench from her pocket as she relayed Deke's instructions. Valery just nodded. He was younger than Deke, and stronger than Svetlana. It made sense. He held the wire cutters between his fists, braced with his feet and legs and squeezed as hard as he could.

With a loud twang, the cable gave way, and the hatch moved, loose against its seal. Valery handed the cutters to Deke, unsheathed the long knife, pulled hard on the hatch to open it fully, reached out with both hands and neatly pulled himself through.

At the metallic snap of the cable being cut, Fang looked up from his work with the ratchet wrench just as the hatch swung open and the dark bulk of a man floated into the airlock, holding a glinting machete.

It was crystal clear that he was being physically threatened.

Fang reached into his leg pocket, pulled out the Black Star Type 54 pistol he had retrieved from his landing survival kit, took careful aim and fired.

69

Skylab

As the Chinese astronaut raised his pistol, Valery twisted to the side, attempting to protect his head.

Bracing for the coming impact.

The 7.62 mm bullet blasted out of the Black Star's short muzzle at over 1,300 feet per second and, in weightlessness, flew true to where Fang had aimed it: the thickest part of the man's body, dead center in the airlock hatch. Fang didn't want the bullet to miss and punch a hole in the pressurized hull of Skylab. But even if it did, there was enough air in the space station that he'd have time to retreat to the safety of his Shuguang.

He still needed several minutes to retrieve what he'd come for.

The bullet covered the short distance down the docking adapter in a hundredth of a second and slammed into Valery having barely slowed at all. It punched a small, neat hole as it entered but inflicted massive damage as it tore through his flesh, exiting in a spray of gore, bone and blood. The now tumbling bullet carried on down the airlock, past Vance's body and in between Svetlana and Deke at the far hatch, continued across the open space of the orbital workshop and slammed to a halt with a metallic bang against the heavy steel lid of the trash disposal airlock.

Its energy spent, it floated slowly up and away, tumbling end over end.

Valery had cartwheeled back with the impact, twisting and sliding along the curved metal walls, his blood spraying and smearing, spattering onto Vance's body and the faces of Svetlana and Deke.

With the threat cleared, Fang pushed off, floated the length of the docking adapter and quickly closed the near hatch. It would take his attackers a few minutes to deal with the injury and come up with a new plan. Enough time for him to extract the prize and get back to the safety of his own ship. He retrieved his floating ratchet wrench and returned to work.

He was still armed, if more self-defense was needed.

On the other side of the hatch, Svetlana yelled, "Deke, find a medical kit!" She grabbed Valery's ankle, tugging gently on it to guide him out into the light of the Skylab workshop.

Yelling in pain and wide-eyed with shock, Valery tried to turn his head to see the extent of the damage. Svetlana saw that the Chinese astronaut was closing the hatch, and guessed she had time to deal with Valery's injury.

"Hold on to this handrail!" she ordered in Russian, pushing Valery's arm towards the blue handrail next to the hatch. She needed him to focus and hold still. He was wearing the blue worsted cotton Russian flight suit tunic and elastic-waisted trousers over white cotton long underwear. "Hold still!" she commanded, and he grabbed the handrail with both hands, moaning in pain. Floating next to his midsection, she inspected the damage.

It was extensive. The bullet had struck his upper thigh, leaving raw meat and splintered bone where it had exited. Blood seeped and spread from the mangled hole. She could see no spurting blood, though, and hoped the major vessels hadn't been cut. If they had been, he'd bleed out quickly, and there'd be nothing she could do about it.

"Here!" Deke gasped, banging to a stop next to her, clutching a white duffel bag marked Emergency Medical Kit.

She unzipped it, flipped up the lid and rapidly scanned the list of contents. Hunting through the internal pouches, she found what she was looking for, pulled out the antibiotic tube, and told Deke, "Find me the cotton bandages!"

Svetlana turned back to Valery, who was watching her through slitted eyes, his face twisted in pain. "You're going to be okay, Valyusha," she reassured him, deliberately using the version of his name his mother would have used when he was hurt. "A serious wound, but the bleeding isn't too bad, and it's a good American kit. We'll get you back to Earth soon. You just need to hold on till then."

She removed the cap on the antibiotic tube and liberally squirted its contents onto the exposed, bloody flesh. Without gravity to hold it, the gel kept curling away, so she daubed it as best she could directly into the wound, Valery cursing in Russian at the pain.

"Bandages," Deke said, holding out a bulky roll wrapped in blue paper.

"Find scissors!" she directed him, and she hooked her toes under a handrail to free up both hands. With her body stable, she peeled and opened the roll and placed a length carefully into the exit wound, doing her best not to touch and contaminate it, hoping it would stanch the bleeding. Deke's hand appeared in front of her holding medical scissors, and she said, "Cut here," pointing with her chin. He sawed across the bulky bandage, and she tucked the severed section into place, Valery gasping at the extra pain.

She took the scissors from Deke and said, "Tape!" As he hunted through the kit, she cut a new length of bandage, then jammed the rest of the roll and the scissors into her thigh pocket and laid the fresh bandage across the wound. The red of Valery's blood had already soaked the first layer.

Deke found a fat roll of white medical tape and began peeling a length off its spool.

"Here," Svetlana directed him, and he attempted to lay it across the bandage. She could see it wasn't going to hold—the tape wouldn't stick to the fabric of Valery's flight suit. With both her hands occupied with holding the bandage in place, she said, "Deke, the scissors are in my pocket. Cut the cloth away!"

She felt him fumbling on her thigh, pulling the scissors out while stuffing the gauze roll back in, and then watched as he cut Valery's blue trousers and white underwear clear, exposing the pink, hairy flesh. With no gravity to drain it, the blood had stayed put, so the skin surrounding the wound was dry.

"Okay, tape now!"

Deke pulled a new length, stuck one end to Valery's bare thigh, pulled it tight across the bandage to partially close the wound and secured it to the exposed skin on the other side.

And then Deke drifted away, grimacing in pain, his hand on his chest.

"Deke, are you okay? I need the scissors and tape!"

He opened one eye to float the gear to her, then put both hands back on his chest.

"Chyort!" she yelled. She caught the tape and scissors and cut four more lengths, sticking them rapidly into place over Valery's wounds, wrapping the leg. She could feel the thigh bone moving under her hands, and guessed it was broken.

The medical duffel kit was floating away, and she reached to grab it, tucking the loose items inside and scanning the contents list again. She riffled through the labeled pouches until she found a cigar-sized aluminum cylinder. Hastily reading the instructions, she popped off its red cap, pressed its blue end against Valery's flesh next to the exit wound and pushed harder until the internal syringe fired, injecting painkiller. He gasped. She set her jaw and repeated the action on the other side of the wound, hoping it was an acceptable amount.

Finally, she pulled out a silver pouch of aspirin, carefully squeezed out four pills and put them in Valery's mouth, one by one, telling him to chew and swallow.

"Voda," he croaked. *Water.*

She turned to Deke, who was now refocusing, looking up at her. "Deke, is there water for Valery?"

"Yes," he answered huskily, and pulled himself cautiously down through the hole in the grating.

While she was waiting, she tucked everything back into the medical kit and hooked it to the hatch handrail by its strap.

Deke floated back up with a squeeze bag of water.

"Is it still good?" she asked.

"Should be," he answered. "Lots of iodine antifungal in it. I took a sip and it tastes okay."

She nodded. "Feed it to Valery."

As she watched Deke put the straw between Valery's lips and open the small valve, she asked, "Deke, are you okay?"

A deep frown crossed his face. Time to be honest. "I'm having heart troubles, but I'm all right now." He shook his head in self-disgust. "It's an old problem."

"Maybe something in the medical kit?"

He shook his head. "Nah. Save it for later if I need it."

Valery moved his head to indicate he'd had enough water, and Deke shut the small valve and stuffed the bag into a leg pocket.

He looked at Svetlana. "Listen to me. We have to stop that Chinese astronaut. It's a matter of national security."

Svetlana frowned. She looked down the darkness of the airlock towards the closed hatch at the other end, considering options.

"He has a gun," she said flatly. "We don't."

The communications box next to them issued a burst of static, and then Kaz's voice came through strongly.

"Skylab, we're back with you through Madrid for the next five minutes. We'd like an update from on board, and then we have a plan."

70

Mission Control

Svetlana's terse description of Valery's gunshot wound and Deke's heart problems momentarily stunned Mission Control.

"Copy, Svetlana," Kaz replied. "Confirm the airlock forward hatch is closed?"

Focus everyone on the primary threat.

"Yes." She considered the new situation. "Can the Chinese astronaut hear us?"

Kaz had asked the same question during the comm outage. "He doesn't hear your transmissions, but he hears our replies. We don't know if he speaks English."

I do, Svetlana thought. *Need to assume he does too.*

Kaz said, "Deke, are you there?"

Deke floated up next to Svetlana and pushed XMIT. "Yep. Feeling weak but okay."

Kaz looked at Jimmy, seated next to him, and then at JW, who was frowning and shaking his head. NASA had only allowed Deke to fly on Apollo-Soyuz because it was intended to be a low-threat, easy mission.

Kaz looked back at Jimmy and gave him a quick summary of what he wanted him to say in Chinese. Jimmy nodded, and Kaz pressed his transmit button, choosing his words deliberately.

"Deke, listen carefully. Shenanigans and spoofing imminent, proceed all haste."

Svetlana frowned at the unknown words, but Deke nodded. "Copy, Kaz, wilco."

He turned to the cosmonauts to clarify, unsure if Valery was even listening. "Houston is about to say and do things to mislead and distract the Chinese astronaut. We need to ignore them and keep working to stop him."

A piercing siren suddenly sounded, oscillating between two shrill notes. A voice came through the speaker box, yelling urgently in Chinese.

Deke spoke loudly over the combined noise to his crewmates. "Ignore it all—it's not real."

He glanced at Valery, floating inert next to them, then looked at Svetlana. Multiple red droplets were drying on her face—small freckles of gore. He felt shaky and dizzy.

"Follow me," he said.

Deke tugged on the handrail and floated up inside the airlock and down to the hatch at the other end. He yanked out his flashlight, looked at the hatch controls and nodded. "Just like I remembered." He explained, "No way to lock this hatch from the other side, so when we're ready, we can just turn the handle and open it."

He moved to the grated round window, taking a quick peek and then pulling clear in case the Chinese astronaut was right there. He reached to turn down the volume knob on the speaker box, muffling the alarms and shouting. He turned to Svetlana, floating in the narrow space beside him, their feet bumping into Vance's body where it was trussed to the wall. He said, "I see him working at the far end to remove a classified piece of equipment. Have a look."

Svetlana stared through the small double-paned window in the hatch. At the other end of the module, she saw that a large metal cover was floating above the man as he worked at the base of a complex piece of hardware covered in cooling tubes and heavy-gauge wire. It had a built-in control panel. *Maybe a laser of some sort*, she guessed, the US taking advantage of the vacuum of space to test it. She shrugged to herself. *We all have secrets.*

She asked, "How long will it take him to remove it?"

"Dunno," Deke answered. "But it doesn't seem like the siren is distracting him."

Distantly, they heard Kaz's voice over the din, and Deke turned the volume back up.

"Kaz, you call?"

"Deke, we have three minutes left before we lose comms, then should pick you up briefly through Madagascar a dozen minutes later. Are the tactics working?"

"Copy, Kaz. Negative."

Kaz's mind raced. *How do I explain this without tipping off the Chinese astronaut?*

"Deke, if we kill buses one and two, you poised?"

Deke thought for moment. "Affirmative. Give us sixty ticks."

Kaz nodded. "You got it. Hack."

Deke reached for his wrist and pushed the stopwatch knob on his Omega Speedmaster. He glanced hurriedly around the airlock. Valery had let go of his knife after he'd been shot, and Deke had seen it somewhere. Near Vance, he realized. He pulled himself down the airlock and probed under Vance's body. *There!* He grabbed the machete's handle and floated up next to Svetlana, handing it to her.

"Any change?" he asked as he pulled his own knife out of his leg pocket.

His voice sounds strained, Svetlana thought. "No."

"Get your flashlight and that wrench out," he ordered. "Houston is about to kill all power in"—he looked at his watch—"thirty seconds. Here's what I want you to do."

71

Skylab

Almost there! Fang was feeling rising triumph. He'd worked his way through the bolts and plumbing connectors, and then he'd retrieved a small hacksaw from his spaceship to cut the multiple power lines. He glanced again down the module at the airlock hatch, seeing the light and dark of movement through the small window. As he sawed, both hands busy, he pictured the motions he would make if they opened the hatch and attempted to rush him. A smooth move to retrieve the pistol from his pocket, an easy aim in weightlessness, then a pull of the trigger. It was public knowledge that the Americans didn't carry firearms on their Apollo ships, and his last attacker had only had a knife.

He ignored the whining false alarm and some American yelling at him in Chinese who didn't speak the language very well. Something about power, but Fang was barely listening as he sawed through the last few strands.

He was about to win.

Suddenly it went dark, and he heard a metallic bang from the other end of the module.

They've killed power and opened the hatch!

The sun had shifted while he'd been working, and the sole small window, below his feet, was now like a spotlight shining up into his eyes. He drew his pistol and pointed it, waiting for his attackers to come into the light. With his free hand, he gave a small tug on the device, and finally it came free.

He saw a quick silver flash of something, and before he could react, felt a hard, heavy blow to his forehead. The impact knocked him back and made him see stars. He blinked rapidly, blindly brandishing the pistol, daring one of them to rush him. As his vision cleared, he saw a wrench tumbling slowly above him and realized they'd thrown it at him.

I'm at a disadvantage, he realized. *Time to tip the odds.*

Fang aimed the gun at the dark behind the module's control panel, where he guessed they would be hiding. He fired three shots in rapid succession and stuffed the pistol back into his pocket. Reaching forward, he grabbed the hatch to his ship, threw it wide open, slung the American hardware down through it and neatly pivoted to follow. He yanked the hatch closed behind him, threw the lever, floated into the narrow confines of his Shuguang ship and closed its upper hatch.

Safe. And alone in the cockpit, as a fighter pilot should be.

Fang smiled as he rubbed his forehead.

Victory.

72

Skylab

"Deke, are you hurt?" Svetlana yelled above the screaming alarms.

No answer. She flicked on her flashlight and saw him huddled on the other side of the docking adapter, his face a mask of pain, his hands against his chest. But he was alive and showed no visible wounds.

The bullets had missed her too. She rapidly pulled herself forward to the hatch that led to the Chinese ship, took her knife in her right hand and yanked with her left on the release handle. It turned and the hatch pivoted open. She floated low to the side, ready to stab an emerging hand or head, but she saw nothing. She braced a foot and darted a quick look.

No one. Just the blank, shiny metal of a second hatch, closed, with no visible access handle on this side.

"Chyort!"

She pulled herself clear and up towards the comm panel.

"Houston, are you there?" The alarms were deafening. She looked for the speaker volume knob and cranked it to maximum. Above it, a MASTER ALARM light was flashing.

She heard Kaz's rapid-fire voice. "Loud and clear, Svetlana, with thirty more seconds in this comm pass. We'll pick you up again in twelve minutes. We see a Skylab depressurization. Recommend you evacuate to Apollo ASAP, closing all hatches."

"How much time do we have?" The most urgent question.

"Depends where the leak is. But we're commanding resupply tanks open now, so you should have several minutes. What happened?"

"The Chinese astronaut fired three shots. Now he is in his ship, hatch closed, with the hardware he took."

"Copy. Recommend you transfer—"

Kaz's voice was cut off.

Transfer what? He'd said they had 12 minutes until the next communications pass. Hopefully the leak rate from the bullet damage would be slow enough that the hatch to their Apollo ship could remain open. But they had to hurry. She tucked the knife away and pushed off, aiming for Deke at the other end. He was floating in the dark with his eyes closed, both hands on his chest.

"Deke! Deke!" she yelled.

His eyes opened halfway, and his mouth twisted in pain. He shook his head. "Heart," he said in a strained voice.

Svetlana grabbed him by the waist and propelled him along the docking adapter, stopping their combined momentum at the far end, next to the Apollo hatch.

"Can you get into Apollo by yourself?"

Deke nodded, reaching tentatively with one hand to grab the curved handrail beside the hatch. He slowly started pivoting himself through, headfirst.

Progress, she thought. *Give him a clear task to help him focus.*

"Get Apollo ready to undock," she said.

As his head and torso disappeared into the tunnel, he gave no sign that he'd heard her.

Svetlana turned and urgently pulled herself back along the length of the docking adapter, feeling her ears pop with the falling pressure. As she passed the control panel, she had a thought. She found the caution and warning controls and pushed the central red and yellow illuminated squares to reset the sensors. The blaring instantly ceased, but she knew it would be back for real as Skylab lost more air.

Still, she was grateful for the temporary quiet.

She pulled with both hands to fly through the darkness of the airlock, and pivoted through the hatch into the yawning blackness of the main workshop section. Far below her, daylight filtered in through a side window. She clicked her flashlight on and saw Valery next to her, holding the handrail, his body stretched out and still. His face looked gray, but he was alert and watching her.

"I heard more gunshots," he said in Russian.

She quickly explained what had happened, Deke's condition and Houston's plan. Then she asked, "How are you feeling?" She turned her flashlight on his leg and was relieved that the covering bandage hadn't soaked through.

"Fine. My femur is broken, but the painkillers you gave me helped. I can move myself okay by hand." He started pulling himself forward into the hatch, and tipped his head towards the tethered duffel bag. "You should bring the medical kit."

She nodded and paused briefly to think as she watched him go, picturing her next few hours. *What else should I bring?* Pushing off hard, she flew down into the center of the workshop. She shone her light on an open panel and scanned for what she might need, then looked around hastily for a bag. Spotting the mannequins against the wall, she floated across to them, yanked one of the white mock heads out of the neck hole, opened its drawstring top and started stuffing items between it. As she counted slowly to 60 in her head, she felt her ears pop again and heard the ship's alarm begin to sound once more.

Time to go. She pushed off the floor and moved through the grated opening and up to the airlock entrance. Houston had said to close all hatches, but Valery had cut the cable to this one. She grabbed the medical kit duffel and pulled herself through, leaving the hatch as it was.

As she hustled past Vance's body, she remembered that Tom was still under the seats inside Apollo. His unsecured weight would be a serious problem as they flew the capsule down through the atmosphere. *Maybe that's what Kaz meant about a transfer,* she thought. She hoped there was enough time. Perhaps Deke had already done it.

She floated out of the airlock into the docking adapter and reached to push the buttons and silence the alarms again. Looking ahead, she saw that Valery was still at the hatch to the Apollo ship.

"What's keeping you?" she asked urgently.

"Deke is partway through, blocking me, and he's not responding."

She floated past Valery, hastily tied off the two bags on a handrail and shone her light into the short tunnel. Deke was doubled up, filling the passage like a cork.

"Deke!" she yelled. She reached in and tugged his arm.

No reaction.

Svetlana squeezed into the narrow space beside him. She short-arm slapped his face, but he still didn't respond. His eyes were closed, his mouth slightly open, and she reached under his jaw to feel for a pulse.

It was there. Very weak and fast, but perceptible small thumps under her probing fingertip.

"Zhivoy!" she yelled back to Valery. *He's alive!*

"Slava bogu," she heard him respond. *Thank God.*

She squirmed up past Deke, spun herself around and tugged on his hands, extending his arms to guide him up and into his seat. The three seats were still lifted from when they'd retrieved Vance's body, and she had to stuff Tom's hooded body to the side as she pulled Deke into place. She fastened the seat's restraint straps across his inert form, wedged herself into a corner and grabbed Tom's leg to steer him down towards the hatch.

Svetlana was sweating heavily from the exertion, and she wiped the salty liquid from her eyes with the back of her sleeve. She found herself gasping slightly as the escaping air got thinner around her.

Hurry! she urged herself.

She pushed Tom's body through the tunnel and out. Briefly, she thought about just leaving him in the docking adapter. But Houston had been specific, so she continued moving the body aft, yelling over her shoulder for Valery to get into Apollo.

The alarms were ringing again, and she punched the buttons once more on the way by, relishing the temporary silence. She positioned Tom's corpse next to Vance's, looped and tightened a loose strap around his ankle to hold him there and pulled herself forward, clear of the airlock. She spun and slammed the hatch closed, locking it and making sure the pressure equalization valve was closed, hoping it would trap Skylab's air on the other side.

Bodies in a small, orbiting bubble, safe for some future ship to retrieve.

Her ears were popping constantly now, and she was urgently short of breath as she pushed off, flew the length of the docking adapter, chucked the two bags through and pivoted into the Apollo transfer tunnel. She felt dizzy as she yanked the hatch against the outrushing air, slammed it closed and threw the large lever to drive its latches to hold it. Instantly she heard the high whistling of air escaping through the equalization valve. Oxygen was pouring from the Apollo spaceship into Skylab's docking adapter and out to the vacuum of space through the bullet holes. It was dark with the hatch closed, so she jammed her flashlight between her teeth as she found the pressure valve with both hands, grabbed its yellow-striped handle and twisted it until it wouldn't move any more.

The whistling sound stopped, but she could hear air flowing and realized it was coming from Apollo's oxygen tanks, the system automatically opening valves to try to get the small capsule back to normal pressure. She was still gulping hungrily for air, but with each breath she got more oxygen into her blood and up to her brain. She took the flashlight out of her mouth, closed her eyes and floated motionless for several seconds, savoring the moment.

Zhivoy!

73

Mission Control

Kaz had an idea. As he watched the Skylab symbol on the front screen map crawl southwards, arcing down across the Horn of Africa towards the communications relay site in Tananarive, Madagascar, he quickly explained it to Chris Kraft.

The flight director listened, thought for several seconds, then nodded. He had Kaz repeat the idea on the Mission Control communications loop and told the flight dynamics officer to run a fast test and then get the commands ready to send as soon as they regained comms with Skylab.

Jimmy Doi was still seated next to Kaz at the CAPCOM console, wide-eyed at the audacity of Kaz's plan.

JW walked forward to stand behind them, grim-faced. He said, "I heard Svetlana say three more gunshots, and it sounds like Deke's heart problems have intensified. We need a medical report from the crew ASAP, Kaz."

Kaz nodded. "We should have ninety seconds of voice comms, maybe two minutes, skirting the eastern edge of Madagascar's range."

He pointed at the notebook on the console in front of him. "I'm making a hit list of items we need to talk to them about." He looked up again at the front screen. "You can see that once we go out of range from Madagascar, this orbit swings too far south for Australia. So we'll have to wait for the *Vanguard* relay ship in the South Pacific." Kaz held his unbandaged hand up in front of his good eye to gauge distances on the map. "That's about a half hour without communication."

JW nodded. "We put some extra meds in the Apollo kit, knowing Deke has a fibrillation history. Here's what you should tell him to take." He'd written the drug names and dosages on a piece of paper and handed it to Kaz. "Deke knows about it, but if he's feeling too bad, Svetlana will have to take care of it."

Kaz took the list and set it next to his own. "What about Valery's wound?"

JW glanced at Jimmy as he spoke. "It sounds like her initial first-aid reactions were good ones. There are oral antibiotics in the Apollo kit, and we'll prescribe some of those, but the most important thing is to get both Valery and Deke back on Earth as soon as possible." He looked back at Kaz and across at Chris Kraft, who was listening from his adjoining console. "Both men's medical conditions are life-threatening."

Kraft spoke to the doctors. "Deke is the only one qualified to run Apollo's systems for undocking, deorbit and landing. Svetlana can help him, but she's just a second set of hands." His gaze was intense. "Do you think you have enough meds on board for Deke to function?"

JW answered. "Probably, FLIGHT, but we really need to get a heart monitor onto him to know for sure."

Kaz added it to his list. "Want one on Valery as well?"

"Yeah, good idea."

"Anything else, doctors?" Kaz looked at the screen. "We have seven minutes until Madagascar."

Jimmy stood up. "I'm going to hit the toilet while we're out of comms, but one thought—I can't see how they can get Valery into a pressure suit with that injury."

Kaz nodded and glanced at Kraft. "FLIGHT, re-entry okay with some of the crew in shirtsleeves?"

Kraft shrugged. "We just have to play the odds. So long as Apollo holds pressure and the landing is nominal, it'll be okay. A couple of Apollo crews chose to land with their helmets off. Here we'll just have to accept the risk of them not wearing the pressure suits." He turned and pushed his transmit button to address all console operators in the room. "Listen up. We have just enough time during this next pass for priority communications with the crew, and then about thirty minutes until we raise them again through *Vanguard*. Everyone review procedures for expedited undock and re-entry, and pass anything urgent to CAPCOM."

The moment Skylab appeared over the horizon near the tall dish antenna in Madagascar, its small, distant radio signal was detected. The data flashed through the comm site computers, African telephone lines and a succession of undersea cables, and appeared on the screen in Mission Control as AOS—acquisition of signal.

Flight Director Chris Kraft saw the AOS and felt the urgency. "FDO, as soon as you have a solid lock, send that command."

The flight dynamics officer had been poised as well. "Copy, FLIGHT, already sent."

FDO's coded signal traveled back through the 10,000 miles of cable and was transmitted by the tracking antenna directly up to Skylab, racing across the sky 267 miles overhead. Skylab's computers read the digital sequence, checked that it was valid and started sending commands.

Commands that hadn't been used in a while.

At the opposite end of Skylab from where the Apollo craft was docked, inside a ring of meteoroid-shielding armor, was a cluster of 22 black titanium spheres, each about the size of a large pumpkin. Filled with nitrogen gas, they were all connected to each other through valves and tubing. When Skylab was launched, the tanks had been filled to their 3,100-pound pressure limit, but over the years the supply had dwindled to 500 psi.

But it was enough.

In response to FDO's command, valves that had been shut tight for nearly a year and a half clicked open. Cold nitrogen gas instantly flowed through a maze of tubes on opposite sides of Skylab, through the valves into a single bent tube on each side, and out to space through a sideways-firing bell-shaped nozzle.

Two simple, invisible jets of nitrogen gas, pointed in opposite directions, their streams aligned with Skylab's hull, meant to turn it like a pinwheel.

At first, there was no visible effect. But slowly Skylab started to turn as if it were on a barbecue spit. As the nozzles kept squirting, the spaceship spun up until it reached the rate that FDO desired. Then little accelerometers sent a command to shut the valves. They clicked closed, leaving the remaining nitrogen gas in the tanks for future commands. Skylab was now slowly spinning.

Just as Kaz had suggested.

"Apollo, Houston, how do you read?" Kaz transmitted as soon as he saw the AOS light, speaking quickly.

Inside the Apollo Command Module capsule, Svetlana had put on a comm cap. "Houston, Apollo, read you loud and clear."

"You also, Svetlana. We have two minutes to talk. Please give us an update." It was the first thing on Kaz's paper list, and he checked it off.

Svetlana had made a mental list. "Okay. Deke, Valery and I are in Apollo, Vance's and Tom's bodies are in the Skylab airlock, and I closed the hatches at both ends of the docking adapter." She assumed Houston would be able to see the data from the Apollo capsule and assess its health, so she focused on the crew. "Valery is in pain, but the bleeding has stopped. He's strapped into the right-side couch. Deke is in the center couch, not feeling good. His heart is unsteady, causing pain, and he's not always awake. Maybe he needs medicine?" She pictured her mental list. "I am fine. One important thing. Make sure you tell Moscow all this too."

"Copy, Svetlana, we will. You're right that Deke needs medicine." He read her the locker location and specific medication container that JW had written down for him. "Also, please put heartbeat monitors on Deke and Valery. They're in the same locker."

He looked at the screen. Sixty seconds left. "The plan is to undock from Skylab immediately and deorbit the three of you to splashdown as soon as we can. I have some urgent switch throws when you're ready."

Svetlana nodded. That was the plan she'd been going to ask for. "I'm ready for switches."

As he read the locations and positions and waited for Svetlana's confirmations, Kaz kept an eye on the clock. He'd set himself a deadline, and they were at it.

"Fifteen seconds left. We'll have you again in thirty-five minutes. Thirteen thirty-two Zulu time. Talk to you then."

"Copy, Kaz. Thirteen thirty-two." Her voice sounded small.

Kaz pictured her alone inside Apollo with the two ailing men. He didn't know if his transmission would make it, but he quickly pushed the button. "And Svetlana—great work up there."

He glanced up at the screen. The green AOS light had extinguished, and below it an orange LOS was now glowing.

Loss of signal.

Kaz had another idea, triggered by something Svetlana had said. He spent several seconds picturing whether it was possible, looking at the world map at the front of the room. *Maybe just. But we need to act fast!* He leaned towards Chris Kraft and quickly outlined the idea. Kraft picked up his phone to make a call.

74

Mission Control

Kaz glanced at the timers on the front screen and peeled off his headset. He had over 20 minutes until they could talk to the crew again through the *Vanguard* communications relay ship. Enough time for him to hit the head and refill the coffee mug JW had brought him.

Several console operators around the room were doing the same, and Jimmy had already ducked out. With undock and re-entry coming, this might be their last opportunity for a while.

Kaz stood, the pain in his ribs dulled by the Tylenol to an intense but livable level. He walked across Mission Control and out the door nearest the restrooms.

There was a lineup all the way out the men's room door. Rather than wait, Kaz turned and climbed the stairs to the third floor, hoping the john there would be less busy. There were several support rooms on that floor that had been used extensively during the Moon landings and Skylab operations, but they were mostly empty now.

As he walked down the third-floor hallway, he heard a voice talking urgently on the other side of a closed door. In what sounded like a foreign language.

Kaz stopped to listen. *Definitely not English.* He moved closer to the door, which had a small square window in it, and leaned far enough over for a quick peek.

A man with his back to the door was seated at the far side of the small room, talking animatedly and waving his free hand as he spoke. Kaz ducked back, risked another fast look to make sure of what he'd seen, and then walked quickly down the hallway to the restroom, his heart beating fast. He pushed the door open, thankful that only two other flight controllers had had the same idea. There was one spot open. He set the coffee mug on top of the white porcelain urinal, unzipped and stared at the wall, thinking as he peed.

Kaz had recognized the man's shirt and hair, and he'd caught enough of the muffled voice to be sure. He shook his head, realizing what it meant, and cursed his own stupidity as several pieces dropped into place. He flushed the urinal, turned to the sink and splashed some water on his face with his unbandaged hand to get rid of the remaining dirt. He caught his own eye in the mirror and asked himself, *What do I do now?*

He used paper towels to dry himself off, retrieved his mug and quickly exited the restroom, looking for a phone.

75

Shuguang Spaceship, Docked to Skylab

Fang was humming.

It was a tune from a movie he'd watched before launch, a song called "Red Star Shines." He didn't have a good voice, but he liked the bouncing melody, and no one else was listening. It sounded just fine to him inside his spacesuit helmet. His hands moved quickly across the control panel in the cockpit. Not rushing. Depending on a smooth, deliberate, physical understanding of how the machine worked, with occasional glances at the checklist clipped to his knee to make sure he didn't miss a step. Just like he'd flown all the aircraft before this one. He was a pilot of methodical, informed habits. Habits that had kept him alive.

He remembered a few of the song's words and sang them. "In the long nights, the red star shines and repels darkness." That made him smile. No red star person had ever seen darkness like what he was flying in now. And he was about to return, triumphant.

Fang reconfirmed that all checks were complete and pushed the button that drove the latches holding Shuguang to Skylab. One last time for the complex docking mechanism to do its job. He stopped humming briefly and listened, nodding when he heard the grinding sound of motors driving gears and cables. He pictured the latches slowly being pulled back, metal claws being retracted, the hardened steel sliding against the hatch until it was just far enough to be clear of the structure. Compressed springs under small plungers had been waiting for this moment ever since docking. Released, they popped up to their full height, smoothly pushing Shuguang away from the heavier Skylab.

Like a kiss to send him on his way. He started humming again.

Strapped into his seat, Fang felt his body float forward with the small acceleration. He counted to 10, in rhythm with the music, to give the ship time to get physically clear, and checked the image in his periscope to verify motion away from the target. Satisfied, he activated his motion control system. Built-in sensors measured accelerations and fired small thrusters to stabilize his trajectory, to hold him on a straight line away from Skylab.

Another line of the lyrics popped into his head. "The shining star passes on for thousands of generations." He felt pride at being a vital part of that history. The Middle Kingdom's first space flyer! He sang the line again, louder, smiling.

His ship suddenly lurched. Fang stopped singing, eyes going to the thruster control system. *Did a jet malfunction?* He could see several jets firing, fighting whatever had caused the disturbance, trying to get the ship back on track.

But his attitude indicator showed him way off orientation, and a glance through the periscope showed Skylab veering away. *It's as if I've been hit!*

Then, through his helmet, he heard the sound of metal on metal, like something being dragged across his hull. His thrusters were firing like mad, trying to counter it, and he stabbed out with his hand to hit the emergency Free Drift button. No use wasting fuel fighting something he didn't understand.

The scraping sound stopped. He checked his display and saw that his ship was slowly tumbling. Through the narrow view of the periscope, he saw the Earth rushing by, and then the horizon, with the blackness beyond. He opened the optical setting as wide as possible to try to spot Skylab, his pulse racing at the thought of an imminent helpless, blind collision.

Fang was confused. What had gone wrong? He cycled through his pressure readings and was relieved to see no obvious leaks. His ship seemed healthy. *So, what, then?*

In the periscope view, the brightness of Skylab suddenly appeared. Fang stared at it for a few seconds and then looked closer, holding a gloved finger against it to gauge motion as it moved across his screen. With his ship's slow tumble, Skylab moved all the way to the edge of his screen and disappeared, leaving it black save for the faint light of stars.

Fang frowned. *Skylab is turning!* he realized. Had a malfunction of his ship somehow caused that? He visualized what he'd just seen in three dimensions and concluded that his ship was moving away from Skylab, so he needn't fear a collision. He took the time to do a systematic check of all Shuguang systems, methodically verifying every pressure, quantity and voltage.

"My ship is healthy," he said aloud. It was calming to hear it.

Something else had made Skylab turn. He pondered for a few seconds, and then his eyes widened. He spoke into his helmet again, angrily. "You bastards!" They had deliberately tried to damage his ship by rotating Skylab's telescope mount into him as he undocked. He revisualized what he'd seen as Skylab moved across his periscope screen. Had there been damage? Fang shook his head. If there was, he'd missed it.

He felt a surge of fury at the physical attack, and with the gut instinct that had made him a top fighter pilot, he had a momentary urge to ram Skylab and the Apollo crew who had threatened him with a knife. *Skylab is an abandoned vessel, adrift in the heavens! They had no right to attack me!*

He took a deep breath. What had Mao said? *The people must move forward at the critical moment.* That moment was now. His ship was healthy. He had accomplished the most complex phases of the mission.

And the prize was strapped securely in the storage space under the head of his seat.

A small smile twitched the corner of his mouth. And then he grinned. They had tried and failed. He would not.

He remembered another line from the song and sang it loudly as he re-engaged his ship's attitude control system in preparation for deorbit.

"In the struggle, the red star shines and shows directions," he bellowed.

He was headed home.

76

Director's Office, Fifth Academy, Peking

The phone's ring was shrill, rattling on Tsien Hsue-shen's desk.

He glanced at his watch, frowning. Almost 9:30 p.m. No one ever called that late with good news.

Despite the hour, he was still in his office, just down the hall from the Shuguang mission support rooms. As director of the program, he needed to be here. Especially at this critical final phase of the flight.

He picked up the receiver and said, "Tsien."

There was a series of clicks and an undulating roar of static, then a distorted voice cut through, talking rapidly, barely understandable.

Tsien listened carefully and then asked the man on the other end to repeat some of the words to make sure he understood him properly. The time lag and noisy signal made it difficult, but eventually Tsien thanked the man for relaying the message, replaced the handset in its cradle and glanced again at his wristwatch. He visualized the world map and Shuguang's current location.

The call had been from his tong contact in Houston, passing on the message that Shuguang might have been damaged by the Americans during undocking. It was still several orbits before the world would turn enough for China to be back under the spaceship's flight path.

Tsien weighed the risks. His contact had also relayed that Fang had been successful in his mission and that the secret American weapon was now on board Shuguang. That took precedence over everything. Waiting only added uncertainty.

He got up from his desk and headed down the hall. *Not totally unexpected*, he thought. It had always been a backup option, and the ship's divers and crew were well trained. Fang had all the necessary deorbit burn information on board. He just needed a decision from Peking.

Tsien's decision. He would tell Fang as soon as he came within range of the first communications relay ship, so they could target the second one.

Tsien was going to bring Fang Kuo-chun home early, to land in the sea.

77

Apollo Spaceship, Docked to Skylab

Svetlana rummaged through the Apollo locker next to the forward hatch, looking for the medication Kaz had specified. She found the pouch labeled Docking Module Pilot and two heart monitor kits, and floated back up into the cockpit with them, strapping herself loosely into the left couch to stay in position next to Deke.

"Deke," she said gently.

His eyes were closed, and his face looked drawn with pain. He didn't respond.

Valery was watching from the far couch. She floated a heart monitor kit over to him and said, in Russian, "Put it on."

She tugged at Deke's flight suit sleeve and said his name louder. "Deke!"

This time, he opened his eyes, blinked a couple of times and turned to look at her.

She held up the medical pouch. "Houston wants me to give you medicine for your heart. It will make you feel better."

Deke nodded, grimaced and asked weakly, "Digitalis? They put some on board for me. Just in case." A ghost of a smile crossed his face. "I think this is the case."

Svetlana nodded, opened the pouch and hunted through the tubes inside, looking for the right one. "Yes, they said seven hundred and fifty micrograms digitalis." She held up a syringe for him to see. "I need to inject you."

He took a breath and twisted, reaching to unzip the upper tunic of his flight suit. "Help me get this off," he grunted.

Svetlana pried the orange-brown jacket off his shoulders and one arm, revealing his white T-shirt underneath. As he pulled the jacket off his other arm, she rolled up his shirt sleeve. There were small alcohol swab packets in the pouch, and she peeled one open and rubbed the wet gauze on Deke's upper arm. "Here okay?" She tucked the loose swab into her leg pocket to keep it from floating away.

"Sure." He looked at her through half-closed eyes and smiled slightly. "Is this gonna hurt?"

She raised her eyebrows. The Star City doctors had given her basic medical training, but she was no nurse. "Probably."

She double-checked that the hypodermic label matched what Kaz had said, unscrewed and pulled off the needle cover, tucking it into her leg pocket, grabbed Deke's arm to stabilize herself and plunged the needle in. She pressed with her thumb until all the fluid was injected, then pulled the needle out.

"Ouch!" Deke said. "Christ!"

Svetlana put the needle cap back on and opened a second swab to wipe off the droplet of blood that had appeared. "That was only two hundred and fifty micrograms. I need to do two more."

Deke looked away as she repeated the process, stowing all the loose bits in her pocket. She found a bandage in the pouch and pulled it tight across the three puncture sites. She looked at the pouch. *We might need to use this again*, she thought, and tucked it into Deke's leg pocket.

She looked at his face. "How do you feel?"

"Like a stabbing victim!"

She frowned at the unfamiliar words, but decided she didn't need to know what he meant. There were more urgent concerns.

"Houston wants heart sensors on you as well as Valery, and said we need to splash down as soon as possible. Here's yours." She handed him the remaining heart monitor. "What do I need to do for undocking?"

Deke thought about it as he slowly lifted up his T-shirt and methodically stuck the cardio sensors in place. Without the high-gain antenna, they would have communications with Houston only about 30 percent of the time. But expedited undocking was pretty simple. They could deal with deorbit targeting during the next decent comm pass.

"Okay," he said weakly. "Here's what I need you to do."

"Apollo, Houston, how do you read us through *Vanguard*?"

Valery pushed the transmit button to answer. "Moment, Houston." He yelled, "Sveta, Houston!"

Svetlana was buried in the nose of the Apollo capsule, reinstalling the docking probe and drogue and closing the hatch for undocking from Skylab. Deke had been drifting in and out of exhausted sleep, so Valery was wearing a comm cap. She pivoted in the confined space, floated up to the left couch and pulled her comm cap back on, reaching to throw the switch for hot mic so Houston could hear all three crewmembers without having to push any buttons.

"Houston, the docking probe is installed, hatch is closed, I gave Deke his medicine, and we connected the heart sensors." *What else is urgent?* "Deke is still sick."

Kaz looked back at JW and Jimmy at the SURGEON console, and both gave a thumbs-up, verifying they were receiving heart data.

"Copy, Svetlana, thanks for the summary. Good work. We have you now for three and a half minutes, will have no comms for nine, and then will have an extended pass as you fly over the United States. The plan is for you to undock and separate now, if you're ready, for splashdown in one orbit near Hawaii." He glanced at JW again. "The doctor thinks the medication should start working soon, so Deke will be able to help you."

Svetlana blinked several times, considering that, and then nodded to herself. "Okay, Kaz, I'm ready to undock."

"Great." He paused. "Is Deke listening?"

Svetlana shook Deke's arm. He had his comm cap on, but he appeared to be sleeping. "Deke!" she yelled.

His eyes opened.

"Deke, talk to Houston!" Svetlana hoped a clear command would cut through the fog.

"Houston, Deke here." He sounded strained.

"Deke, loud and clear, you up for an undock and re-entry?" Kaz looked left and made eye contact with Chris Kraft, assessing Deke's capability. They needed him.

"Yeah, Kaz, we can," Deke answered slowly. "The jabs Svetlana gave me feel like they're kicking in a bit." He fought to think clearly. "We won't be able to get suited in time, though. You okay with us re-entering just wearing flight suits?"

JW cut in hurriedly on the Mission Control loop. "FLIGHT, we're getting good heart telemetry. Valery's looks a little fast, with his injury and loss of blood. Deke's pulse is very high, irregular and weak, hopefully improving soon."

Kraft gave him a thumbs-up.

Kaz answered Deke's question. "Deke, we've discussed that and are okay with unsuited re-entry. We're looking at your switch config now, and you have a GO for undock and expedited manual separation."

Svetlana asked, "Has the Chinese ship undocked? Will we collide again?" She was back down by the forward hatch, following the wall placard checklist, venting pressures for undock and checking for hatch leaks.

"Apollo, Skylab accelerometers saw him undock thirty-three minutes ago. He should be clear."

Deke had been looking at the instruments. "Kaz, I see us having a steady unexpected roll rate. You okay with that for our undock? I could cancel it out once we separate and get clear."

"Yeah, Deke, the roll rate should be fine for you to undock. We made a late decision to spin Skylab to try to swat the Chinese ship with the telescope mount as he undocked. Accelerometers show we may have dinged him." Kaz thought ahead. "NORAD will be tracking him soon."

"You tried to swat him?"

Kaz could hear Deke chuckling. A good sign.

"Nice move."

"Thanks. You're on the axial end of Skylab, so you'll be clear." Kaz glanced at the timer. "Fifteen seconds until we lose you. Talk through Goldstone at thirteen thirty-two."

Deke glanced at the instrument panel timer and forced himself to do the math. Nine minutes from now. "Copy, thirteen thirty-two."

78

The Pentagon, Washington, DC

Defense Secretary James Schlesinger was furious. He'd just gotten surprising rapid-fire calls from both the NASA administrator and the chairman of the Joint Chiefs of Staff.

He hated being surprised.

Schlesinger glanced at his hastily scrawled summary notes on his broad desk. The Chinese had successfully docked their new secret manned spaceship with Skylab, claiming that the orbiting workshop was an abandoned vessel. They had subsequently stolen the Project Seesaw beam weapon test hardware, and successfully undocked after a battle that injured the Apollo crew and damaged Skylab. And now NORAD was confirming that the Chinese spaceship was maneuvering, changing orbit to set up for re-entry. Possibly into the ocean near one of China's communications relay ships.

The NASA administrator had said that one of his ops people in Mission Control, a Navy officer, had come up with a suggested course of action that required the highest level of approval. As the former director of the CIA, Schlesinger knew about the project, and now he briefly pondered it, looking at the clock on his Pentagon office wall.

The Chinese were clearly in the wrong. They had violated the Outer Space Treaty and were now in possession of something of great strategic significance to the United States of America.

He plucked the handset off his phone receiver and dialed the Oval Office directly.

Dorothy Downton, Ford's private secretary, answered. "Good morning, Office of the President, may I ask who's speaking?"

"Secretary Schlesinger here. Please put the president on ASAP."

"I'm sorry, sir, but President Ford is in a meeting. May I—"

Schlesinger interrupted her. "This is urgent. I need to talk to him right now."

There was a brief pause. "Yes, sir, I'll get you the president."

Downton got up, walked quietly into the Oval Office and got Ford's attention. Frowning, he excused himself from his meeting with a congressman and followed her to her phone.

He grabbed the handset. "President Ford here. What's up, Jim?"

Schlesinger described the situation, the extremely short time window and the limited options, stressing that China was clearly the aggressor and in the wrong. He knew that last piece would be important for Ford, who, as commander in chief, had to make the call.

"Will these actions and outcomes remain classified?" Ford asked. A key question.

"Yes. We are within our rights, and we don't need to tell anyone. The Chinese are in no position to tell the world what they've been doing." He paused and simplified the issue. "It's a classified military problem, and this course of action makes it go away."

Ford pictured the possible outcomes and how he would defend them. This was an obvious threat to the United States that he could solve right now.

He decided. Glancing at Dorothy, he made it official.

"The use of Project Spike is approved."

79

Groom Lake, Nevada

The horn blared on the wall in the Quick Reaction Facility, a building on the edge of a secret airfield on a high-desert lakebed. It was a remote classified Air Force base known to people stationed there as Groom Lake; its official Nevada Test Range name was Area 51.

The on-duty Air Force pilot, Mac Heuser, had been lounging in the facility's small canteen, chatting with his intelligence officer. Mac was wearing his flight suit and boots as required, but he'd never expected to actually hear the horn.

"Holy shit!" He sat up, staring wide-eyed at the intel officer, his heart racing. He jumped to his feet and ran out of the canteen and into the attached hangar, towards his jet.

Mac's F-106 was kept plugged in, all electronics and navigation equipment running and updating targeting datalinks. Mac sprinted to the ladder, where his g-suit and helmet were hanging, hurriedly put them on and scrambled up the metal rungs. He vaulted over the sill onto the ejection seat as his crew chief raced up after him, moving swiftly to get him strapped in and connected to the plane.

The F-106 Delta Dart. An old design, built as a pure 1950s interceptor, but still capable. It had a manta ray–shaped delta wing to allow it to maneuver in the thinnest of air. It had no gun, and no ability to carry bombs. No extraneous weight or drag. Everything was purpose-built to enable it to carry a missile to high altitude as quickly as possible.

Then fire it.

Mac glanced at the instruments and dials, checked that all switches were set, raised his left hand and spun his pointer finger. The crew chief had already hustled down and pulled the ladder away, and now signaled for the airman to flow air to start the engine. The start cart screamed, air blasted through a tube into the turbine, and the engine wound up and lit.

A cacophony of noise, with the purpose of getting the F-106 airborne ASAP to meet the threat.

The hangar was open at both ends so the pilot could push up power and taxi out fast, not worried about his jet blast. The radio frequency was preset, and Mac pushed the transmit button on the side of the throttle in his left hand.

"Ranch Tower, Spike One, ready for takeoff."

The tower controller had received the scramble alarm as well and was watching the F-106 taxi the short distance from the QRA to the runway.

"Spike One, cleared for takeoff on three-two."

No further instructions needed from the tower. Everything else would be handled by NORAD.

Mac did an abbreviated check of key systems as he taxied fast onto runway 32, not stopping, advancing the throttle into full afterburner. The jet leapt ahead, sucking in the thin, hot high-desert air, spewing it out the back in a tube of fire. He raised the nose, slammed the gear handle up and turned left to follow the guidance on his instruments.

His jet had the Hughes MA-1 integrated fire-control system, linked to NORAD's Semi-Automatic Ground Environment network so the aircraft could be steered by mission controllers deep underground in Colorado.

But what really mattered was slung under his right wing. A long, sleek blue tube with a pointed black nose and four white tail fins.

Project Spike.

Mac engaged the Hughes autopilot, still in full afterburner, and the jet turned left, racing skyward. A computer deep beneath the rock of Cheyenne Mountain, 500 miles away, was calculating the trajectory, steering the jet towards its target.

Mac watched the path they were following and monitored the plane's systems, his flesh and blood as much a part of the machinery as the pumps and valves. A weird role for a fighter pilot. Like a babysitter riding a remote-controlled dragon. But a vital role. He checked the datalink, saw the approval message and reached for the switch that armed the missile.

Permission to fire. He was the final link.

A light illuminated on his guidance display. Already going Mach 1.2, he pulled firmly back on the U-shaped control stick, squishing himself into his seat at nearly four times his normal weight, raising the nose into a 65-degree climb, following the steering. He checked the stick forward to hold the angle precisely, and at exactly 38,100 feet, the F-106 automatically launched the missile. It streaked out from under his wing, racing away in front of him, leaving a trail of white smoke pointed skyward.

Spike was on its way.

With his part of the mission complete, Mac exhaled and relaxed, took control from NORAD and rolled the airplane upside down, smoothly pulling the nose back down towards the horizon. Feeling his pulse slowing, he started a long, sweeping, descending turn back towards Groom Lake.

Mac checked his gas—not a lot, but enough. He glanced at the angled cockpit mirror that allowed him to see over his shoulder, towards his jet's six o'clock. The narrow column of white was there in the sky, a bizarre vertical contrail, starting to dissipate behind him.

Visual proof of what he'd just done. Not a test.

The first-ever operational firing of the Project Spike anti-satellite missile.

88

Earth Orbit, above the United States

It looked like a very large tomato can. A fat metal cylinder with a super-cooled central infrared seeker and 64 small surrounding solid rocket motors to steer it. Rising at extreme speed out of the atmosphere, into space.

Like a powerful giant had thrown it.

It had no exploding warhead. To work, the guidance had to be perfect, counting on the violence of a high-speed impact to cause the desired destruction.

The Project Spike missile fired from the F-106 had accelerated and pointed the tomato can exactly on its way. As it closed on the target, everything depended on precise small nudges from the small rocket motors to ensure a bullseye.

But only seconds before impact, the Shuguang capsule fired a thruster, correcting its orientation. There was no time for Spike's projectile to respond. Spike had been designed for intercepting simple, predictable satellites, not self-propelled spaceships.

At tremendous speed and by the slimmest of margins, Spike missed, whizzing by in the silence of total vacuum. Going so fast that Fang couldn't have seen it even if he'd had windows.

The metal can, lobbed high above the Earth, was slowly pulled back by gravity until it fell into the atmosphere, heating rapidly with the friction of the surrounding air and burning up in a quick flash of incandescent light.

An insignificant man-made meteorite that had failed to do its job.

81

Apollo Spaceship, Earth Orbit

Hundreds of switches. Toggle switches, rotary switches, thumbwheels, push buttons and circuit breakers, seemingly squeezed into every corner of Apollo. Svetlana shook her head, frowning. Why did the Americans make their ship so complicated?

She'd gotten Valery and Deke tightly strapped into their couches and was following Deke's vocal direction. Both she and Deke held checklists, verifying they made no mistakes. So far, so good.

Weird that I've already flown an Apollo re-entry and Deke hasn't, she thought. But that first time, she'd been strapped into the right-hand couch, with no responsibilities. This time, she was the one doing the work, with deadly seriousness, glad for any way that she and Deke could help each other.

Houston had tracked them closely as they crossed the United States and had updated their navigation accuracy. There had been several key switch throws, called up to them by Kaz in Mission Control as they'd passed over Madrid and Madagascar, getting them ready for the deorbit burn. They had one last communications pass over the Orroral Valley tracking station in Australia, and then they would re-enter the Earth's atmosphere.

"Apollo, Houston, how do you read?" Kaz was concentrating hard on the stream of updated data on his console screen.

Deke answered, "Loud and clear, Houston."

"Copy, Deke, looks like you had a good deorbit burn, and we're updating your tracking now. Seems right down the center. We see you've jettisoned the Service Module on time. Entry interface in three minutes."

"Roger. Still expecting about four g?"

Kaz listened briefly to an update from the flight dynamics console and replied, "Max g should be three point six, Deke." He glanced at JW and Jimmy at the SURGEON console. Hopefully not too much for Valery's makeshift leg triage. And Deke's heart.

Svetlana asked, "Houston, might the collision we had with the Chinese ship have damaged our heat shield?"

There had been an intense discussion in Mission Control about that. "We don't think so, Svetlana. The Service Module covered and protected your heat shield until you jettisoned it, and only a very deep gouge could have affected it. Our data didn't show enough change in velocity for that level of damage."

I sound too wishy-washy, Kaz thought.

He glanced at Kraft, who shrugged and quietly said, "If it was actually damaged, there's nothing anyone could do about it anyway."

But Kaz needed to give them something. "Apollo, we're confident that your heat shield is fine."

Svetlana had tipped her head to the side, listening to Kaz's tone of voice. *Easy for you to say*, she thought. *You're not piloting this ship. But good to hear anyway.*

Kaz glanced at the front screen. "All telemetry looks nominal, Apollo. We show you in good config for atmospheric interface and reentry. Weather in the landing zone is reported as clear skies, light winds, minimal ocean swell. You'll splash down in dawn light, just before sunrise. The crew of the USS *New Orleans* is on station, helicopters airborne, ready to welcome you home."

Deke replied, "Copy, Houston, thanks. We'll talk to you after the blackout zone."

Kaz had the entry chart open on his console. The long, straight line on the map as Apollo descended through the atmosphere was cross-hatched where the high energy of re-entry would heat the air around the ship, turning it into ionized plasma, blocking communications until it slowed.

"Copy, Deke. Talk to you then."

Under his console, out of sight, Kaz crossed his fingers.

82

Mission Control

Kaz's console phone rang. He picked up and recognized the voice on the other end. He listened carefully to the updated plan, quietly suggested a couple of changes and then pushed the glowing button to hang up.

He leaned left to speak in a whisper with Chris Kraft, rapidly explaining what was about to happen. Kraft stared at him, not pleased. Mission Control was the flight director's turf and responsibility, and he kept high awareness and a tight rein on all activities in the room. But after several seconds, he grudgingly nodded. This superseded his authority, and it needed to be dealt with quickly.

Kaz peeled off his headset, stiffly stood, his ribs aching, and walked back one row to talk with JW and Jimmy at the SURGEON console. Both medical men looked up at Kaz as he approached.

"How are their heart rates looking now, doctors?"

JW looked puzzled, clearly wondering why Kaz had come over to his console to ask this question. But he answered, "For Valery, it's the same as it was, but that will likely change with g onset. Deke should be good, thanks to the meds Svetlana gave him." He looked Kaz over and asked a question of his own. "How are you holding up?"

"Still some pain on my left side, but I'll get through it."

Kaz leaned to look at the data display on JW's screen, then walked around behind him, reaching to point at one of the numbers being projected. For balance, he placed his damaged right hand on Jimmy's shoulder, fingers gathering the cloth of his shirt. Jimmy looked up at Kaz, frowning.

Kaz, still staring at JW's screen, tapped it with his left pointer. "What's this?"

When both doctors looked to see what he was asking about, Kaz gave a sudden hard pull left and down to yank Jimmy sideways out of his chair and onto the floor, where he could kneel on him, the pain in his ribs be damned.

To Kaz's surprise, it didn't work.

Jimmy reacted in a blur, his left arm whipping up to knock Kaz's hand off his shoulder. With his right, he grabbed his heavy ceramic coffee cup and swung it across the console, hot coffee spraying, aiming at Kaz's crotch. It landed. The pain doubled Kaz over. Moving at what seemed like several times normal speed, Jimmy grabbed Kaz's arm, yanking him down to hit him in the face with the mug.

"Hey!" JW yelled, throwing himself sideways between the two men to protect his wounded friend, catching the swinging mug on the back of his shoulder.

Jimmy spun out of his chair and landed catlike on flexed legs, facing Kaz and JW. He pivoted quickly and kicked, his hard leather shoe arcing high, striking JW in the chin and knocking him back. Kaz saw his chance when Jimmy's foot was still in the air and kicked him solidly between the legs. Payback.

Jimmy grunted and fell clear, curling in agony for a moment before he scrambled back to his feet. Kaz was upright and facing him. Jimmy's eyes flicked to the right, and then he looked left over his shoulder, sizing up an exit route. Behind Kaz, a dazed JW slowly got to his feet, his hand cradling his jaw. Around them, every flight controller had stopped what they were doing, some standing to see, shocked at the spectacle of a fistfight in Mission Control.

The front side door of Mission Control burst noisily open, and two men in uniform moved purposefully through it, rapidly climbing the steps towards the SURGEON console, one with his pistol drawn. At the same time, a man and a woman came quietly through the room's rear entrance and stood at the end of the SURGEON console, blocking any exit.

The leader of the two men stopped, pointed his pistol one-handed across the console and spoke loudly. "James Doi, you are under arrest for treason and being an accomplice to murder." Holding up a Houston Police Department badge in his other hand, he began to read Jimmy his rights. The second, larger man, wearing a DIA uniform, walked around Kaz and JW, warily approached the taut crouched figure and commanded, "Lie down on your stomach!"

Jimmy didn't move.

"You better do what he says, Jimmy," Kaz said quietly. "You're beaten, alone and out of options."

When the big man loudly repeated his command, Jimmy relaxed like a marionette whose strings had gone slack. His arms dropped to his sides, then he knelt, fell forward onto his hands and lowered himself onto his chest, his head turned, his eyes still defiant.

The DIA agent placed his boot heavily on the small of Jimmy's back, pulled handcuffs from his belt and bent down to pin Jimmy's hands behind him. He said, "Thanks, Commander Zemeckis. We'll take it from here."

Kaz reached to steady himself on the console with his left hand, grimaced from the pain and turned to JW. "You okay, Doc?"

"I'll live," JW said, cradling his chin. "Though my ex-colleague may have broken my jaw."

"I hope not. Thanks for covering my back. I'll explain all this once Apollo is safely in the water."

Gingerly, every part of him pulsing in pain, Kaz walked back to his console. He was putting on his headset when Chris Kraft calmly and clearly addressed the room.

"Everyone take your seats and listen up. Sorry for the interruption, but we had an official police matter that needed to be dealt with. It does not—I repeat—it does not affect what's going on now with the Apollo crew. As the officers finish their work here, I need everyone to focus on the final stages of re-entry, descent, splashdown and support to the on-scene recovery team." He looked around the room, deliberately ignoring the commotion as the officers hoisted Jimmy to his feet. "Any questions?"

The room was silent. The four officers formed a tight cordon around Jimmy and swiftly escorted him out of the room as everyone turned to watch.

"Okay," said Kraft. "Let's close out this mission properly."

83

Earth's Upper Atmosphere, Pacific Ocean

There had been damage to the spaceship.

Unseen by the crew, the metal-on-metal contact of the collision had gouged a hole through the protective Service Module covering and had scarred the thick ablative heat shielding on the capsule's belly.

As it plummeted into the upper reaches of Earth's atmosphere, the orientation control system automatically sensed the slight difference in drag from the predicted models. The small thrusters easily handled it, correcting for the asymmetry.

But the heat produced by the thickening air molecules colliding with the capsule at Mach 25 caused the temperature to rise rapidly. By the time the drag from the air had slowed the ship to Mach 24, the outer edges of the shield were already at 3,000 degrees and climbing. The superheated air discharged energy as light, bright flashes and a red-yellow flickering enveloping the capsule like sparks around a glowing blast furnace, and intensifying.

A probing tongue of heated plasma curled around the edge of the capsule in the lee of the windblast. As it gained strength, it reached farther, tasting the gouge in the smooth heat shield surface.

A fire-breathing dragon of immense power, sensing a weakness in its prey.

The collision had cut a notch deep into the epoxy resin of the heat shield, down almost to the brazed steel honeycomb underneath. The superheated tongue, pushed ever harder by the thickening air, was far hotter than the melting temperature of steel. The shield's supporting ribs began to soften and spatter, collapsing on themselves, widening the gouge. The relentless heat moved deeper, spraying molten steel slag onto the aluminum alloy of the ship's hull.

The engineers had added magnesium to the aluminum to raise its melting point, but it was not nearly enough to withstand a heat shield failure. As soon as the splattering steel and plasma jet raised the local temperature above 1,200 degrees, the pressure hull of the ship turned to liquid, like ice under a blowtorch.

The hull was breached. As the ship plunged through 240,000 feet, 45 miles above the endless blue of the Pacific Ocean, the air inside the ship began hissing out through the melted hole.

The blasting sheet of superheated flame was relentless. It cut through support braces, fluid lines and pressure tanks under the ship's lower floor. In seconds, electrical power was shorted, thruster fuel lines were severed, and the main oxygen tank exploded. The ship was now a dead hulk of wounded metal, a man-made meteorite, racing ever faster under the relentless gravitational pull of the Earth.

The crew, starved for oxygen, lungs collapsing, lost consciousness within seconds.

The burn-through damage dragged the ship to one side, turning it like a broken badminton birdie. The attitude control thrusters had been firing near continuously, fighting it, but as soon as their lines melted, they stopped. The ship leaned more and more and suddenly began to spin. That exposed the unprotected upper aluminum hull to the fiery blast of re-entry friction and pressure. The capsule became a flaming pinwheel, shedding external antennas and skin, and then the contents of the spaceship itself.

Traveling at Mach 21, at 220,000 feet, the capsule catastrophically failed and came apart.

Strapped into that hellish tumble of searing flame and wild violence, the crew died.

84

The USS New Orleans, *Southwest of Hawaii*

She was an Iwo Jima–class amphibious assault ship, pale gray above the Pacific deep blue, with a flat upper deck for her helicopters. The ship's captain, Ralph Neiger, was standing out on the upper flying bridge, wearing his dress whites for the big day, hatless in the wind. He held his binoculars up, scanning the darkness of the early-morning sky to the southwest. Looking for a streak of light.

So far, nothing.

Behind him, the predawn glow of the rising sun was starting to illuminate his ship. He'd already deployed two Sea King helicopters with frogmen in blue wetsuits aboard, ready to jump into the ocean and recover the spaceship when it splashed down at 05:20. Ralph checked his watch and looked up again. It was two minutes to when the parachute was expected to deploy, at 05:15.

They'd had to scramble to be on station. The splashdown had originally been scheduled for four days from now, but there had apparently been problems on orbit, so they'd had to steam out of Pearl Harbor at full speed, directly to their current location. Word was, there were injured crewmembers on board, and the plan was to hoist the entire Apollo capsule under one of the Sea Kings and set it directly onto the deck of the *New Orleans*. Neiger leaned to the side to look over the railing and spotted his ship's surgeon standing on the main landing deck below. He also had an emergency medical team on board one of the helos, just in case.

He looked at his wrist again. Less than a minute. He let the binoculars dangle from their strap, figuring he'd have a better chance of spotting the Apollo capsule with his naked eyes.

There! He saw a quick flash of color against the darkness and snapped the binoculars back up to look closely. He'd been briefed that there should be three parachutes, high enough that they would catch the morning light.

Suddenly, three big red-and-white chutes filled his magnified vision, billowing and pulsing, followed by a glint of the capsule suspended beneath them.

Ralph smiled in amazement as he watched. Just a few minutes before, that ship had been in space, and now here it was, right on time and on target.

He lowered the binoculars again and stepped through the hatchway onto the bridge, looking for where he'd put his broad, gold-braided white cap.

Time to get ready for the crew welcoming ceremony.

85

Director's Office, Fifth Academy, Peking

Tsien Hsue-shen felt sick to his stomach as he pushed his office door closed, walked to the desk and collapsed into his wooden swivel chair. He eyed the small wastepaper bin on the floor beside him, waiting for the wave of nausea to pass.

He'd been standing behind the mission director when word had come from the Yuan Wang tracking ship in the Pacific Ocean. The encrypted signal, sent by high-frequency radio to the tall receiving antennas along China's coast and then by telephone lines to Peking Mission Control, was definitive. China's first astronaut, Fang Kuo-chun, was dead, and his Shuguang spaceship was lost, pummeled and melted into misshapen fragments during re-entry, its high smoke trail visible to the tracking ship. The few heavier pieces that had survived re-entry had fallen at terminal velocity, splashing violently into the water, the hot metal hissing and rapidly sinking into the inky depths of the endless ocean.

Tsien raised his eyes to look at the small photo on his desk of his wife and two children, taken on that pivotal day in 1955 when they'd boarded the SS *President Cleveland* in California to begin their new life in China. In the photo, his wife, Ying, was smiling, while he was doing his best to look stalwart and confident for his family, even as the wind blew his thinning black hair up into a wispy horn. Their children's faces were the ones that reflected the fear and uncertainty they'd all felt.

What will I tell Ying when I get home? Today was supposed to be our triumph! His eyes filled with tears at a second realization, and he closed them. *What will I tell Fang's widow?*

Tsien sat for several seconds seeking calm. Then he opened his eyes and swiveled to face the photo of his leader, Chairman Mao, hanging on the wall. In the iconic image, a small, benign smile played on the great man's lips. This was the man Tsien saw when he visited Mao in his chambers—not the coughing, partially paralyzed ruin that remained. This was the man who had inspired him after the American humiliation, who had helped him rise to a position of power in the People's Republic.

What will I tell him now?

A furtive thought flashed through Tsien's head. *But how much longer will Mao live?*

Tsien had risen to the highest levels of his discipline in the United States, had been struck down unjustly and had risen again to his role here as director of the Fifth Academy of China's Ministry of National Defense. Today had been a tragedy, no question, but along with it had come many gains. The rocket had worked, and the Shuguang vessel had successfully docked with Skylab. Their intel on the docking mechanism and the existence of the American beam weapon had been correct. The details would, of course, be kept secret, but the Americans and Russians now knew without doubt that China was a major player in spaceflight. A nation to be respected and feared for her growing capability.

Tsien squared his shoulders as he thought about it.

The anti-satellite decoy rocket that they had fired from inside Soviet territory had remained undetected by the Russians long enough that the truck had successfully recrossed the border into China. The ploy had been Tsien's idea, and it had succeeded in sowing great anti-Russian suspicion among the Americans. He'd seen that suspicion clearly in Bush's eyes. Fertile ground for China, and especially for Mao's likely successor, whether it was Hua Kuo-feng or Teng Hsiao-ping. Tsien knew both men, and knew that they respected him and his work.

Tsien's eyes had dried. Despite the losses, he would be okay. He was still fit and strong at 63, and there was still much to do. For himself, for his family.

For China.

EPILOGUE

Rose Garden, the White House

"Let me say how humbled, saddened but also proud I am to be here today and to participate in this ceremony."

President Ford stood at a slender mahogany podium on the White House Rose Garden lawn, with flowering rosebushes, trees and the pillars of the West Colonnade behind him, one hand rising to briefly touch the line of neat stitches still showing along his hairline. Rows of folding chairs had been set up on the grass in a semicircle facing the podium, while the haphazard tripods and cameras of the press were scattered behind a low barricade that separated them from the assembled guests. Secret Service agents were posted at intervals behind Ford and around the perimeter of the garden, and security surrounding the entire White House grounds was on high alert.

Ford alternated between looking up at the cameras and down at the US crewmembers' families who were seated in front of him. "Lives were tragically lost, American and Russian, in the noble pursuit of exploring the universe at the same time as deepening the cooperation between us."

No mention of China, nor of a traitor being arrested at Mission Control, nor of the anti-satellite missile launches. Those details had been immediately classified, and the issues were being worked both diplomatically and at several levels of government. Not something for a garden party. Especially not today.

The three surviving crewmembers, one American and two Russians, stood next to the president. After splashdown, they'd been taken directly to the medical facility at Tripler Army Medical Center, near Pearl Harbor. As soon as they were treated and certified well enough to travel, Air Force One had flown them directly to Washington.

Kaz was standing at the back of the crowd, watching. *Deke looks normal enough*, he thought. Now on proper heart medication, Deke was standing somberly beside Ford, wearing the plaid suit and broad tie his family had brought from Houston.

Beside him was Valery Kubasov, with a chair behind him if he needed it. For the moment, he'd chosen to stand, propped on crutches. Kaz couldn't see any sign of a cast underneath the trousers of his dark suit and wondered just how bad the gunshot injury had been.

Svetlana glanced away from the president and caught Kaz's eye across the crowd, holding his gaze for a moment. She was wearing a knee-length pale-yellow dress with matching shoes, and Kaz guessed the Soviet ambassador, seated in the front row, had provided the clothes for both cosmonauts. *She looks good*, he thought, *even tanned— maybe she caught some Hawaiian sun while her crewmates were in the hospital.*

As she turned again to listen to Ford finish his remarks, Kaz could see her lips moving as she quietly translated for Valery.

A man's voice broke into Kaz's thoughts. "A tough day."

Startled, Kaz turned to see that General Sam Phillips, his mentor and former Apollo program director, had quietly walked up next to him.

His eyes on the crew, he asked, "How are your own injuries healing?" Phillips was wearing his Air Force dress blues, the four silver stars shining on his shoulders.

"No permanent damage, thanks, sir." Kaz couldn't keep the bitterness out of his voice as he looked back at the mission's survivors. "It should have been all six of them standing there today."

Phillips nodded. "An inglorious ending to the Apollo era. And a grim retrieval task for the Space Shuttle, if we can get it flying in time."

The president was now presenting the three crewmembers with the NASA Distinguished Service Medal, pausing with each of them for a private chat and a photo as he pinned the medals in place, then solemnly shaking hands.

Phillips leaned closer to Kaz and spoke quietly. "Did you hear what we uncovered about Jimmy Doi?"

Kaz met his gaze. "No, sir. I haven't heard a word since his arrest in Mission Control."

"His father was a US citizen, but he had Japanese parents, and they were all sent to a desert internment camp in Gila River, Arizona, from 1942 through 1946. Their business and belongings were confiscated, and when they were finally released, the family had to start over from nothing. Doi's mother was Chinese, and during those years, it seems she taught the boy a lot more than Mandarin." He pursed his lips and shook his head. "An unsurprising permanent distrust and deep-set anger towards the United States. Best guess is, he was recruited by Chinese intelligence while he was at med school."

Kaz nodded. "Probably learned his fighting skills in that internment camp too."

Ford was now standing in front of Svetlana, fumbling for an appropriate way to pin the medal on her dress. With a smile, she took the medal from him and did it herself, thanking him.

Kaz looked at General Phillips. "I hear you're retiring soon, sir—that true?"

Phillips smiled. "I've got a likely job lined up with a defense contractor, and I've been promising Betty for years that we'd eventually settle in California. Looks like that time is now." He returned Kaz's direct gaze. "More importantly, what are you going to do?"

They were interrupted by a crackle through the speakers as Ford returned to the podium for a final word. "I have been in direct contact with Secretary Brezhnev, and we jointly wish to express our deepest respects to the fallen crew and their families. To honor them, the Congress of the United States of America has posthumously bestowed each of them with the Congressional Gold Medal, our highest honor. In addition, Alexei Leonov has been promoted to major general in the Soviet Air Forces, and Tom Stafford to lieutenant general in the United States Air Force."

Ford left the podium to present the medals to the American families, and the formality of the event quickly broke up as he moved around, speaking with the relatives and the Soviet representatives. Deke joined his family, leaving Svetlana and Valery on their own.

Seeing a rare opportunity to have a word with them, Kaz said, "Not sure, General, but I'll figure something out." He shook Phillips's hand and walked quickly around the end of the chairs to join the cosmonauts.

"Valery." Kaz came to a halt in front of Kubasov. "I'm Kaz Zemeckis. I was one of your CAPCOMs."

They shook hands awkwardly around the crutches, Kaz helping the cosmonaut steady himself.

Valery looked up at Kaz, a trace of a smile crossing his face. "I know, Kaz. Thank you for . . ." He hunted for the words. ". . . your help. It was very important."

Kaz nodded and released Valery's hand, then moved on to Svetlana. He was sweating under his suit—it was noon on a late July day in Washington—but Svetlana looked cool as she, too, shook his hand.

"Yes, thank you for supporting us, Kaz. It was a very hard mission."

Kaz let go of her hand and stepped back to address them both. "My deepest condolences on the loss of Alexei Leonov. He was as good as it gets." He pointed at Valery's leg. "How's it healing?"

Svetlana spoke for her crewmate. "They inserted a long metal rod in his leg where the bone broke and locked it into place with screws. It's strong and stable, and it will heal." She shrugged. "Valery says he feels lucky. He's not sure our doctors in Moscow could have done this."

A Soviet official approached them and spoke to Valery in Russian.

Kaz looked at Svetlana and gestured towards a refreshments table in the corner of the garden. "Can I get you a drink?"

She glanced briefly at the Soviet delegation and nodded. "I know no one here. I'll come with you."

"Cheers," Kaz said, raising his plastic cup of ice water, emblazoned with the White House seal.

"Na zdarovya," Svetlana responded. "To health."

They were standing well clear of the press and the crowd, in a shaded corner of the garden.

"So you've flown two Apollo missions," Kaz said. "That's more than most American astronauts." He nodded towards the families, still talking with the president. "More than Deke."

She regarded him somberly. "But both bad missions, where people died." She took a deep breath and let it out, to help clear her thoughts. A wry smile curled her lips. "Russian men think women are bad luck on airplanes and spaceships." She looked directly at Kaz. "Maybe you agree? You Americans don't let women fly in space at all!"

"You're right, we never have. It's a lingering symptom of our Puritan history. I think it's stupid to exclude the capabilities of half the population, but attitudes may finally be changing." Kaz took a sip of his water. "NASA's getting ready to select its next group of astronauts. Now that Apollo is done, a lot of the old guys are leaving. This new class will be the ones who will fly the Space Shuttle. Rumors in the office are that women will be included."

Svetlana thought about that. "I've seen that the Space Shuttle designs show seven seats. So most crew won't need to be piloting." She looked at him. "Will everyone need two eyes?"

Kaz laughed, then caught himself. This was meant to be a solemn honoring of everyone who had taken part in the mission, especially those who hadn't come back. "That'll never happen. But we did just fly Apollo-Soyuz."

She raised an eyebrow at him.

He chuckled again and corrected himself. "I mean Soyuz-Apollo. Maybe there'll be room in the Shuttle program for international astronauts."

Svetlana regarded him thoughtfully for a few seconds, and then she moved closer and asked quietly, "What happened to the Chinese spaceship and astronaut? I tried to find out in Hawaii and on the airplane here, but no one will tell me."

What am I allowed to say? Safest to stick to things the Soviets already know. "We tracked it as it went across Australia, but it never showed up over America. The Chinese had a communications relay ship stationed in the ocean under its flight path. We assume they attempted a deorbit to splashdown near that ship, but we don't know if they succeeded or not." He took another sip. "We're asking our territories and consulates in the South Pacific islands if anyone saw a re-entry trail in the sky, but so far, nothing."

She pressed him. "The Soviet Union keeps surface ships and submarines in the international waters of the Pacific, and so does the United States. Someone must have seen something."

Both were aware that she was right and that he knew more. The US Navy had, in fact, assigned a submarine to shadow the Chinese vessel, and it had reported no capsule splashdown. But that was classified.

Kaz shrugged. "You'll have to ask your navy when you get home." He glanced at the Soviet delegation. "Have they told you when you're leaving?"

Svetlana nodded. "Immediately. Valery and I are on a flight this evening."

Kaz felt an unexpected pang, and realized he'd hoped to have more time with her. He saw her staring at him, and he covered his reaction with a question. "Will they fly you in space again, do you think?"

She looked away. "Not likely. Two flights are often enough for one cosmonaut." She made a wry face. "I'll probably get assigned a ground job at Star City or in Moscow. Maybe I'll go back to test flying for the Air Forces."

She looked back at him. "What are your plans?" She paused to give her next question extra meaning. "Might you be in Star City?"

Surprised, he said, "Unlikely, but you never know." He held up his plastic cup. "If I am, it'll be your turn to buy."

"Svetlana!" Valery's voice carried across the crowd. "Para!" *It's time!*

She waved to show she'd heard and handed Kaz her half-full cup. "Do svidanya, Kaz. Do you know what that means?"

"It means 'goodbye,' right?" He couldn't believe how disappointed he felt that she was leaving so soon.

She smiled. "Nyet. It actually means 'until I see you again.'"

Her eyes twinkling, Svetlana turned and walked away.

AUTHOR'S NOTE

The Reality Behind Final Orbit

Most of the characters, events and things in *Final Orbit* are real. This made creating the plot a complex and endlessly challenging jigsaw puzzle — to stay true to fact and history while building a plausible, exciting story for Kaz and Svetlana.

Here's a quick list of the real people and true history, to save you from bothering some unfeeling artificial intelligence. Note that, for authenticity, I used the 1975 English spellings of Chinese places and names throughout.

REAL CHARACTERS

Aaron (the bomber). Pseudonym used by the Weather Underground for their primary bomb-maker, Ronald Fliegelman

Brand, Vance. Astronaut, US Marine Corps fighter pilot, Lockheed test pilot, Apollo-Soyuz crew member

Bush, George H.W. Chief of the US Liaison Office in China 1974–76, later US President

Cheney, Richard. Assistant and Chief of Staff for President Ford 1974–76, later US Vice-President

Colby, William. Director of the Central Intelligence Agency (CIA) 1973–76

Crippen, Bob. Nickname "Crip," astronaut, US Navy test pilot, pilot of first Space Shuttle flight, friend of author

Fang Kuo-chun. Chinese astronaut selectee 1971–72, People's Republic of China Air Force fighter pilot

Ford, Gerald. President of the United States 1974–77, spoke with the Apollo-Soyuz crew from the Oval Office and welcomed them post-flight in the White House Rose Garden

Ford, Jack. President Ford's son, one of four children who occasionally went on official travel with their father

Heard, Jack. Harris County Sheriff, responsible for the Houston area surrounding NASA's Johnson Space Center

Hill, Clint. Secret Service agent who leapt on the convertible to shield Jacqueline Kennedy after the assassination of JFK in Dallas in 1963

Kissinger, Henry. US National Security Advisor 1969–75, Secretary of State 1973–77

Kraft, Chris. NASA's first Flight Director, Director of the Johnson Space Center 1972–82, full name Christopher Columbus Kraft Jr.

Kubasov, Valery. Cosmonaut, civilian engineer, Soyuz-Apollo crewmember

Leonov, Alexei. Cosmonaut, Soviet Air Force Major General, fighter pilot, world's first spacewalker, Soyuz-Apollo crewmember, friend of author

Lunney, Glynn. NASA Flight Director, manager of the Apollo–Soyuz Test Project

Mao Tse-tung. Chairman of the Chinese Communist Party 1943–76, founded the People's Republic of China in 1949, died after an extended illness in September 1976

Neiger, Ralph. US Navy Captain, commander of the USS *New Orleans* 1973–75

Nixon, Richard. President of the United States 1969–74, visited China and the Great Wall in February 1972

Phillips, Sam. USAF General, Apollo Program Director 1964–69, USAF Systems Command Commander 1973–75

Schlesinger, James. US Secretary of Defense 1973–75, formerly Director of the CIA and Chair of the Atomic Energy Commission

Slayton, Deke. Astronaut, USAF test pilot, NASA Director of Flight Crew Operations, Apollo-Soyuz crewmember, who lost half of his ring finger to a hay bailer on his family farm in Wisconsin, long disqualified from spaceflight for heart fibrillation

Stafford, Tom. Astronaut, USAF Lieutenant General, test pilot, Apollo-Soyuz crewmember

Stovel, Richard. Lieutenant General in Canadian Air Force, NORAD Deputy Commander 1974–76

Teng Hsiao-ping. Chairman Mao's military Chief of General Staff 1975–76

Tsien Hsue-shen. Chinese-born US scholar, MIT/Caltech professor, NASA Jet Propulsion Laboratory cofounder, sent to Germany by the US Department of Defense to retrieve rocket secrets in 1945, arrested in 1950 under McCarthyism, deported in 1955, founded China's nuclear and space programs as Chairman of the Fifth Academy, Director of the National Defense Science Committee on Space

Wang Tung-sing. People's Republic of China's Deputy Minister of Public Security, at one time Mao's chief bodyguard

APOLLO-SOYUZ A 1975 joint project between the US and the USSR for astronauts and cosmonauts to rendezvous and dock in space, demonstrating cooperation and peace. The Soyuz had only two crew but had previously flown with up to three. The burnt glue smell post-docking was real, and unexplained.

AREA 51/GROOM LAKE A highly classified CIA/USAF base in the Nevada desert.

ATS-6 Communications relay satellite providing near-continuous coverage and high data rate for Apollo-Soyuz, much improved over NASA's Spaceflight Tracking and Data Network ground site dish antennas.

BLACK STAR TYPE 54 PISTOL Standard Chinese sidearm since 1954, with a five-pointed star engraved on the grip.

CHINESE ASTRONAUT PROGRAM Called "Project 714" for its start date of July 14, 1970, to develop the Shuguang ("First Dawn") manned spacecraft for launch in 1973. Astronaut selection began in late 1970; initial screening resulted in 88 People's Liberation Army pilot candidates. After further medical and political scrutiny in the first half of 1971, 20 finalists were selected. Canceled by Mao in 1972.

CHINESE GANGS With the US easing of Asian immigration in 1965 under the Hart-Celler Act, Chinese tongs and triads deepened their crime organizations in major-city Chinatowns. Mao's Communists used the patriotism of triads and other secret societies as their needs arose.

COMANCHE 250 A Piper four-seat, retractable, variable-pitch airplane built from 1958 to 1973. The author has a '59.

CZ-2A Rocket; CZ stands for Chang Zheng, meaning "Long March."

DEFENSE INTELLIGENCE AGENCY The DIA is the US military equivalent of the civilian CIA.

DONG FENG Meaning "East Wind," China's first intercontinental ballistic missile.

FEMALE ASSASSINS Two women tried to shoot President Ford in September 1975: Lynette "Squeaky" Fromme and Sara Moore. Fromme was a member of the Manson Family cult, and Moore was inspired by the Symbionese Liberation Army and also recruited as an FBI informant. Fromme misfired; Moore missed by inches.

FEMALE COSMONAUTS The first woman in space was Valentina Tereshkova, who flew solo on Vostok 6 for nearly three days in 1963. The next was Svetlana Savitskaya, a test pilot and 1970 world aerobatic champion. She flew in space twice in the early 1980s, including doing a spacewalk, and eventually retired from the Russian Air Force with the rank of major.

FIRE DRAGON A Chinese multistage rocket, the world's first, used as a cruise missile in naval battle in the 1270s.

KAUAI TRACKING STATION Communications relay site in Hawaii, part of the global NASA Spaceflight Tracking and Data Network.

KETTERING GRAMMAR SCHOOL UK science teacher Geoffrey Perry used radio tracking of satellites as a way to inspire his students from 1964 to 1984. They were the first to detect several Soviet launches and spacecraft, sometimes ahead of the Pentagon.

KING'S INN The biggest hotel near the Johnson Space Center, used regularly for NASA visitors and meetings from 1967 to 2004.

MACHETE Included in every Apollo survival kit in case of an emergency landing in a remote Earth location.

OUTER SPACE TREATY Signed by many countries starting in 1967, it forms the basis of international space law. Taiwan ratified the treaty in 1971, but China called that "illegal" and only signed in the early 1980s, well after the events of this novel.

POLLY RANCH A suburban Houston community based around a private runway, with houses and hangars combined. Several astronauts have lived there, and still do.

PROJECT SEESAW US Advanced Research Projects Agency's particle beam weapon, under development from 1958 to the 1970s, a predecessor to President Reagan's "Star Wars" Strategic Defense Initiative.

PROJECT SPIKE USAF anti-satellite program to launch a missile from a F-106 interceptor, controlled by NORAD's Semi-Automatic Ground Environment (SAGE), canceled before first test. Later developed into an ASAT missile launched from an F-15.

SECRET SERVICE Provides protection to US political leaders; had female agents starting in 1971.

SITUATION ROOM A secure facility inside the White House since 1961 for the president and senior advisors to make decisions about national security. It's also used for classified global communications.

SKYLAB America's first space station had three crews of 30, 60 and then 89 days duration in 1973–74. Its orbit decayed faster than expected, and Skylab burnt up on July 11, 1979, with some pieces falling on Australia.

SR-71 BLACKBIRD Supersonic high-altitude reconnaissance aircraft based at Kadena, Japan; Mildenhall, UK; and Beale Air Force Base in the US.

STAR CITY Location of the Yuri Gagarin Cosmonaut Training Center, 30 miles east of Moscow, where all cosmonauts have trained since 1960. The author also trained there, and was NASA's Director of Operations in Star City.

SYMBIONESE LIBERATION ARMY A US militant terrorist group from 1973 to 1975 that committed murder, robbery and the kidnapping of newspaper heiress Patty Hearst. The name came from the word "symbiosis," meaning "of all struggles."

THUNDERBIRD A Ford two-seat coupe built from 1955 to 1957 as a competitor to GM's Corvette Stingray. The author has a '55.

TRIPLER ARMY MEDICAL CENTER The Apollo-Soyuz crew was taken to this Hawaii hospital after splashdown, because of accidental breathing of hypergolic gases during re-entry.

U-JOINT Fort Terry's Universal Joint was a favorite hangout during the Apollo era. During the Space Shuttle years, it became the Outpost. The author spent many an evening there, and his picture joined the hundreds on the walls. It closed in 2009 and the building burned to the ground in 2010.

WEATHER UNDERGROUND A US terrorist organization opposed to American imperialism, active from 1969 to 1976. In 1975, the Weathermen bombed the State Department, the Department of Defense and a New York bank. They usually phoned in warnings prior to bombings to avoid bloodshed.

ACKNOWLEDGMENTS

Writing this book took intensive, far-ranging support and research, far beyond my capability and expertise. I am forever indebted to each of these friends for their multifaceted help, insights and corrections. Any mistakes that did sneak past the filter are all mine.

Alex Shifrin—Russian proofreading
Alison Faraday—help with Kettering Grammar School history
Alla Jiguirej—lifelong friend and Star City sage
Anatoly Zak—creator of the incomparable www.russianspaceweb.com website
Andrew Yee—friend and China space consultant
Bart Hendrickx—expert author of *Russian Life Support Systems: Vostok, Voskhod, and Soyuz*
Bill Reeves—friend and longtime NASA Flight Director
Bob Behler—SR-71 pilot
Bob Crippen—friend, NASA astronaut and real-time support expert on Apollo-Soyuz and Skylab
Chuck Lewis—NASA Flight Director for Skylab
Drew Swenson—Skylab 3-D modeling expert
Eric and Terry Fan—friends, artists, coauthors and Chinese cultural consultants
Evan Hadfield—son who suggested several key plot ideas and twists while floating in an inner tube

Gene Kranz—the archetype of a NASA Flight Director and expert on Mission Control details
George Abbey—friend, Johnson Space Center Director and deep expert on NASA and world space programs
Jason Garkey—friend and expert on Pentagon inner workings and layout
Dr. JD Polk—lifelong friend and NASA medical expert
Jeff Peer—friend and deeply experienced fighter/test pilot
Jeremy Hanson—friend and astronaut
Jonathan McDowell—world expert on space history and orbital mechanics
Kata Hadfield—daughter and trusted proofreader
Kate Fillion—coauthor and keeper of my handwritten notes while I piloted Soyuz
Ken Cockrell—lifelong friend, astronaut, musician and deeply connected pilot
Kristin Hadfield—daughter and trusted proofreader
Larissa Okhrimovich—Star City history expert
Li Juqian—professor at China University of Political Science and Law
MiZai Hadfield—daughter and provider of insights on China
Neil Hutchinson—NASA Flight Director for Skylab and Apollo-Soyuz
Ray Porter—narrator for the entire *Apollo Murders* series of audiobooks
Rich Graham—SR-71 pilot and author
Rob Wilson—firearms expert
Rusty Schweickart—Apollo astronaut, friend and possessor of deep corporate memory
Sasha Lavrov—Star City life support systems expert
Steve Jurvetson—friend and insightful collector of Apollo and Skylab artifacts

My deepest thanks go to Jon Butler (impetus and key support), to Rick Broadhead (unflagging attention to detail) and to Anne Collins (patience, unparalleled editing perspicacity and confidence).

Most of all, my eternal gratitude and love to Helene for everything as we create and share this grand adventure together.

CHRIS HADFIELD is one of the most experienced and accomplished astronauts in the world. He was the top test pilot in both the US Air Force and the US Navy, and a Cold War fighter pilot intercepting armed Soviet bombers in Canadian air space. A veteran of three space flights, he served as capsule communicator—CAPCOM—for 25 Shuttle missions, as NASA's Director of Operations in Russia and as commander of the International Space Station. Hadfield's books *An Astronaut's Guide to Life on Earth*, *You Are Here* and *The Darkest Dark* have all been international bestsellers and topped the charts for months in Canada. His two previous novels, *The Apollo Murders* and *The Defector*, were both instant number-one bestsellers.